Praise for Tim

"Voicy, playful, heartbreaking, and ultimately perfect. I felt every possible emotion while I read this, and hugged the book when I'd finished. *New Adult* is delicious. It is everything I love about reading."

—**Christina Lauren**, bestselling author of *The Unhoneymooners,* for *New Adult*

"Sweet and swoony—the perfect treat. A delightful romantic comedy that satirizes the wellness world with pitch-perfect wit. I adored it."

—**Kate Spencer**, author of *In a New York Minute,* for *New Adult*

"*New Adult* is an escapist time-swap romance wrapped in a deeply emotional coming-of-age story about trying to become the best version of yourself. Magic crystals, a nefarious wellness company, and nods to *13 Going on 30* add to the novel's hilarious adventures in time travel, but the beating heart of the novel is its tender friends-to-lovers romance, its complex family dynamics, and its flawed hero. Achingly romantic, tremendously funny, and often bittersweet—this is Janovsky at his absolute best!"

—**Alison Cochrun**, author of *The Charm Offensive* and *Kiss Her Once for Me,* for *New Adult*

"Brimming with all the heart and humor you'd want from its clever time-bending conceit, Janovsky left even this old adult believing anew in the redemptive power of second chances."

—**Steven Rowley**, bestselling author of *The Guncle,* for *New Adult*

"A joy-filled story about first love and finding yourself, *Never Been Kissed* is a nostalgic but still totally fresh read that's full of heart. Wren is an absolutely adorable rom-com hero, and his movie references make this the perfect romance for film buffs."

—**Kerry Winfrey**, author of *Waiting for Tom Hanks,* for *Never Been Kissed*

"An enchanting debut! Full of hope and heart, *Never Been Kissed* is a sweet second chance romance that captivated me with its charming characters and delightfully cinematic setting."

—**Alexandria Bellefleur**, author of *Written in the Stars,* for *Never Been Kissed*

"Full of heart and hopefulness, swoon and serendipity, *Never Been Kissed* reads like a cinematic classic that should be viewed upon the big screen at Wiley's drive-in. In a world that tends to idolize toughness and masculinity, Janovsky serves us a rare treat by creating a cast of emotional, romantic human beings who are strong BECAUSE of those traits, not in spite of them. Perfect for fans of Becky Albertalli, this dazzling debut shows that we're all worthy of love, forgiveness, and yes—romance."

—**Lynn Painter**, author of *Better Than the Movies* and *Mr. Wrong Number,* for *Never Been Kissed*

"A cinematic daydream guaranteed to steal your heart, *Never Been Kissed* is a delightful debut. The perfect balance of charm, swoons, and unforgettable laughs. Readers will be deeply in love with this second chance romance!"

—**Julian Winters**, award-winning author of *Running with Lions,* for *Never Been Kissed*

"*Never Been Kissed* is a wonderfully upbeat and sweet blend of self-discovery and second chance romance. This book warmed my heart—I can't wait for readers to fall in love with Wren and Derick!"

—**Suzanne Park**, author of *Loathe at First Sight*, for *Never Been Kissed*

"*Never Been Kissed* is an absolute delight! Wren is the hopelessly romantic film nerd I was missing from my life. I ached for him as he sussed out his dreams for his future, navigated his own sexuality, and blossomed into his first love. I caught myself cheering out loud for Wren and for Derick, gobbling up every word as fast as I could to get to their HEA. This story will thaw even the coldest heart and leave it with the warm fuzzies. A stellar debut from a fresh, new voice."

—**Xio Axelrod**, author of *The Girl with Stars in Her Eyes*, for *Never Been Kissed*

"A tribute to movies, drive-ins, and figuring out who you truly are, *Never Been Kissed* is a pitch-perfect second chance summer romance. Watching Wren and Derick navigate their past and their present while fighting for their community and what they believe in will make you want to cheer. This book made my queer heart so very full and deeply happy: everything a rom-com should be."

—**Anita Kelly**, author of *Love & Other Disasters* and the Moonlighters series, for *Never Been Kissed*

"In this sparkling debut Janovsky offers a queer romance YA readers are going to gobble up. Its uplifting message of identity and belonging will resonate with readers of all ages, and the quirky nostalgia-filled setting is the perfect backdrop for all the first time falling in love feels, which lead to a standout swoon-worthy romance readers will want for their keeper shelves!"

—**Annabeth Albert**, author of *Conventionally Yours,* for *Never Been Kissed*

"Grab the popcorn and curl up with *Never Been Kissed.* Timothy Janovsky is an incredibly gifted storyteller—his unputdownable debut novel brims with sparkling wit, high stakes drama and a swoony, slow burn romance worthy of the classic movies that Wren, the book's flawed but lovable cinephile, holds dear. I can't wait to read what he writes next!"

—**Erin Carlson**, author of *I'll Have What She's Having: How Nora Ephron's Three Iconic Films Saved the Romantic Comedy,* for *Never Been Kissed*

"Janovsky captures, so poignantly, that feeling of figuring out who you are and where you belong (and who you belong with) that makes new adult romance so universally addictive. This sweet, heartfelt slow burn smells like fresh cut grass and popcorn, sounds like the buzz of cicadas and the fizzle before a firework bangs. It feels like the long-awaited heat of your crush's breath across your collarbone. *Never Been Kissed* reminds you of that exhilarating time when firsts feel like forevers."

—**Ruby Barrett**, author of *Hot Copy,* for *Never Been Kissed*

"This is holiday rom-com perfection. Sparkling with a gloriously fresh, witty voice and timely messages of healing and hopeful new beginnings, *You're a Mean One, Matthew Prince* is tender, sexy, and deeply heartfelt—a new all-time favorite!"

—**Chloe Liese**, author of the Bergman Brothers series, for *You're a Mean One, Matthew Prince*

"*You're a Mean One, Matthew Prince* is a funny, heartwarming pop of Christmas sparkle with a protagonist whose selfish ways are so entertaining to read that I'm almost sorry he can't be bad forever—but with as funny as Matthew is when he's wicked, his redemption arc is equally satisfying, sweet as a chai sugar cookie, and I was rooting for him and Hector, as well as the whole town, from the moment Matthew Prince stepped into Wind River in his Gucci boots."

—**Sarah Hogle** author of *You Deserve Each Other* and *Twice Shy,* for *You're a Mean One, Matthew Prince*

New Adult

TIMOTHY JANOVSKY

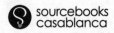

sourcebooks
casablanca

Copyright © 2023 by Timothy Janovsky
Cover and internal design © 2023 by Sourcebooks
Cover and internal illustrations by Monique Aimee
Internal design by Laura Boren/Sourcebooks

Sourcebooks and the colophon are registered trademarks of Sourcebooks.

Published by Sourcebooks Casablanca, an imprint of Sourcebooks
P.O. Box 4410, Naperville, Illinois 60567–4410
(630) 961-3900
sourcebooks.com

Cataloging-in-Publication Data is on file with the Library of Congress.

Printed and bound in the United States of America.
LSC 10 9 8 7 6 5 4 3 2 1

THE LAW OF ATTRACTION:
Thoughts are a form of energy...
Like attracts like.

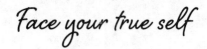

PART ONE

BLACK OBSIDIAN

Face your true self

Chapter One

Jokes, they say, are a lot like life and love: all in the timing.

Right now, I should be planning out the jokes for my next open-mic stand-up set, practicing the punch lines that are going to bring the house down, but *no*. Instead, I'm doing *this*.

Come quick. It's an emergency, I type before throwing my phone on the bed like it's a bomb and assessing the unmitigated disaster that surrounds me.

Ever since my sister announced her surprise engagement and subsequent blowout wedding, my timing has been *way* off. Like, life-in-utter-disarray off.

Case in point, I'm midcrisis on a Saturday night, running majorly late to meet someone, and banking on my best friend to come through with a fix like he always does.

Footfalls bound down the hall to my right. The door flies open, and a frenzied Drew—all six-foot-three of him (90 percent limbs, 10 percent miscellaneous) thrusts the fire extinguisher we keep stashed under the kitchen sink into my bedroom, nozzle first. "I told you not to light any more of those Doop candles if you're going to take a nap," he shouts. "You flail in your sleep. You're a flailer!"

He points and weaves, clearly trying to decipher where the fire is.

There is no fire. Not this time, anyway. Just socks. Lots and lots (and *lots*) of discarded socks, dumped from an overturned drawer and sprawled all over the floor. Tall socks. Short socks. No-show socks. Socks with zany patterns and TV show quotes and corgi butts printed on them. But sadly, detrimentally, no dress socks.

There is, however, dress sock. Singular. And I am now dejectedly holding it up for Drew to see.

"It's not an I-accidentally-started-a-small-fire-by-flailing emergency. It's a do-you-have-a-clean-pair-of-dress-socks-I-can-borrow emergency." I look back down at my mess and correct myself. "Even dirty dress socks would suffice at this point." I'd buy my own if I were in any kind of financial position to do so. Perks of being a struggling stand-up comedian with a tip-based survival job.

Drew retracts the extinguisher, powering down from red-alert mode. "You couldn't have texted me that instead of making me think our entire building was going to burn down again?"

"Where's the fun in that? Where's the *drama* in that?" I waggle the sock in his face for emphasis, which he swats away, left eyebrow twitching. The one with the tiny scar above it from when he had to get stitches in high school after a bookshelf-building attempt gone wrong. "Sorry, but in fairness, how was I to know the Go to Sleep, Bitch candle was going to put me to sleep in literal seconds? I don't fuck with witchcraft."

Drew snorts. "Of course, blame witchcraft and not your shifts that sometimes last until 3:00 a.m., or your off-again, on-again insomnia."

"I know you don't believe me, but there is totally something weird about where my sister works," I protest. Doop claims to be a lifestyle brand, and yet they operate more like a cult. A very trendy, very wealthy, very health-conscious cult. It's creepy. "And they definitely put something in that candle." What else would I expect from a company that started as a popular anonymous blog and rapidly became ubiquitous in the world of "wellness"?

"I bet the Doop higher-ups possessed your body in your sleep and forced you to knock it over too." Drew's accusatory expression is completely unwelcome here.

"At least I acted quickly!"

"Yes. Your prompt yelling of 'Drew! Drew! Fire! Fire!' was both chivalrous and helpful."

I would dispel that absurd rumor if it weren't completely true and I weren't talking to the world's leading Nolan Baker Bullshit Detector. "At the very least, nobody was hurt and the damage was minimal."

"True," Drew concedes. "But we definitely lost our security deposit."

"Which is not a problem, considering we're going to live here together forever and ever until we're gray and wrinkly and senile, and then nobody will ever know about the unsightly singe marks until we're dead and buried." I shoot him with my most winning smile. "Won't need that money when we're in side-by-side burial plots somewhere shady and beautiful, perhaps with an oak tree and a bench."

Drew's expression warms. Red rising to the tops of his cheeks, matching the stark red of his hair that has always made him easy to pick out even in the largest of New York City crowds. Well, his hair and his previously mentioned height.

He's basically a giant. A gentle giant. A gangly gentle giant who is looking at me like I just solved the universe's oldest riddle. "You have it all figured out, huh?"

"Indeed." I give his cheek a light, friendly smack. "What I don't have figured out is what I'm going to do about this sock-cession..."

"Are you saying 'succession'?"

"No. Sock. Cession." I chop the air with each syllable. "A recession of socks."

Drew goes from looking at me like I hold the key to enlightenment to looking like I've swallowed said key and now we're going to have to wait days to weeks for me to poop it out. "Clue me in here."

"As in the value of my socks has greatly declined due to the fact that half of them have holes in them." I gesture to the pile on my left. "And the other half don't have a match." The sad, single socks sit on my right. An apt metaphor for my life.

Drew assesses the situation before dropping to his knees and doing his damnedest to find a perfect, put-together pair. How sweet and naive he is to think I haven't scoured. Haven't hunted. Haven't prayed to Saint Anthony even though I'm as unreligious as they come. "How did such a deficit come to be?" He's evidently flummoxed by this, even if my general brand of disorder is commonplace by now. "Did you buy a million single socks or something?"

"Honestly?" I give him my best deadpan. "I blame the candle."

That gets a laugh out of him. "I'll be right back." He edges out of the room slowly. "Don't cause any more chaos while I'm gone."

I cross my heart with my pointer finger and wait seconds for him to return from his own bedroom. It's a sneeze-and-it-shakes small apartment.

"What do you need the dress socks for?" he asks once he's back, gracing me with a neatly folded pair of navy blues.

I flop way down onto my mattress, which doesn't have a bed frame (I like it like this, I swear), and slip the socks on, pausing over what to say. Drew and I have a no-lie policy as all the best best-friendships do, but in this case, I have to tread lightly. The last thing I want to do is let Drew, the bestower of blue socks, know that I'm slightly embarrassed and a little miffed over my evening plans. "I'm, uh, meeting someone."

His expression sours. "I thought we had plans to catch up on *Drag Race* tonight. This is the second time you've canceled this month alone. You didn't put anything new on our Google calendar..."

It's funny how so much of my life is *ours* regarding Drew and me. This is *our* apartment. What he's referencing is *our* joint online social calendar. These blue socks, for all intents and purposes, are now *ours*.

A lot of *ours,* but there is no *we*.

"Sorry. It was a last-minute thing," I say, not meeting his eyes while pretending to be amused by how big his socks are on me. You know what they say about guys with big feet…

"It takes two seconds to update our calendar." *Big* amounts of skepticism.

He's right on all counts. It would've been exceptionally easy to add a blue color block, the same shade as these socks, to the shared calendar that's meant to make our lives easier by blocking out work shifts (red), nap schedules (purple), nights we may want to bring another person home so the other should make themselves scarce (blue), et cetera, et cetera.

But the truth is, Nolan Baker using the blue is a rarity. Almost unheard of recently. "I have a…*date*." I nearly choke on the word.

There is an excruciatingly lengthy silence. "What happened to the whole *I'm not going to date anyone until I've become a successful stand-up* thing?" he asks with a jagged edge to his voice.

The other truth is, Nolan Baker using the blue is a rarity (almost unheard of) because he's been in love with Drew Techler for a little over two years. But that's an admission only someone with a decent pair of matching dress socks is allowed to make. Love is not for those without a bed frame. Or so I'm told.

"That was all before my sister decided to be selfish and go and get herself engaged." I groan, crawling over to the open closet. I struggle to prepare myself for the onslaught of shoes. Being crushed by Mount Ve-*shoe*-vius sounds better than having to face Drew about my feelings.

"Ah, yes. Love. The most selfish thing you can give another person."

I don't even justify that with a proper response because I can't. I snort…or grunt…or something else stupid comes out of my mouth while I sort through the wreckage that is my belongings and try not to think about the inconvenient, nebulous love lodged in my stupid heart.

When my sister and her coworker announced their engagement to my whole family and told them Doop was footing the bill for an all-expenses-paid wedding as a marketing stunt, everyone else shrieked with excitement while I dutifully smiled, participated in the toast, and then sprinted to the bathroom to comb through my contacts for a suitable date. Even though the little audience in my brain was chanting: *Drew! Drew! Drew!*

Ted Grindr was a no-go because of his BO. Bill Tinder was a ghosting situation. Lamar Bumble was a chronic dick-pic sender. My phone was a long list of failed connections and missed opportunities, but I couldn't give up the search so easily.

Baker family functions, for me, go a little something like this:

Well-Meaning Family Member: "Are you still doing that comedy thing?"

Me: "Yes, Great-Aunt (think of the oldest, crotchetiest name you can think of), I am."

Well-Meaning Family Member with an Old, Crotchety Name: "That's nice. Your Uncle (insert creepy, generic name here) showed me one of your videos on *the* Facebook."

Me: "Oh, that was nice of him."

Well-Meaning Family Member with an Old, Crotchety Name: "Yeah…it wasn't my cup of tea."

That's not even to touch upon the "Isn't New York City expensive? How do you afford it?" and the "Isn't New York City dangerous?

Do you carry pepper spray?" and, by far my favorite, "Isn't New York City full of *the* gays? Shouldn't you have a boyfriend by now?"

All that passive-aggressive care is uncomfortable. I need a buffer by my side. Especially for an occasion as lovey-dovey as my sister's wedding to her well-to-do, Connecticut-bred boyfriend. Without a plus-one, I'm going to stick out like the black sheep who can't stop *baaaaaaaaah*-ing loudly for attention.

"So, you're dating again because your sister is getting married?" Drew asks, obviously not grasping what I'm getting at.

As I carefully inspect the precarious shoe situation, I say, "I don't really think of it as dating. It's more like...*shopping*. Shopping for a wedding date. I'm basically going to the mall."

"As someone who lives and dies by romance novels, I don't love where you're going with that analogy." Drew has always been the one in our friendship with the mushy, hopeful heart, and honestly, that's part of the problem.

Not that he has a mushy, hopeful heart. I love that about him. Gah, *love*. Jesus.

It's more that he's a lovebug through and through, and if I take the wrong step toward him while bumbling my way through adulthood, he could end up splattered on the sole of my shoe. A fate far worse than loving him from afar. At least from afar, I can't fuck it up.

That's what I'm telling myself, anyway. A smaller than small part of me knows I'm being governed by fear here.

Fear of awkwardness, rejection, having to find a new living arrangement because I've irrevocably fucked up the best friendship I've ever had by choosing to catch feelings after one almost-magical New Year's Eve.

Drew wants it all. The commitment. The cute Instagram photo shoots. The getaways and late-night phone calls. The whole works.

I think I want that stuff too. I think I want to give him that stuff.

But I can't plant romantic roots until I'm firmly progressing on my career path toward comedy stardom. With my family breathing down my neck, seemingly ready for me to fail, I need to prove that this move to New York City was for *something*.

For now, I'm fine—or pretending to be fine, depending on the day—with casual, don't-bring-him-back-to-the-apartment flings. It all provides ample fodder for my stand-up material. Leave the strings for the puppets, I always say. (I don't really, but maybe I should start?)

Which is why when I turn around with two pairs of matching shoes, one in each hand, I'm hit with a niggling sense of mourning.

There's Drew. Handsome as ever, even in a pair of pale-pink sweatpants and a matching crewneck. Someone who would make an excellent wedding date, and an even more excellent life partner. Someone who supports me and loans me socks and has kissed me on exactly two occasions (once for practice, once for…*pleasure*?) and hasn't curled away in disgust—which has happened to me in the past, mind you! But in fairness, I had eaten a shitload of garlic knots before said kiss, so I was basically vampire-repellent and this dude was wearing guyliner and a vintage My Chemical Romance T-shirt. You do the math.

I can't even keep a pair of damn socks together. How on earth could I keep a couple together when one half of that couple is *me*? Drew deserves more, better, *the world*. All I have to offer is this: half-heartedly begging for a pair of clean, matching socks on a Saturday night mere minutes before I need to leave for a date I don't even want to go on with a guy named Harry who's way out of my league. Honestly, Harry and I might even be playing two different ball games, but he asked me out and I'm really in no position to upset a potential wedding date at this juncture.

"Which pair?" I ask, forcing myself back to earth.

Drew deliberates with keen eyes. "Neither of them match the socks. And, now that I'm looking, the socks don't match the pants. Do we need to get you a sticker system so you know what goes with what?"

"I could always lie and say I'm color-blind."

"You could always stay home and watch *Drag Race* with me like you promised," he says.

Drew isn't exactly a social butterfly. When we moved to New York City from our New Jersey suburb together (my idea, mostly) after high school graduation, I was the one forcing him out of the apartment on a Friday night. I was the one nudging guys to go up to Drew and ask for his number. It's not that Drew isn't friendly. He's got the kindest smile and the weirdest sense of humor, but outside of our apartment and the bookstore he works at, he's more bashful than you'd expect from a guy who takes up so much physical space. Whose bright-red hair and fair skin literally demand your attention in every room he enters.

I look him right in the ice-blue eyes and urge myself not to get lost in them. Not even for a second. Because if I do, there's no going back. I'll be in lounge pants and a John Mulaney T-shirt before I can even cancel on Harry.

Harry! I check my phone and remember I'm going to be late. Probably later-than-late now, but I'm hoping this guy is one of those dudes who finds messy, blundering guys charming. I grab the nearest, least wrinkly shirt I can find and throw it on. "As much fun as *Drag Race* sounds, I have to go. If you're still up when I get back, we can roll a joint and watch and bitch, but right now I need to make sure I'm not flying solo at my sister's wedding." Drew visibly sags at this. "Tonight, why don't you read that hockey player/swimmer romance you've been excited about? What was it called again?"

"*Rink or Swim.*"

"There we go! I knew it had a silly name." All his favorite books do, but I don't even make fun of him for it. He's never once made me feel bad for the number of times I rewatch a streaming stand-up special for the quiet comfort and familiarity. "Read that, and by the time you're done, I'll be back and you can tell me all about it. Okay?"

He nods. "Okay."

I'm hustling toward the door, scooping up my keys, my wallet, my light jacket.

Stupidly, I kiss him on the cheek even though I know I shouldn't. Even though I know his soft, freckled skin under my lips will make my heart flutter. Even though I know it's going to make giving Harry a chance a zillion times harder than it should be. But I do it anyway because I'm a fucking rebel literally without a cause, and when I pull back, Drew smiles the friendly smile that powers my days, keeps me up at night, and never ceases to buoy me.

"Wish me luck?"

"Good luck," he says genuinely.

And then the door shuts between us.

Chapter Two

THREE MONTHS LATER

The elevator doors open onto the Doop headquarters.

Natural light spills in from floor-to-ceiling windows across the way, reflecting off glass pendants that hang from the ceiling at regular intervals above the open work space, which is bustling at this hour.

The whole floor is awash in sandy tans and muted pinks, evoking the West Coast with such ardent effectiveness that I can almost imagine the elevator is a teleportation machine that spit me out somewhere in beachy California.

Most offices have chairs, but Doop has rolling, plush stools. Instead of couches in their waiting area, they have cushions on the floor complete with lumbar support. On the walls, one might expect beautiful but nondescript photography or paintings that spark conversation, but the anonymous founder (or *guru*, as they prefer to be called in profiles) has opted for sparse white walls. The guru once said in a long-form interview, "Blank space inspires limitless possibility."

All it inspires me to do is to tag THIS IS AN EXPENSIVE SCAM in red spray paint across them. Too bad I don't have a graffiti-art kit. All I have is a bag of CeeCee's belongings for her penultimate wedding dress fitting. As mister of honor, I'm keeper of the undergarments, courier of the heels. I hoist the bag under my arm as I step off.

Before I ask the kindly, stylish guy behind the circular, panopticon-esque reception desk about my sister, I check my phone for word from her. I spot a few different messages instead. One's from Harry: Don't forget. Dinner on Thursday night with my parents. I'll pick you up from the club at 7.

Drew's luck before that first date did the trick. I've successfully maintained a casual relationship with Harry the working director.

I type back: Can't wait!

Even though really, I've been *waiting* all week for an excuse to fall out of the sky, asteroid-style, as to why I can't make it. Meeting the parents is a big step, and as Drew loves to remind me, I'm supposed to be steering clear of strings-attached entanglements unless by some miracle I become a famous stand-up in the next several days. Even so, I'd prefer those strings be golden and attached to Drew. But in my head, I know I need to keep those strings as untangled as possible until after the wedding, until after Harry and I can part ways amicably, until…

"Welcome to Doop," the guy in the tall swivel stool says with eyes that sparkle almost as brightly as the orange, salt-rock lamp plugged in nearby. "What can I doop—Whoops, I mean *do* to make your day better?" Then, his voice dips. "Sorry, I'm new!"

"All good," I say, knowing full well that CeeCee had recommended I apply for this exact job a few months ago when the previous receptionist got promoted to executive assistant in the beauty division. Because the job I have now is, apparently and vocally, a blemish on our family and a source of near-constant debate. I peer down at the receptionist's nameplate. "*Ryan*, can you tell me if CeeCee is available?"

He fiddles with a very loud, rose-colored mouse as he squints at an enormous Mac screen. "I forgot to put my contacts in this morning," he explains. "But I'm not seeing a CeeCee."

"You're not seeing much of anything," I joke to lighten the mood, but he doesn't laugh. "I mean, without your contacts." Usually when I have to explain a joke, the laughs never come, but I swear this dude nearly topples off his stool when he finally gets it.

"That's a good one." He's wiping his eyes, which is both over the top and good for my ego. "Might she be under a different name?"

Oh, right. "*Cecelia* Baker?" I forgot that, when she got in at the ground floor here, she swapped out her New Jersey nickname for her full name that no one ever uses. She said it "fits in better with the culture at Doop." Which makes sense, given how I feel both underdressed and overdressed in a pair of rigid jeans and a T-shirt with a vintage Coca-Cola logo on it that Drew bought me for my birthday a few years back. I should've just worn a flashing sign that said: *Look at me, I ingest filth!*

"Ah, yes. Cecelia Baker—our blushing bride—is in a marketing meeting in the Lavender Lounge," he says. "Are you as excited about the wedding as we all are?"

"Yeah…excited for it to be over," I say with a laugh that doesn't come out right. All jokes, no matter how absurd, have a nugget of truth underpinning them, and I've perhaps shown too much truth to Ryan, a total stranger, in this moment. "I mean, weddings bring a lot of stress on families, and I already get a lot of stress from my family without a wedding." Damn, I must be a broken vending machine because I'm dropping bars without any buttons being pushed. "Sorry, you didn't need to hear all that."

"No," Ryan says with a smile that doesn't reach his eyes. "Here at Doop, we encourage sharing your truth and living your best life."

His smile paired with the generic platitudes give me the creeps. "Well, if you want my truth, you can pay to hear it at my next stand-up show at the Hardy-Har Hideaway. Sadly, my best life won't be here for another seven years. At least according to my life plan," I say to cut up the awkwardness. "Anyway, when will my sister be available?"

Ryan doesn't even look back at his computer, a new glint in his eyes. "She should be done in about ten minutes. Can I get you anything while you wait?"

I'm *early*? The only time in my life I've ever been early was when I was born a week before my due date, and Mom had to have an emergency C-section because the umbilical cord was wrapped around my neck. Nolan Baker: bringing the drama since Y2K.

I eye the cushion area before asking, "Which way is the bathroom?"

I get a bit lost following Ryan's directions, which were long-winded and roundabout. While the main area is open concept, the left side is a maze of corridors, various glass-box offices, and painted chalkboards denoting space sign-outs and upcoming meetings. That's how I find myself doubling back until I've weaved down a hallway to avoid an oncoming cart.

When I turn, I'm staring down a hallway that doesn't look like the others. The lighting is darker, nearly ominous, and the walls are more of a slate gray. Multiple signs reading AUTHORIZED PERSONNEL ONLY and RETINA SCAN REQUIRED hang at various intervals, making me wonder what kind of Matrix-level nonsense they're up to.

I'm about to take a photo and send it to Drew with a million exclamation-mark emojis when I hear: "Nolan!"

I jump at the sound of CeeCee's voice behind me, like I'm a tween again and she's caught me stealing her *Seventeen* magazines. "Hi. Hey," I manage.

"What are you doing down here?" she asks. She's wearing an oversized beige cardigan over a white linen-silk-blend blouse and a matching skirt, all assuredly from the Doop spring collection with some up-and-coming, eco-conscious designer. She taps the toe of her loafer with supreme impatience. At some point, she stopped acting like my older sister and started being like a second mom.

"I, uh, got lost on the way to the bathroom," I say, voice pitching higher at the end as I scamper to her side like the people pleaser I am.

"Okay, well, come on." She leads us back to the elevator bay and presses the down button, already sliding on her amber-tinted sunglasses that are more for aesthetic than anything else. "Have you given any more thought to working here?" CeeCee asks.

"Given any more thought to working in the place with the anonymous founder and sketchy, secret hallway? Yeah, no thanks," I say. It's a new excuse, at least in my never-ending parade of them since the bachelorette party from hell where she basically announced in front of the entire bridal party that I was working a dead-end job and needed a life makeover. Drew got an earful about that when I got home. I never even brought it up to Harry. As far as Harry knows, I'm never not a good time.

CeeCee is carefully observing the numbers on the elevator sign climb while she says, "It's not a sketchy, secret hallway. It's the Doop Lab."

"Which is where you…?"

She shrugs with the shoulder not currently hefting her over-stuffed vegan-leather attaché. "I've never been down there."

"Wait, you've worked here for five years and you've never been in there? Not even on an introductory tour?" I suddenly get the sense that I'm being watched. When I glance back, Ryan's eyes are trained on me (was he lying about the contacts?) until he notices me noticing him, at which point he picks up a phone that hasn't rung.

Okay, I'm really creeped out. The ding of the elevator nearly makes my skin spring off.

CeeCee steps in first. "I work in marketing, not product

development. I'm swamped enough with my own projects. There's no reason for me to go snooping into the Doop Lab, okay?"

I feel distinctly like I've seen something I shouldn't have. All that hallway needed was flickering lights and a screeching violin score to have been straight out of a sci-fi/horror flick.

"Speaking of, there's an opening in my department with the social media team," she says, so blasé, nails tapping out an email on her phone.

"I have a job," I snap. There are only so many times you can fight with your sister-slash-second-mom about your life choices. "Just because you don't like it doesn't mean it's not true."

She folds her arms over her chest as the elevator begins its descent. "I never said I don't like it. Just thought you might be ready to settle into a career."

I hug her bag to my chest, right up against my fitful heart. "I have a career. I'm a comedian." Though that is feeling less and less true the longer I stagnate, but I won't admit that. Most certainly not to her. CeeCee and I are not the kind of siblings who have heart-to-hearts.

"The social media team could use a comedic voice to spice up their content, so it's too perfect to pass up," CeeCee argues.

"Social media content creator for a fad lifestyle brand is not in my five-year plan," I retort, standing my ground but keeping my tone as calm as possible.

"Because that plan's going so well for you," she snaps back, eyes fierce over the top rim of her sunglasses. I mask the upset by looking away, which I think softens her. "Just please consider putting in an application. It would make Mom and Dad happy. They may not even hire you."

"Love that vote of confidence," I say as the elevator stops.

"Jesus, I'm just trying to help." She's always trying to help, which leads me to believe she thinks I'm helpless.

I wave the bag of her unmentionables in her face. "I'm the one who's supposed to be helping *you* right now," I say. The last thing I need is this argument brewing between us all day. I want this mister of honor business to bring us together. *Back* together. The way we were as kids. Friends, or at the very least *friendly*. And that won't happen if we're at each other's throats over nonsense like where my paycheck comes from.

The doors slide open with a *whoosh*, letting in a rush of cold air and a slew of workers.

"Whatever. Sorry I said anything." CeeCee doesn't even wait for me as she strides across the lobby.

Outpacing me in every respect.

Chapter Three

"Nap on your own time," Wanda, my boss and this club's owner, crows, slugging me with a slightly wet tray from the kitchen.

My eyes snap open, and I'm rushed back to the bleak reality of sticky floors, drunk tourists, and the pervasive scent of trying-too-hard-to-impress-your-date. Don't get me wrong. The Hardy-Har Hideaway is a New York City staple and one of my favorite places on this godforsaken planet, but it's much less illustrious on nights when you're hocking nachos and mopping up spilled beer pitchers instead of soaking up the spotlight in front of that famous redbrick wall and weathered, painted sign.

"I don't pay you to doze off in the middle of my club, got that?" Wanda warns in her stern but fair tone.

She's right. She pays me to take orders and bus tables, so I accept the tray while simultaneously accepting the fact that after four years of paying my dues in the everybody-knows-everybody comedy scene, I'm still making a living as a server, not solely slaying onstage.

On my way to table twelve, where a gargantuan stack of soggy napkins and half-drunk cocktails awaits me, I sneak peeks at the girl performing tonight: Taylor Pemberton, a club newbie—spunky, blond, sporting a pair of bright-purple combat boots. She's shaky yet still commanding the room with every tug of the mic cord, every cheeky wink.

She's a gentle reminder of how far I've come from my open mic days.

After countless workshops, networking events, showcases, and classes, my stand-up skills are sharp. I know they are. My skeleton is made up of 206 funny bones rattling around inside a relatively attractive skin suit—modesty, meh. Who needs it when you're twenty-three and already hosting your own night in New York City?

Granted, it's Monday nights, but *still*. Major.

I only wish that meant something to my family. Meant more in terms of fast-tracking me for global stardom.

Part of the reason I took this job was so that I could get paid to learn by example. Soak up some genius by sheer proximity. And I figured getting in the good graces of Wanda Howard, the queen of comedy club owners, wouldn't be a bad bet either in my five-year plan for success, which dovetails into my ten-year plan for comedy domination. A plan that most resolutely does not include a detour into working for Doop.

CeeCee's insistence that I start in on a real career has been trailing me all week like a piece of toilet paper from a Port-a-Potty that I can't get unstuck from my shoe.

"Down in front!" a belligerent man at table twenty spit-shouts in my direction. No wonder I have a bad back at my young age. Half my job is ducking out of the way of confrontational audience members.

When I dare look over, the man's much-younger date is laughing like he's all the comedy she needs. Taylor up onstage—bless her heart—has been reduced to background noise on somebody else's expensive night out.

One day, I'm going to be the kind of comedian you can't keep your eyes off.

If only I could snap my fingers and make *one day* into today.

I squat down lower, shoes squelching in an unidentifiable puddle, wishing I had a pair of toxic-waste gloves to handle these crumby plates caked with queso. I bring them into the back, through the unwieldy swinging doors, and go to town in the slop sink with a fireman-grade hose. Right beneath the slosh of the spray I hear Declan, my coworker, shout: "Nobody panic, but Clive Bergman is here!"

My heart does a pratfall inside my chest. "What did you just say?" I ask, turning without thinking and jettisoning a geyser of water clear across the kitchen. Declan, in a blur of long hair, jumps out of the way before I baptize him in tap. "Sorry!"

"Watch where you're aiming that thing," Marco, one of the line cooks, hollers from his station, sidestepping the spillage on the way to the fryer.

I nod before bouncing my attention back to Declan, who has begrudgingly gone to get a mop. "Did you say Clive Bergman?" Clive-fucking-Bergman is a big deal in the scene right now. He's a late-night fixture at the Broadway Laugh Box—*the* crown jewel of New York clubs, the place I've been dying to get an audition.

"Yeah," Declan clarifies, kindly cleaning up my mess. "Apparently his cousin has a spot in the open mic tonight. Clive's mentoring him. Damn, those rookies on the bill don't even know they're being handed an opportunity on a silver platter."

"Or a death sentence," Jessie, the nonbinary bartender who gets more tips than anyone in this joint for their flirty service and creative drink specials, says right before receiving major death stares. "What? Bomb in front of a headliner and you're basically dropping your pants and taking a dump onstage."

"Call it performance art and maybe you can get booked at the MOMA," says Marco with a laugh, underscored by the Tater Tots rising from the frizzling oil vat.

Jessie comes over to me, picks up a dish, and starts helping. "Don't choke tonight."

Jessie's worked here almost as long as I have, and from the outside, we don't look like the type to become fast friends. Their style is street-chic: buzz cut, a myriad of piercings, the ever-expanding pin collection that covers their dark-wash denim jacket, and a shaved slit through one eyebrow. My style is whatever's clean. And yet, this place, this job, has bonded us.

Jessie isn't a comedian but does want to break into the industry on the business side, and they know that even though I've graduated from open mics to more paid, pro stuff here, I use the open mics as a chance to work out new material. Take big swings I wouldn't in front of bookers.

"I don't have a slot," I say. "I have dinner plans."

"Okay. Simple solution. Cancel them."

"I can't. They're with Harry."

Their blank stare speaks volumes before they splash me with soapy water from the sink. "Context!"

"The guy I've been...*seeing* for the past three months." Though I suppose *the guy I've been in an arrangement with for the past three months* would be more accurate.

"You're seeing someone? And that someone is not your gorgeous, redheaded, sweetheart-of-a-roommate Drew?"

I unclench the hose and point it in their direction. "You are the only person I told about my feelings for him—while I was high, mind you—and I'd appreciate it if you stopped blabbering that all over the city!"

"Eight-point-four million people live in this city, and every single one of them could tell you love him just by the way you look at him." Even Jessie, a staunch singleton who openly mocks lovebirds, gives me a pointed look.

"You would be clambering for a plus-one to your sister's wedding too if your ninety-year-old grandfather had put out a personal ad in his nursing home's weekly bulletin asking if any of the residents had single, gay grandsons for me."

"That could be the premise for a pretty sick reality show," Jessie says, drifting off into a brainstorm the way they do when any potential business tangent catches their attention. "Eh, maybe not. Too messy. But you should use that in your set. It would kill."

"I would if I had a set to kill tonight. The slots on the website book up in advance." I wish I had a crystal ball to have seen this coming. As much as I want to make good on my promise to Harry, I only agreed to dinner because he agreed to be my date to CeeCee's wedding despite our relationship consisting mostly of sex and small talk.

"What am I always telling you?" Jessie scolds. "You're talented, Nolan, but when it comes to managing your career, you're seriously farsighted. You're not going to get where you want to go in the future without making good use of the here and now."

I return to sulking and soaking the dishes. "Good thing I'll have you as a manager when I make it big and I won't need to worry about any of that. You'll handle it all, and I'll just be responsible for the jokes."

"You better not be joking about *that*. That's my dream job." They gaze off wistfully. "While I wish we were in that era already, we're not. We're here scrubbing dishes, which means you need to be getting as much stage time as possible, especially stage time in front of Clive-fucking-Bergman."

"Don't you think I know that? I'm stuck between a rock and a hard place here."

"Ew, Nolan, I don't need to know about Harry's hard place..." They swat me with a nearby rag and, okay fine, I crack a laugh. Because laughing feels better than stewing. "I'm sure Harry will understand if you're a little late."

I pause over this, considering how punctual Harry is for everything and how he appeared majorly peeved when I arrived late to our first date. Which didn't even seem to matter once we ordered because he spent the whole meal monologuing about being a director. I barely got a word in edgewise. Regardless, he's used to timetables and planning and making sure people are where they're supposed to be when they're supposed to be there, which gives him major wedding date points. "I'm not so sure about that."

"Okay, well," they huff, visibly growing frustrated, "what is for sure is that I know you, and if you pass up this opportunity, you're going to be kicking yourself forever. Just like how you passed up that opportunity to tell Drew about your feelings after Near Year's Eve two years ago until it was too late!"

After Drew and I kissed for the second time, drunk and casually pairing off when the clock struck midnight at a party in Alphabet City, I debated coming clean to him about my sudden, swoopy feelings. But I waited, playing it all off as just *one of those things* until he eventually started seeing someone from one of his lectures, and I realized it was better this way.

That's when I resigned myself to: *from afar, I can't fuck it up*.

"Again, with the loud projection of my love!" I push the memory of the kiss and my unsaid words aside.

"You want loud? I CAN GET LOUDER!" Jessie's challenge is backed by many years of yelling orders through the window to our cooks. "Who's the funniest guy I know?"

"I am!" I shout back, feeling the adrenaline begin to surge, needing to channel this whole conundrum into something actionable.

"Who's going to be a famous stand-up some day?"

"I am!"

"Who's going to go up to Wanda and *demand* a spot in tonight's open mic?"

"I AM!" I stop jumping when that registers. "Wait, I'm going to what?"

"Yeah, you're going to *what*?" Wanda asks, appearing again out of thin air.

Wanda's got many talents, but chief among them is sneaking up on people. The famous golden clipboard has replaced the tray in her hands from earlier. My heart hitches with unbridled anticipation at what that clipboard symbolizes.

Quickly, I finish shoving the plates into the industrial-grade washer. With caution to the wind and Jessie's encouraging eyes on me, I say, "Throw me a bone and sneak me into the lineup tonight."

She hits me with a withering look. "Let's see…" She runs the eraser end of her No. 2 pencil down her list. "We're full up. You lose. Good day, sir."

My shoulders slump. "There's nothing at all?"

"There's maybe some wiggle room at the very end of the night if you want it," she says, knowing full well I don't.

"Nothing earlier?" I regret the question as soon as it slips out of my mouth, but Clive might leave by then if his cousin has already performed.

"Why? Is that past your bedtime?" she asks, goading me as she always does for being the baby on staff. "Thought you'd be all rested up after that catnap I caught you taking."

My cheeks grow hot. "Ha, good one. Sorry about that. Everything is haywire with my sister's wedding coming up. It's just, well, I was hoping to work out some material in front of a really good audience." I hope she gets my message. Spelling it out will only make my plight more desperate.

"Are you suggesting some of the crowds my club attracts aren't *really* good?" Wanda squints in challenge, staring down at me from atop her three-inch heels. Being a comedian means serving yourself up for scrutiny night after night, which largely lets you check intimidation at the door with your coat. Hecklers don't usually make me flinch, but Wanda still intimidates the shit out of me, even after three whole years working under her.

"No, not at all! They're all really good. They're just not all… *loose*?" I'm grasping at straws here.

"If you're looking for loose, you've come to the wrong club," she huffs. "Try Candiez up near Times Square." She's on the move again, zipping out of the kitchen and back out onto the bustling floor.

"Really crushing it tonight with these zingers, Wanda," I say to her still-beelining backside. "Maybe you should do a set. Dust off the old joke book."

"Now I know you're not trying to butter me up for a slot tonight." She stops near the bar, where Jessie takes up their mantle once more.

"You call it buttering up. I call it paying compliments where compliments are due." I'm batting my eyelashes, but she can't see given how dim it is in here. She turns and mutters something sardonic to Jessie, who hits me with pity eyes. I hate pity eyes more than I hate drunk patrons who don't tip.

"Give Nolan a break," Jessie says, oozing their usual charisma. "He upsells more drinks in a night than some of these newbies do in a week." Jessie punches me encouragingly on the shoulder before scooting past to take an order.

After a lengthy groan, Wanda relents to the simple facts. Those drink sales and door fees are how she's stayed successful all this time. "Give it to me straight first. Why tonight? What's so special about tonight?"

It's clear she doesn't know who's here. I jut my chin in the direction of a tall dude with tied-back hair, one leg crossed over the other, a notebook open on his table beside a pint glass and a pitcher. "You know I've been working on getting an audition with the Broadway Laugh Box. I have the tape. I only need one more late-night reference. He could be that one."

"Trying to graduate outta my ranks?" she asks. I don't think she loves being thought of as a lily pad and not a launch pad.

"You know I'm grateful for everything you've done for me. You're a legend and this place is iconic."

Her smile is tinged with something somber. "If you'd care to politely remove your lips from my derriere, I can maybe do some rearranging for you." I'm about to hug her, but she stops me with an authoritative hand. "Just…this…once. Got it, Maggot?"

There's less bite than expected to the age-old nickname.

One of my first nights here, I was tasked with taking the over-stuffed trash out to the sludgy dumpsters after close, and Wanda stumbled upon me practicing my tight-five.

"Not bad, Maggot," she said.

Thinking she'd just spaced on my name, I said: "It's Nolan, actually."

"I know it's Nolan-actually, Maggot." She chuckled to herself, slinging a small plastic bag of personal trash from her office into the massive, reeking receptacle. "You're hanging out by the trash piles, practicing your material in the hopes your dreams won't be crushed before you grow wings and become a fly."

"Ah, like a maggot."

"Aren't you quick?" she joked at my expense, stepping closer. She wore a black blazer over a T-shirt that read CLITERACY, the letters forming an optometrist's eye chart. "I always say comedians reproduce like flies. Every year, they descend upon our city like an infestation of excited maggots. The open mics are swarmed. The showcase prices skyrocket. Just a bunch of wriggly kids fighting for resources. Only the strongest few will undergo metamorphosis into full-fledged comedians, and even then…flies only live for about fif-teen to thirty days."

"That's if they don't get swatted down first."

"Exactly." Wanda offered me a hit of her vape, which I took. The cotton-candy scent was dreamlike and intoxicating, searing my nostrils so I'd never forget her imparting wisdom. "This business is tough. Don't let anyone—and I mean *anyone*—try to squish you, Maggot."

And with that, she was gone.

Chapter Four

"Is that what you're wearing to dinner with my parents?" Harry asks, with an air of judgment that doesn't bode well for the course of this unfortunate conversation.

We're on the sidewalk outside the club, bathed in the neon glow of a blinking sign. I glance down at my black wrinkly T-shirt, my scuffed-up red Converses, and my stylishly ripped jeans. My find-me-relatable show outfit. I know it. Harry, with his perfectly styled, spiky black hair, olive skin, and gym-built body dressed in crisp slacks and a casual blazer—my fashion antithesis—knows it. "I'm going to be late for dinner."

"You told me you requested off after seven." He's discernibly annoyed by this turn of events, his eyebrows converging into one mega eyebrow of disapproval.

"I'm doing the open mic."

"On the night my parents flew in from Ohio to take us to dinner at a very nice restaurant with a two-month reservation wait list?"

"Two months? What, do the servers ask, 'Would you like still, sparkling, or water from the fountain of youth?'" His grunt tells me he's in no mood for my cutesy diversionary tactics. These days, I'm a rip-roaring avoidance machine, and right now, I wish I could avoid the inevitable fallout of the decision I'm about to make.

Don't let anyone—and I mean anyone—*try to squish you, Maggot.*

"Nolan, open mic can wait. Go inside, get changed as quickly as possible, and let's go." His bossy, all-business attitude was part of the reason I was interested in him in the first place. When he slid into my DMs after a show I absolutely slayed, he told me he hadn't laughed that hard in years. I liked that I was the one person who could crack his hard veneer, and it didn't hurt that his get-it-done attitude extended into the bedroom, the primary arena where this relationship (or maybe *arrangement* is still a better word) has developed.

"I'm sorry. I can't do that." I stand up taller, only slightly wounded by the way he says *open mic.* As if he, like my family, thinks what I do, what I *love*, is a wasted pursuit. "There is someone really important inside that I need to be seen in front of."

"And there are two really important people waiting inside a restaurant in Midtown eager to meet you."

"They will! Just a little later than anticipated." His mouth drops open, but no words come out because we're interrupted by Jessie shouting into the alley.

"Nolan, you're on deck!"

"Be right in!" I call back before grabbing Harry's free hand. "Please don't be too upset with me. I didn't plan for this to happen. I'll do my tight-ten, change, and book it to the subway. They'll be too busy catching up with you to even notice I'm missing. Tell them I got held up at work. They'll understand."

"They might, but I won't." He runs an aggravated hand across his clean-shaven chin, clearly thinking something through. Something bad. "I won't ever understand why you put comedy before everything and everyone else."

"Whoa there," I demand, anger cooking underneath my skin. I would try to keep my voice down if this wasn't Manhattan, a borough in a city known for loud, dramatic displays on public sidewalks. "You've known me for, what? Three months? We've been on six, maybe seven actual dates. You don't know me like you think you do."

"Oh yeah? I know you well enough to know that we've only been on *five* dates because *you* canceled one for a last-minute stand-up gig, one because *you* got invited to a last-minute special taping, and another because *you* got in late from an all-night networking drink-a-thon and were too hungover to meet me for brunch, which, by the way, was supposed to be followed by a matinee of *Hamilton*," he says, words like pointed daggers.

"You were going to take me to *Hamilton*? I didn't know we were at that level. That's, like, the queer equivalent of a marriage proposal."

"You literally invited me to your sister's wedding!" His arms flap at his sides.

I don't dare divulge my ulterior motives. The truth that when I saw his DM in my inbox, I was wooed by his impressive résumé, his squeaky-clean internet presence, and his disarming smile. He seemed like the kind of guy who owned—and didn't have to rent, like the rest of us plebeians—a tuxedo. Not Mr. Right, but Mr. Pick-the-Chicken-or-the-Fish Right Now! "You didn't have to say yes!" I protest, aggravated and wishing I'd never broken my cardinal no-dating rule for *this*.

"I said yes because I like you!" he cries. "Or *liked* you. I'm really not sure right now."

It's a diplomatic answer that would be charming under differ-ent circumstances. I shrug one shoulder, at a loss. "I don't know what you want me to do. I wouldn't ask you to miss an important rehearsal."

He scowls. "That's different. Directing is how I pay my rent, live my life. Not the thing I do after serving reheated foods and watered-down drinks to out-of-towners."

Ouch. I thought him being in the arts would at least make him sympathetic to my situation. Instead, he's standing there, discrediting me to my very core. He shouldn't get to hold this much power over me when I don't even like him that much. I thought that feeling went both ways; I was just a placeholder for him to get off with and monologue at until someone better came along, but the evident upset on his face says otherwise.

Jessie's back at the door now, shouting at me. "Nolan, wrap this up and get your ass in here! Wanda's getting angry. You're on in three minutes."

I swallow any unsaid, hurt words. "I have to go, okay? I'll be twenty minutes late. Thirty, tops. Order an appetizer. Enjoy some shrimp cocktail. You love shrimp cocktail! And later? Later, I promise to make it up to you." I waggle my eyebrows in an ill-advised attempt at seduction. "I might even do that thing I said I wouldn't do because it seemed unsanitary but have thought it over and would totally do on this one occasion as a li'l treat. For *you*."

Should I wink? Too late. I've winked. God, if I ever wondered why I wanted to be a comedian, it's this. The ability to make every situation cartoonishly awkward with minimal effort.

"You know what, Nolan? Be as late as you want." He holds his hands up in defeat, backing down the sidewalk with no regard for anyone trying to get around him. "Better yet, don't come at all. Save yourself the trip and the 'li'l treat.'"

"Are you…are you breaking up with me right now?" I ask, watching in horror as my perfect wedding date—my buffer—slips away.

"Yeah, I am," he declares, no holds barred.

"After I offered to do the Chris Evans in *Not Another Teen Movie*? Cherries and all!"

A chortle to my left makes me realize a few people vaping and chatting outside the comedy club have stopped what they're doing to take in the scene. One might even be surreptitiously filming this on her phone. Embarrassment races through me.

"I'm not interested," Harry snaps. "And, for the record, if you listened to anyone but yourself, you'd know I'm allergic to shellfish!" He turns away in a hurry, marching off in long, stomping strides.

I stammer, properly hurt by his insult and thrown off by the onlookers. "Well… Well, then it's a good thing you're breaking up with me and not coming to the wedding!" I yell after him. "There's going to be shrimp! So much shrimp! All they're serving is shrimp!"

Instantly, Jessie's outside, jostling my arm and yanking me toward the door. "Are you the new Bubba Gump spokesperson or something? Get your ass inside, now!" They really have all the makings of a cutthroat manager.

I take one last look at Harry's gym-toned backside before he disappears around the corner.

Fine. Whatever. Good riddance. I'd rather be dateless for the wedding than miss this.

Jessie's pushing me down the Hardy-Har Hallway of History— the dark passageway between the green room and the stage where Wanda displays photos of all the famous comedians who got their start here. The faces on the walls of all those who've come before me, memorialized in red frames with sloppy Sharpie signatures in the corner, whiz by. Some of these people have gone on to world tours, to Netflix specials, and to movie franchises. To fame and fortune, awards and first-look deals. These are my idols, and one day, someday soon, my face is going to be among them.

I made the right decision.

I blow away the post-breakup brain fog as best I can, enough to hear the emcee's loud introduction: "Give it up for our very own homegrown comedy cool kid. Emphasis on the kid, light on the cool. Heeeeeeeeeeeere's Nolan Baker!"

I push out from behind the curtain, the spotlight slapping me with so much force and heat that I nearly keel backward. As soon as my eyes adjust and I spot Clive with a freshly filled lager by his left hand, I throw on my show face. Only problem is, when I step up to the mic stand, innumerable pairs of eyes looking at me expectantly, my whole set flies out of my head.

It's like a bad dream. I glance down, and at the very least, I'm not in my underwear. Even though I did put on a scandalous black pair tonight, which I assumed I'd be showing off for Harry.

Harry. Did I ever really like him, or did I just like that he liked me enough to be my wedding date? The latter seems more probable, and yet his rejection still throbs inside my chest like a beesting.

The belligerent man from earlier, unimaginably drunker than before, shouts, "Get on with it!"

An uncomfortable laugh rolls through the room, and flop sweat starts on my brow. God, I can't bomb in front of Clive Bergman. My reputation will be ruined. I can kiss the Broadway Laugh Box goodbye like I kissed Harry goodbye.

Without an opening line, I take a breath and fall back on my improv training, allowing a truth bomb to trip off my tongue: "Sorry, I'm a little shaky. I just got broken up with." Tension takes over the crowd. "Not, like, a couple hours ago or days ago. I mean, literally right before I stepped onstage. Right in the middle of the sidewalk outside. He dropped me like burnt pizza crust on a dollar slice after a drunken Saturday night out."

One or two tentative laughs ring out. They loosen my muscles. Remind me that I own this stage. This is my time, and I'm going to take it and wring it out for all its worth, regardless of Harry's rejection. I can use this feeling as fuel.

"When you think about it, being broken up with is a lot like being pizza crust. You're half of what you once were, still hoping someone finds you delicious, and waiting on a rebound rat to come make a meal out of ya." There comes the first proper laugh from the audience, including Clive, who I see out of the corner of my eye lift his glass in commiseration and write something down in his notebook. "If there are any hungry subway vermin out in the crowd tonight, meet me out back by the dumpsters after my set. I'm back on the market and happy to give you a taste."

Losing Harry doesn't seem like so much of a loss anymore because by the end of the set, I've won over the crowd, including Clive. And that? That's the only true thing that matters.

Chapter Five

Thirty minutes before my big audition, Jessie and I stand holding hands outside the Broadway Laugh Box, a white brick building squished up against a faded orange town house. The club itself is a narrow building, barely a sliver, and if it weren't for its bright-blue script sign overhead, you might walk right by without noticing it.

New York is like that. Even the extraordinary places blend in because everything holds something extraordinary to someone here.

Two weeks ago, I impressed Clive with my set, got the reference I needed, wooed the booker with my tape, and now I'm here. *My* extraordinary place is welcoming me through its doors for the first time. It's both a breath of relief and a bullet train of anxiety through my gut.

A text pings in from Drew. When I open my messages app, I swipe over the stagnated thread with Harry. A few times over the last two weeks, I considered sending him a text, leaving him a voicemail, trying to explain the situation to him better than I had outside the club.

But what's the use? Even if he forgives me, there's no way he'll still be my wedding date, and frankly, after his parting words, I'm not sure I'd want him to be. If he doesn't believe in me, he sure as hell doesn't deserve an open bar, a pricey entrée, and my best dance moves.

Besides, maybe him breaking it off with me at that exact moment was the best thing that ever happened. The jokes it prompted got me here, didn't they?

Forgetting about Harry, I tap Drew's contact photo—a cute picture of him at the Whitney Museum looking up at a beautiful piece of art. His message: We still on for lunch today?

Quickly, I type back: Shit. Sorry. I forgot. Big audition today. Big. HUGE!

I know he'll soften at the quasi–*Pretty Woman* reference. I've been so focused on preparing for this audition that I've let all my other obligations slip. Even my social ones.

Drew's typing bubbles appear and disappear a few times. Nervous already, I'm expecting a thought-out diatribe about updating our Google calendar. Instead, I get: Break all the legs, Nolan. xo

My heart does a one-eighty, pitter-pattering for Drew and his understanding sweetness. I tap out a thank-you and a smiley face before Jessie demands my attention with a squeeze of the hand.

"In the name of the setup, the punch line, and the holy booker, we pray," Jessie says, bowing their head, so I do the same. "Oh, divine comedienne in the sky, please bless Nolan Baker with the clarity to remember his set, the bravery to deliver it with gusto, and the confidence to leave them in stitches. Amen." They glance at me expectantly. "Now you say it."

"*Ahh*-men," I say like I'm thanking the universe for their beautiful creation.

"Bastard," Jessie mutters with an eye roll before tugging me in to face them. "You. Got. This." They punctuate each word with a sharp poke in the center of my chest. "Walk in there like you deserve to be there because you do. Say it back to me."

I take a deep breath, looking Jessie right in the jade-green eyes that are even starker thanks to their fresh buzz. "I belong in there."

"Why?"

"Because I'm fucking funny!"

"Yeah, funny-*looking*," says a short, scraggly white-bearded man rolling a shopping cart full of empty soda cans past us. As soon as he rounds the corner, cackling all the while, we burst out laughing too.

"New York," I say. "Always keeping me humble."

Two-and-a-half weeks later, I'm sitting in Wanda's office before a shift, stuffing my face with another slice of humble pie.

"'I'll call you.' That's what he said, I'll call you," I say to Wanda while clutching my phone, staring at its black screen. I can hear the booker's southern drawl that would've been more at home in the Wild West than on the West Side. "It's been so long since the audition, and nothing. Radio silence. Don't tell someone you'll call and then don't call!"

Truthfully, the audition didn't feel great. Maybe it was the material. Maybe it was me.

The prayer Jessie and I sent out into the universe went half-answered. The booker chuckled a few times. Nodded a few times. But for the most part, he seemed in a better mood when I arrived than he did when I left. A definite bad sign.

Jessie was more optimistic about the whole situation. "He was probably just deliberating. Seeing where you'd fit best in the lineup they have. Don't stress so much about it. Did you do your best?"

I lied and said, "Yeah."

"Well, then you did what you could and your best deserves a doughnut."

So I ate a glazed doughnut the size of my head and tried not to obsess over it.

Yet here I am, preparing for another crummy shift at my crumby (*Ba-dum-tss*) job…obsessing over it. Probably a reticent side effect of my ADHD. Rejection-sensitive dysphoria coming on strong in the face of no news, which I'm taking as bad news. Bad news that is making me seriously reconsider this career I've put my all into with such little return.

Wanda leans back in her red chair, wavy hair fanning out behind her. "That's the business, Maggot. It's a waiting game, not a wish machine. I thought you knew that by now."

"I do," I say unconvincingly, looking around at all her accolades up on the wall. She was a star touring act for a while in the nineties before she gave it all up to come back and work here. The road was too hard for someone with chronic pain. At least here, in a stable location, she has an office to come back to when she needs to get off her feet and an apartment close by when her migraines set in with a vengeance.

"But," she says, "you were hoping it would be different for you. Am I right?" She takes my silence as an answer. "I've seen it all before, Maggot. Being talented and catching a break are not linked. Sometimes the funniest comedians fizzle out before they even get started. Sometimes hacks become household names. It's the luck of the draw."

"What if," I begin to ask, "I feel the fizzle starting?" Ever since CeeCee began to push the office jobs at Doop on me, I've been questioning my life plan. By twenty-five, I swore I'd have graduated to a bigger club and be regularly gigging on the road for a big name. By thirty, I told myself I'd be that big name, selling out theaters with my face on T-shirts. I'd have a gorgeous apartment, a dependable man (cough—Drew—cough), and an adorable corgi named Milkshake.

All those well-laid plans seem a million years ahead of me, completely out of reach.

Can't I skip to the good part?

Or, at the very least, skip past CeeCee's wedding so I don't have to show up alone?

"Only you can decide when to throw in the towel," Wanda says in a way that's stern but not patronizing.

"The ladder to success just seems so steep and tall, and I'm hanging for dear life from a low rung," I tell her, drained. "If I fell, I probably wouldn't even break a bone."

She gives an understanding nod, hair bouncing along. "So jump and find out. You can always start climbing again."

I take her words to heart.

Defeat follows me like a shadow out of her office. I know she wouldn't say it, but I could tell even she was a little disappointed. Not *in* me, but *for* me. She wanted to see me grow, fly.

Fly. It felt for a second there, hearing Clive's glowing approval a few weeks ago, that I had finally sprouted wings. Too bad I can see the hot-pink plastic swatter in my mind's eye headed straight toward me.

What I don't see headed straight toward me is the very real swinging door as I walk into the back for the start of my shift, completely lost in thought. The saloon-style piece of wood comes flying back at me. For a second, the only sound I hear is an unfortunate crunch, and then unfathomable pain spirals out from the center of my face.

Chapter Six

"Maybe it's broken and insurance will cover a nose job. How New York glamorous is that?" Drew asks from the craggy blue chair in the corner of the urgent care exam room, tabbing down a page in the romance novel he's been reading. "I think you could look really good with a Jennifer Aniston or a Kim Kardashian. Oh, hold on a second, wait!" He pulls up his phone and shows me the first picture in a hasty Google image search. "Your face shape would complement a classy Elizabeth Taylor nose."

"While I appreciate your optimism," I groan from behind the absurdly large ice pack I'm holding to my aching, throbbing face, "I was quite fond of the nose I already had, so this is more of a loss than you'd think."

He sits. "Should we have a moment of silence then?"

His joke makes me crack both a tiny smile and a bone somewhere south of my eyes. "Fuck! Don't make me laugh. It hurts more when I laugh!"

"Sorry, sorry," he says, patting my knee, which hasn't stopped bouncing since I sat on the cushy examination table after walking the few blocks from the Hardy-Har Hideaway. Drew's soothing touch somehow shuts off those fast-firing neurons. I calm down some—he's good at helping me do that, always has been—even if the pain radiating from the center of my face won't subside.

"Thanks for meeting me here," I say. Drew showed up to urgent care in record time, all the way from the bookstore in Brooklyn. It's not exactly a speedy subway commute given the walk and the train schedule, but like magic, he appeared in the waiting room before I was even called in by the burly nurse in Baby Yoda scrubs.

"Of course," he says, so reassuring it could bowl me over. "It's not every day your best friend calls to tell you he's suffered a Brittany Murphy in *Uptown Girls*."

"*Swinging door*," we both recite in unison.

"An underrated classic." I smile, but even that hurts. I bet I look like a rabid raccoon, dark bruising beneath my eyes where the blunt force of the old door smashed me in. I pull the gauze out of my nostril, happy to see the bleeding has ceased.

Drew is the paragon of concern as he leans forward, resting his elbows on his knees. "I can't believe you didn't see that door coming. What were you doing?"

I close my eyes. "Thinking about how I can't do anything right." That statement somehow hurts more than my nose.

"We don't have enough time before the doctor arrives for me to dissect the multitude of ways you are wrong about that," he says in a disarming way.

I pull the ice pack away to give Drew a good hard look at the wreckage that is my once moderately attractive face. He makes a good show of pretending not to grimace. "I'm going to be reminded of my failures every time I look in the mirror or take a selfie until this eggplant heals." Even pointing at my nose makes it feel like it's swelling more.

"Put the ice back on and take a deep breath," Drew says. The breath helps. His presence helps more. God, I'm an asshole, but at least I have the best friend in the entire world.

Drew has been one of my best friends since freshman year of high school. We met while hiding beneath bulky hoodies in the back of a Pride Alliance meeting, and we've been inseparable ever since. He's bookish, lanky in an imposing way, and graduated in the top ten percent of our class. I'm a loud class clown type, wearing a jester cap in my yearbook photo to prove it. On paper, we shouldn't have made sense, except coming out in high school can be a bitch, and our growing text chain became a haven for commiseration and late-night plans to sneak out to the elementary school playground where we'd smoke a reasonable amount of pot and bemoan suburbia.

Before graduation, I sat my parents down and told them I was leaving behind the college scholarship for New York City comedy. I was met with resistance, until Drew stepped into the picture and made it semi-okay.

Drew the Optimist. Drew the Safety Net. Drew the Sensible and Constant. Drew the only reason my parents even remotely let me go.

Drew eventually decided to attend a CUNY school, so my parents knew he'd look out for me just as he always had throughout high school.

I miss those high school days where we could laugh at everything and nothing because we weren't adults yet. Real life was still a couple years and a train ride away.

However, right now, it still seems a bit like I'm playing at being an adult, not quite crossing the threshold into responsibility. Like in that Britney Spears song from the feature film *Crossroads* we watched with my sister during a sleepover, except replace girl with boy and woman with man and, okay, maybe it's not so much like that after all. But the sentiment of the lyrics rings true.

Drew stares at me across the way, eyebrows waggling a mile a minute, trying to elicit another laugh. That's always been our thing, who can make the other laugh more, but…nothing. Not even a chuckle from me this time.

It's not the pain, which is upsetting. I can usually find the humor in everything—that's my *job* as a stand-up—but the longer I sit here, the more I can't help but wonder if I've become the butt of my own joke.

Did I set myself up for spectacular failure by chasing a pipe dream to New York City? What do I have to show for toiling away for four whole years? A fucked-up nose, a shattered five-year plan, another failed relationship I didn't even want, and a silent love I'm pretty sure I do want, even though I can't let myself pursue it.

CeeCee's frequent emails about open Doop positions swim into my mind. I can't believe I'm even entertaining the idea of applying, but I also can't believe I'm here right now with a potentially broken nose and a languishing dream.

"You're a saint for showing up. An A-plus emergency contact." I offer Drew as close to a smile as I can muster in this moment. "I know you like to read on your breaks, so I'm sorry to pull you from that."

"Please," he says, holding up the book with an illustrated cover of a man in a hockey uniform and a woman with a foam finger looking longingly at each other across a crowded arena. "This is a four-star book at best and you're a five-star friend. The face-sitting scene can wait."

The door flies open with a *whoosh*, prompting some major PTSD. I will never look at doors the same way again.

In comes a young, fast-talking doctor with her hair pulled back and a short, bearded nurse in tow. The doctor takes one look at my bulbous nose and declares: "Oof. Yup, that's broken." She inspects me closer, scrunching up her features as she does. "Probably a fracture, to be exact. I can't imagine you'll need surgery, but it's hard to tell with all the swelling. Let me feel around."

"Hey, Doc, buy me dinner first," I joke, because that's all I can do right now to not start crying.

The doctor, not finding me funny in the least (join the club!), ignores me as the nurse readies a needle on a nearby rolling tray. When he sees the nervousness on my face, he says, "Believe me, you're going to want this."

The doctor asks me to lie back, strapping on a pair of white latex gloves. I gulp back a wad of panic spit as my heart starts racing. Coming closer, the nurse blocks the clinical overhead light, making the doctor look like a menacing shadow figure. I flinch, but within seconds, Drew is scooting his chair up on the opposite side of the table and rustling around for something unseen.

"Is it okay if I'm here?" At first, I think Drew is asking me, but then I notice he's looking at the doctor.

The doctor nods. "You're good there for now."

Drew leans in, paper crinkling loudly beneath his elbows, and grabs my right hand in his. Small gentle strokes of his thumb crest over the back of my shaking hand. I keep my head still but shift my eyes toward his face, full up with another big smile, though I can tell there's some worry in the deep wrinkles on his forehead. He devilishly widens his eyes at me and then begins reading in a whisper, breath ghosting over the hot shell of my ear.

"'Jenna arches her back with pleasure as she sinks lower onto Preston's tongue. All that chirping out on the rink during an intense hockey match has made his tongue dexterous, adventurous...'"

I'm too busy laughing—really laughing—to even notice the piercing needle or the tingling, numbing sensation that sweeps straight down to my toes.

Chapter Seven

My broken nose broke the camel's back.

The urgent care bill mocks me from my bedside table, a staggering red amount circled at the bottom that causes my anxiety to skyrocket each time I so much as glance in that direction.

Over the next few days, I hole up in my room. Wanda keeps me off the schedule so nobody has to see my garish face, and I binge reality TV to try to make myself feel better.

Spoiler alert: It doesn't work.

In my cave, shades and curtains drawn, with distance from the club, I decide it's time to throw in the towel, as Wanda put it. With no word from the Broadway Laugh Box, with my friend request to Clive on Facebook sitting in limbo, with no certainty in my career and no steady-enough income, it's high time for a change.

It's never too late to make a change.

The Doop slogan in its looping, pleasant typography stares at me from the application screen CeeCee emailed me a few months ago. Do I dare?

If I quit comedy, at least for the time being, I can't keep working at the Hardy-Har Hideaway. Even if I'd miss Jessie, Declan, Marco, and the gang, I can't be reminded of my failed pursuit every time I clock in. It would only make the transition to offstage life harder.

Comedy has been my dream for an eternity, and I've been striving for this audition for almost two years, but going back to the club now feels like returning to my kingdom after a hero's journey without the head of the beast I was sent to slay. No sword or armor could protect me from how cast out I feel.

Given that CeeCee already offered to put in a good word for me with HR at Doop, I'm practically guaranteed the job. I'd end up like Ryan, that hapless guy at the front desk, filling my days with mindless tasks to help sell a brand I don't believe in, that may or may not be doing witchcraft behind a retina-scan doorway, that cheats people out of their money so they can make money.

Capitalism. Gotta love it.

Before I begin filling out the application, I text CeeCee to hold myself accountable: You win. I'm applying to Doop.

She writes back: Ha. Ha. Your funniest joke ever.

Post-submission, swallowing my pride, I send her picture proof of the screen that says, "Thanks for your application!" and then my phone lights up with her contact picture. An incoming call. I go to answer it, but then I hear Drake's "Take Care" booming from a Bluetooth speaker hidden somewhere in the hallway. I decline CeeCee's call so I can see what's going on.

My door opens a crack and in pops one pale leg like a showgirl.

Right as Rihanna begins to sing the song's hook, Drew makes his grand entrance in a ridiculously short nurse costume, skirt swishing with each swivel of his hips. Pinned in his hair is a white cap with a red cross stitched on the front. He carries a comically large prop needle that squirts water onto my floor. "Care for a little *exposure* therapy?" he asks, pumping his chest to the beat.

He's seen way too many episodes of *Drag Race*. The showmanship is next level.

I'm erupting with laughter over this absurd display as he

continues a mildly awkward dance around my room—not quite sexual but not *not* sexual—carrying a tray with a tiny cup of Tylenol on it. "Time for your medication, Mr. Baker."

"Please," I play along. "Mr. Baker is my father. Call me Nolan."

"Alrighty then, Nolan. Open up." He bends over in a way that suggests he's showing off his cleavage and not a flat chest speckled with a light smattering of red hairs. "Say 'ahhh.'"

"Ahhh," I echo.

Drew breaks the act by laughing heartily. Our gags always go a little far.

"Where did you get that outfit?" I ask when we both calm down.

"My cousin came by the shop to pick up one of her preorders today. I remembered she was a nurse for Halloween last year, so I asked if she could bring the costume. We're about the same size." He takes a seat on the edge of my bed, stopping the music and smiling warmly at me.

"'About' is the operative word there. You're busting out of this thing." I point at a seam begging to break free right at his shoulder peak. I'm flush with a thought of what that outfit ripped off and flung to the floor might look like.

It's not as if I've never seen Drew naked before—all freckles, limbs, and plentiful hairs the color of autumn leaves dappled in sunlight. But this probing thought is different. It strikes my chest, snakes south through my stomach, and settles somewhere low in my gut.

Drew inspects a fraying area around his midsection. "Shit. Can't believe I'm going to IOU a slutty nurse costume to my cousin. Is this rock bottom?" He laughs.

"You're definitely asking the right person."

My joke is met with a pinched-mouth expression. "How are you feeling?"

"The swelling has gone down, and my face doesn't feel like it's on fire anymore, which is nice." I dry swallow the two pills he's brought me. "I have an appointment with the ENT in two days. They said they can reset the fracture and put me in a cast now."

"How long will you have to wear that?"

"Ten days. Which means…"

"You'll be wearing it at CeeCee's wedding."

"Bingo." Groaning, I fall back on my pillow, nearly kicking my laptop. I'm already deep in a money hole over the urgent care visit and now this procedure. A full-time job with real benefits would be a godsend right now, even if it's with Doop. "Weddings are kind of traps when you think about it. Trapped in a room with a bunch of people you know and don't want to talk to, and then another bunch of people you don't know and don't want to talk to. Weddings could be emails."

"Subject line: We Did It! Send Gifts."

"It would save everyone a lot of time and money." I pick up my phone, ready to jot this down in my notes app. There's a nugget of a joke in here somewhere. But then I stop myself.

If I'm leaving the Hardy-Har Hideaway, I probably won't be performing for a while. New material needs to take a back seat to this new life that may include a desk job at Doop.

Could it also include Drew in a different role?

Drew sets his tray down, tugging at the hem of his skirt, trying to make sure it doesn't ride up too far. Which is impossible. I can see the edges of his baby-blue boxer briefs beneath the lattice of his stretched-to-the-max fishnets. I never noticed how thick and bitable his thighs were before.

Drew says something I don't catch because I'm attempting to shake the thought of what the heat of his skin might feel like in that spot. In the face of all this other change, I sense my feelings for Drew growing larger and louder inside my chest. Impossible to ignore. My brain itching for stimulation, newness, and *him*.

"It won't be all bad." Drew rolls so he's on his side, looking up at me, finger absent-mindedly toying with the dangling string on my hoodie. Like he's a tabby cat. A really cute tabby cat in a silly costume.

"How so?"

"It won't be all bad because," Drew says, "all the attention will be on CeeCee."

"You say that like it's a good thing."

"It is a good thing," he says, "since it means there will be so many regimented activities and meals and photo ops. Not to mention the open bar and the dancing. I'm merely trying to point out that you won't be the one in the big white dress."

"So I shouldn't show up in my flawless recreation of Princess Di's wedding gown—train, veil, and all?" That would add a whole new dimension to the black-sheep role I've been given in the Baker family.

"You would certainly turn heads." Drew lies back, splayed out across my bedspread, the fabric of his costume pulling tighter, and tighter, and…

"Like you in that costume," I say without thinking.

"Oh, uh, thanks." He's blushing so hard as he sits up.

We let my words lie between us. I can tell I've surprised him, and I know for certain I've surprised myself.

"Want to help me make dinner? I got all the ingredients for Bolognese," Drew says. It's clear he's flustered and trying to change the subject. I don't blame him. I've made an immaculately awkward mess in as little words as possible.

"My favorite," I chirp like I'm newly surprised by his thoughtfulness and completely undisturbed by what I just said.

I leave behind my blanket cocoon and my trashy TV show (and maybe my neediness too) to help him boil, slice, and simmer.

He sheds his nurse outfit before we start, which is a bit of a bummer but understandable. He trades it out for sweats and a crewneck that says "Open a Book. Open Your Heart."

It's been a while since we've done this together. Our work shifts are always in opposition. He spends his days at the store. I spend my nights at the club. When we catch a rare moment with each other, we're smoking a bowl on the fire escape or binging the latest episode of *Drag Race* in our brief period of overlap.

These last few days have reminded me what our true dynamic is like. As Drew readies the meat sauce in a large silver pot and I prepare a few pieces of garlic toast in our toaster oven, I really lay it all out for myself.

We live together. We're cooking together. We take trips upstate together to pick apples and take in the fall foliage. The only parts of a relationship we don't do are the kissing or the sexing. And not all queer relationships even have those parts...

If I'm rethinking my career, maybe I could rethink my relationship with Drew too. A desk job would mean we'd both be home nights, I'd have a steadier stream of income, and the pressure to perform wouldn't hit so hard.

I've already said something out of left field tonight. Why not add another big swing?

"Drew?" I ask, as he taste tests his creation, *mmms* without a self-conscious care, and then meets my eyes. Happy. "What would you say if...I asked you to be my date to CeeCee's wedding?" He chokes on the meat sauce in his mouth, eyes widening to alarming proportions. I haven't seen him this shocked since he found out mass market books were going to be made bigger and his whole shelf aesthetic was going to be ruined. "Jeez, you don't need to gag over it. A simple no would've sufficed."

Grabbing the nearby dish towel, he wipes his mouth, blue eyes watery. "That wasn't a no-choke"—he pauses to cough and catch his breath—"That was a...was a surprised choke. A really surprised choke." He's blushing again now.

"A good surprised or a bad surprised?" I ask, ready to backtrack at a moment's notice should he answer in the negative. My nervous heart skips several beats.

He bites his lip before saying, "Are surprises usually good or bad?"

"Uh, yeah? Getting a brand-new car for your eighteenth birthday: good surprise. Finding out you have chlamydia after having sex on the second date: bad surprise." I don't add that I speak from experience. On both accounts.

"Good point." He looks all stern and sensible. It's infuriatingly wonderful. While he mulls this over, he moves to the fridge, produces a freezer pack of peas, and wraps it in a clean dish towel—blue with a floral pattern. His long deliberation makes me wilt, until he presses the makeshift ice pack gently to the center of my face, certain not to cause me any undue harm, and grins. "Are you serious about this?"

"As serious as I am about scoring tickets to Matteo Lane's next tour, yes." I shoot him with my best pity-me eyes. Damn, as someone who hates getting them, I certainly have no qualms about inflicting them on others. "I need a buffer. Please, be my buffer."

"The four words every man longs to hear." His eyes drift away.

"Drew..." I hold my breath.

So many minuscule choices fell into the blender of my life and churned out the sludgiest smoothie imaginable. Instead of gulping it down with my nose plugged—not like I could do that anyway in my present state—I'm throwing it out and starting a new one from scratch. Something heathy with, like, acai and shit. Something Doop might feature on their website.

Lord, help me.

I'm tired of being stuck in the same spot, doing the same things that aren't working anymore. Forget my arbitrary rules and my refrain of *from afar...* Comedy has hurt me a thousand times over, but Drew—gentle, careful, sweet Drew—would never, *could* never.

Finally, he nods, a roguishness flitting across his expression. "Then, I'll be your date."

"Really?" Suddenly my last hope feels utterly hopeful.

"Yeah," he says, checking on the pasta. "You know how many romance books I've read. I may not have been to many weddings before, but I've picked up so much. I'm going to be the best damn wedding date. Even a fictional character couldn't compare."

If Drew and I were characters in one of those books, we'd go into the wedding as friends and come out as romantic partners. I clutch tight to that burst of hope and ignore the niggling in my gut that screams *What about your dreams?* Because maybe having it all was asking the universe for far too much.

Stardom was a shot in the dark, and Drew is the light at the end of a long tunnel.

"I'm looking forward to it," I say, heart fluttering, and for the first time when talking about CeeCee's wedding, I realize I'm telling the truth.

PART TWO

CLEAR QUARTZ

Look deep within

Chapter Eight

Love is in the air.

Literally.

From the trellised roof of the outdoor space, heart-shaped golden bulbs hang down over the venue. Even turned off, they sparkle, catching the fading spring sun as they twist in the breeze. It's beautiful, and my excitement hasn't waned.

Love is by my side.

Drew stands to my right, holding my hand in his as the wedding photographer sets up for the pre-ceremony family portraits.

I don't know if it's the ambiance, the way Drew's blue tie brings out his eyes, or the last six days that we've spent excitedly talking about how wasted we plan to get while dancing our asses off, but whatever the case, I think tonight's the night I tell Drew about my withheld feelings.

Love is…about to get real.

As if this day weren't massive enough.

My parents stand nearby, glancing around like they hope someone will ask them to be of service. Mom's in a peacock-blue lace dress with short sleeves and buttons up the front. The color complements her every-season tan. Mom loves the sun and it loves her right back.

Dad, much pastier given his aversion to anything outdoors, wears a tan suit with a matching peacock-blue tie. He looks like a high schooler costumed for the spring musical, waiting for his cue to go on. Dad lives in Wranglers and old T-shirts at the hardware store he and my uncle own and work at.

Well, *worked* at. Ever since his depression diagnosis, he's stepped back from the day-to-day. Uncle Stew has him working from home, making calls, filing papers. I can imagine this isolation makes the depression worse, but as CeeCee likes to remind me, I'm not a doctor, so my input is unwelcome.

And he seems in good spirits today. They both do. That's what counts.

"Are you sure you're not in too much pain, Nolan?" Mom asks for the third time today, over-worrying the way she's prone to. Better than last night at the rehearsal dinner when she spent half the meal on WebMD seeing if there were any chronic conditions or lingering symptoms that could spring up after a fractured nose.

"I'm fine. I promise." Drew squeezes my hand tighter, and the sentiment grows truer. This week alone, Drew accompanied me to my ENT appointment, surprise ordered us takeout from my favorite Italian restaurant, and even let me choose what we watched curled up on the couch on Thursday night. It's been bliss—comedy and the club the furthest things from my mind.

Until Dad asks, "What is it you were doing again?" I was sparse with the details when I called them (work, accident, ow).

Mom jumps in. "Did you forget to wear the nonslip shoes I ordered you? If you're going to continue working in a kitchen, you have to be more careful."

"I don't work *in* a kitchen, Mom."

"You work *around* a kitchen, which is *like* working in a kitchen, and I read online that nonslip shoes are important, and the ones I sent you had the best reviews online. Did you read the reviews when I sent you the link?"

"I honestly don't remember," I say. "But I probably won't need them anymore because I put in my two weeks' notice and applied for the social media position CeeCee recommended me for at Doop."

Mom practically vibrates with excitement the second I finish my sentence. "Oh, Nolan. That's wonderful. Have you heard about the first interview? Benefits? Next steps?"

"Not yet. I think most of the company had their hands full with this." I gesture at the grandeur around us.

Doop employees, all camouflaged in formal attire and artfully hidden headsets, are scurrying around like mice in Cinderella's room, tidying, fixing, and making sure everything is perfect for what is meant to be the ultimate fairy-tale wedding of this century and the next.

The Flamhaff Hotel, a former factory turned boutique hotel and to-die-for wedding venue, is completely decked out for my sister's big day. A wall of cascading flowers and feathers that reads #DoopThereItIs and #QuakerWedding, which is a hybrid of Qualley (James's last name) and Baker (CeeCee's and my last name)— slightly unfortunate because it looks as if this is a wedding for the guy on the oatmeal box—lays the backdrop for our photos.

Dad furrows his brow. "That's the kind of job you want?"

Mom lightly smacks Dad in the stomach before I can answer. "Of course that's the kind of job he wants, Carl. It's full-time with insurance. We don't have to worry about what he'll do in a few years when he can't be on our plan anymore." I'm already dreading that day. The copay while on their insurance was already astronomical.

"Yes," Dad says, clearly a bit miffed about the smacking, rubbing the spot with his right hand. "I'm only asking because I know how much the comedy club means to him." Dad's understanding eyes land on me. He's never said it outright, but I've always sensed he was a quiet champion of my comedy dreams. He showed me my first stand-up special. Took me to my first comedy show. Like many men from his generation, he isn't much of a talker, but we shared a language through laughs, the jokes we both found funny, that bonded us more than words ever could.

"It's okay," I tell him. "I don't even have the job yet, so we'll see what happens. Maybe it'll be good for me. At the very least, it'll inspire some new material." *Even if no one ever hears it*, I think before shaking that thought away.

As if sensing my discomfort, Drew jumps in. "I think congratulations are in order, Mr. and Mrs. Baker. You must be overjoyed." Drew gives good parent to the point of envy. Even in high school, he had a way of wooing everyone's guardians with a boyish smile and an offer to help with the dishes.

Mom immediately bursts into happy tears, as if completely forgetting the previous conversation. "I can't believe my little girl is getting married." Her eyes land on Drew. "And that my little boy brought you as his date. We always thought you two had a special bond. Nolan needs someone sturdy to lean on."

"I'm not a bicycle, Mom. I don't need a kickstand." Even when the kickstand in question looks as fetching as Drew does in the same suit he wore to our high school graduation. He's always been this tall and lanky and perfect, even if I didn't see it back then.

"I know, I know. I just worry. We worry." She says that like it's breaking news, taking Dad's arm and stepping in toward his side, using him as a human shield against the gusty springtime breeze so it doesn't mess up her hair. "Thank you for taking care of our son," she says to Drew.

"It's my pleasure," Drew responds, directing his sparkling smile at me.

That smile quiets my discomfort and makes my knees buckle in a good way.

"The Doop job will certainly quell some of that worry," Mom adds. "Look around; they did all this for CeeCee. Imagine what they could do for you."

I know what she's insinuating. That someday, when the time is right, Drew and I will walk down the aisle together. I like the idea, but it's a bit premature. We'll see what happens tonight, after the ceremony and the drinks and the dancing, when I plan to come clean about the love I've tucked away for too long.

"I don't think they'll be doing something like this again. They clearly blew a big chunk of their yearly budget," I say, tamping down the nervous excitement gurgling in my stomach.

Dad's already off on another thought. "Once we're done with these pictures, don't let me forget to have one final man-to-man chat with John before the ceremony."

"Carl, it's James," Mom says.

Dad reddens but holds his ground. "That's what I said."

"No, it's not, but it's fine."

"I know our daughter's fiancé's name, Dana. It's all over the place."

"Well, then you slipped up. No harm, right?" Mom looks at me and Drew for backup.

"Right, it happens to all of us." My offer is met with even more resistance, Dad's face growing ruddier. He hates being pacified. I get that from him.

"Maybe, but it doesn't happen to me." He jabs his thumb into the center of his chest before stalking over to stand behind the photographer.

I don't remember when the slipups started exactly, but if I had to guess, I'd say it was around the time CeeCee went off to college. I recall Dad setting the table for dinner and putting out a plate and utensils for CeeCee, even though she was away at Penn State.

He'd look at me when I reminded him, as if reappearing from a misty fog, and say, "Right. I knew that. Force of habit. You do something for eighteen years, and it sticks. It'll unstick sooner or later."

Later never came.

That thought gets whisked away as soon as CeeCee steps out onto the terrace in her ivory, cap-sleeved wedding dress, hair down, tulle cathedral veil sweeping behind her. Her smile is radiant.

I saw her in the fittings, but this is a whole other level of stunning. She's always gorgeous, but today especially so. Mom's crying again. Dad's crying. And, dammit, I'm tearing up too, which makes CeeCee upset.

"Stop it!" she cries with a wavering smile. "I'm already going to cry during the vows. I need this makeup to hold." The four of us huddle in for a family hug, something we haven't done in a long time. It's nice. I breathe this in.

Before I know it, we're being arranged and then rearranged. Again and again.

The cameraperson appears disgruntled behind her equipment, squinting and sighing when they can't get the shot right. "We're getting a lot of glare off that nose thing. Can you take that off?"

"Uh, no, it's kind of taped to my face." I knew something like this would happen, yet I wasn't prepared for how ruffled it would make me feel.

The cameraperson presses a palm to their forehead. "Okay, can we powder it, maybe?"

A makeup team trots into frame, pushing their brushes in my face, powder flying and making me sneeze, which undoes their work. "It's fine. I'll just not be in the picture." I step aside, cheeks hot with embarrassment.

I expect Dad to speak up for me, but surprisingly it's CeeCee who isn't having this. "Nonsense. It's a family shot. You're family. They'll edit the photo later." She smiles at me, *really* smiles at me, which is new and nice and appreciated. "Make it work," she says, using the iciness she usually reserves for me and funneling it at the photographer.

"I really don't want to ruin the shot," I whisper, testing this new niceness.

"The only way you'll ruin the shot is by not being in it," CeeCee says, surprising me even more. A surge of emotions crackles through me. Miraculously, I feel like a proper part of the family unit. Not the Lego that got lopped off and is now lying in the middle of the floor waiting to be stepped on.

Posing for a picture we'll cherish forever, I don't feel so out of place. Even with the eye-drawing splint taped to my nose, I belong. Of course, I had to change a few key aspects of myself—namely my job—but that seems small in the grand scheme of things, right?

The cameraperson whispers something to their assistant, who's trying to reposition the lights to the best of their ability. It's not until a redheaded knight steps up with a large umbrella branded with the hotel's name and glittery logo on it that a solution arrives. "Will this help?"

Drew stands far enough to the side to be out of the shot, but his height allows him to position the umbrella in a way that casts a shadow right over my face, blocking the rays from reflecting off my splint. "Easier to brighten up his face in post than edit out the glare, yeah?" Drew says, as if he's been hiding a secret knowledge of photography in his back pocket for this exact occasion.

Drew. Wholly wonderful Drew, who I should've asked to be my date from the very beginning because nobody knows me like he does and nobody else's thoughtfulness could ever compare.

Certainty curls up inside my chest like a dog in the sunshine. Tonight's the night that I let those eight letters, three words, and one big meaning out from the locked vault inside my chest. I only hope he receives the treasure I've hidden inside as warmly as he's smiling at me right now.

I mouth a thank-you to him right before the shutter goes off.

Chapter Nine

"You survived it," Drew says to me a short while after the ceremony, surprising me with his arrival. I was having some alone time out on a balcony overhanging the terrace where party people mill about and snack on hors d'oeuvres.

Drew hands me the signature cocktail from the open bar—a dirty martini with a sprig of rosemary speared through a swollen olive at the bottom of the shapely glass. "What a ceremony."

"It was beautiful." I say, wistful. When I passed CeeCee James's ring, in that fleeting moment of contact—sun setting, eyes glimmering—we clicked back into our old selves. And I cried.

When the happy couple kissed, dusk blanketing the outdoor terrace, the twinkle lights strung overhead blinked on, and Taylor Swift's "Lover" played on piano filtered in from the other room. The romanticism was all-encompassing, and I thought, *If a desk job gets me all this, maybe it won't be so bad.*

"I'd like to thank pomegranate mimosas, sheer willpower, and…" I hover over the word for a second. "*You*, Drew." It's a sweeping statement brought on by the day. The unexpected emotions. The about-face that happened when my sister exchanged her beautiful vows. Whatever our petty disagreements in the past, I melted into a puddle of brotherly love.

As CeeCee and James walked back down the aisle, together, outside arms raised in triumph as if to say "We did it, world! We found our perfect match! Take that!" a Hunger Games cannon sounded in my mind, signaling the death of our childhoods. We'll never be young and messy together again.

Once this campaign launches, CeeCee will go on to a bigger salary, move out of Jersey City, join a nonfiction book club, take up gardening her own vegetables, and maybe have her first kid. And, where will I be? Hopefully here with Drew, flipping the page to a new, fresh chapter that I've been too preoccupied and scared to write.

"What did I do besides show up and look pretty?" Drew asks, winsome, running his thumb across his cutely dimpled chin. I know my fears about taking a step out of the platonic and into the romantic are founded, but I've got wedding glitter gunking up my heart, and my whole body is aching for change.

Good change. A new start.

I brush a stray hair out of Drew's eye. "You were here for me. You ran interception with my parents. You saved the photos. I don't know what I did to deserve you." After I say it, I shudder a little. "In my life, I mean. I don't know what I did to deserve you in my life."

Down below, the Doop staff and hotel staff work together to transform the indoor-outdoor space for dinner. Long communal wooden tables. Centerpieces of wildflowers. Tall candles and golden cutlery. They move with precision and intensity, yet here, as I gaze into Drew's eyes, they are a blur of peripheral motion.

"Just trying to make good on my declaration of being the best wedding date there ever was." He sips his drink, which I think is an attempt to hide his blush, which has already spread down his neck and under the collar of his crisp white shirt.

"We're only at the halfway point of this thing, and you've passed that test with flying colors."

"Don't tally the score just yet. There's still a meal to eat and some dancing to do."

I roll my eyes. "Unless you start eating with your feet or request the Electric Slide, I think it's safe to say you've secured gold status when it comes to wedding dates."

"I see your Electric Slide and raise you a Cotton-Eyed Joe."

"Oh, yeah? If you request the Cotton-Eyed Joe, then I'm hell-bent on doing the Cupid Shuffle."

"God, no. Anything but the Cupid Shuffle. I'll have the directions stuck in my head for at least five days."

"Don't test me, Techler. I'm a menace when it comes to line dances."

He steps closer to me, our cups almost clinking. If I didn't know any better, I'd think he was putting the moves on me. Is he thinking what I'm thinking? His breath smells like gin and vermouth, a taste that would be so much less satisfying if I got it from my own glass. "When pushed, I can be even more menacing…"

He tilts his head down toward me. The two of us are basking in a nighttime glow, an event-day high. I lengthen my neck, curious. So damn curious. "How so?"

My eyes become a ruler, taking detailed measurements as the inches between our lips become centimeters and the centimeters become millimeters. We hold there for what feels like forever, hovering over the precipice of the impossible. Am I imagining this?

Suddenly, he whispers, "Gangnam Style."

My immediate laughter gets interrupted by Drew's upturned lips crashing into mine.

I'm not imagining this in the slightest. No, I'm kissing Drew Techler. His silky tie slips between my fingers while his hands dome around my face, careful our noses don't bump. Not that I'd notice. Breath hot, heart racing, I'm too busy relishing this, feeling his pulse drum into my palm at the base of his neck. It's heaven.

When he pulls back, I stumble off-center, stunned, clutching my burning cheek. I accidentally spill part of my drink over the ledge, narrowly missing the head of an unsuspecting guest in a mint-green gown. Thank God the olive stayed put.

Afraid someone might look up and see us, I take Drew by the hand, jerk him inside, and ditch my martini glass behind a portly clay vase—no evidence, no crime.

Relaxing, I laugh a little to myself. "I'm such a fucking klutz. Goddamn."

"At least you're a handsome klutz." Drew reaches out to smooth down my lapel where he'd rumpled it seconds ago.

"You…kissed me," I say finally, a little awestruck. Our first *real* kiss. My lips still tingle. His fingers are so close to my neck again. Any moment they could be walking their way up toward my jaw, tracing a line back to my mouth. A place where his mouth just was. All hot and bothered and fantastic.

"I did," he replies, less brazen than before. "And you kissed me back?" The question lingers.

"I…" His touch is amazing, making it nearly impossible to answer as my throat jams up with giddiness. "I did. And, listen, there's something I've been wanting to tell you…" My heart pounds and adrenaline surges. This is it. The perfect segue. My confession is about to trip right off my tongue when my phone starts buzzing in my pocket.

Dammit.

When I don't recognize the number on the screen, I sharply hit *Ignore.* "As I was saying…"

"Who was it?" Drew asks. We're in a corridor now, hidden and a bit dark.

"Spam, probably," I say, annoyance lingering over the interruption. "Now, where were we?" I lean in again, swathed in the joy and the charming albeit heteronormative displays of love, ready to tell him everything I haven't had the guts to say previously.

The roar of the party is feet from where we're standing, but it's no match for the roaring inside my head. The floating inside my chest. The buzzing against my leg. Against my leg? "Shit, it's the same number. *And* I have a voicemail?"

"Jeez, spam is getting way more aggressive these days."

I'm a firework show of frustration as I ask, "I should take this, right?"

Drew nods, practical. "Could be important."

"Ugh, fine." I groan, feeling all the air fly out of me. "I'll take it."

He shoves his hands, which were just roving all over me, into his pockets and backs away. "I'll make sure that woman you almost assaulted with a martini is okay." I thank him, then the door clicks shut behind him. He waves at me through the window, and my heart squeezes.

I answer the phone in a huff. "Hello? If this is a telemarketer, I want you to know you may have just ruined a pivotal moment in my not-quite relationship with my best friend, so this better be good."

"Nolan Baker? This is Clive Bergman." If I were still holding my martini glass, it would be on the floor right now, alongside my jaw. "Am I catching you at a bad time?"

I glance out onto the wedding through the tiny window in the door before moving away from it, muffling the noise by cupping my hand around the end of my phone. "No, this is a great time. Excellent time. Couldn't be better."

Cruising down the hallway, I jiggle a bunch of handles.

Locked. Locked. One gives way, but I'm accosted immediately by two Doop employees dressed in all black who are poring over goody bags. "Hey, you can't be in here!" a familiar one shouts while the other shields their activity from view.

Okaaaaaaay.

"Everything good?" Clive asks as I discover a housekeeping closet, flip on the light, and shut myself inside so nobody overhears or interrupts. "I got your number from the booker at the Broadway Laugh Box. I hope that's okay."

"Yeah, totally. That's great. Excellent—"

"Couldn't be better?" His smile comes through in his voice. "To make a long story short, my usual opener for tonight caught a nasty flu and can't come down to perform. I liked what I saw of your set a while back. It was just the right amount of unpolished energy I like to have at my shows, and the booker here said you left quite the impression."

"I did?" I ask, shocked. "I mean, thank you. That's really amazing to hear, but what are you asking exactly?"

"I was hoping you could come down to the Laugh Box in about an hour and do a tight-ten." My heart and my stomach meet in the center of my torso, twist around each other, and then explode. This is everything I've ever wanted. Only to me would it happen on the night of my sister's wedding and Drew's and my first real kiss.

Catastrophe. Why must my life always be in complete and total disarray? I thought I was taking actionable steps in the opposite direction.

Putting Clive on speaker, I check how far the Broadway Laugh Box is from my location. Without any unnecessary roadblocks, I can get there in forty minutes on the subway. Maybe even sooner if I call a rideshare.

But the ironclad itinerary is a familial anchor in my pocket. I'm due to make the grand entrance with the rest of the bridal party as soon as CeeCee is done changing into her shorter, flirtier reception dress—equally as expensive for less fabric (make it make sense). Then there's the first dance, Dad's speech, the dinner, slow-dancing deliciously close with Drew, possibly on the verge of beginning something extra special.

I can't dip.

"You still with me, Nolan?" Clive asks.

I wish I *were* with him. In Midtown, prepping for a big gig. A gig that could open so many doors for me if I nail it and allow me to withdraw my Doop application. Get my five-year and ten-year plans back on track. But, of course, once again, my family steps between me and the dreams I'd just folded like a winter coat for storage in the attic during the summer months. I sigh. "Yeah, I'm still here, but I can't. I'm sorry. I won't make it in time."

My body grows leaden. If I thought my comedy career died at my audition, this was its zombie resurrection, only for it to be killed again by a vigilante farmer with a shotgun.

"Ah, all right. You do you," he says, when what he really means is "blow your chance if you wanna."

"Thanks for thinking of me." I don't get it all out before he hangs up.

This is the adult thing to do. Isn't that what my family wants from me?

That doesn't stop me from calling Jessie to tell them what happened.

"Oh my God! Call him back! Call him back right now, Nolan!"

"I can't just dip! It's my sister's wedding!" I shout. "Plus, Drew and I just kissed! Like, real kissed. There was even some tongue!"

"Uh, shit, okay," Jessie says. "First off, congrats on the tongue-kissing. That's rad, definitely need to hear more about that later. Second, read me your itinerary. There has to be a way to do both, right?"

I speed down the list. "Thoughts?"

"Go now!" they shout like that was obvious the whole time.

"Skip the dinner, and you'll be back in time for the speech. If anyone asks, play up your IBS. Easy-peasy, lemon-squeezy. You're welcome."

It does make sense, and it wouldn't be hard to pull off.

Don't let anyone—and I mean anyone—*try to squish you, Maggot.* Wanda's words are always there when I need them.

With blinders on, I say, "You're right. You're the best!"

"I know I am! Keep me posted."

With that squared away, I don't second-guess myself. I'm not letting another chance slip through my fingers. Immediately, I redial Clive's number and tell him I changed my mind.

On the way out, I open my text thread with Drew to see a message waiting.

Drew: I told your great-aunt Judy it was me who almost showered her in martini. We had a good laugh. 😄

Drew: She asked if you were still doing "that comedy thing." I didn't know what to say...

What I want to type back is: "Yes, Great-Aunt Judy, I am!" But instead, I say: Big news! Had to step out. Be back soon.

In an instant, I'm out the door.

Chapter Ten

"What's with the getup?" Clive asks.

It's absurd that I made it onto two trains, through six stops, down busy sidewalks, and not once did I consider that I was still wearing my wedding suit. I must look like a straight-up clown to Clive. Hair a mess, tie loose, nose still stinted. I shrug like this is my everyday wear. "What can I say? I like to make an entrance."

Clive nods in appreciation and extends a hand decked out with multiple rings; a stringy bracelet hangs from his wrist. "Nice to see you, Nolan. Thanks for coming down. What made you change your mind?"

We start walking back toward the green room. He skips any formal tour or introductions with any of the staff. I'm his special guest, and it's clear from everyone we pass that Clive is held in high esteem here; thus, by extension, so am I. It's a welcome change over the blatant disregard I get from most at the Hardy-Har Hideaway. "Let's just say the circumstance changed suddenly."

Speaking of circumstance, I pull out my phone. I've got three missed calls from Drew, and a few texts as well. "Hey, it's none of my business, man. I get it. Save the real shit for the stage."

Clive leads me into a communal room. A few vanity mirrors with burnt-out bulbs, crimson walls, and paper clippings framed and hung with no regard for organization. A white guy in a backward hat rolls a joint on a nearby table, while two women sit on a faded leather couch in the corner, scrolling their phones and sighing.

"Crew, this is Nolan. Nolan, this is the crew." Nobody looks up from what they're doing. Weed Bro gives a little grunt. "Make yourself at home. We'll get you out there soon. The house is about to open."

I thank him before he disappears. Uncertain where to sit given the vibe of the room, I find a corner and lean up against the least cluttered wall. I pull out my phone to sort through my notifications.

Where are you going?

What happened with that phone call?

A bit later: Can you please text me back? I'm getting worried.

It's all too much to type, so I slink further into the corner and call Drew instead. He picks up right away. "Nolan, thank God. Where are you? I went up to our room to look for you. They did the entrance dance without you."

"I know. Look, don't freak out," I preamble.

"Is this about the kiss?" Drew asks, voice soupy and concerned.

"What? Oh my God, no. This has nothing to do with that," I reassure him.

"Are you sure? Because if I scared you off, I can leave. I don't want to—"

"Drew," I cut in lovingly. "The kiss was *amazing*. And do you know what else is amazing? The Broadway Laugh Box finally called. That was Clive Bergman on the phone. I'm here. I'm going on as his opener."

I expect excitement, but instead I get exasperation. "What?" he asks. "You're in Manhattan? You know they're about to serve dinner, right?"

"Yes," I say quickly. "I'll do my thing onstage, finish up here, and slip back into the party right on cue for my mister of honor speech. CeeCee will be wowed by my heartfelt yet hilarious words. Everything will be perfect." I keep my voice as light as possible to remain convincing.

"What am I supposed to say when someone asks where you are?"

"Tell them my stomach was bothering me. One of the hors d'oeuvres. I stepped out to run to the pharmacy," I say right as a stage manager enters the room with some important information. "Drew, I have to go. It's almost showtime. I'll be back before you know it."

"Uh…okay?"

I hang up, certain my plan will work.

It's foolproof.

I'm a fool.

As usual, the audience is slow to take their seats. Front of house is swamped. The servers are racing to fill drink and food orders before the main acts take the stage. I'd be pinching myself over being one of those main acts if I weren't punching myself for being reckless.

Weed Bro from before, who ventured outside to smoke when one of the Phone Girls complained, bolts back into the room, out of breath. "Shit. You're not going to believe this. Two guys booked the same table. Some mix-up with the box office. One of the dudes was already drunk and he threw a punch. A fight broke out."

Phone Girls, having exhibited no signs of life other than apparent disgust for reality, perk up, demanding more details. When Weed Bro's info is not enough, they race out to see the commotion for themselves.

Instead of staying behind, I make my way in the direction of the stage, stomach sinking lower with each damn step. I need to find Clive. Maybe he'll understand or offer advice. Something tells me I can trust him.

I find him backstage, eyes closed, AirPods in. He's doing some kind of tai chi, shifting his weight while his arms flow freely. I hate to break his preshow calm, but I'm in a crisis. "Clive, do you think we're going to start soon?"

He pops out one pod. "Not sure. Security is escorting the men out of the club now. It wouldn't be a comedy show without seventy delays. Have you got somewhere to be?"

"Yeah, sorta." I hook my hands behind my neck, suit jacket riding up constrictively. "You see..." And then it all comes pouring out. The wedding. The stress. The five-year plan. The ten-year plan. How I just quit my job for a corporate position at Doop, thinking my comedy career was over before this miracle occurred.

I'm glad Clive was already in a zen place when I found him. Otherwise I'd probably stress him out by sheer proximity, burying him under my rapid-fire words.

Blinking back at me, he takes it all in, then looks me dead in the eyes. "I can't tell you what to do, Nolan, but can I offer you some advice?" I've never nodded faster in my life. "Doors in this business slam shut more often than they open. If you leave now, *I* won't hold it against you, but the booker, the owner? Can't say anything for certain, but they don't take kindly to no-shows."

My hooked hands find their way into my hair, raking with such furious concern I could pull each strand out by its root. Make a sculpture of my stupidity with them. "So, in other words, I'm in deep shit either way?"

"I might've used different words, but yeah, sort of." His calmness falters. "If you're as hungry for this as I think you are—I mean, hell, you left your own sister's wedding, which, *daaaaaaamn*—then it

seems like an easy choice to me. This career comes with big sacri-
fices. Are you willing to make them?"

My mind's eye flickers to CeeCee, Mom and Dad, Drew, James
and his many Connecticut-bred brothers. The other guests, the offi-
ciant, a nearly drenched Great-Aunt Judy and the plate of organic
lavender-honey-basted chicken they probably had to throw out
because I was nowhere to be found.

How happy they all were that I was finally "settling down" into
the life they wanted for me.

I have to hope that on the other side of this, they'll understand
that giving up on my dream for Doop would've never fulfilled me.
I might've found contentment, but not true happiness. Don't they
want me to be truly happy?

When they ask why I did it, I'll say: Opportunity knocked, and
I had no choice but to answer. They may not like it, but they'll have
to respect it.

Life is a series of in-the-moment choices, snowballing into an
always uncertain future. Other people can weigh in on my choices
all they want, undermine the career I've been striving for, but at the
end of the day, I'm the only one who has to live with those choices.

I choose my dream.

And I absolutely, positively *crush it.*

Chapter Eleven

Cloud Nine carries me all the way back to Brooklyn. I keep pinching myself, tiny reminders that *I fucking did that.* I brought the house down at the Broadway Laugh Box.

There wasn't a dry eye in the audience from everybody laughing so hard.

When I reenter the wedding venue, they're getting ready for the bouquet toss, which stops me in my tracks.

Wait. That can't be right. My phone died before my set and nobody had a charger handy, but I couldn't be that late, could I?

CeeCee, looking radiant with a dancing-induced, newly married glow about her, is sauntering to the center of the floor wearing a full smile.

I find myself smack in the middle of a group of onlookers who are shuffling forward with anticipation.

My heart glitches as I realize just how poor my calculations had been.

Maybe they pushed my speech back. Maybe I'll give it after this.

I turn away, attempting to extricate myself from the crowd and ask someone who works here, but my escape gets blocked off.

I pivot back, look up, and notice the bouquet of roses, dahlias, hydrangeas, and plum branches arcing in my direction. Dread clatters in my stomach. All I can think is: *Please, universe, don't give me this kind of attention. Not here. Not now.*

The floral arrangement bounces off the hands of a bridesmaid in front of me, smacks me in the face, and then lands in my shocked, shaking hands.

I spit out a few stray petals before opening my eyes.

CeeCee's death glare pins me to my spot in the crowd, swiftly squashing all the good post-show vibes. I gulp back a thick wad of spit.

She's going to get me alone and tear me limb from limb. She's going to save parts of me and pass them off as a new Doop product—rejuvenating skin serum made from the blood of your enemies.

Before I have a proper moment to react, CeeCee's gracious, captivating smile returns, and the dance floor opens back up. The sconces get dimmed, and some Jennifer Lopez throwback song pumps up the place. I have to face the music of my own actions. *Waiting for tonight! Ohhh.* More like, *Waiting for a fight! Uh-oh.*

I approach CeeCee, semi-prepared with an ironclad apology and explanation. "You missed a spot," I say lightheartedly, pointing out a few errant petals that got stuck on her dress.

Her laugh is humorless. "You missed a bunch." I can tell she's covering up her rage with Mom-asking-for-the-manager niceness. "How's your stomach? Drew said you had the shits."

To save face, at least in front of her friends, I take the jab. "Damn flaxseed muffins. My body hasn't had a healthy food in it in forever. I live on a diet of nachos and ramen these days." CeeCee's friends, Doop employees or worshippers who take full advantage of CeeCee's friends-and-family discount, all cringe. "Can I speak with you for a second?"

"We're speaking right now."

I glance at our audience. "Alone."

She relents, though she's visibly unhappy about it.

Out on the garden terrace, nighttime chill whipping up and door shut behind us, CeeCee drops the act, voice dripping with poison. "I want you to leave."

"What? I—"

She grabs the bouquet from me, throws it on the ground, and stomps on it like it's on fire. "That"—she points at the trashed flowers—"is what I think of whatever lie or excuse you're about to feed me. I know exactly where you were."

"You do?"

"When you moved to the city, I asked you to turn on your location status so that if I ever didn't hear from you, I could look on my phone and make sure you were at home or at work, safe."

I completely forgot about that. It's a small reminder of what our relationship was like before this city and our differences weaseled their way between us. "In fairness, I could've been murdered in either of those places and you'd have been none the wiser..."

"Stop! Just, stop, Nolan. Jesus, is everything a joke to you?"

"No, look, I didn't just dip. An opportunity presented itself and I thought I'd be back in time. I swear. CeeCee, I killed it. I wish you could've been there."

"Been *there*? When you were supposed to be *here*? That's rich, Nolan. Really rich." Her voice has grown sharper, angrier. "One day. One day it gets to be about me, and you...you go and do this!"

"If only the speech had been twenty minutes later..." I regret it as soon as I say it.

"I can't believe you're trying to make yourself into the victim right now. Actually, knowing you, I can!" she shouts, before seeming to remember that the party guests, including the people who employ her, are on the other side of the doors.

"If you could just listen to me for a second—"

She points a French-tipped finger at me. "That's your problem.

You think everyone needs to be listening to you. All the time. Center of attention. Jokester, class clown, comedian. The world according to Nolan Baker. Stop being so selfish and grow up already."

The doors open, and Mom steps out. "What's going on here?" It's clear she senses the tension like an impending storm. "CeeCee, they're ready for you to make your grand exit. The car is here to take you to the airport."

There's a long, contentious silence between the three of us, until CeeCee takes a breath, thanks Mom, and starts for the door. Before she makes it to the other side, she turns back and says, "I'm never going to forgive you for this. I hope you know that."

"Oh, CeeCee, you don't mean that," Mom says, but a crack in her voice undercuts the sentiment.

"I do mean it. Never." CeeCee freezes me with her ice-cold stare.

"Let's not let the night end like this." Mom steps between us, playing peacekeeper.

"My night *isn't* going to end like this," CeeCee says sternly. "My night is going to end with a bottle of champagne in a first-class cabin on the way to Hawaii. Nolan, you've already messed up my wedding. I won't let you mess with my honeymoon, too, by making me late." After a pause, she adds, "I hope you get the life you deserve."

Those words wrap around my heart like shackles, in sharp contrast with the freedom and elation I felt onstage earlier. I wish I'd handled it better, but still, against all odds, I don't regret going. How could I when I can still hear the ghost of that receptive audience? I had them in the palm of my hand.

The door slamming shut makes me jump. I pull my suit coat tight around me, waiting for Mom to say something. To comfort me, maybe?

"Where have you been?" she asks, sounding small.

"Something came up."

She shakes her head, short, brown hair bouncing around her face. "I'm very disappointed in you right now, and so is Dad."

"Where is Dad?" I ask, veering us off-topic. "I don't recall seeing him after the bouquet toss."

Mom winces with her inhale. "He's…upstairs resting. It's been a long day. He got tired." She's wringing her hands, uncomfortable probably. "Changing the subject won't fix things, you understand? I don't know what's gotten into you lately."

"Why do you always take her side?" I ask, unmasking some of my pent-up resentment. My success onstage tonight has planted confidence inside me that's taken hold; it won't allow me to hold back.

"I'm your mom. I don't take sides."

"It feels like you do. It's always felt like you do." It's hard to admit that, maybe after all these years, moving away and finding my voice, I still crave Mom and Dad's approval. That their dissatisfaction makes the commute every morning from New Jersey, hops off the bus at Port Authority, and cuddles up next to me in bed when I wake up. When I look myself in the mirror to brush my teeth and my hair, it stands beside me, reminding me that, as the free-spirited artist, I've somehow let the whole family down by existing.

Mom purses her lips. "I try my best, every day, to be the mother you children need, and maybe I've fumbled a few times along the way. That's life. This wasn't a fumble, what you did today. It wasn't a mistake. It was a willful choice. The wrong choice."

"Wrong for you and CeeCee, maybe," I say. "But right for me." I remain firm in that. Tonight's gig is a giant step toward a successful future. Why can't anyone else see that?

Mom frowns. "I can't believe this. On what should've been a lovely day for your sister and the new son we're welcoming into our family."

"More like replacement son."

"Why would you say that?" She can't stop shaking her head.

"Because it's true, isn't it?" Sadness cranks through my veins, dissolving the last of my high from the show. Mom is seemingly speechless. "I was amazing today. The best I've ever been, and I can almost hear the doors of opportunity flying open for me, but that won't ever be enough for you, will it? You'll always wish I were more like CeeCee. You'll always wish I'd grown up into a James."

I wait for an answer that never comes. Instead, I get: "After today, it's clear you're a long way from being done with growing up."

I want to rebuke that. Rebuke that to hell! But I get interrupted by a deeply tragic cover of "Whoomp! There It Is"—the hip-hop hit from the '90s—changed to "Doop! There It Is" for this occasion. "I'm going to see your sister off."

Without another word, she ducks inside past the gauzy curtains.

Alone, I pick up the remnants of the bouquet CeeCee stomped on. Petals are strewn like puzzle pieces across the brick. Some drift off on a spring breeze to be lost, and I wonder if, like these flowers, this mess is unfixable.

I don't know what possess me to, but I hug the flower stems and branches to my chest and carry them inside. There's something wrong about leaving them to rot out there, to lie until the cleaning crew sweeps them away.

On my way out, following the flow of the crowd, I look for Drew but don't spot him before I'm pulled aside by Ryan, the Doop receptionist I met a few weeks ago. He holds out a peacock-blue gift bag with a golden, twisty handle. "Don't forget your party favors." He wears an unsettling, unwavering smile, and I'm hit with the memory of those employees in the secret room from earlier. The dark hallway at their offices. That stupid candle.

Peering past him and around the room, I notice everyone else exiting has a white gift bag. "Why's mine a different color?"

"These are for the bridal party only. Extra special Doop products inside," he chirps. "Picked specifically for each of you." To make matters even more unsettling, he winks. Oh God, is that what I looked like when I winked at Harry? Note to self: No more winking ever again. I accept the bag and start off. "Oh, and Nolan?" I turn back, more than ready for this exchange to be over so I can find Drew. "It's never too late to make a change."

Words get stuck in a traffic jam behind my lips. I'm paralyzed by that grating piece of advice until Ryan takes the bag back and swivels it around. Stamped on one side is:

DOOP
IT'S NEVER TOO LATE TO MAKE A CHANGE.

Oh. I forgot. It's the passive-aggressive tagline for this whole sham brand.

He passes it back with one more smile. "Take care, Nolan Baker."

Chapter Twelve

Drew, an absolute sight for sore eyes, is perched on the clean white duvet on the far bed when I arrive back to the hotel room. After the high of the crowd and the crush of my family's disappointment, I'm emotionally drained, and Drew, I know, will revive me, maybe even share in my previous excitement.

He's facing away, staring out the window. Moon and city lights shimmer across the ripping surface of the East River beyond the pane.

The lamps in the room are dimmed to an ambient glow, and the flat-screen TV is on at a dull roar, some TBS syndicated movie from the early 2000s I'm sure Drew has seen a million times is playing. A song I remember being on a playlist I made as a kid underscores a slow dance scene.

I drop my goody bag on the desk. "I'm so happy to see you." Drew doesn't turn to look at me. Or, move at all, really. His shoulders are hunched, closed-off. He's probably tired.

I slip off my shoes, and then tiptoe across the carpet so I'm in front of him. "My family is majorly pissed, but, Drew, I rocked my set tonight." When he finally looks up to meet my eyes, I notice that his are bloodshot. "Have you been crying?" Then I notice his suitcase is repacked, zipped, and standing on its wheels beside him. "Are you leaving?"

"You put me in an impossible position," he says, voice barely above a croak.

Dread returns with a vengeance. "I know. I know. I'm really, I mean, *really* sorry about that." He's stopped blinking, and he's staring straight through me now like he's got X-ray vision. "I really thought I'd be back in time."

"You had me lie to your family," he says with a level of frustration he usually reserves for solving the Sunday crossword.

"Yeah, I shouldn't have asked you to do that," I admit, shame starting to mingle with the dread.

"But I did it because…" He takes a deep breath and then makes a tearful confession. "Because, Nolan, I love you."

His words don't compute at first, as if I'm hearing them in another language being spoken in another room. "I–I love you, too? I don't see what you—"

"Not like that." He runs a hand down his face, muscles loosening, only to snap back into a rigid, tense state of unease. "Not as a friend. I'm *in* love with you. I've been *in* love with you. For a long time."

My heart starts pounding, and my ears start ringing. He beat me to the punch. He's just confirmed that he returns my feelings. I should be overjoyed, but I'm so bogged down with emotional overload, winded with whiplash.

"I thought today was special. That maybe if I was the perfect wedding date, you could see me, too, in a different light," Drew says. "Or at least start to."

"I didn't need to start to," I say, untangling my tongue. "Because I do. I already do. Love you, I mean. I was going to tell you earlier. I love you, Drew." My words run together, frantic to make this right.

He lifts his chin, lip wobbly. "You do?" I nod in confirmation, slow and heavy. "How can one piece of news be both elating and heartbreaking?"

The day is a blur of events, but I haven't forgotten about our kiss.

Now, remembering the heat of him pressed against me, I'm unable to respond in any articulate way. "I don't know what to say to that."

"You don't have to say anything." Drew stands, pulling on the handle of his suitcase so it glides along behind him. "Because I decided that I need time away from you."

His words sucker punch me. "Ouch." It's all I can say, really, to verbalize the pain that's vaulting through my heart. I feel like a crash-test dummy being repeatedly driven into a wall. The positive adrenaline constantly giving way to a devastating airbag blow.

"I'm sorry, Nolan. That didn't come out exactly right. There's a lot going on in my head right now."

"Didn't you hear me, though?" I ask hoarsely. My wellspring of tears replenishes. "I love you too. I love you back. I've been sitting on these feelings for probably as long as you have, waiting for the moment when I could stop aggressively clutching my career aspirations and give myself over to them...*you*." Because from afar I couldn't fuck it up, right?

He shakes his head. "You basically stood me up at your own sister's wedding."

"When you say it like that, it sounds bad, but I promise it was for a good reason."

"Really?" he asks before audibly swallowing. "You're worried about whether I'm hearing you, but I don't think you're hearing yourself."

"What I'm hearing is that you're starting to sound like my family." My defenses are fired up. "You think I should give up on my dreams too? Become a servant to Doop and the corporate machine?"

"Never," Drew says, and I know he means it, which only makes this situation worse. "I hope you get everything you've ever wanted, but I—I need some time to figure out what *I* want, independent of you. Especially since your words and your actions don't exactly line up."

"Wait, what?" I notice the suitcase again. "Where are you going? If you're going home, let me come with you. We should talk about this."

"We just did. Talk about it, I mean." He pauses only long enough to look back. "I'm going to stay with my cousin for a bit. Take some time to go home and visit my mom. Then, when I'm ready, I'll come back to the apartment to let you know what I've decided."

"Decided? About what?"

"About whether I'll stay for another year or not."

My ears must be deceiving me. "Hold on, you're considering moving out?"

His nod is grim. "Our lease is up in two months anyway. After tonight, I need my space. I think you might too."

As the suitcase starts rolling again, my mind sputters and restarts. Suddenly, I see this for what it is. A joke. Drew is playing the ultimate prank. Cruel, maybe, but his commitment is damn near perfect. Laughter, sharp and high-pitched, springs out of me. "Okay, you got me. You can drop the act now."

"What?" he asks.

"This. You're joking, right?" It's a bit garbled because of my unsettled laughter. "You can't be serious."

He holds up a fist in front of his mouth, shutting his eyes, cheeks growing redder than I've ever seen them. "I wish I wasn't serious, but at least one of us has to be. I don't think I can be in love with you right now because I don't think you have the space in your life to love anything more than comedy. Goodbye, Nolan."

The thud of the door catalyzes my laughter again. The tears come second. Spilling from my eyes in salty waterfalls. I slink over to the bed, clawing my way up the duvet until my head hits the pillow.

Curling up in the fetal position, I lie there like that for a long while. Laughing and crying. Crying and laughing.

The movie Drew had on in the background comes to an end. A familiar eighties song cranks over the credits. For some reason, this only makes me cry harder.

Hours pass, and I accept the fact that I'm going to sleep in my very expensive suit, except sleep never visits me. I can't stop thinking about how much I gained and how much I lost in the same fell swoop.

The pros and the cons sort themselves into neat lists inside my head. Somehow, even through my tears, the pros seem to win out. The relationships can be mended; the opportunity was once in a lifetime.

It's selfish to admit, but I'd do it again. Sure, there are changes I'd make, but I wouldn't take it back entirely. Not for a million bucks.

No matter how spent I am or how tired I feel, the minute I close my eyes I'm met with a greatest hits montage of disapproving looks and harsh words. Propping up the pillows, I fiddle with the remote, channel surfing until I land on QVC, and when a middle-aged woman trying to sell me a foot bath doesn't hold my attention, I surf away on my thoughts again.

This will blow over. They can't stay mad at me forever. Everyone needs sleep and time and space and, for one person in particular, a spirited honeymoon to forget this ever even happened.

In another world, another life, they should be ecstatic for me. Tonight (or last night at this point) I might've secured a permanent spot at the Broadway Laugh Box. I might've even clinched an opportunity to go on the road opening for Clive. Who knows what tomorrow holds for my comedy aspirations?

When the woman with the blond bob on TV gets tapped out by a woman with a brown bob and the foot bath becomes a standing desk and rolling chair combo, my eyes wander from the screen and land on the goody bag I dropped with a flourish on the nightstand.

What had the weird Doop employee said? All the products were picked out especially for us? I'm not certain why CeeCee thought I needed a dried flower crown. Or is it a wreath? Either way, it's now on my head, adorning me as the reigning King of Chaos.

As I set aside a blush-pink mug and a botanical serum, I find a small velvet sack with glittery stars all over it. When I undo the tassel and dump the contents into my hand, I find a collection of crystals and a folded-up piece of paper with the color and texture of parchment.

I'm a natural-born skeptic. I don't believe some hunk of rock can cure you or fix you or change your fate. Though I didn't believe the Go to Sleep, Bitch candle could cause me to pass the fuck out right away either...

As I unroll the tiny, scroll-like piece of paper, I'm surprised to find that, tonight of all nights, maybe I *want* to believe.

In this collection, you will find clear quartz, black obsidian, hematite, rose quartz, malachite, citrine, and pyrite. These specially shaped crystals were chosen in consort to help the user manifest their ideal future.

Instructions:
Hold the crystals close to your chest.
Set a strong intention.
Visualize the ideal outcome. Speak it into the universe.
Place crystals under your pillow for sleep.
Wake up rejuvenated and ready to start anew.

What kind of "Princess and the Pea" nonsense is that?

Pushing all the junk to one side of the bed, I slog into the bathroom, wash my face, brush my teeth, and contemplate a hot shower before ultimately deciding that that's too much work for my sleep-addled, emotionally drained body. I return to the room, turn off the TV, strip down to my underwear, and hop under the covers, hoping dreams will come and whisk me away somewhere pleasant and unscrewed.

They don't.

No matter how dark I make it. No matter how cold I set the thermostat, its continuous hum becomes less like a white-noise machine and more like a marching band. I even switch beds, wondering if maybe one mattress is softer than the other, attempting to convince my mind it no longer needs to be awake, alert, *thinking*. The second mattress is, for some reason, plusher, but Drew's scent lingers there—Dove soap and lavender.

Maybe I am a Hans Christian Andersen character after all, and I'm passing the queen's test tenfold. Only trouble is, my prince just walked out on me.

When the clock finally blinks 3:13 a.m., I throw off the covers and shuffle like a zombie around the room.

In my shuffling, I notice the scroll with the crystal instructions is flipped over. On the back is the Doop logo with its foreboding slogan: *It's Never Too Late to Make a Change.*

That's what everyone in my life wants from me. Change. Change in attitude. Change in behavior. Change in goals. Everything that makes me *me*. That list doesn't even include the changes *I* want. Change in address. Change in relationship status. Change in job title.

Sleep deprivation wins out as I reread the instructions, cradling the crystals close to my heart chakra, and set my "intention." Whatever that's supposed to mean.

"I intend to become successful, happy, and universally loved…

Annnnnd I intend to prove everyone who doubted me wrong." Maybe it's petty, but it's truthful, and damn, am I in for a dose of truth after the day I just had.

I close my eyes, and the ideal future—successful comedian, together with Drew, everyone proud of me—becomes a whimsical paint-by-numbers image in my mind, so serene and awesome that I almost forget how badly shit hit the fan today.

I feel like simply saying my intentions out loud isn't enough, so I blow on the crystals as if they were casino dice, jiggle them around in my hand, and let them loose beneath my pillow so they land in a random assortment that is sure to hurt my head no matter how I position it.

With my eyes heavy and my heart heavier, I flick off the light and allow my thoughts to drift back to that wonderful world where everything is at my fingertips and life is but a laugh.

A long, hearty, nothing-really-matters laugh.

PART THREE

PYRITE

Panning for fool's gold

Chapter Thirteen

"Whoomp! There it is!" Tag Team shouts at an earsplitting volume.

I'm jolted from sleep with so much frightening energy that I snap up, and in my closed-eyed frenzy to reach for the remote or my phone, I topple overboard. *Whoosh.* Straight to the floor like a sack of potatoes rolling off the bed of a truck.

There was definitely a bedside table within arm's reach when I went to sleep last night. Did one of the housekeepers come in here and feng shui the room while I was sleeping?

This hotel had weird energy from the moment I stepped foot in it yesterday. The by-product of a Doop-affiliated wedding, no doubt. I wouldn't put it past the staff here if they did a little redecorating in the dead of night, regardless of guest status.

Now that I think about it, this faux sheepskin rug—faux sheepskin, why do I even know that from feel alone?—was not here when I went to sleep last night. I think I'd remember this cloud-like texture under my bare feet as I got ready.

Maybe I was sleepwalking. That would be a first for me, but after the atrocious day I had, I wouldn't be surprised if my body decided to revolt against me as punishment for my sins.

When I roll onto my side, I'm inches from a dresser, stained a deep black, with silver handles. A matching mirror hangs above, and a silver vase is perched on top. Fresh-cut flowers fill the air with strong, sneeze-inducing fragrance. Those weren't there yesterday.

I go to rub my eyes and notice the splint isn't there anymore.

When I touch it, my nose doesn't hurt at all. This is somebody else's nose. Like one of the fancy celebrity ones Drew was showing me at the urgent care. I squish and I flick at what almost feels like an applied prosthetic.

A deep voice comes from above. "Are you picking your nose?"

On the edge of my bed is a naked man. A chiseled, black-haired, full-mast morning-wood man covered only by the satiny white sheet I slipped out of minutes ago.

Okay. *I'm dreaming.* I'm dreaming, and all I need to do is pinch myself to wake up back in the Flamhaff Hotel in Brooklyn. Simple.

Pinch once. Twice. Nothing. Third time's the charm?

"You good? What are you doing down there?" the man asks, even though it took him quite a long time to check on me after the fish flop I did.

Wait. Whoa. What am I saying?

Who is this man? And why is he in my bed? Is this even *my* bed? This has to be a dream. I just didn't pinch myself hard enough.

"Ow!" I squeal after making my forearm turn red.

I shoot back, suddenly scared. My head bumps a built-in book-shelf that's fully stocked and organized by spine color. This was also not here last night. *None* of this was here last night. I am in a com-pletely different room, in a completely different place, and I have no idea how I landed here.

"Who are you?" I ask. My mind is a hailstorm of swirling gibberish.

The Adonis with the attractive case of bedhead quirks a brow. "Hit your head that hard, huh?" He asks it in a sexy way, not a concerned way, which makes me think those crystals caused a possession. Some wellness spirit inhabited my body, made me way more confident than I actually am, and helped me land a smokin' hot piece to bang away my bad-day woes.

The crystals.

They're obviously causing me to hallucinate.

I jump to my feet and reach for my pillow, but the Adonis dives in the way. "Coming back to bed?"

There's a certain timbre to his voice that's oddly familiar. I don't have a spare second to think about where I've heard it before, though, because he's reaching out a hand to touch me, which I very much do not want.

"Why so skittish? You certainly didn't mind my hands all over you last night." He's smoke and velvet. Golden seduction under those thin, luxurious sheets.

Maybe the crystals caused me to black out.

Though that doesn't explain what app I used to find this guy and how I blacked out so badly that I don't even recall sleeping with him.

Seriously, he's got the kind of body you'd remember. He's got guy-on-an-underwear-package body. I've got good-for-what-it-is body, so the two don't exactly match. Except…

I pivot slowly, remembering the mirror above the dresser, and when I see what's reflected at me, I let out a scream so bone-chilling I might as well be in a haunted house.

I'm having a straight-up Jamie Lee Curtis *Freaky Friday* moment. I'm…I'm…*old*.

Okay. Not *old* exactly, but *older* than I was when I went to sleep, that's for damn sure.

My face has grown fuller, eyebrows arched and plucked sharper. My hair, previously oily and uncared for, is a voluminous dark-brown mane that could be slicked back and styled in so many ways. Even my skin, which was blotched with connect-the-dots acne from working around greasy foods, has evened out into a supple, moisturized visage a serial killer might want to skin and wear. A personal goal of mine, though I'd never admit that morbid secret.

As my eyes scan lower, my shirtless torso reveals itself. While it's a far cry from the Adonis in the bed, I'm worked out and tightly toned in a manner that suggests I have a personal trainer, or at the very least a Peloton.

This surprise is…pleasant, to say the least, but still wildly confusing. I'm in a body I don't know. Sure, my eyes are the same—hazel—and I didn't mysteriously grow any new appendages that I know of.

Wait. Curiosity kills the cat as I pull the elastic waistband on my expensive underwear to see what I'm packing. I am both disappointed and reassured to find one part of me mostly unchanged.

"Is the microphone hot?" Adonis asks, apparently undisturbed by me screaming my head off seconds ago, smoke and velvet turned up so high it's like I'm at a goddamn magic show. A sexy magic show. Where instead of rabbits, they pull vibrators out of the top hats. Note to self: Magic Mike but *literal* magic.

I turn back, flushed hot with the embarrassment of being caught checking myself out. "I'm sorry. What?"

"I asked if it was time for the open mic." His smirk is artful, and it would be arousing if I weren't so utterly confused and scared by what's going on here. "I'm ready to take the stage."

"In this case, the mic is my…" I point downward, and he nods, coming closer with a growl. I push out a hand, palm finding warm washboard abs that are too rock-solid to be a mirage. "Nope. Sorry. The mic is—uh—broken."

"Broken?" Adonis's eyebrows go up. "I didn't think I worked you that hard last night."

The idea of not remembering last night, not even a smidge,

sends me flying to the other side of the room. The last person I remember touching me—so tenderly that it just might make me cry at the thought—is Drew.

I wish I could call Drew right now. Get him to help me sort this out. He's always been levelheaded when I dive into the shallow end of a problem. He probably doesn't want to hear from me after last night—our confessions of love still churning hot in my memory—but I *should* call him.

I'd disappear into a bathroom or closet or any other confined space where I could be alone to do so if I had any idea where I was. In the world or in this space. Left or right, every closed door is a game of guess-what's-behind-it that I'm not in the mood to play. Judging from this room alone, this place seems palatial.

Figuring Adonis must be some sort of crystal-induced manifestation anyway, I put one of my therapist's tricks into practice. I plant my feet, close my eyes, and perform a few four-seven-eight breaths to ground my mind and right my senses. Surely this will all be gone once I'm done.

"Are you sure you didn't hit your head too hard when you fell out of bed?"

My eyes snap open at the question, and Adonis stands, entire body now on full display, a beautiful crime scene I can't tear my eyes away from. He scoops up his boxer briefs from the floor and wiggles into them.

Unfathomably, I think he's real. So I take the excuse he's handed me and run with it. "You know what, now that you mention it, I am more groggy than usual, and I'm having trouble remembering last night."

His striking green eyes bulge. I swear I've seen those eyes before. "Should we call a doctor? We can't have you forgetting stuff. Especially not your set for the big show. Jeez." He's off toward the door, opening it to reveal a long hallway and a trail of clothes like bread crumbs.

When I step out behind him, I realize that this isn't a hotel; it's an apartment. It's far too lived-in while also being meticulously clean, which means I'm not the one maintaining it. We pass two more bedrooms (one turned into a home gym), two bathrooms, and a curved staircase that leads to God-knows-where (heaven, maybe?) before entering a solarium-like open living space where all the orange curtains are drawn.

I go to the nearest one, part the center, and look out. I'm greeted by a magnificent waterfront view, but this time it's not the East River; it's the Hudson.

Somehow, I made it to a penthouse on the Upper West Side overnight.

I unlatch the lock and fling open a door leading out onto a wraparound terrace. There's a blue café table and chairs to my right. To my left, a comfy-looking outdoor couch sits with string lights, not dissimilar to the ones from CeeCee's wedding, strung above. Plants in full bloom peek out of robust clay pots speckled around the brick walkway.

Adonis steals my attention again as he rummages around inside for his phone, checking the glass coffee table and then the spotless marble breakfast nook. "Is there anything I can get you? Tea, coffee, an ice pack? Do you think you're concussed?"

I must be if this is real and I don't remember coming here. This is paradise.

"No, not concussed. Just fuzzy. I feel... *fuzzy*."

Adonis is a bit more frantic now, flinging throw pillows off the couch. His hands stop and hook onto his hips, where deep v-lines taunt me. "Oh, in that case, you had a lot to drink last night, not to mention the weed brownie, and maybe some poppers? It was a wild after-party."

"After-party?" I don't remember CeeCee's wedding itinerary having an after-party on it, nor would it have ever included weed brownies and poppers. Those are two items on Doop's do-not-use list.

"Yeah, for Taylor Pemberton's comedy special taping. Are you sure you're not concussed?"

"Taylor Pemberton got a special already?" The shock wears off immediately when I remember that I'm somehow inhabiting a waking dream. Or nightmare. Or alternate universe. Not quite sure on the details just yet.

Adonis doesn't hear me, because he opens a door across the room and out scampers the floofiest, smiliest corgi I ever did see, shedding fur everywhere he goes. "Good morning, Milkshake," Adonis coos. A tag is jangling around the dog's neck as it leaps across the room, sniffs my feet, and then promptly starts humping my leg with so much force for such a small dog that I nearly topple over.

"Hey, stop that. You at least have to buy me a meal first," I say, using my go-to line.

"Since when?" I hear Adonis ask from the other room with a laugh. Okay, I seriously don't love that. "Where is my damn phone?" he cries. "This happens every time I come over here. We strip in three different rooms and I forget where everything is."

I pull my focus from the frisky dog, who's moved from my leg to the leg of a seafoam-green couch. "You said, 'every time I come over here.' This isn't your place?"

He pads back into the room, barefoot, holding a pair of designer jeans and a plum-colored jacket. "Okay, you're officially scaring me. What's your name?"

"Nolan Baker."

"Middle name?"

"Christopher."

"Age?"

He stumps me there. I want to say twenty-three—the age I was when I went to sleep—but something fishy tells me that's no longer the truth. I stammer for a few seconds before he comes to an alarming conclusion. "You're dying. That's it, you're dying. You better not die, okay? You have so much coming up in the immediate future, and if that fall… Shit, if that fall is part of the reason, I was the only one here. I'm going to be questioned, and I shouldn't have even been here."

"Sorry to interrupt your spiraling—and as a professional spiraler, may I just say, you're doing a great job—but can we pause for a second?" I try to regain my senses, failing mostly. "Why shouldn't you have been here?"

"Because we told everyone we wouldn't do this again." He gestures down at his still half-naked body. "And look at us. In your apartment. Doing it again."

I nod with feigned understanding, heart rate picking up speed. At least now I know this is my apartment. How I came to reside in it at this current moment in time—what even is *time* right now?—is still anybody's guess. Panic is a cauldron overflowing inside my gut, but I have to at least play along since I see no immediate way out of whatever this is. "Right, right. Of course. But, if you had to…in your own words, describe *why* we weren't to do this again, what would you say?"

Scrubbing a hand over his chiseled features, he says, "Because we're in a bit of a personal and professional gray area, given that I'm your director."

"Director for what exactly?" I ask.

He crosses the room in three impressively long strides (it's a *big* room) so he's in my face. "Follow my finger." Annoyed, but wanting this interrogation to be over with, I do as he asks, looking up and down and left and right as his pointer finger roves and circles. That's when I notice more of my surroundings. Posters, pictures, dozens of them, with my face on them. Those dreamed-of SOLD OUT banners slapped across them. Is that me and Hannah Gadsby? Me and Ali Wong? Me and Nathan Fielder?

"What gives?" Adonis asks. "You look fine, but you're acting weird. Can you stop being weird so I can stop panicking?"

Oh man, he thinks *he's* panicking?

I still have so many questions stacking up in my brain. My eyes are darting around the room taking in all the images of me that aren't the me from last night but are various versions of me I've never seen and never been. But I must've been, right? There can't be photographic evidence of a me that never existed.

My frazzled brain spits out only two explanations I haven't yet considered:

+ I was drugged last night, dumped in a million-dollar fun house, and everything happening here is all an elaborate trick for which I'm being filmed to air on a prank show.
+ I've somehow time-jumped into the future.

It says a lot about me that the first option seems far more feasible and somehow preferable.

Adonis takes my blank stare for what it is and restarts his hunt for his phone, which he finds, inexplicably, in the Nutribullet on the counter. It says even more about me that I'm both proud I'm accomplished enough to own a Nutribullet and ravenous for a strawberry-banana smoothie.

"I'm not weird. I promise." Though it's a lie, and a promise I shouldn't make, because clearly something is off in a major way, but this man does not seem like the right confidant for that information. I don't even know his name, and asking seems like it would only rile him up more.

Looking unsure, but apparently willing to let it go, Adonis gets fully dressed and collects the rest of his belongings. "If you're sure. You'll call if you get blurry or dizzy or fainty or whatever?"

"If I check any of those boxes, I'll be sure to call." I won't, because I don't know if I have a phone, where I put it if I do, or what contact I should look under to call him if I found it. But fake reassurance seems like the safest bet in this unimaginable circumstance. While I don't want to be left alone in a haze of panic, I don't think I have a choice if I plan on figuring this all out.

He comes over and kisses me on my cheek, still smelling heavily of whatever debauchery we got up to last night. "I need to get out of here before Jessalynn comes to give you your rundown for the day. They'll have my head if they see me."

No more is said before he escapes around the corner and through the front door.

Finally, I'm alone. Still freaked out. But alone.

Creak. Cra-creak.

Well, not quite. I turn to find that ridiculously horny corgi going to town on one of the beige throw pillows that landed on the floor. He does his thing while staring right at me, almost defiantly.

"Guess it's just you and me, Milkshake." As soon as I say it, the corgi turns away and picks up speed. "Men," I grumble to myself before navigating back to the bedroom. It's a maze in here.

In my hunt through the main bathroom (spotless), the walk-in closet (bigger than my bedroom in Astoria), and the dresser drawers (who knew one person could own so many pleasure devices?), I abandon the phone altogether when I remember what I stuck under my pillow. With a loud "aha!" I rip the pillow off the bed, expecting to find those Doop crystals glinting in the sunlight pouring in from the ginormous, well-washed windows, but all I see is empty space.

And then a buzzer goes off.

Chapter Fourteen

When I open the door, I'm met with yet another recognizable face that I can't put a name to until they open their mouth and a far-too-familiar voice pipes out.

"If you're planning on denying it, save us both the time and don't." Jessalynn, the one Adonis was so hell-bent on avoiding, turns out to be none other than Jessie, my coworker at the Hardy-Har Hideaway, except older and without the buzzed hair and beat-up trainers. In their place, they've got a short, stylish haircut and red-bottoms that must have cost a pretty penny.

They push past me into the apartment, a whir of bags and brashness. Gone is the chumminess of two aspiring entertainment workers suffering through a poorly paying job. Jessalynn—clearly a combination of Jessie and their middle name Lynn—has a sleek business aura so severe it could poke your eye out.

"Let's take the meeting up on the deck. The weather's divine," they say before gliding up the sweeping staircase with carpeting down the center and ivy growing up the railings. Milkshake follows me over, but as I begin to climb, he lets out a bark.

"Aw, such little legs," I coo before hoisting him up. He's heavier than he looks, but I've got strong biceps now, so it's no big deal. This part I could get used to.

Outside, there's another garden with an unparalleled view of New York City that makes me feel like I'm hanging out with the clouds. The sun's only a shout away, bathing the rest of the skyline in late-morning light. My Astoria bedroom looked out onto a brick wall. This is...wow.

I feel lucky. Panicked still, but lucky that out of all the universes or futures or whatever, I landed in this one.

From a chair in a corner, Jessalynn unpacks a briefcase, laying items out in a neat array on a table, continuing where they left off. "I don't know why Harry thinks that ball cap and sunglasses combo as he exits your *private* entrance and then ducks into a taxi a block away is going to fool anybody. As if I don't have the height, weight, build, complexion, and penis size of every man you've ever been with memorized in case I need to lawyer up over a broken NDA."

While there's lots to unpack in that worrisome statement, I go for the lowest hanging fruit. "Harry?" Adonis couldn't have been the Harry who dumped me outside the club before CeeCee's wedding, right? Though, I'm sort of seeing the resemblance despite multiple features that have been plumped, set, and injected during the intervening years.

"Yes, Harry Stokes. The man who ran out of here." I'm having a hard time imagining what could've brought us back into each other's orbit. "The man who's directing your special, thanks to you and your need to prove everyone wrong by being the bigger person." They freeze, drop their head, and then pick it back up like a robot rebooting. "Sorry. You know I love your moxie. It's what sells out shows and pays my bills. It's just been a rough morning. The venue booker pushed back our viewing, which means we could've taken the interview with BuzzBang. Then, I was trying to call you, but you weren't answering your phone because you were BuzzBanging Harry, so I'm a little tense at the moment. My knots have knots have knots."

I stand there in bumbling silence, realizing that Jessie has become my manager just as we always talked about. It dawns on me that I'm inhabiting the future we envisioned. I'm stupefied by this. The intentions I set with those crystals miraculously came true.

Jessalynn continues. "Look, I'll drop it right after this, but why Harry, huh? Were Lance and Marc and Jean-Luc not available? Because it's a bad look for you to be hooking up with someone on the artistic team."

"Wait, sorry, so Harry and I aren't...." I let the question trail off, trying not to alert them of my state of utter what's-going-on-dom.

"Together?" they ask, sounding incredulous. "I should hope not."

I nod. "Right, because we weren't a good match."

"No! Not that. Who gives a shit about that?" I come over to sit, and they smack me in the arm like I'm a younger brother who's misbehaving, which makes me think about CeeCee and the fight and the wedding. I should call her too, but where is my damn phone?

"You shouldn't be with Harry because you're Nolan Baker, famously single, anti-love comedian. Do you know how bad you being in a relationship would be for the brand we've worked so hard to cultivate? Cynics are our target demographic and our lifeblood. If you started drinking the romance Kool-Aid, we'd lose our fan base, our sponsorships, everything." Their eyes grow deadly serious. "So, tell me. I know it gets lonely at the top, but are you and Harry more than—or thinking about becoming more than—BuzzBang Buddies?"

I didn't even know Harry was Harry until a couple minutes ago. "No." I don't know if that's true. It just seems to be what they need to hear, so I'm happy to give them that.

"Fantastic. Now," they say, eyes sparkling, a smile manifesting where a stern frown was before. "Look what just came in." They gesture to the table at three different poster mock-ups. They're all a slight variation of the same image. I—the me from the mirror, not the me from yesterday—stand wearing a full suit and no socks in the center of a mess of cut up roses, greeting cards, and cutesy stuffed animals. In my right hand, I hold up a heart that is dripping fake blood down my forearm. The title is script and oozing: *30 Times Two*.

"I don't get it, Jessie." I'm pointing at the title.

They give me a disgusted look. "First of all, no one has called me Jessie in a good five years. Second of all, you were in the Netflix pitch meeting when we conceptualized it. It's supposed to be ironic because it's a sixty-minute special, so thirty-minutes time two. Plus, you're thirty and it's 2030."

Holy. Fucking. Shit. If Jessie—*Jessalynn*—is to be believed, I've missed seven years.

"Okay, something weird is going on." My chest grows tighter.

"I'll say," they actually say, pressing the back of their hand to my forehead. "What did you take last night?"

"Nothing!" I shout, finally breaking. "I went to bed twenty-three, and now I'm thirty and living here and doing whatever this is." I flail my arms in the general direction of the posters, which are mostly cool but also a tad concerning. That prop heart looks slightly too realistic for comfort. "I have no idea how any of this happened."

Jessalynn stares at me for a long time, seemingly searching for something in my expression. At first their gaze is serious, and then it cracks. "I would love to be the test audience for another one of your character-based bits, but now is not the moment. Now is the moment to select a poster for the special so we can get in the waiting car downstairs and go to the theater."

"Theater?" I'm incredulous, winded, and lost. I want everybody to slow down and for someone to explain this to me with preschool-level simplicity. "Didn't you hear what I just said?"

They roll out their neck. "Yes, and I know you love a bit. It's what the fans adore about you. It's what I adore about you. But another thing I adore about you is your pickiness when it comes to promotional materials, so please, pick one or pick none, but at least give me something to send back to the team."

Realizing that protesting is futile, I shuffle numbly back into my seat and inspect the posters again. Even though this is all mystifying, I have to admit that I look like a goddamn superstar in these. All hot and funny and in on it. I may have missed all the work it took to get here, but through some stroke of sheer luck and will (and maybe those damn disappearing crystals), I ended up in an echelon of comedians I only ever fantasized about.

For a minute, I let that sink in. It would be amazing if it weren't crisis-inducing.

"That one." I point to the middle option where I'm brooding but smirking. Approachable yet above it all.

"Excellent. You're a gem. Now, please put on something presentable. We're going to be late to the theater."

"The theater?" I ask again as we move back inside.

They click their tongue at me, shoving me in the direction of my gargantuan closet. "Yes, the theater. I don't send you itineraries every morning for my health, you know."

When I think about what happened when I shirked my last itinerary, I follow their instructions.

· ✦ ·

"This is the Brooklyn Academy of Music," I utter, awed, as I'm rushed out of the back of the car. Sunbeams streak over a glass awning that slopes overhead, while a red sign with vertical text races up the front exterior.

"Yes, great deduction skills, Sherlock," Jessalynn says. "Madison Square Garden was too big. Joe's Pub was too small. Let's hope, for your sake, Goldilocks, that this venue is *just right*. We're running out of time."

I roll my eyes at their mixed metaphor before an idea amuses me. "Detective Goldie Sher-locks, a reformed trespasser investigating the crimes of burglars, bandits, and other atrocities against bears."

"Cute," Jessalynn says, pushing us through the entryway and into a lobby that has an industrial art-gallery feel to it. "Write it down. Save it for when a publisher asks if you want a book deal. We all know it's coming sooner or later. You're nobody in comedy until you've written a memoir, a humorous collection of essays, or an adults-only picture book."

Before they can make another pointed yet accurate observation, a short Asian woman with medium-length dark hair wearing a white button-down shirt appears with a portfolio under her arm and two flutes of champagne in her hands. "Nolan Baker, how kind of you to join us today. I'm Cassandra Yuen. It's a pleasure."

"Sorry we're late," Jessalynn concedes while taking the drinks, their tone laced with subtext: *Divas, am I right?* Their knowing looks confirm that I'm the diva in question, and they've both been around the block with more than a few. Never in my life have I had the opportunity to play the diva.

Maybe leaving CeeCee's wedding was a major diva move, but who knows what time warp or wormhole I slipped through to end up here? If I'm lucky, in this reality that never happened.

"No need to be sorry." Cassandra's smile sparkles with politeness. "We're thrilled you're considering our lovely space for your special taping. I'll show you around."

The tour takes us through the front-of-house area and the control booth. Cassandra weaves an oral history of the space, and I barely touch my bubbly, enraptured by every word she's saying. Our three sets of shoes click down storied hallways, while I consider that nobody has ever tried to woo me to do comedy somewhere before. I've always been the wooer.

It's a swap of fates.

When we enter the theater proper, air saws out of my lungs in amazement. It's stunning. Weathered, antique pillars. A gilded, rounded proscenium is adorned with a painted image of a warrior riding a four-legged creature, arrow drawn back in battle. The space is awash in mossy green, muted peach, and gold. So, so much gold.

It's worn, like all the clubs I've performed in, but alive with so much elegance. I would pay good money for the privilege of standing on that stage. Turns out, in this life, people are going to pay *me* to perform on it.

"Do you like it?" Cassandra asks after pointing out a few of the finer points: the sound system, the seating capacity, the sight lines, and the plentiful space for the Netflix film crew to come in and do their thing.

Jessalynn jumps in. "Nolan likes many of the venues we've scouted, so we'll save any deliberations for once we've made our final decision."

I don't pout or say anything to the contrary. Instead, I let Cassandra lead the way backstage; rows and rows of flipped-up seats flit by in my periphery. I imagine them filled with eager audience members, ready to laugh and love me.

Goose bumps appear on my arms when I step on the stage for the first time. Cassandra is too busy regaling Jessalynn with information about the lighting rig, so I take the opportunity to stop and inhale this moment. Even amidst the chaos, a stage is still where I feel most at home. No matter the year or my age.

Facing out on the auditorium, I stare up into the balcony, overwhelmed by this sudden change in the trajectory of my life. None of this can be real.

Cassandra's voice breaks my reverie. "Can we hear a joke?"

"What?"

She motions for me to step forward a foot or two. "Pretend your microphone stand is there. Tread the boards a bit. Try out some material. I think you'll find our theater is quite responsive. Many performers say it has a palpable energy."

Jessalynn shrugs, checking their phone. "Go on. Do something. It's a good idea."

I get excited all over again. That surging adrenaline that always comes before I launch into a joke. "I was broken up with recently. Dumped right on the sidewalk like the crust on a dollar slice of pizza after a drunken night out." I take a studied beat. "When you think about it, being broken up with is a lot like being pizza crust. You're half of what you once were, still hoping someone finds you delicious, and waiting on a rebound rat to come make a meal out of ya."

Cassandra's laugh is exaggerated yet truthful, and it prompts me to turn back. Jessalynn's harsh stare roils through me. "That was excellent," Cassandra says. "Let's continue."

As Cassandra starts ahead, Jessalynn asks in a whisper, "What was that?"

"What was what?"

"That old, crusty-ass material. You're not reviving those jokes for your set, right? You understand this is your first special. If you blow this one, there might not be another."

"Really packing on the pressure, huh?" I don't have any new material. Seven years have flown by. What kind of jokes could I come up with while missing key memories?

Switching to false friendship mode, they link an arm in mine. "No, not at all. You're a fucking star, and I'm just making sure you shine the brightest you possibly can. Okay?"

Our little aside is interrupted by Cassandra unlocking the

dressing room. It's spacious, clean, fancy—meant for a world-class headliner to luxuriate in.

"Take a look around." Cassandra doesn't need to tell me twice. I inspect my new self in the mirror, go for a spin in the chair, and soak in the general ambiance. "Of course, we have full staff to decorate the space and provide refreshments to your liking. Anything you'll need will be accounted for. Jessalynn did us the courtesy of sending over your rider early."

"Rider?" I ask.

Jessalynn cocks an eyebrow at me. "Your list of requests as per a contract."

"Right, my rider." They say requests, but I know they mean demands.

"The espresso machine will be an easy get," Cassandra says, opening her portfolio and checking off a list. "As will a Lovesac, but we will want to know your color, fabric, and size preferences for napping reasons."

"I'm going to be napping here?" I ask.

"During tech…" Jessalynn is clearly growing more annoyed with me each time I open my mouth.

"Bottles of Hennessy, Patron Silver Tequila, Grey Goose Vodka, Jack Daniels, and Heineken will be available to you at any time via a fully stocked fridge we'll have installed," Cassandra says. "We'll be certain to get the extra-long bendy straws and specific kind of glasses you requested as well. And we also have someone on call to be your personal gum-throw-away-er."

Jessalynn smirks at this. "He really hates having to touch it after he chews it."

"Makes perfect sense," Cassandra says. And if she finds this ridiculous, she makes no show of it. A consummate professional. I, on the other hand, am agape at all this nonsense. Shame ping-pongs around in my head. "Lastly," Cassandra adds, "we've ensured no one on staff the night of or leading up to your show will have the name Drew."

My chest tightens. "Excuse me?" I ask. Hearing his name spoken aloud in this strange reality makes my heart tumble into my stomach. Brings last night—*my last night*—into sharp focus again. I can hear Drew telling me he loves me and minutes later telling me he needs time away from me. It crushes me all over again.

"We received explicit instructions," Cassandra says, pulling me from the recent but somehow not-so-recent memory.

Jessalynn steps in. "That's exactly right. He wouldn't be the anti-love comedian without being able to hold a nearly decade-old grudge, right?" The two share a clipped, for-show laugh, while I try and fail to process this.

I take it things with Drew have not improved in the seven years I've somehow soared over. That can't be possible. I was so certain when I went to bed last night that my actions were absolvable, over time and maybe with some groveling. I was right about the career benefits, but I guess I was wrong about the relationships being salvageable.

Discomfort becomes a fourth person in this room, breathing down my neck.

I gulp back the panic and say, "Excellent," as bottles of champagne are brought in.

Chapter Fifteen

I'm day-drunk by the time Jessalynn drops me back off at the apartment.

Drew's name and my complete lack of control over my life and timeline led me to down a full bottle of champagne all by myself, which spawned a burp fest and an uncomfortably bumpy, queasy ride back. I've got sea legs as I stand on the sidewalk, swaying.

Jessalynn, behind a pair of larger-than-life sunglasses, glares at me through the open back window of the car. "Sober up, babe, and polish that material. We may have a venue now, but that won't matter if the jokes are shit. Rehearsals start next week. Got it?"

"Got it," I say, because I'm at a loss.

The car speeds away.

Back in my extravagant apartment and still floored by the square footage, which sits somewhere north of four thousand—I asked!— and impeccably put-together interior design, I forage through the kitchen for sustenance. Anything that will quell my stomach cramps.

Even though I'm apparently in possession of state-of-the-art appliances and tools to cook homemade pasta (who am I?), the fridge, cabinets, and walk-in pantry are devoid of food, which leads me to believe that I don't spend much time here.

"So many food preppery…preppering…preparatory? Come

on, mouth. So many *prep* tools and no ingredients to do the prepping with," I drunkenly grumble to myself, slamming shut the fridge with a tablet built into the door beside the ice dispenser.

"Would you like me to go out and grab something for you, Mr. Baker?" comes the sound of a masculine voice that's so soothing and melodic, it could only be coming from the robot that lives inside my futuristic (or is it now-istic?) fridge.

"I can't believe this thing talks." I begin inspecting the tablet, which is far more complex than my seven-years-younger mind can even compute. I had just gotten used to having an Alexa in our apartment. Now I have a fridge that can do my grocery shopping for me. "Yes. Poke-ay Bow-el," I enunciate, and then realize that sounded like *bowel* (which in fairness is what I'll have to tend to as soon as I eat one). Also, nothing's happening on the screen. I *tap, tap, tap,* while saying, "Poke bowl."

"Looking up Pokémon recipes…" an even-toned feminine voice purrs from the door. Why'd the voice change all of a sudden?

"No, no. Poke bowl!"

"Looking up Super Bowl recipes…"

"Okay, now you're just mocking me."

"Mr. Baker," comes the sound of the deep, masculine voice again. I flip around with a start when a hand clasps my shoulder. As I jump back on wobbly legs, my hands fumble across the counter for something to protect myself with. You'd think a building that houses a famous comedian would have better protection against intruders.

On instinct, I hoist up the nearest object, which is…a whisk. A not-scary, ineffective whisk. What am I going to do, *beat* him to death? *Ba-dum-tss.*

"Who are you and what are you doing in my apartment?" The whisk wiggles in my hand. I've imbibed and I'm scared, which is a bad combination.

"Mr. Baker. It's me. Antoni. Your first assistant." He's wearing a checkered button-down, navy-blue chinos, and an expensive-looking belt. He holds a tablet, a stylus, and a glass of water.

I set down the whisk. "*First* assistant?"

"Yes. I'm the daytime assistant. Jerome is your nighttime assistant." He hands me the glass of water. "Jessalynn said you might need this. Drink up."

"There's nothing in here, right?" I've lived in New York City long enough to know not to accept drinks from strangers. Except in this instance, I suppose Antoni isn't a stranger. If he's to be believed, he's got my whole life cataloged on that tablet.

"No, there's nothing in there. Just filtered water." He flashes a trustworthy smile.

I gulp it back. "What do I need a nighttime assistant for?" I ask, wiping my mouth on the back of my forearm.

He checks his notes. "Uh, well, I'm not here to know for sure, but Jerome has logged: booking cars, VIP bottle service, spontaneous trips, off-menu room service, after-hours gym access, and the occasional bedtime story."

"Bedtime story?"

"Yes, you're really into the Game of Dark Dissension series, but you say reading gives you migraines and the audiobook narrator"—he defers to his iPad, reading directly—"sounds like someone you used to know and never want to think about again as long as you shall live."

It has to be Drew. Sometimes, when he read a passage in a book he really loved or one that made him laugh, he'd come bursting into my room without knocking to read it aloud to me. No matter the time of day. No matter how long the excerpt. I loved that.

Sadness ties a tight bow around my heart. "I really said that?"

"According to the log."

"You keep a log?"

"For general records, upkeep, taxes, and your business manager."

"Jessalynn?"

"No," he says, starting to sound spooked by my game of Twenty Questions. "Jessalynn is your talent manager. You have a business manager who's solely in charge of your finances. Are you sure you're okay? Should you lie down?"

I seriously wish everyone would stop asking me that. Of course I'm not okay. Seven years have passed overnight. I'm lucky I'm not curled up in a ball on the floor right now.

"No, I'm just hungry. I get confused when I'm hungry." I clutch my stomach to really sell it. "A poke bowl would be excellent."

He's already putting on an indigo jacket and grabbing his bag. "The usual okay?"

All I do is nod, having no idea what the usual is. Some strange part of my brain is wondering how much my taste buds could have changed in the intervening years. When I was a kid, I hated soup, but practically lived on grilled cheese and Campbell's tomato when I first moved to New York. What if I'm into slimy squid now or something else revolting?

Without time to harp on that, I decide now is the moment to snoop for answers. I finally find my phone in the bedroom. Scrolling through my contacts, I search from my go-to's. Mom is mysteriously missing. No Dad either, but a plethora of *Daddy* variants. *Daddy Steve. Daddy Mark. Daddio.* I really must get around.

When I try the number listed for CeeCee, I get a woman named Cécile who I apparently met four years ago in Provincetown while singing along to a Billy Joel cover concert. Sounds about right, but not who I was looking for.

Since my parents never did social media, I scavenge for signs of CeeCee on all the apps I have downloaded and am already logged into. Some, with their eye-catching logos and confusing interfaces, make me wonder how I ever learned to navigate these newfangled grids and no-scroll feeds. After clicking away from several CeeCee Bakers who aren't my sister, I find who I'm looking for.

In her profile photo on an app with a French-looking name I can't even pronounce, CeeCee and James smile brightly in front of a calm ocean. Tapping to see more, I come to the hopeless realization that I've been blocked. On every app. You'd think after seven years we'd have reconciled our stupid fight over a missed speech.

My recklessness reared an unfortunate end. I had been hoping the wedding would bring us closer together, but my rash decision clearly ultimately severed our already weak connection. I feel mortified, crushed, and completely alone.

Seven years lost over a few hours and a career gained. Suddenly, I'm not sure I'd do it all over again, even if it did net me millions.

That petty fight reminds me of the second big fight I had last night. Or whenever that was at this point.

Apparently, I hate Drew so much that I can't even have somebody working near me who shares his name. I've spent seven years without my best friend, and I have no memory of them, but that doesn't make it any less awful.

I'm not delusional. I knew it would take time and work and, again, *groveling* to earn a spot back in his life. But maybe time is not the all-powerful healer I assumed it to be.

A slithery feeling coils through my chest. It reminds me that there must be a darkness that's grown inside me over the past seven years that I'm unaware of. I wish I could cut it out before I have to confront it.

My thumbs can't move fast enough, and still, I end up disappointed by the results. Drew isn't anywhere to be found in my phone. Relationship erased from the server. I shouldn't be surprised or devastated, but of course I am.

Out of curiosity, I launch a search for Drew Techler, independent bookstore. Sure enough, there he is. My heart twitters at the sight of him, even on a screen.

Bearded and bespectacled now, Drew smiles in front of a bookstore in Queens, holding a stack of books before an exquisite window display. Zooming in, however, I notice none of those books are romance novels with illustrated characters on the covers or soft, bright colors. His comfort reads. His favorites.

The books in the window display are thrillers, mysteries, and horror novels with titles like *Kill or Be Killed* and *Can't Keep a Secret*. Spyglasses and monocles and houndstooth hats are arranged in a way that make it look as if the books are investigating a crime. A slightly raised tape outline of a body can be seen down below.

The store's signage reads: Bound by Mayhem Bookshop.

It's a far cry from Eight, Three, One Books, the silly, lovey-dovey name Drew had doodled on card stock and stuck up on the dream board in his room in our Astoria apartment.

Seven years can change so much.

Knowing I have nowhere else to turn, I decide I need to see Drew. Even if it's from afar. Even if it's just for one second. I need to know he's okay, even if we aren't.

His confession of love rocks me fresh and anew each time I think of it. I don't know how I'm supposed to pretend it happened seven years ago when it happened yesterday, but I'll have to try, at least at first, so I don't freak him out.

As if he knew the perfect cover, Milkshake waddles over with a red leash dangling from his tiny, cute mouth. Eyes hopeful, he wiggles his butt, and I can almost hear him say, *Let's go, slowpoke!*

Wait, *did I* hear him say that? Maybe we're microchipped and can read each other's minds.

That thought is how I know I'm still drunk. Too drunk to

presently confront Drew. I pour myself a glass of water and give myself a little bit of time to cool off and sober up. Sitting in a nearby chair, I realize that I don't know what my limits are in this body because this body is on loan for the time being. It's like high-stakes Rent the Runway, except I'm wearing a model and not just an outfit.

Thirty minutes later, feeling clear-headed, I stuff Milkshake into a harness, latch on his leash, and head out with directions to Bound by Mayhem Bookshop chirping from my phone.

Chapter Sixteen

The window display at Bound by Mayhem Bookshop is even more garish in person. A gruesome hodgepodge of corn syrup blood and yarn tied to various pushpins tacked to author photos, all edited to look like mug shots. It's a messy feast for the eyes, if said eyes were hungry for gore, gore, and, uh, more gore.

Judging by the lack of patrons going inside, I'm not the only one worried my life would be at risk if I stepped across the threshold. Luckily, I'm across the street while Milkshake does his business on a nearby fire hydrant. With a baseball cap sitting firmly on my head and sunglasses perched on my nose, I'm incognito.

Not even five steps from my apartment building, I was monsooned by people asking for photos and autographs. The first wave was manageable. The second, larger wave, however, was all-encompassing. Fighting for air as people flung their phones in my face was not as fun as I imagined it would be in my teens, dreaming of celebrity for myself.

When I spotted a clear opening, I sprinted away, ducked into the first souvenir shop I could find, and decked myself out in I HEART NYC apparel. Seven years may have passed, but tourists—thank God—are still as tacky as ever.

Milkshake and I shuffle through the crosswalk when the signal lights up. I coach myself into a reasonable breathing pattern. *This is*

Drew, I remind myself. *He'll believe you. He'll know what to do. Don't panic. More than you already are…*

"What the *hell* are you doing here?" My heart spiders up into my throat when I look up and place the source of the voice. Drew hulks over me with broader shoulders, a rounder face, a scraggly full beard, and tortoiseshell glasses. He's hot. A downright well-read hunk, which is an unproductive thought to be having since, just like the last time I saw him, he's pissed. "You didn't think I'd miss you stalking me across from my shop?"

In fairness, he was probably leering in the window, hoping to catch an unsuspecting passerby to assault with scary books. I wish I'd concocted a good cover story on my trek over here. My head is empty aside from the incessant refrain of: *What in the living hell is happening?*

"Well," Drew huffs, crossing his newly muscular arms over his chest, "what do you have to say for yourself?"

"Very little at the moment," I utter. The pictures I saw online did not do him justice. Drew's amped-up hotness has thrown me for a loop. Also, his stern, gruff tone. The night of CeeCee's wedding, he spoke to me with a soft upset that lapped over me and tugged me under, ultimately drowning me. This, what I'm being met with, is a hardened aggression that can only come from years of strife.

Milkshake takes this as his moment to introduce himself, lunging toward Drew's closest leg and making it his own personal pony. As if this weren't already going poorly. "Down, Milkshake. No. Bad dog." Helplessly, I glance up at Drew. "He's got good gaydar, huh?"

Drew clicks his tongue, carefully shaking Milkshake away, not even faking a smile. I really thought Milkshake's cute face would sweeten this encounter. He had to go and ruin it by being a horny menace who then promptly plops over seeking belly rubs. He really must be my dog—desperate for attention. "This is ridiculous, and you look ridiculous too," Drew says.

I peer down at the hot-pink tank top hastily tugged over my electric-green T-shirt, and he's right. I look like a Disney Channel star at best or a watermelon at worst. "I didn't realize I was going to get mobbed when I left my apartment to come here, so I had to throw on the quickest disguise I could find."

His eyebrows furrow. "You, Nolan Baker, world-famous comedian, didn't think you'd be mobbed by fans if you left your apartment alone?"

"Yes," I reply, knowing how ridiculous that must sound.

"All that partying the reporters say you do must really be killing your brain cells." He pinches the bridge of his nose right below his frames and closes his eyes before taking a deep inhalation of breath, unstiffening a tad. "At least I can rest easy in the knowledge you still haven't figured out how to color-match your wardrobe."

"Never too late to try the sticker thing," I half-joke, attempting to shake off the stinging insult, even if those presumed partying ways weren't *my* direct actions. This is somehow still my life, and if I don't figure out how this happened or how to fix it, it will remain that way. I'll be saddled with the consequences of my own mistakes plus the mistakes of another me.

Drew's face corkscrews into a new quizzical expression. "You remember that?"

"Like it was yesterday." Because in my reality, it practically was.

He drops the defensive posture, instead choosing a level of open exasperation I've only seen from him when a book marketed as a romance defies the HEA rule. "When I said that I didn't want us to be in contact anymore, I meant that. Full stop. Now, please leave." When he turns to go back inside, I'm hit with the image of him turning to leave our hotel room after admitting he needed to figure out what he wanted without me.

Those emotions still fresh and surging inside me force me to plead, "Drew, wait. Please. Can we talk?"

His headshake is instant and resolute. "No, Nolan. We talked six years ago. You had your chance." The door jingles closed behind him. Of course Drew would put twinkling welcome bells on the door to his murder shop, a small remnant of what could have been.

The memory of what *we* could've been, had I been braver and less stubborn and hadn't prioritized my career over everything else, wills me inside after him. I was right in my assessment from across the street. There is not a single living soul in here. Not even a curmudgeonly bookstore cat leaving hair wherever she trots. Everything has a pristine, untouched quality about it. Not unlike the castle library in *Beauty and the Beast* before Belle's arrival. "What happened to Eight, Three, One Books?" I ask as he whips back around ready to roar at me.

His visible anger falters but he avoids my question. "No dogs allowed in the store." He points to a sign behind me with cartoon drawings on it, a circle with a slash through them.

"Is it a safe neighborhood?" I ask. "I can tie Milkshake up outside if you have, like, a bowl of water I can give him."

"Great, but what do we do about you?"

"Good one," I say, wishing I knew what the hell I did to deserve an insult like that. Aside from skipping out on my sister's wedding and basically standing him up, which admittedly was not my brightest moment.

His gaze is fierce as he says, "There's an urgent care in the neighborhood if you need help tending to that burn." Time has made him sassier.

"Like the one you met me at when I fractured my nose?" Instinctually, I reach up to touch my face to remind myself how real this is. How my nose is completely healed and a different shape. My features have been reorganized into camera-ready symmetricity.

I wait for Drew to comment on this, but then realize he won't.

My image is splashed across subway stations on old posters announcing dates for my last tour. He's seen the changes in me gradually over time. I, on the other hand, haven't had a chance to come to terms with them. "Remember when you said I'd look good with an Elizabeth Taylor nose? Is this one closer?" I ask, hoping to shuffle up his memory deck to happier times.

"That was seven years ago. Why would I remember that?"

"You remember how many years it was," I counter. The number seven has been rattling around in my head all day, leaving me breathless with wonder and taunts of *why*. Why that many years? Is it because I'm thirty now? New decade, new career, new *everything*... "You also knew how many years it's been since we've spoken."

He flips up his hands. "Not everyone is rich and famous and has people to keep their calendars for them. I run a business. I do tend to know what day, month, and year it is on top of being able to do basic math." Leaning against a book display, as if my presence is making it impossible for him to stay upright, he stares up at the ceiling. "It's kind of hysterical that you remember I said you'd look good with an Elizabeth Taylor nose when we were in our early twenties but conveniently don't remember when I told you to fuck off and never see me again."

In our previous years of friendship, I got on Drew's bad side only once. Shortly after we moved in together, I accidentally forgot to pick up a package from the mailboxes—a one-of-a-kind collectors' edition of one of Drew's favorite romances with sprayed edges and a foiled cover. They had printed a limited run that Drew had paid a pretty penny for and woke up extra early to secure a copy online.

Too bad by the time I remembered, the package had been stolen.

Drew didn't curse. He didn't even yell. He calmly told me how he felt, which was almost worse. It made me look inside. Investigate the selfish parts of me. The ones that seem overblown in this timeline.

Milkshake sits at my feet and lets out a whimper, as if he knows this conversation is going poorly. That my mind is moving in a million directions. "I wasn't there..."

Drew scoffs, disbelieving. "Really? I distinctly remember standing in your new apartment across from you when you got back from your first tour with Clive, telling you that I never wanted to see you again, and you saying I didn't know how to take a joke." Hurt crisscrosses in his eyes, magnified by his glasses. "I suppose a hallucination of you said that? Maybe a hologram? Your Madame Tussauds wax figure with a voice box?"

I shake my head, unable to grasp the right words. "No, it was me," I say, motioning to my body, "but it wasn't *me*." I point from my head to my heart, praying he gets the message.

"What? Are you trying to tell me you've changed since then? I don't believe that," he spits out. "I don't believe that one bit." He moves farther from me, putting the register between us and nearly knocking his head on a severed-hand decoration dangling from a nearby shelf. The whole place has the vibe of a half-assed escape room where all the clues are lodged inside hollowed-out books.

"Well, this is going to be even harder to believe," I say. Then, I pretend he's still twenty-three-year-old Drew and I'm still twenty-three-year-old Nolan and we're high on the fire escape of our old shoebox apartment, and I confide in him. He may hate me, but I attempt to appeal to our history. I call on him to help, or at the very least tell me I'm not losing my mind over a set of crystals.

All he does is blink. And blink. And blink some more.

Bang. He slams his hands down on the counter, making Milkshake jump and move to cower behind me. "Where are they?" Drew asks, head turning every which way.

"Where are what?"

"The hidden cameras. The crew. Where are they?" he asks.

Clearly, he's assuming I've bugged his shop for a prank show, which, *wow*. "I refuse to be the butt of another one of your jokes. Haven't you hurt me enough?"

His anger mutates into audible sadness. It fills the whole store, so potent I could almost choke on it. "Drew, I'm telling the truth. It sounds absurd, I know. I swore this was a dream, yet I haven't woken up. This body is not mine. This life is not mine. I wish I could explain it better, but I can't. Last night, you walked out of our hotel room after telling me you loved me but needed space, and this morning I woke up in an apartment I've never been in next to a man I thought I'd never see again."

Maybe it's hope messing with my vision, but I could swear Drew cringes at the mention of another man in my bed. The nearly imperceptible squeeze of his body is gone the minute he shakes his head. "I lost my trust in you a long time ago. Maybe you *believe* what you're saying is true, but I'm not your person anymore. I haven't been for a long time."

Any optimism I held drains out of me and swiftly gets replaced by desperation. "But, Drew, please. I need your help!" Milkshake howls alongside me, underlining my plight.

"I can't help you!" Drew snaps.

"Oh, are you closed?" In the howling and shouting, neither of us heard the twinkling bells over the door. A stunned elderly gentleman with tufts of white hair sticking out over his ears stands with his hand still on the doorknob, one foot inside the shop.

Drew shakes off our fight like water droplets right out of the pool. "No, we're open. My apologies. Please feel free to browse and let me know if you need any assistance." Before my eyes, he transforms into the supreme professional he's always longed to be, in an environment so antithetical to everything he loved when I knew him.

I couldn't have caused this drastic shift, could I? I'm only one person. My actions don't reverberate that widely.

As soon as the man picks up a hardback on the far side of the store and begins reading the jacket, I turn back to Drew, face-to-face with his stormy expression. "Fine, I understand. I won't bother you again. I'll, uh, go find CeeCee. She's blocked me on everything, but I'll show up at the Doop offices, I guess. Maybe she can help. See if they'll let me in and tell me what the hell they did to those crystals." Drew's expression is a neutral mask, even at the second mention of the crystals, which I hoped might intrigue him. "Wish me luck?" I ask, like I used to in the old times, which were really yesterday times. Only not for him.

He opens his mouth, and it seems like he's about to say something unexpected. My heart ignites for a moment, only to be extinguished when he grabs a stack of books, turns away, and says dismissively, "Good luck."

Chapter Seventeen

Drew's luck doesn't work this time.

Perhaps because he didn't mean it when he said it.

Or perhaps it didn't work last time either. I had nearsightedly convinced myself it did. And then proceeded to pitch my life into turmoil anyway.

I dropped Milkshake back off at the apartment and fed him before snagging the poke bowl Antoni left out for me on the island. On the subway ride to the High Line, I shovel food into my mouth with gilded, reusable chopsticks. This body may be borrowed, but I intend to treat it right while I've got it.

I can't stop replaying the hostile words Drew spewed at me. That was clearly a deep hurt manifesting into an uncharacteristic rage. Though, I suppose, after seven years, I'm not an expert on what's characteristic for Drew anymore.

He did say in the hotel room that he needed to find out what he wanted independent of me. Is this what he wanted—*who* he wanted to be?

I ponder that question for so long that I nearly miss my station.

Depositing the last of my tuna, ponzu, sesame oil, and avocado into a nearby trash bin, I stare up at the regal tower of glass and steel, bracing myself for my first encounter with CeeCee in this new timeline.

The rooftop is a tree-lined garden much like the one in my new apartment. Folks in ties and skirts lounge by the ledge, looking out onto the water. Terraces hang from the right side over the High Line, where couples take springtime walks and buy gelato from carts. A memory of Drew and me there when we first moved to New York City arises, sharing one tiny cup of stracciatella with two flat spoons in the sweltering heat of July.

The future felt rife with sweaty, beautiful possibility then.

Strange that the future is now.

Inside, Doop's name doesn't appear anywhere on the commercial signage in the massive, marble-floored lobby. Their upper-level office space, with sandy tan and muted pink accents, yoga mats instead of foosball tables, has seemingly relocated.

When a Black man wearing nearly imperceptible earbuds comes up beside me, I politely ask for his attention. "All good?" he asks.

"Not quite," I say, frazzled. "Doop...they, uh, moved?" I point to the board where their name has been replaced with a tech company's.

"Yeah," the man says with a laugh.

"Do you happen to know where?"

"Sure," he replies, "the graveyard where all fad businesses go when they die out." The shock on my face must look like hurt because he adds quickly, "Ah, damn. Sorry. Did you work there or something?"

"No, but I know someone who did. I thought I'd find her here."

He nods, eyebrows raised. "We're all looking for that special girl, aren't we?"

"It's my sister," I tell him. "And I'm gay."

Turns out the future isn't any less heteronormative than the present.

"Ah, shit. Well, right on, bro," he says before popping back in his earbud and starting toward the elevator bay.

Leaving me alone to wonder: *What do I do now?*

Three days.

It takes me three whole days to fill in the gaps of my memory.

Luckily, full-time rehearsals for my comedy special—which I'm anxiously dreading—don't start until Wednesday. Jessie— Jessalynn, argh, that's going to take some getting used to—granted me the privilege of a few hours off today between fittings and photo shoots and interviews and meetings and one mandated session with a chiropractor. (God, I'm old enough to need a chiropractor!) Hours I should be using to learn the script "I" had already written, chock-full of jokes that make me cringe.

So in a stellar act of avoidance, I'm filling my time with healthy amounts of sleuthing about myself. Playing private investigator by snooping into my own life, clicking through photos of me on stages I've never seen in cities I've never been to beside celebrities whose names I don't know. They could be politicians or singers or actors and I wouldn't know a thing.

There's:

Me on top of a pool table in a dive bar in Nashville.

Me on top of a barn roof in the middle of a cornfield, some-where in the Midwest.

Me on top of a couch on a late-night talk show, giving major Tom Cruise on *Oprah* energy.

I'm gathering that my recklessness leads me to stand atop things that generally aren't meant to be stood upon, which wouldn't be concerning if in every photo, I wasn't holding a bottle or a bong or both.

I'm thirty. Shouldn't I have set the partying ways behind me at this point?

Some of these images are as recent as last week.

Is this why Drew wrote me off? After ditching out on CeeCee's wedding, did I become a raging party fiend to fill the hole where love used to be?

I wish the questions would stop, especially since every answer only opens another can of stinky, muddy, wriggly worms I can't seem to hold onto for longer than a second or two.

I'm anew yet the same, changed in body but not in mind. Difficult, but I'm trying to latch on to the comfort of anything I'm familiar with. Too bad the internet is a cesspool of the unknown, and I'm not just talking about the new widgets I've been struggling to parse out.

With Milkshake curled around my bare feet with one of his stuffed duck toys, I switch to a new tab and return to my deep dive on Doop. Needing a break from my own face. I read:

The Death of Doop:
How a Lifestyle Brand Became Lifeless

The business went belly-up four years ago. The offices were open one day and closed the next. Most of the employees were unaware their workplace was folding, as is indicated in many social media posts and interviews. There are rumors in deep forums that Doop was working on secret projects and products with no plans of releasing them to market, but they're all unsubstantiated. While posters are vague about what "secret projects" means, a strong part of me wonders if that secret hallway had anything to do with it and if those crystals that I can't seem to find anywhere are included.

Two days ago, I tore this place apart looking for them. My penthouse looked as bad as my Astoria bedroom did after the sock-cession. Closets were flung open. Expensive clothes piled high on the floor. Pots and pans littered every countertop and table.

The crystals were nowhere to be found, which leads me to assume they transported me here and then…disappeared? Disintegrated? Are they still under my pillow seven years ago and I'd need to go back in time to get them again?

Thank God I had Antoni and Jerome's help putting everything back where it belonged, given that I have no idea where anything was to begin with.

The buzzer's grating growl goes off, echoing through the mammoth apartment, scaring Milkshake from his sleepy, sunshiny spot and waking me from my all-consuming spiral. Groaning, I ask into the high-tech receiver, "Who is it?"

"It's Drew."

Those two words send a shock wave through my entire body. I've never hit a button faster in my life—the portion of my life I can remember, anyway.

A click sounds on the other end, a door unlocking. Like a teenager, I slide over to the nearest mirror, raking my hands through my hair, and do my best to make myself appear presentable when I haven't showered, shaved, or changed out of my pajamas. Arguably, Drew has seen me look worse.

Minutes later, Drew stands outside my door with a reusable shopping bag that reads BLOODY GOOD BOOKS in one hand and a bottle of whiskey in the other. My heart splutters. I can't help it. He looks even more haggard than he did at the store, but this time there is a tender sort of beauty beneath his new burly, pinned-up look.

"Hi," he says, tentative.

"Hi," I echo back, brushing granola-bar crumbs off my T-shirt. "Come in?" I don't mean for it to sound like a question. Not entirely. It's just… "I'm surprised to see you," I blurt out.

He dips his head. "Yeah, well." A pause of what feels like the length of a pop song goes by. "I realized after I left my apartment that I should've contacted you. Then, I remembered I don't have any way to contact you, so I was going to say I was in the neighborhood. That's what I rehearsed on the way over here, but that's a complete and total lie, and I figured you'd know that since you claim to know me. The old me. Not the me now. What I'm trying to say is that—"

Gently, I grab his shoulders to ground him. The way he always used to do for me. I shouldn't, not in this timeline, but it's an impulse. "Drew," I say, "take a breath with me, okay?"

Quick inhale. Long exhale. He relaxes, until he notices the position of my hands. I wonder if he ever succeeded, over the last seven years, at falling out of love with me. There's that old scientific myth that every seven years your body replaces itself, old cells long gone to make way for new ones.

Science may have proven that false, but I'd also argue that science at large probably has no idea about the time-traveling crystals I had in my possession, so anything is possible.

"I'm good. I'm fine." Drew's tone is curt and his stance is guarded, yet he still hands me the bottle of whiskey like it's a peace offering.

"What's this for?" I ask.

"We're going to need it." He shakes the bag, and a small, compact item rumbles around beside the outline of a book. Drew's never without a book. At least that aspect of him hasn't changed.

Inviting him inside, I'm intensely curious about what he meant by "we're going to need it." Is he here to tell me to fuck off again or stage an intervention over my outrageous time travel story? Or maybe (most hopefully) he's ready to hear me out.

I bypass a grand tour, considering even I'm still having trouble deciphering which door leads to the guest bedroom and which door leads to what I can only describe as a shrine to myself. That room is unnerving. The accolades and photos and memorabilia from tours I never took. A cardboard cutout of me lurks in there like a monster beside a picture of me posing with my wax figure. It's uncanny valley to the highest order.

I instruct Drew to make himself comfortable even if I, myself, am still uncomfortable in this modern, maximalist place full up with items I always dreamed of having but, now that I have them, spark very little joy.

The robotic vacuum cleaner that turns on each time it senses or hears a spill never ceases to scare the shit out of me and send Milkshake into a barking, agitated tizzy. The smart mirror somehow seems to both not respond to my touch and distort my reflection, frustratingly not serving either of its intended functions. And a Grammy Award? Well, turns out a Grammy Award is just a statue that collects dust like every other item you place on a shelf for display. It's worth is purely extrinsic.

"Sorry," I say, self-conscious from the sensation of Drew's eyes on me from the sofa beyond the island. "I know this must seem like I'm still doing a bit, but I swear I don't have any idea where the glasses are in this kitchen. Truthfully, even if I was consciously in this timeline, I might not even know. Seems like there are people and robots to do everything for me." On my tiptoes, I try to reach for a high-up cabinet in the corner.

Suddenly, Drew's beside me. Crowding me. My nose is inundated with the scent of rosewood, blackberry, and a light hint of whiskey. Was that bottle already open? Maybe he took a swig to bolster himself before coming here. He opens the cabinet without incident, and of course, there are the glasses. "I believe you," he says—finally, shakily—while pouring.

"Thanks," I say, distracted by the brown liquid sloshing into the glasses. "Wait, what?"

"I believe you," he repeats, arresting me with his pale-blue eyes. Eyes that have aged with such grace, yet now hold something darker in their irises.

"You do?" He nods and hands me the glass, as if the alcohol is both an apology and a justification. "What changed?"

Before he gives me a straight answer, he clinks our glasses together, drains his whiskey with a full-body shiver, and serves a second for himself, tongue seemingly more relaxed. "I couldn't stop thinking about what you said in my shop."

"Which part?"

He heaves out a breath. "The part about you going to find CeeCee at the Doop headquarters. I think I was so thrown off by you being there in my store so out-of-nowhere that it didn't register that Doop had closed. The 'new' Nolan would know that," he says, which explains why he isn't being nasty. Not that the nastiness was undeserved the first time. "I tried to rationalize it by thinking it was all part of your prank show act."

"You do know I don't have a prank show, right?" I ask. "At least, not one that I'm aware of, anyway."

"Yes," he says between sips. "I looked you up."

"I looked me up too." I shudder again. All those lurid photos send me chugging back my own whiskey and then taking the bottle into the living room to sit. "It was *not* pretty."

"You forgot your glass," Drew says, shaking it in the air.

"I'm a twenty-three-year-old magically trapped in my thirty-year-old body. I'm going to drink from the bottle," I say as he grimaces. "What? We can share. I don't have cooties. Unless that's a

disease now, then maybe I do. I truly know nothing about myself."
Unthinkingly, I begin patting myself down with all the vigor of a TSA
agent doing a full-body search.

Wow, I bet I don't even need to take my shoes off at the airport
anymore. I'm famous!

Drew's across from me in three strides, giving me a scrupulous
once-over as I explore the parts of me that were once hollow and
now bulge, the spots that were once soft and are now hard.

I stop the patting as heat rises to my cheeks for thinking about
hard things right now. Under Drew's gaze, this already off-kilter
world flips completely upside down. I pass back the bottle before I
drop it and the automatic vacuum revs into gear.

"Your Wikipedia page doesn't say anything about you having
cooties, so I think you're okay," Drew says, loosened a bit from the
whiskey. Milkshake makes a home on Drew's lap, settling him even
more. "Let's get back to why I'm here." He produces a pair of glasses,
not all that unlike the ones on his face right now. Sexy-librarian style.

"What are those?" I ask.

"Blue light glasses."

"Seems like everything is a screen now. My fridge is even a
screen! You'd think they'd have invented blue light contacts or blue
light Lasik surgery at this point."

When I came to accept that it had been seven years since
I opened my eyes, I half expected to see flying cars outside my
window, but nope. Everything is just a little newer, a little brighter,
a little *louder*.

Drew shakes his head. "There's a lot of new blue-light-blocking
technology, but that's not the point. These are from seven years ago."

"I never saw you wear those around the apartment," I say.

"That's because," he says ominously, "they're from the goody
bag I got at CeeCee's wedding."

Chapter Eighteen

Drew's blue light glasses can read your mind.

If you put them on and look at a screen, it pulls up the image of whatever thought crosses through your head, not only eliminating blue light intake but cutting down on your overall screen time by not having to type, wait, or scroll to get your result.

At least that's what Drew says. I decide I need to test them for myself.

Embarrassingly, the first time I glance at the computer screen, a long feed of photos of Drew and me together spanning from high school until CeeCee's wedding day pop up in various overlapping windows. Reaching for the mouse, I exit them all out, but my mind, trickster that it is, thinks up more happy memories of the two of us. The rest appear in tinier and tinier frames until every screen in the room is overtaken.

Class trips. School plays. Queer clubs. Smiles for days.

Drew is seeing all this too.

I rip the glasses from my face. "Whoa."

"Trippy, right?" he asks, a bit rosy-cheeked from the deluge of old photos.

"Majorly." Turning the glasses over, I inspect the rims for cables, plugs, chips, sensors. There's nothing telling except the Doop logo scrawled in a small font across the arms. They are as unassuming as the pair Dad used to wear as readers to peruse the Sunday paper before heading to the hardware store.

"I've looked a million times since I saw you in my shop," he says. "There's no reasonable explanation. The night of CeeCee's wedding, I went through the bag and found these. After reading the directions on a tiny paper scroll, I tried them out. Glanced at my TV, up popped my favorite movie. Glanced at my phone, there was a dozen-year-old text thread from my dad on my birthday, apologizing for not showing up. I thought I was too drunk and I was seeing things. The next morning, I vowed I was going to try them again, except I got too scared and never did."

"But you kept them?" I ask.

He nods sheepishly. "I was in a state of paralysis over it. On one hand, I wanted to regain my bearings and try them again to make sure I wasn't losing my mind. On the other, I wanted nothing to do with them." He swallows loud enough for me to hear across the room. "I remember wondering if maybe you were right about that Go to Sleep, Bitch candle."

"Oh my God! I forgot about that." A whirring kicks up in my brain. "I got that in the goody bag from CeeCee's bachelorette party, and then later I stumbled down this retina-scan-only hallway in Doop while meeting CeeCee for a dress fitting. You don't think..."

He shakes his head. "I don't know what I think. All I can say is that if glasses like these exist, then crystals like the ones you described can exist too." It sounds as if there is an apology laced into his speech. Reassurance races through my nervous system, calming me more than the whiskey. Having Drew believe me is a surefire step in the direction of figuring this out. At the very least, I don't have to sort through this alone. "Can I see them?" Drew asks after a minute.

The reassurance stops dead in its tracks. "I can't find them." He can provide proof of his experience, and all I have is the empty space under my pillow. How far can you suspend your belief before reason runs out?

"You lost them?" he asks, probably thinking the worst of me, assuming that in the last seven years my bad habits have only been exacerbated.

"They disappeared," I tell him. "I searched this apartment top to bottom. Unless I have hidden chests or secret passageways, I think it's safe to say they're either back with my twenty-three-year-old self or they're lost to the sands of time."

Time has become such a meaningless expanse. It's always been intangible, but now it's almost completely irrelevant. Tomorrow is the faraway future. Yesterday was the very distant past. Drew, befuddlement etched across his brow line, is my only hope in the now. And I can't risk losing him again.

"Guess that means you can't just try the crystals again," he says, tracing an image into the condensation on the sides of his glass. Half-melted ice cubes clink together as he thinks.

"No, and I can't get ahold of CeeCee, Doop is done for, and the internet has been no help in sourcing the crystals because I can't for the life of me remember their names."

"What do you need their names for?"

"The scroll said the *specific combination* was for manifesting your future. I don't think any old crystals will do." I rack my brain for as much information as possible. "I think the shapes of the crystals mattered, too, but everything is hazy right now."

He worries his lip, picking up the bottle of cheap whiskey we've basically drained at this point. "I don't think we're going to find any answers at the bottom of a bottle."

We're. The word makes my heart sing. I spent so much time pouring over *we* vs. *ours* that I never stopped to appreciate how lucky I was to have an *ours* to begin with.

"You mean there's no secret message from Doop down there?" I ask jokingly. "No tea-leaf-type reading or proverbial wisdom etched onto the bottom?"

He places his left eye at the top of the neck. "Afraid not." A smile hints at the edges of his lips when he looks back up. Maybe it's from the alcohol. Maybe it's me.

I hope it's me.

But the hope is outweighed by overbearing guilt. Guilt for actions I have no recollection of. So I broach a topic neither of us is and likely never will be ready for. "What happened between us?"

"I might need another before I answer that," Drew says, shaking the empty whiskey bottle, still devoid of any secret notes or portentous imagery. Not at all jarred by my abrupt change in subject, given he used to be well acquainted with my ADHD.

When I return from my hunt for alcohol, finding a particularly pricey bottle with a gift tag still attached in a cabinet in my shrine-room, Drew is wearing the blue light glasses. Pulled up on the TV is a YouTube video of me at the Broadway Laugh Box. The upload date is a few months after CeeCee's wedding. For some reason, I'm wearing the peacock-blue suit again.

Now that I think about it, in many of the photos adorning the walls, I'm wearing a suit. Not the same one, but a similar cut. All in bright, vibrant colors. It's as if it's become my go-to costume. It's vastly different from the casual, relatable look I turned out for the folks at the Hardy-Har Hideaway, which leads me to believe this "new" Nolan dresses up to be above his audience.

"Should I have gotten something harder? Absinthe? Moonshine?" I ask, sitting down next to Drew on the couch. As I pour, I'm careful not to invade his space. We no longer hold that familiarity. He won't rest his head on my lap. I won't stroke his hair, even if it is just as red and thick and luscious as I remember. We aren't settling in for a *Drag Race* marathon. *Drag Race* might've been canceled at this point.

Oh, who am I kidding? Drag Race is forever.

Drew coughs into his hands and slides the glasses off, but the video stays—presumably until the next wearer thinks up another site. The shaky YouTube video starts playing from the middle when Drew hits the remote.

I'm wearing a shit-eating smirk, holding a wired microphone. "I was in love with my best friend for a while. That's not the joke, but thank you for laughing. It is funny. Being the gay boy cliché like that. I found out recently that he was in love with me too." Aww's sound off in the crowd, tinny due to the low quality. "Thank you for the aww's. It is cute. Or it would be cute had you been listening. I said 'was.' As in the past tense of is. Seems like *some* people need to retake elementary school English class.

"No, in all seriousness, he told me he didn't think he could be with me because, and I quote, 'I don't think you have the space in your life to love anything more than comedy.'" I hold as tension overtakes the audience. "Clearly he's never seen me devour a whole banana pudding from Magnolia Bakery. True love is spending two hours on the toilet for ten minutes of creamy banana bliss."

Bathroom humor was never a part of my sets. I avoided jokes like that for their cheap laughs and easy punch lines, but it kills the crowd and shows up often in the script for my special that I've been combing through. In the video, I'm soaking up the attention, mugging to extend the joke.

"In a way, I think that's how our relationship would've gone in the end. Sweet on the tongue, heavy on the stomach, and then straight down the toilet." The self-satisfied pout on my face is aggrandizing and grating. I want to slap the smug punk onstage even though that punk is me. "But it's alright, I wish him all the best…all the best punishments in the seventh circle of hell."

Quickly, I grab the remote and stop the video. My heart is racing.

Sweat beads at my hairline. Cramping, my stomach feels as if it's trying to evacuate my body. I can't bring myself to look at Drew. Those haunting words vibrate here between us. History, unbeknownst to me, pushes us farther apart.

I'm so lost in my own head that I don't even register when he stands, bag hiked up to the top of his shoulder. "I should go," he announces, crossing in front of the TV and moving toward the door. Milkshake is hot on his tail.

I call after Drew on autopilot, "No, you don't have to go." There's so much more I want to say and so few words to say it in.

He keeps his back to me, hand poised on the doorknob. "That's not the only skit," he says gravely. "And I–I think you should see it. I just can't. Not again." I can hear the strain in his voice, sense the tears welling behind his eyes.

Part of me wants to go to him, hug him from behind, absorb the blow of your best friend publicly stabbing you in the back for nothing more than a dozen laughs. Only, I'm the knife-wielder. There's metaphorical blood on my hands. I don't know how to reconcile that or make it better.

"Okay. Um, how will I—"

"You know where to find me," he says, abruptly exiting. Milkshake, seemingly as sad as I am at this, whimpers and scratches at the bottom of the door.

Needing the comfort, I go to Milkshake, scoop him up, and scratch him behind the ear. We return to the couch. I hover over the play button, knowing what I'm about to witness must only get worse or Drew wouldn't have left. Wouldn't have been upset over this still.

"Let's see how much damage I caused this time." I sigh, snuggle Milkshake, and prepare for the worst.

Chapter Nineteen

"I'm a terrible person!" I announce, out of breath as I burst through the front door of Bound by Mayhem Books.

Since it's nearly 7:00 p.m. on a Tuesday night, a Tuesday I spent at a torturous rehearsal spouting off jokes that I didn't write and that don't reflect my values, I assume the store will be as devoid of customers as it was when I first visited. However, a group of four, including Drew, sit on folding chairs in a circle at the center of the store, books open in their laps. Their aghast looks are hardly a warm welcome.

"Oh," I stammer, peering around at the elderly folk eyeing me suspiciously. "Sorry to interrupt. I'll, uh, come back later." Without thinking, I'd bolted out of rehearsal and straight to the store, disregarding Jessalynn's insistence I go home instead of going out to party. Little did they know, I was making my way to Drew.

"We're almost finished here," Drew says.

"We can skootch over. We don't mind skootching, do we, gang?" comes from the older Black man closest to me.

A tall white woman with long gray hair grabs a folding chair that's been leaning against the wall. "Pop a squat if you care to." After practically running the whole way here, I do care to, and I thank her.

The third person, a scrawny man wearing a zigzag-printed button-down, gives me a wicked eyebrow. "Aren't you that vulgar comedian?"

No hangs on the tip of my tongue, but I can't say no, so I nod.

"Wouldn't kill you to clean up your act. Back in my day, comedians didn't need to say all that shocking stuff to get a laugh," he tuts, slouching back in his chair and angling away from me. As if my presence alone is a scourge.

The woman waves him off. "Oh, Peter, pipe down. Your day was when the dinosaurs roamed the earth."

"You're not far behind him!" the first man, Xavier—so says his name tag—jokes with a laugh.

Drew claps his hands, smiling. "Okay, okay. Let's get back to the book, shall we? I want to hear everyone's thoughts on the big killer reveal. Peter, would you like to start?" Drew is good at politely commanding the room back to attention, I notice, so at ease in that role with people he's clearly comfortable with.

"I thought it was hackneyed," Peter spits out. Guess I'm not the only object of Peter's grumpiness. "I called it that the mailman was the killer the whole time. You could tell by page fifty."

"It was chapter three for me," says the woman. "He knew too much about the protagonist's life. Plus, the long-lost twin trope? Give me a break."

"I liked it," says Xavier, sounding a bit bashful. "Sometimes stories that hit the beats we expect are just as satisfying as the ones that blow our minds. I thought the writing toward the end there was really poetic and the themes tied up really nicely."

Drew chimes in. "I agree. There's comfort in revisiting the tropes we know and love. I think there was something quite interesting to be said about how torturous reconciling our pasts can be when we're trying hard to change our future. The psychic told him his family would be his downfall. Ironic that he didn't even know the family member who would commit the crime."

"Have you read it?" the woman—Jolene written on her name tag—asks me.

"No, I haven't read anything in…" I fumble for the right wording. "A *while*. But it sounds interesting. Even though I don't know the story like you all, I am a writer. As a comedian, I have to plot out stories and jokes, and to speak to Drew's point, sometimes the tried-and-true method is the most successful mode of getting your point across. It may be overdone, but it's been done so many times for a reason. Think about how many observational jokes begin with 'Have you noticed…' and then the comedian shares some universal insight about traffic or family or airline food. It's how you observe the airline food that dictates whether the material is successful or not."

Drew offers me an appreciative if hesitant smile. "That's an excellent point, Nolan." His eyes flick away quickly, reminding me of the awkwardness from our last encounter. I may be up to date now, but that doesn't mean Drew wants anything to do with me.

About twenty-five minutes later, a timer sounds off in Drew's pocket. "That's our meeting. I'll announce next month's pick later in the week and you can pick up your copies by Monday."

The small group scatters. Peter issues me another grouchy glare, but Xavier and Jolene say they hope to see me at their next meeting, which will not happen considering I only stumbled into this one by complete accident. Much like this timeline.

Drew and I stay behind to clean up. As I grab a paper plate covered with cookie crumbs left under Peter's chair, I'm hit with flashes of busing tables at the Hardy-Har Hideaway. It's mind-boggling to think how far I've come in seven years, how much attention and wealth I've accumulated by selling my soul in a pretty sucky way.

"The book's themes were a little too applicable for comfort,"

Drew says, offering me the open side of a trash bag. Where's that robotic vacuum when you need it? "Your past popping up into your present hits a bit too close."

"Tell me about it." I follow him into a back room that turns out to be his office. The desk from his old room in our apartment is there, cluttered with papers and an old laptop.

"Now, what was it you said when you entered earlier?" Drew asks. His expression lets me know he remembers full well and is toying with me a little.

I smirk. "Should I make my entrance again?"

"By all means."

With a dramatic flair, I exit the office and then burst back in. "I'm a terrible person!"

"I concur," he says smugly, now sitting in a rolling chair with his legs kicked up on the desk, ankles crossed, exposing tall, blue socks like the ones he gave me for my date with Harry. "I take it you watched the rest of the video."

"And every other video I could possibly find. The world's longest, darkest rabbit hole. I can't believe I wrote all that material. I mean, the stuff about you was bad, but the stuff about my family..." I wince, thinking back on the way I made CeeCee out to be a monster, my mom out to be overbearing, and my dad... Well, I didn't say much about him, but he was incriminated by association. "I spun that whole wedding situation in such a dishonest way."

He nods and shrugs. "We all want to be the victim. Unless you're in one of these," he says, tapping a finger on a stack of nearby hardcovers. "Then you *definitely* don't want to be the victim."

A laugh warms me momentarily. Enough of a reset to allow me to ask another question that's been plaguing me. "Why murder?"

"What?"

"Sorry, I mean, what happened to Eight, Three, One Books? You never answered me the other day. Bound by Mayhem seems a bit off brand for you," I reply. "Obviously I know now that a lot can change in seven years. It's just, I don't know…"

"Are you asking if I pivoted from romance to thrillers and mysteries after everything went down between us? And if you are, do you really want to know the answer? Because I've never lied to you, and I'm not about to start now," he says matter-of-factly.

"Yeah, I want to know," I tell him. Because I'm not stupid. I know the answer. But like watching those videos, I need to hear it to come to terms with the true scope of my actions.

He sits up straighter. "It wasn't a sudden change. It happened gradually after CeeCee's wedding. Little by little, those love stories stopped ringing true to me. The fantasy they sold felt completely out of the question, so I found another genre to love, and when it was finally time to open a store of my own, I knew I still wanted it to be a specialty shop for underserved readers, so I learned to lean in to the carnage."

"Oh." The syllable slips out of me, realization dawning that I'm a joy thief. My actions stole a crucial part of Drew's identity.

"It wasn't all you," he says, a surefire attempt at making me feel better that doesn't work. "It was life. It was my mom's relationships when I was a kid. It was the crappy, app-based dating culture in this city. It was long hours and high standards and moving out of our place."

At least I'm spared the pain of remembering Drew haul his bags out of our minuscule Astoria apartment. It was hard enough seeing him wheel that suitcase out of our shared hotel room. Seeing him leave for good would've gutted me.

He continues, "Over time, I just decided the whole situation was a wake-up call. Love isn't for me, and I'm fine with that."

"That…that sounds awful sad."

"It's not," he says certainly. "It's freeing. I don't believe in love. At least not the way I used to."

"Neither do I in this timeline, apparently." Those posters Jessalynn showed me illustrated everything. All those crushed-up flowers, reminding me of the bouquet CeeCee stomped on in the hotel courtyard, prove that I've cast off love in the exact same way.

"And you're rich and famous, so it can't be sad. Right?" Drew asks, and I can't tell if it's a rhetorical question or not. "It is what it is."

The resignation in his voice is too much for my already-ravaged heart to handle.

"I'm sorry, Drew," I blurt out, knowing I should've said this earlier. "I'm sorry for ditching out on the wedding. I'm sorry I made you feel like you weren't important to me. You are and always have been one of the most important people in my life. My last life and this bizarre one that I've tumbled into. I'm so sorry that I acted against that."

Drew nods, visibly taken aback. "Thank you."

"Part of me always thought words were just words—things that could be tossed off and used for a laugh—but after watching those mean videos, I realize that words can be weapons." An understanding that once seemed out of reach hits me over the head. "Using those weapons for protection is not an excuse when I was never under attack to begin with. I take full responsibility for that. Anyway, that's all I came here to say." I wait but he doesn't speak. Maybe he's stunned. Maybe he's letting it sink in. Either way, it seems it's time for me to go. "I'll leave you to close up and leave you alone indefinitely, like I promised."

I'm halfway to the front door when Drew stops me. "I could use some more help." When I look back, one corner of his mouth tips up slightly.

I'm more than happy to offer it. Anything to not go back to that massive, lonely apartment full of gadgets I can't work and trophies I didn't earn and dark rooms I don't need. We complete the tasks on his list in relative, companionable silence. It shuts my brain off for a while.

I watch Drew, through the front window, sweeping the sidewalk outside and can't help but mourn the loss of those seven years, wondering what we might have experienced had I not murdered our friendship over a career opportunity. I would've had a partner in my rise to fame, someone to keep me grounded and levelheaded, and to love me back to sense. He would've had support opening his bookstore—a bookstore where love stories could flourish. Milkshake would be *ours*, and he would lounge around the store, greeting customers and spreading merriment.

When the last book has been placed on its rightful shelf, Drew clears his throat, pulling me from the fantasy. "Since you helped me, I'll help you."

"With?"

"Getting back."

"Yeah, right," I say with a laugh.

"No, I'm serious. I have a plan." Why I would've thought otherwise is beyond me. "The book inspired me, actually."

"You want me to fight for my life against a murderer who also happens to be my long-lost twin?"

"No, though that would be quite entertaining."

"Okay, I know I'm an awful person in this timeline, but I don't think I deserve *death*," I say, trying to make light of a situation that couldn't be more leaden. "At least, I don't think so."

"I don't think so either," Drew says, coming out from behind his desk, shrinking the margin of space between us. Where I'm a run-on sentence, he's a concise clause. Always so sure in what he's trying to say. "After the inciting incident of the book, the protagonist—he's almost killed, it's a whole thing—has to retrace his steps, reach out to the people he saw that night, and enlist experts for help."

I play with a grouping of pens poking out of a holder by the register. The holder is skull-shaped and the pens stick out of the eye and mouth holes—gross. "Okay, but who's going to help me? Nobody is going to believe my ludicrous story. Hell, you didn't even believe me until you remembered those freaky glasses. We can't just go around showing people those."

"We ask people who already believe," he says, with more certainty than anyone discussing time travel should have. "Psychics, shamans, healers, and crystal shop owners. Some of them are bound to know more than we do, at least when it comes to which combination of crystals might help you… Wait, what is it you said they did again?"

"Manifest your future," I recite. Annoying that I can remember that and not the names of the crystals. My mind was mush by that point. "I could maybe pick them out if I saw them. By color or something."

"Exactly!" Drew exclaims, stepping closer. There's excitement in his gait. "If we can jog your memory enough, maybe we can figure this out. Plus, there's one other line of defense."

"Which is?"

"Former Doop employees."

"Who do we know that worked at Doop aside from CeeCee?" His pinched expression says it all. "I told you she's blocked me. I can't reach her."

"I have her personal email," he says, which shocks me and touches me in equal measure. I can't believe he's kept in contact with my family even after falling out with me. I wonder if it was a small way to stay connected to me or purely a necessity given how close we were growing up.

"Where is she?" I ask.

"Colorado. She works in insurance now," he says. My first thought is: Wow, she must be miserable. What I think she loved about Doop was the open offices, the products she believed in, and a group of freethinkers. Insurance sounds about as soul-sucking as working at the DMV.

"How do we know she won't just delete an email from me? She might think it's a prank or spam, or worse, she might just not care." I'm certain she's seen those comedy tapes I cringed through. I practically added devil horns to her head in every story. Forgiveness won't come in the form of a desperate email, but maybe it's a start...

Drew nods. "Since we're supposed to be estranged now, she's bound to be surprised and respond to one of us, right?"

And that's how our mission begins.

PART FOUR

ROSE QUARTZ

Crack open the heart

Chapter Twenty

Dearest CeeCee, I type before backspacing and groaning.

I try Hey, Sis and Sup, girl and Long time, no talk, but no greeting conveys the panic and apology of seven years lost and mistakes made and help needed.

Eventually, I settle on sending:

Hi, CeeCee,

I recognize that you likely don't want to hear from me. Why would you? I lambasted you in front of many an audience. I get it. But...I'm kind of in a pickle and you might be able to help. So, here's the *dill*. (See what I did there? Pickle joke...)

I need to ask you about the goody bags from your wedding. Something strange has happened, and I think Doop had a hand in it. I'm being purposefully sparing with the details because every time I try to type them out, they sound more and more absurd. Could I call you sometime?

Of course, no pressure.

All my best,
Your bro

P.S. Sorry if my pickle joke was *sour*!

We don't hear from CeeCee over the next few days.

I wasn't holding my breath over it anyway.

I'm too wrapped up in our three-pronged plan of attack.

Prong one: Fill in my memory gaps so as not to majorly alert anyone presently in my life to the farcical predicament I find myself in.

Prong two: Track down crystals that may have been included in that goody bag.

Prong three (my little secret): Win Drew's forgiveness. For real.

He may be willing to help me, but I have a sneaking feeling he's doing it to get rid of me. The vortex of time split open when I jumped. That much is certain. Drew's always been a do-gooder. Letting me lose seven years of my life, existing in the body of someone I don't even recognize, would weigh on him, no matter the hurt between us. Knowing he could help but didn't would be wounding.

I must accomplish all of this before the Netflix special taping. It's imperative that I make it back to my proper timeline before committing those uncomfortable jokes to tape forever.

That's why we're here, sitting close on one side of a velvet-draped table, a woman wearing more bangles than should be legal across from us. A deck of cards has been shuffled, drawn, and decoded one by one. They are...*not good.*

"For the past, we have the Nine of Swords," Lucille says, tapping the edge of her card with a long, painted nail. "It represents deep anxiety and fear. There was a huge stressor in your past." Lucille is probably in her late-sixties, long dark hair raining down over a crimson-colored peasant blouse.

"No kidding," I say, thinking about the pressure to perform, to achieve, to live up to my family's demands and be the romantic ideal. "Tell me something I don't know."

She must take that as a challenge and not the defensive joke I mean it to be. "Suffering in our lives is as much up here"—she presses her palm to the center of her forehead—"as it is out here." As she gestures around, I take stock of the room with its plum-painted walls, candelabras, and dark, heavy curtains. Lots of distractions for what feels like poetic nonsense. Even so, I'm in no place to say so or judge. "Would you like to hear about your present?"

I look to Drew, who had his reading before mine, rife with positivity and hope. I'd be annoyed if he didn't deserve all that. His nod prompts me to continue.

"We have here the Devil."

"Oh dear God."

"God can't really help you now," says Lucille ominously. "No, I'm just kidding. Usually it means hedonism, materialism, addiction, the works." I think about the photos I found of myself online. The drinking, the drugs. Harry in my bed and on my payroll. The items in my apartment that serve no function other than status. "But there is a flip side."

"Which is?" I ask.

"Freedom and pleasure."

Those ring true too. It's clear the financial security I've found in this career has unshackled me from the uncertain chaos of my old ways. Of living paycheck to paycheck, tip to tip. Operating on energy drinks and the absolute will to succeed. "Those don't sound too shabby." I smile at Drew, who has his eyes laser-focused on the final card in my reading.

"Don't get too cocky now. We've still got the future." The grim reaper is displayed on the card, white flowers blooming beneath his pointed staff. The skull face gives me the creeps. "*Death*."

"That seems hardly fair. Everybody dies," I say with a nervous laugh. "That's in everyone's future."

Lucille doesn't look up as she speaks. "There's loss and grief on the horizon for you, child." Her voice possesses a new, fierce conviction that scares me into belief.

Worry mounts inside me. If she's telling the truth, has this seven-year jump set destruction into motion? In the cards, maybe she sees my untimely demise. I used those crystals, gamed the system, and now time is going to come crashing down around me. Claim me for the dirt and the weeds.

I clutch at my tight chest when suddenly I notice Drew's hand twitch below the table. It appears as if he wants to touch me, to soothe me. But his hand goes still again, remaining firmly in his own lap. What I wouldn't give to feel the warmth of his palm on my skin, allow it to cut through my anxiety and inject a balm straight to my soul. "It's okay," Drew whispers with a nudge of his elbow, which helps some.

"He's right," Lucille says. "It will be okay. As I mentioned, there is always the inverse. Out of death can come rebirth. A new cycle and a fresh start."

If this nightmare has shown me anything, it's that I desperately need one of those. I've isolated my family. Lost my best friend's trust. Succeeded only so much that I stood on their backs and spat on them to get here. I don't deserve any of the fame I've gotten.

I'm surviving in a constant state of mortification and shame.

I offer a waning smile without forgetting why we're here to begin with. "Let's hope that's it. Do you happen to have any, uh, cleansing agents, maybe? Like, sage or herbs or *crystals* perhaps?" I'm being leading, but I'm itching to get out of here.

Lucille perks up at the mention. "You've opened your mind to the healing power of our earth's rocks? I wouldn't have expected that. You seem so clogged." No matter which way I spin that, it is unequivocally an insult. Her eyes are a scrutinizing scan. "I may have something for you. Hold tight."

Once she's disappeared behind the curtain, I have a moment to absorb that Drew's elbow is still lightly touching mine. A reassuring sensation. My insides are a war zone: joy over the comfort of his slight touch and terror over the cards still mocking me from the table. "We need to get me back ASAP!"

"Okay, I hear you, but they're just cards. They might not mean anything."

"Uh, hello? They were *just crystals* until they flung me into the future!" I shout-whisper, scaring myself with my own voice.

Drew's blue eyes are squinted. "I understand this is stressful, but we're not going to figure this out by panicking, okay?"

I wish I could take his advice like a shot of tequila and let it loosen me up, shake the fear off, but it feels unfeasible.

After an exhale, I say, "I'm worried. What if I ripped a hole in the space-time continuum? What if I'm in for a world of punishment? What if those crystals were a barter with the devil like the one on the card and he's sucked out my soul?"

"That sounds like a questionable erotica plot," Drew jokes, an obvious bid to distract me. "And I've read my fair share of questionable erotica to know."

"That card does look quite BDSM-y," I point out, noting the silhouetted humans bound by the neck. "Wait, are they naked?"

"They are," says Lucille upon reentry. She holds a fancy cloth, a bevy of crystals collected inside. Maybe from her private collection. Maybe from a stash for sad saps like me. "I had those cards custom made. I even provided the models."

Okay, now I'm worried she's got a secret sex dungeon, and we're about to become her latest prisoners.

Lucille lays out her spread on the table beside the cards, which I'd prefer to forget about. "Do any of them call out to you, Nolan?"

I inspect them all, but only two of them churn up memories: a clear, pointed obelisk-shaped one and a smooth, rounded, heart-shaped pink one. I point to them enthusiastically, not mentioning our true intentions for coming here. We don't need someone like Lucille asking too many questions, because even if she may claim a connection to the larger spiritual realm, I have a feeling literal time travel trumps all that.

Lucille smiles. "Good eyes. The quartz duet. Clear quartz and rose quartz in combination can be powerful since they're of the same family. Perfect for processing big emotions and manifesting trust and harmony."

Maybe she *is* super connected to another realm. How else could she know how badly I want to make it up to the man sitting next to me? Drew's pointer finger traces the divot above his upper lip. I wonder if he's registering the irony as well.

I consider the other crystals once more, but for various reasons— their shades, sizes, general vibes—they don't dredge up anything mentally for me. Which makes me think this quest will be harder than I originally considered. Part of me was hoping we'd snag all of the crystals on this trip, but it's the specificity that's bogging me down.

"I'll just take those two. How much?" I ask immediately. I'm ready to be out of this shop so those haunting cards can't stare me down from the tabletop any longer.

"Twenty each, but I'll go for thirty-five for the pair." Momentarily, I worry I can't afford that. Days ago, I wouldn't have had that kind of cash on me, and if I swiped my debit card it would've probably shredded itself in protest. Now, all I need to do is fish into my wallet and there's a fat wad of bills waiting for me.

I hand over the cash, she hands over the crystals, and then we all walk out of the room and into her kitchen. Yes, we agreed to tarot appointments in some stranger's apartment, but desperate times call for desperate measures, and here I am, turning to the very trinkets I once openly mocked. They may be my only hope.

With the crystals tucked safely in my jacket pocket, Drew and I shuffle about for a second on the sidewalk. "That was...something," I say to break up the silence.

"At least we got some of what we came for." He pulls his MetroCard up on his phone, alerting me that our time together for the day is ending. Disappointment hops up into my chest, wishing we were riding the subway home together like the old times, sharing a single pair of wired earbuds while listening to whatever audiobook Drew was listening to at the moment. He never ceased to blush if a sex scene came on unexpectedly.

"Maybe even more than we bargained for," I joke to squash the tension and discomfort. "I'm going to be scarred by those scary cards for eternity."

"If you even remember them," he says.

"What do you mean?"

One shoulder goes up in a noncommittal shrug. "We don't know how this works. If the crystals get you back, you probably won't remember any of this." There might be a note of sadness in his voice, but maybe I'm overthinking it. "I only say that because you have no recollection of the seven years you missed. I can't imagine you'll get to keep memories you never made."

"Guess I should live it up while it lasts, then," I tell him, encouraging myself. "Hey, would you maybe want to get dinner and drinks? Jessalynn hasn't sent me any frantic texts, so I assume I don't have anywhere to be for the rest of the night." I truly can't bear the thought of sitting in that spacious apartment alone, curled up with Milkshake, who may or may not be able to read my mind, with nothing to do and no other human around.

I miss the comfort of knowing Drew is on the other side of a paper-thin wall. My new apartment is like a fortress of solitude.

Drew's eyes grow apologetic, and words I'd rather not hear follow. "I don't think that's a good idea."

"Right, sure," I say, trying and failing to temper the rejection. "But, um, why exactly?"

He sighs. "It's just that I think we should keep our interactions to the crystal hunt. Keep things less complicated."

"Of course, because they're so uncomplicated now." I mean to say it as a joke, but it comes out like cutting sarcasm. I think about what he said about not believing in love the way he used to. I think about the comedic reputation I've established in this timeline.

Drew probably has a point, even if I don't like it. Trying to get back to the place we were at on the night of CeeCee's wedding before I ran off would be messy. This whole time travel situation is already complicated enough. But does that complication also extend to a friendship?

I can't think of anything in my real timeline less complicated than the beautiful friendship I shared with Drew. It was my keystone, and only now that I don't have it do I realize just how quickly the archway of my life could come crumbling down in its absence.

"Sorry, no. I understand. I should probably get back to learning my set before rehearsal." I suppress an eye roll at the thought of spending time with those ridiculous jokes and stupid punch lines that feel gross to say aloud, even while alone in my apartment.

"And I have stuff to do at the store." It sounds like a lie, but I don't test it.

We both nod. Both stand there. Both let the city and the sidewalk and soundscape of honking swallow us up. Drew makes the first move by offering his hand for me to shake. The formality punctures me.

"Can we at least hug?" I ask. It's only afterward that I realize how childish the question sounds. "We don't have to, you know, if that will complicate things too much." It's selfish, really. To crave comfort from someone so set on pulling away. Though in fairness, I pushed first. And this time, I can't even blame the unfortunate events of the lost seven years. I pushed the night of CeeCee's wedding, so I have no right trying to pull him back in.

No right. But I am anyway.

I think Drew senses this, our friendship sonar not completely dashed to pieces. Tentatively, he says, "Sure, we can hug, Nolan." And as soon as he opens his arms, I fold into them, channeling all my love and care into the palms of my hands as they press into his back. I memorize the rise and fall of his collarbone beneath my cheek, subtly inhaling the scent of him, which, mixed with Lucille's incense, is sweet and intoxicating.

"Did you just sniff me?" he asks, sounding somewhat amused but mostly concerned.

Guess I wasn't as subtle as I thought. "No, sorry." I back away, embarrassed. "I had a sniffle. All that incense bothered my sinuses," I lie, forgetting that he's the leading Nolan Baker Bullshit Detector even after all these years. Thankfully, he doesn't push me on it.

"Take some Sudafed and get some sleep," he says sternly. "Text me and we can schedule our next plan of attack."

"Will do."

As I turn to go, I sense an acute connection to the crystals jangling around in my pockets. A light breeze blows over my shoulders, whispers hope into my ears, and I realize that I may be overwhelmed by this new reality, but I won't, under any circumstance, let it beat me.

Chapter Twenty-One

"What were you doing canoodling with Drew Techler outside of a tarot shop?" Jessalynn asks, shoving their tablet in my face. On it is a trashy news site showcasing a picture of Drew and me hugging outside of Lucille's place. Whimsical, light-up signs cast a purplish glow over our heads.

There I am. Midsniff. Damn. Can't pass that off as allergy-related sniffling in the slightest.

"Uh, we ran into each other," I lie, tucking the two crystals into the nearest drawer and closing out the browser tab where I was searching for nearby metaphysical shops so Jessalynn doesn't see. They've already come in guns blazing, eyebrows cocked. I don't need them asking questions about the store I've flagged for Drew and me to visit tonight.

My many searches for "manifesting your future" suspiciously turned up nothing of note, almost as if any helpful record had been wiped out. Not even the mind-reading blue light glasses Drew left behind were of use to me because my memory of the crystal collection is still watercolor-painting blurry, so they kept opening and closing new tabs without stopping for me to read anything.

I guess piecemeal is the only way we're going to get this done, unless my mind snaps into clarity anytime soon.

"Right, so I'm to believe you've suddenly taken an interest in spirituality and warmly receiving former friends who've on more than one occasion sent you cease-and-desist letters?" Jessalynn asks.

"Cease-and-desist letters? More than *one*?" The videos I watched when Drew came here must've only been the tip of the iceberg of my betrayal.

Jessalynn gapes at me. "Please, Nolan, for the love of all that is holy, your metaphorical marbles? Pick them up before I trip on them and crack my skull open, 'kay?" It's a demand, not a question. I swivel away from my desk to face them. "I'm sure the stress of the special is getting to you," they continue. "It's weighing on me as well. But you can't be sleeping with Harry and hugging Drew and visiting psychics. You just can't."

In a world filled with yeses, it seems Jessalynn is the hard-ass hoarding all the noes. But are they necessary? "What's the big deal? It was a hug."

"I wish it were that simple. It's never just a hug with you, Nolan," they say, clacking their fingernails together in apparent frustration. "I work day and night to ensure your brand is consistent, your fans are fed, and you arrive sober-ish and on time for all scheduled appearances and shows. When you do something that threatens one of those three things, I have to put my red-bottomed foot down. Do you understand?"

Feeling chided and childish, I intone, "Yeah."

"Good. That means no more sleepovers without NDAs, no more surprise visits with card readers, and no more Drew Techler. Kapeesh?"

"Kapeesh," I reply.

Except the *kapeesh* only holds for about six hours.

After texting Drew a profuse apology involving the hug, the sniff, and the subsequent internet uproar over "raunchy comedian

Nolan Baker reconnecting with former flame Drew Techler," I told Drew I had another lead on crystals.

I meet Drew in lower Manhattan on a Monday night standing outside a metaphysical supply store called Stop, Rock, and Roll. I know their name is a play on what to do if you ever catch on fire, but I wonder if they know how much like counterculture protestors they sound. *Down with Elvis*, their signage almost screams.

The spring air is brisk, reminding me of the night of CeeCee's wedding. Drew wears a thin dark-blue cardigan that brings out his eyes, which are full up with confusion when they land on me.

"What exactly are you wearing?" he asks, pressing down the amusement that tickles the side of his lip.

I do a twirl and win that smile fully. "What, you don't like it?" I combed through an image search of me for the last seven years, and I learned that during the day I usually wear upscale designer-casual in muted tones, and onstage, I'm always decked out in a tailored, colorful suit. Today, I'm donning a ratty, tie-dyed camp T-shirt I found at a secondhand store, a pair of distressed bell bottoms, and Jesus sandals with a broken strap. "It's my disguise."

"What are you disguised as? A cut ensemble member from a community theater production of *Hair*?" he asks, probably recalling the terrible musical production his college put on for freshman year parents' weekend that we laughed about for weeks. So, so many flopping penises. And we went with his *mom*.

"Very funny. Do you remember those black hoodies we bought at the mall in high school so we could sneak out to smoke at the playground on school nights?" Drew nods, expression glazing over with what looks like nostalgia. "Well, after that photo of us hit a few headlines, Jessalynn has me on lockdown. Says us being seen together is bad for my brand. Hence the ridiculous getup." My eyes sweep the street. Nobody is looking too long or hoisting a camera, so I'd say I'm in the clear. "Let's get inside before I test my luck though."

Beneath the magenta-and-yellow awning is a swath of greenery. Hanging plants rain down upon numerous tiered shelves of potted succulents in all shapes and sizes. We practically have to hatchet our way through the jungle just to step inside.

Past the terrariums, Buddha statues, and a dream-catcher display, we enter the crystal section. Rows and rows of buckets are lined up, crystals in every color of the rainbow gleam in disorganized piles, while the larger cuts are displayed on glass shelves along the walls. Some have even been fashioned into pieces of jewelry; necklaces are pinned up on white boards so you can see how low they hang, and bracelets are draped over mannequin wrists for a better view of the craftsmanship. Mom would love one of these.

I know it would make more sense if Drew and I split up to divide and conquer, but this place is such a maze, I could get lost in here. Besides, after Jessalynn told me about the cease-and-desist letters, I'm starting to think there's more to the story than what I've seen on YouTube.

"So, I know we're supposed to be sticking to the crystal hunt, but Jessalynn told me about how you legally tried to stop me from telling jokes about you, and I hope this isn't terribly awkward, but..." I grow nervous, which is strange because aside from my romantic feelings for him, I've never been afraid to talk to Drew about anything. "I was wondering if you'd tell me your side."

Drew stops appraising a yellow stone to look at me. The glazed expression is back, but he answers easily after a moment. He's had much longer to sit with this than I have. "I think you got a good rise out of the crowd with that first set, so you made me a permanent part of your act. That whole confessional angle was really big in your industry at the time. When you went on the road with Clive, you kept adding more and more material about it. At first, I rolled with the punches, figuring it was your way of processing the situation and none of my business, but then your star started to rise and people started recognizing me."

That explains how those articles cropped up so quickly after our trip to Lucille's. Nobody had to do much digging to identify the red-haired hottie I was hugging. He was getting media attention alongside me. I hate that I added that stressor on him. "Shit," I mutter.

He scrubs a hand over his wary face. "It was awful. Bad enough I had to be reminded of you when I went on social media or turned on the TV, but to have people from our past reaching out to me, asking if I knew about it, sending me videos." Distress torques his brow. "My mom even started getting asked about it."

Drew's mom, Belinda, was always a marvelous free spirit. She worked at Bath & Body Works during the week, painted on weekends, always had a different boyfriend, and probably knew about all the pot we were smoking but never said anything because she knew we were "good kids." She was a reliable mom who loved Drew, but it was clear to me fairly early on in our friendship that if she could be a painter in New York instead of a single mom in New Jersey, she would be.

"You're kidding," I say. It's bad enough I dragged Drew down, but taking his mom into the mud by association doubles the suffocating impact. Drew shakes his head, moving away to hold up a different crystal. I shake my head right back. That one doesn't look like any of the ones from the goody bag, nor am I ready to drop the subject just yet. "Does your mom, like, hate me?"

"You know my mom—or, *knew her*, anyway. 'Hate' is not in her vocabulary," he says, not nearly as reassuring as I'd hoped, but it makes a certain sense. "She processes things differently. 'Art it out, Drew,' she kept telling me."

"Did you?" I ask, worried but trying to keep a calm composure. "Art me out of your system?"

He laughs, shaking his head. "No, but I did benefit from her doing it."

"How so?"

He scrunches up his nose. "Not sure I should say."

"Come on, what is it?" I've seen the bad parts of this life. Nothing can hurt me more.

"She painted some anti-fan art of you and sold the pieces online."

"For how much?"

"Let's just say hate might be worth more than love in this lifetime," he says, skirting around the answer.

I stand there, stunned by how far removed I feel from myself, no better than the dirt trekked in on the floor being ground into the carpet with each passing person.

Drew notices me shutting down. "Jeez, sorry, I really shouldn't have brought it up."

"Did the money go to good use, at least?"

He nods, offering a conciliatory smile. "Helped me open my shop, so, um, yeah. I'd say so." My dream indirectly got Drew his. Both of them warped and unrecognizable from the fantasies we shared with each other seven years ago.

"Good," I say, coming back to life a little. "God, I don't know how many times I can say it before it loses all meaning, but I am so, so sorry. I'm not just a terrible person. I'm a full-blown asshole."

"Why does Full-Blown Asshole sound like the name of a ska band?"

"Jeez, seven years and people still know what ska is?" I ask, needing the distraction but not letting it stay. "Seriously, how can you joke with me right now? I ruined not just your life but your mom's." That alone downright destroys me.

Drew stops his search at the jewelry display, new lines grooving across his forehead. "You said it yourself, *you*"—he waves a large hand up and down my body—"yes, but *you*?" His hand stops inches from my temple. I'm tempted to tip into it. Make a point of contact. "I'm starting to differentiate the two."

"How?" I ask. "Even I'm losing myself in the mess of me, and I'm *me*!"

"Because…" His voice trails off. "I just can. I can't explain it. I can't explain anything that has happened since you dropped into my shop, but while we're working together I'm choosing to forgive you and accept the situation. You have to accept it too. We don't have another choice."

Hearing him say this provides a deep sense of relief. Fighting the situation won't fix it. We're in it. Maybe not *together* exactly, but at least in proximity. For now.

"But is being around me right now causing you more pain?" I ask, fully ready to vanish into thin air if he says yes. He fiddles with a ring—a silver band and a purple stone. "I don't want to cause you more pain."

It's stifling enough that I caused him any pain ever. Drew Techler is the singular person that least deserves life's shit, and I became the leading shit-slinger.

Though maybe I was always the shit-slinger. I was the one always late with the rent. I was the one constantly forgetting to update the calendar. I was the one setting tiny, isolated fires from candles Drew warned me not to light. Maybe he was scooping up my shit faster than I could notice I was slinging it.

"Nolan, I'm not just doing this for you. I don't know if this is a parallel-universe situation or a time travel situation or a completely different situation that I can't even possibly perceive, but maybe if I help you get back, things will…" His voice dwindles to a quiet rumble. "Shake out differently?" There is evident hope wound into those words, and I inhale as much of it as possible, allowing it to penetrate the walls of my heart.

"I get it," I say. Because I do. Now it makes sense that if he gets me back, maybe that hurt won't ever happen. We can create a different ending for ourselves. If I jumped time, as I suspect I did, I can go back and make different choices. But... "What if, like you said the other day, I get back and I don't remember any of this?"

While I was spiraling, Drew circled around a display, getting lost behind hanging ornaments that appear to be melted down into wavy, pink swaying pieces affixed to the ceiling. When I join him, I notice he's holding a black crystal skull as if at any moment, he's going to give a Shakespearean soliloquy about time and fate and wanton bastards. Instead, all he says is, "I have to believe you will remember, because I won't be able to forget."

I let out the deepest exhale, allowing Drew's reassuring words to sink in. He's right. Whatever this is, it's monumental. Maybe unprecedented. We may be the only two to ever navigate this, and that impression, regardless of timeline, won't be easily erased. Drew's spirit, both then and now, will stick with me. Somehow, I'm sure of that, and my heart pitches toward him.

He sets the skull back down with a thud that hurts my ears and draws my eyes. There, next to the skull, are a few smaller black beauties that jog my memory. The small card in front of them reads: *Hematite stone and black obsidian.*

"Those!" I shout without regard for the other customers across the store. The names are familiar.

I take one stone from Drew's hand and cross to the wall by one of the display cases, which has a poster with descriptions on it. I read: "'Obsidian is good for the Law of Attraction.' Unhelpful, but *okay*. Not sure what that means. The other, hematite stone...clears your mind."

Drew steps in beside me, and my mind really does clear for a second. If I tipped slightly to my left as my finger scanned over the lines of text, our shoulders would brush, our shirts would bunch. "'Helps provide clarity in the face of confusion,'" we end up reciting in near-perfect unison.

"I'm pretty sure these are two of them," I heave out. "I'm less confident about their shapes, but they're small enough to fit under my pillow, which seems like a good sign." My heart ticks into hyper, cheerful motion.

Then my phone cuts our outing short. Jerome, my night assistant, must've ratted me out, and now Jessalynn is in my ear demanding to know where I am, who I'm with, and when I'll be back. I lie about two of the three.

When I slip my phone back into my pocket, I look at Drew, disappointed we won't be able to collect the rest of the crystals today. "I wish I didn't, but I have to go."

"I understand," he says. "We've got time."

"Maybe. But I'm not exactly sure time is on my side." I let out a rueful laugh that he matches. Then, his blue eyes land on mine, and he's no longer *looking* at me but rather *considering* me. It's in the soft set of his brow, and it sends a thrill through me.

Regardless of Drew's forgiveness, I want so badly to turn back the clock, and these black stones might help me do that, so I hold tight to Drew's firm belief. That at the end of this, I'll return, I'll remember, and I'll do everything I can to ensure he and I don't end up here like this: stilted semi-strangers clinging to hope while scouring a crystal shop for a lifeline.

Chapter Twenty-Two

Have you heard from CeeCee? I text Drew during a break at rehearsal for my special.

My email inbox floods daily, but all I do is scour it for CeeCee's response, and I always come up empty. In my real timeline, hearing from CeeCee was a rarity until I became her mister of honor (out of sheer nepotism), and when I did hear from her, just seeing her contact pop up on my lock screen sucked all the energy out of me.

Now each notification ping is a tiny burst of hope that it's her.

I'm let down every time.

When I don't hear from Drew right away either, I decide to start drafting a second email to CeeCee on my walk to the refillable water station in the hallway outside the Forty-Second Street rehearsal studio we're renting (and practically living in) until we move out to Brooklyn for tech:

CeeCee,

I know I was vague in my last message. Purposefully so. But I'm realizing now that maybe you thought that was someone trying to impersonate me. I swear, I'm not a rando fishing for your social security number or to harvest your organs. Though, I suppose a rando fishing for your social security number and your organs might say that to throw you off their scent...

I guess you'll have to trust me. Impossible, I'm sure, given I've sullied your name with my assholery.

Sorry about that.

Is this a terrible way to apologize for what I've put you through? Definitely. But I have no other way to contact you, and I *am* sorry.

God, this is getting long, but what I need to say is: those crystals in the goody bag made me time travel.

That also sounds like something a scammer/organ harvester might say but—

"You're phoning it in," Harry says, stomping up to me in the hallway wearing an irremovable scowl.

His abrupt arrival causes my thumb to slip. I meant to save that message to drafts, but instead, I sent it out into the universe, unfinished, unedited.

Oh well. CeeCee's probably not getting these anyway.

"Sorry, what?" When I look up, I notice Jessalynn is standing behind him, appearing both austere and apologetic. They unbutton their crimson, studded blazer and fold their arms across their chest. Feeling like Mom and Dad are about to ground me after finding gay porn on the family computer's browser history, I slip my phone in my pocket and give them my attention even though I'm parched.

Harry's frustrated sigh flings me back to the night he broke up with me outside the Hardy-Har Hideaway. Time has turned him into an Adonis but hasn't softened his easily triggered temper. "You're delivering the joke like you're reciting the Pledge of Allegiance. It's a rote snoozefest."

I should be offended by this, but I know he's right. The twenty-three-year-old inside wants to argue that it's not me, it's the material that goes low when it should go high. Michelle Obama would be deeply disappointed in me. Great, now I'm wondering if Michelle Obama has ever run for president... Time-jump brain farts are inundating.

"Are you even listening?" Jessalynn snaps.

"Yes, of course," I lie, because I sense part of Harry's annoyance is a by-product of those gossip-rag photos of Drew and me. In this timeline, I clearly was never taught to keep the personal and the professional separate. My former friend is my manager, blurring the lines between chumminess and capital gain. My former flame/recent fuck buddy is my director, a huge middle finger to decency. Instead of saying any of that, I apologize. Like I'm becoming so good at.

"We've worked too hard for this special to tank, which is why I'm booking you a warm-up gig," Jessalynn says.

"What kind of warm-up gig?" I ask, dreading having to do these jokes any more than necessary before completing the crystal hunt and getting me back. Hopefully.

"Maybe at the Broadway Laugh Box as the surprise headliner. Take you back to your roots," they say offhandedly. Sounding as if the Broadway Laugh Box, my former pinnacle, is now a bottomless pit they'd rather not think of. "Let you perform in a place you're comfortable before moving into the theater. I think it will be good for you."

My brain whirs. "What about at the Hardy-Har Hideaway instead?" I ask. I spent more time at the Triple H than I did in Drew's and my apartment—it was my second home. There's no stage in the world I'd be more relaxed on.

Jessalynn's face scrunches up with disgust. "You want to perform at that dive?"

"It's where I got my start."

"For autobiographical purposes, you got your start with Clive at the Broadway Laugh Box," they inform me. "We need to stay consistent, and the Clive connection is far more interesting than you serving reheated spring rolls to stingy tourists at a B-minus club."

"Ouch," I say.

"Oh, don't give me that. You buried that past alongside me, and you know it," they say, not realizing that I truly don't. The more I piece together from the last seven years, the more I want to tear it all up and set it ablaze.

"What about all the good times we had there? All the dreaming about the future?" I ask. "Let's stomp all over our old stomping ground. It'll be fun." I'm flying by the seat of my pants.

Jessalynn looks to Harry for backup. All he does is shrug.

"Fine, just this once." My chest loosens, allowing more optimism to swoop in. Jessalynn must read it on my face because they squelch it quickly. "Don't get too excited. You're doing the show front-to-back as written for the special. No ad-libs. No new stuff. Promise?"

"Promise," I say because it's the only leverage I have to get what I want.

"Good," Jessalynn says. "Wanda won't love hearing from me, but I'll make the call. Now get back in there and please, please, *please* KO some punch lines!"

.⁺✦⁺.

No word from CeeCee. Sorry. 🙁 Drew's text pings in a little after eight.

That's okay, I type back. I emailed her again but still radio silence. It was a long shot anyway.

Our whole plan is a long shot, but I'm trying to remain positive. Or as positive as I can be given the circumstances.

I'm sitting in the green room of the Hardy-Har Hideaway, getting ready for my set and saying hello to the budding comics who come up to me to tell me they love my work or that they "saw me when…" It's gratifying, but in truth, it's ridiculous. Mentally, I'm right where they are, even if physically I'm at the top of my form.

As I look around, I realize this place has lost what little luster it used to have. Wear and tear doesn't even begin to describe how run-down Wanda's place has gotten. Time has not been kind, and that doesn't sit well with me.

To assuage some of the discomfort, I text Drew again: What are you up to tonight?

Nursing a whiskey and finalizing the next book club pick, he responds. I'm picturing him in a nice robe and slippers, laid back on a recliner, a stack of books and a stout glass on a table by his side. In this fantasy, he's smoking an old-timey pipe and a roaring fireplace is nearby.

A second message from Drew comes in: Nothing exciting.

I hate that he feels the need to qualify that, as if I have any room to judge him. Are you looking for some excitement? I send back.

It's way flirtier than I intend to be, given his vocal aversion to love and my realization that keeping things platonic while we try to get me back is healthier, but it's out there. My twenty-three-year-old impulses are not getting filtered out by the thirty-year-old wisdom surely stored somewhere inside me.

Damn, you'd think after seven years Apple would've implemented an "unsend" button for those messages you invariably regret.

Drew says: I could be... and the regret flows away.

That text could totally be the whiskey talking, yet I don't let that stop me from sending: I'm doing a set tonight at the Hardy-Har Hideaway. Want to swing by?

I know it's a risk, but a risk for friendship is a risk worth taking. Drew made clear that we should keep our interactions contained to the crystal hunt, but it's hard to stop reaching out when he's the only person who gets me. He's always been that person for me. In the past, in the present. In this life, and surely in the next. I know he said he wasn't anymore, but our connection feels too inescapable.

I don't know, he types, it's late.

Come on, Old Man. I've got a lot of power here. I can get my assistant to hook you up with the best table AND free drinks, I type. I hope my offer sounds appealing. Having one familiar face in the audience would surely make this easier and more fun.

More than two drinks and my acid reflux starts acting up, he sends back sans emoji. The joys I have to look forward to in older age. Weird to think that this doesn't put me off in the slightest. I'd happily supply Drew with all the Pepcid he needs to enjoy his night. I'd even put on that ridiculous nurse costume he got from his cousin and deliver it to him on a tray if he asked. Anything to be around him more, to take what I can get after I hurt him so badly in both timelines.

Fine, 2 drinks and anything off the menu, I counter.

Fried foods are just as bad for acid reflux, Nolan.

The stern tone of his text makes me tingle. Only a little. Triple H does a salad that is distinctly not fried and definitely salad-adjacent.

Mmm. Appetizing.

How about this? I get my assistant to hand deliver you a poke bowl from my favorite place and have your drinks only made with top-shelf alcohol? I respond. At least that way the acid reflux will be worth it.

I wait with bated breath for his answer. When are you on?

About an hour.

I smile when I see: I'll be there.

And sure enough, when I step up onstage, there's Drew wearing a slight smirk, double-fisting his two drinks with a half-finished poke bowl on the table in front of him.

Just his presence alone in that button-down floats me as the crowd around him erupts with pleased shock over my arrival. It cushions the blow of having to deliver half-baked jokes with sour punch lines laced with negativity. Every time I get uproarious laughter over something awful, all I have to do is look to Drew—his chopsticks hovering midair in entertained disbelief—and know I'm not alone in this half dream, half nightmare.

Chapter Twenty-Three

"The prodigal son returns," Wanda says with a hint of iciness upon wandering into the green room after my set. Her curly hair has gone gray. Fuller too. It's nice to see she hasn't retired her CLITERACY T-shirt, which she wears proudly as she steps up to hug me.

"It's so good to see you," I coo, trying to gauge where I stand with her. Wanda was like a second mom to me. Losing her respect would gut me even more.

She pulls back to look me over. "Is it? You seemed less than pleased when I came to the New York stop on your tour a few years back. Honestly, I was shocked when I got the call from Jessie— excuse me, *Jessalynn*." Wanda's eye roll is fabulously over-the-top. "Guess you both reinvented yourselves since the days when you were washing my dishes."

I'd happily scrub, mop, and wash anything Wanda asked me to if it meant getting back to my own body and my own life. I hate the way she's looking at me as if I have red horns poking out of my forehead, the Antichrist of comedy.

"Well, I'm here now and the crowd was excellent," I say, even if I did notice some empty tables toward the back, which rarely ever happened when I worked here. Live comedy was the place to be every night of the week. A date spot, a chill hang. Tonight, I got the vibe that most of the attendees had been turned away at other theaters or clubs and found themselves here when they were out of options.

My appearance was the only thing that perked them up.

"Lying doesn't change the reality, Maggot." She's fiddling with a peeling piece of paint on the wall beside the mirror. "Guess I can't call you that anymore either."

I chuckle. "Does that mean I'm a fly now?"

"Not just a fly. *The* fly."

"Ew, like that grotesque horror movie?"

"If the wings fit." It's not a compliment. The paint chip peels off, and she chucks it in a nearby trash bin with a hiss of dissatisfaction.

It's a testy question, but I ask anyway. "What did you think of the set?"

She purses her lips, probably trying to decide how honest she can be with me now that I'm a *someone* and not just the someone who sells the most drinks on her staff. "It was certainly in line with the character you've cultivated."

"Character?" I ask.

She nods. "Yeah. You dress like a man and act like a boy. There's a comedic duality to the narcissistic shtick. It works for you." Her smile is weak. "I have no place to critique what sells." This is strange to hear. Back in the day, which was only maybe a week or two ago in my real time, Wanda never withheld when offering me feedback, always pushing me to be the best stand-up I possibly could be. Her harshness was how I knew she thought I could succeed. She saved the gratuitous praise for those whose egos would never withstand this business.

"What if I said I hated it?" Jessalynn would probably have a stroke if they overheard me ask that. Too bad. It's the truth. "What if I said I felt slimy up on that stage tonight and doing those jokes for a special feels wrong?"

The crystal hunt starts banging pots and pans in the back of my mind. Tonight was a nice diversion, but I'm serious about getting back to my proper timeline before the special. Committing those jokes to tape for millions of viewers to watch would tarnish my ultimate goal forever.

I wish I didn't have to act normal and follow my predetermined schedule, but Drew made clear that if I started acting erratically and began shirking my responsibilities, we'd have a whole other set of problems to deal with.

Wanda pauses for longer than I expect, maybe puzzling over what to say next. Maybe recognizing the old me underneath the tailored Willy Wonka–colored suit and slicked-back hair. "Then I'd say trust your gut, but don't be surprised when the bottom falls out." The Wanda I know and love pokes through the nice veneer, reminding me that even if this life is confounding to me, it's still mine. I'm the consciousness inside this body, and it's my choices steering the ship. If I want to rock the boat, then so be it.

"Thanks," I say, renewed somehow. "I needed to hear that."

I grab my bag and start toward the exit. Wanda lets out an *uh-uh* and leads me toward the back, the door that opens into the alley. "Too many fans know you're here tonight because of social media. There's a mob out front."

A mob of fans just for me was always a part of my wildest fantasies, but now the thought of stepping out into the spotlight as this manchild Wanda described ties my stomach in knots. Somehow, I braided together all my worst qualities and made them a brand. Distilled them into millions of dollars. The American dream is seriously fucked up.

So am I.

Out in the back, in the alley where Wanda first called me Maggot, beside the dumpster that still reeks with food scraps, Wanda hugs me again. Harder this time. "For a while, I was afraid you'd forgotten where you came from. Thanks for wanting to perform here tonight. It's going to boost us for the next few weeks." It's then that I realize how hard the Hardy-Har Hideaway has been hit over the intervening years. One night here means fans will show up for many more to come in the hopes that I'll reprise my set. Jessalynn would never allow that, but I'm glad it did some good.

"Thanks for having me," I say. "I guess the saying 'You can't go home again' isn't true after all."

Her smile grows stronger, more genuine, and before she lets go, she drops another wisdom bomb on me. "Home always holds the answers."

After saying our goodbyes, I shoot off a text to Drew asking if he went home already. He doesn't need to respond, because when I walk around the corner, he's standing on the edge of the sidewalk in his oxfords, unsuccessfully trying to hail a cab.

I call out to him and he turns, the back of his coat catching the breeze and setting everything into dreamy slow motion. Those two drinks, not to mention the whiskey he was nursing before he left home, cast a warm flush across his cheeks. His shy smile is spotlighted by the nearby streetlight. "Great set," he says as I approach.

I echo Wanda's sentiments: "Lying doesn't change the reality."

"Okay, then it was pretty cringe," he says with an honest chuckle. "But I laughed a bit, and you looked very handsome." We both freeze. Clearly, the drinks are talking for him. "And the poke bowl was delicious," he adds quickly, moving the conversation along.

Once I tame my blush and recover from the compliment: "It's my usual. Isn't it weird that I have a usual at a pricey poke bowl place? Before this whole ordeal, I existed entirely on a diet of ramen, egg sandwiches from the bodega on our corner, and your leftovers."

"The three major food groups," he jokes. "Though I'd have preferred to eat my own leftovers. Can you even call them leftovers if you didn't eat the meal originally? It's just a small portion of old food at that point."

"Sly observation there, Techler. Sure you're not the stand-up comedian?" I give him a playful punch in the arm the way we used to. The way that seems childish when shared between two thirty-year-old men on a New York City street in late spring. But not in the bad way Wanda described my ghoulish onstage "character." This is authentic to us. Who we've always been to each other. Even if we're mostly repressing that for the sake of the crystal hunt.

"No, I could never keep a comedian's hours," Drew says, glancing down at his watch. "Speaking of, I have to get back. I've got a delivery coming in early for the shop tomorrow." Responsibility has always been integral to his makeup. Something he must've gotten from his dad, whom he rarely talks about.

Before he has a chance to flag down the oncoming cab, I ask, "Can I give you a ride?"

"You drove here?"

"Let me rephrase," I say. "Can I have my driver give you a ride?" I point across the street to where a woman in a white shirt and black pants leans up against a large SUV, patiently waiting.

Drew shakes his head. "It's really out of your way. There's no need." He's stepping out into the street again, looking like an Alanis Morissette lyric come to life, so I reach out and grab his hand. The warmth of his palm and the surprise on his face cause rapid-fire fluttering in my chest.

"I'd really like the company," I say. "Besides, I owe you for coming all the way out here tonight. I never would've gotten through that without you." Again, I realize I'm speaking recklessly. From afar, I can't fuck things up. I learned that hardily in the last timeline. I can strive for a revival of our friendship, but that's it. No more because *more* could prove catastrophic.

Except, he came. He's here. Looking striking and tentative, yet grateful and beautiful. And if I can squeeze even a silent car ride beside him out of this night, then I want that. There's nothing inherently *complicated* about sharing a back seat, is there?

A couple minutes later, Marjorie, my driver, holds the door open for us as we scoot into the back seat. "Where to?" she asks when she's buckled into the driver's seat.

Drew gives her the address of the bookstore.

"What, are you going to sleep in your office until the delivery arrives?"

"No, I live above it," he says, which makes perfect sense to me. Quaint. Homey. "The opportunity presented itself when I was searching for retail space, and I fell in love. It's a tiny one-bedroom. Maybe even smaller than what we had in Astoria. Just enough for me and my books. It's not much, but it's home."

I nod. His words remind me of what Wanda said. *Home always holds the answers.*

Home seems so far away.

I miss the silly things, the ridiculous places. The movie theater that hadn't been updated since the eighties. The defunct hot tub in our backyard. The Stone Museum where we'd gone on class trips in middle school.

"Holy crap," I whisper to myself, fingers unable to move fast enough as I search my phone. The place pops up with hours of operation.

"Everything okay?" Drew asks.

I show him the screen. "Do you remember the Stone Museum?"

"Yeah, we had senior prom at the wedding venue there."

Flashes of that night come back, of *kissing for practice*, but I push them down. "Right, but the museum itself had a store full of stones and *crystals*." Realization dawns over his expression. "They're open this weekend."

Before Drew gets out at his place, we make plans to trek out to New Jersey early on Saturday to see what we can dig up, and I might be overthinking this but he appears excited. I might even go and visit my parents, see where I stand with them in this timeline and maybe learn more about how else I can reach CeeCee.

"Thanks for the ride," Drew says, hunched in the still-open door.

"Thanks for showing up for me," I reply.

"Thanks for bribing me to show up for you with delicious drinks." Do I detect a note of flirtation in his voice?

Reaching into my bag, I pull out the box of Pepcid I had my second assistant, Jerome, grab from the drugstore on his way back from the poke place. "Thanks for suffering eventual acid reflux."

He seems taken aback by the gesture, turning the box over with a disbelieving grin on his face. "This whole night has been worth the eventual acid reflux," he says, with such sincerity and sweetness that I could lean across the seat and kiss him. But I won't. Obviously.

Except then he leans over. Further. No more than an inch or so. But it's perceptible enough that my heart pulls me toward him. Anticipation makes a dramatic entrance.

"Good night, Nolan," he says, keeping this delicious bit of distance between us. "See you on Saturday."

The sound of the door closing barely registers underneath the pounding of my expanding heart that echoes *Saturday, Saturday, Saturday*...to the tune of an Elton John song my dad used to love.

Chapter Twenty-Four

On Saturday, my morning off, Drew and I sit across from each other on an NJ Transit train, his long legs bracketing in my shorter ones as we both stare out the window, watching homes and trees and trains on parallel tracks blur by. That's sort of how I feel right now: like a fast-moving train that suddenly switched directions, and now I'm flying backward at hyper speed, unable to be seen by the naked eye.

A few stops before ours, Drew reaches into his satchel and produces a paperback book, which he hands to me. "What's this?" I ask.

"It's the next pick for my book club. A tiny gift in exchange for the Pepcid from the other night," he says shyly. "Which I may or may not have desperately needed when I realized I was all out of my own. Do you think those crystals gave you psychic powers too?"

I shake my head. "Nope, pretty sure it was just the time travel," I reply, turning the book and inspecting the stepback. It's a contemporary adult thriller titled *Fare-Thee-Wellness* all about a murder at a lifestyle company that sounds eerily familiar. The cover features a brunette in a pair of amber-tinted sunglasses that I swear I've seen CeeCee wear before.

"Apropos, no?" Drew asks, pushing his own glasses up his nose.

I nod, head loaded up with new thoughts. "There isn't any info about the author in here." I search the jacket copy for the mysterious

R. U. Low's headshot, even flip through a few pages, but come up empty. "This is obviously a pen name."

"Very little is known about him. He wanted to remain anonymous when the book published last year so the story could speak for itself," Drew informs me. "The book was a runaway success, so the publisher wanted to lift the veil to create buzz for the paperback release. He agreed to do one in-person event. Guess where?"

I smile, quirking an eyebrow. "Bound by Mayhem Books?"

"Wow, you're good," he says sarcastically. "Are you sure about the psychic powers? Anyway, the publisher was looking for a quirky store with a lot of ambiance to host the reveal at and, well, bookstores don't get much quirkier than mine." I love how proud Drew sounds as he says this. Even if Bound by Mayhem Books wasn't his original dream, he's still content with the business he's created.

Laughing, I tab open to the first page. Read the opening line. *The body was found by a receptionist beside the Zen garden right after the company-mandated morning meditation session in the Love Yourself Loft.* I chortle to myself. The writing style is vaguely familiar, but I don't have the time to deduce where from because we're pulling into our station, and above the crystal hunt, I'm just excited to spend a full day with Drew.

$$\cdot \, {}^{+}\!\!\not\!\!\!+\, {}^{\cdot}$$

The Stone Museum in my hometown is just as strange as I remember it being.

Our rideshare takes us through the towering front gates. A signpost is stuck with wooden arrows pointing every which way to various weird attractions.

To our right, an old oil tank was turned into an ogre—green, mean-looking, and lurking in the nearby copse. To our left, a field of brightly painted tires gives way to a disused helicopter and an even more impressive tank. A dinosaur made of old bicycle parts presides over them, giving *Jurassic Park* a run for its money.

I recall being enamored by this labyrinth as a child. Skipping with CeeCee through the defunct driving range. Playing games of hide-and-seek along the short fairy trail festooned with bird feeders, where statues of winged mystical creatures mingled with the real-life winged creatures that came to munch on the seed left every morning by the owner. He was an older man with a penchant for turning junkyard scraps into silly creations that made kids smile.

The driver lets us out in front of the museum proper, which isn't much more than an archway into an open-air exhibition of fossils and gems and minerals (oh my). It's right beside a single-story building with a tiny screening room for educational materials and a rather extensive gift shop. Despite this attraction being entirely free, it's rarely known to those outside our pocket of New Jersey, and mostly afloat because of the ginormous banquet hall that became a staple for weddings and proms, including Drew and mine.

It dawns on me that we are thirty here, close to marrying age. If I do have to stay this way forever, would I be emotionally mature enough to pursue something with Drew? Could I learn to live without those seven years of memories while making amends for them all the same?

No, I can't think about that. This crystal hunt *should* work. I'll get back to my real timeline, fix my mistakes, and forge a better future where maturity and marriage will come with experience and time and no expanse of missing memories.

Drew points to a sign written in red marker that's taped to the door: BE BACK SOON. When Drew jiggles the handle, the door to the gift shop is locked. "Bad timing," he says. "Weird sign too. Soon? That's such a proximate word. It only has meaning if we know when they left. How are we supposed to know when they left?"

"That sign," I say as we begin to stroll around the grounds looking for an employee, "is hardly the weirdest thing about this place." To prove my point, we enter a cave where a beat-up Trans Am spray-painted to look like a tiger is bursting through a gaping hole in the wall. A motion sensor makes it honk loudly at us. Drew jumps. "God, I'm glad this place is still here. A weirdo's paradise."

"I always found it kind of creepy," Drew says before clocking the shock unfurling on my face. "I moved here when I was a teenager, so I never came here on class trips or with my mom or anything. My only frame of reference for this place was prom." His neck and face turn ruddy, so he angles himself away from me.

He's gone and poked the sleeping bear of our past with a prom-sized stick. That was the night when, overcome with magic and imminent change, we first kissed. *For practice.* It didn't mean anything on either end. At least, I don't think it did.

I offered to help him get his first kiss out of the way so he wouldn't be nervous when he met up with his "summer guy" on an upcoming vacation, and he accepted the offer.

Nothing more than an exchange of lips.

But now, being back here, I get the strange sense that I might've missed something.

It appears as if Drew is about to say more, but someone interrupts us first.

"Need a map?" asks a woman about my height whose hair is pulled back in a tight ponytail, a chestnut-colored flannel knotted around her waist. "Sorry I wasn't here when you arrived."

"All good. We'll take the map," Drew says, stepping forward to take the pamphlet, obscuring his face again. Even though I know it's still red from thinking about our high school selves.

She inspects us both. "You two with the scout troop?"

"No," I say, and then watch as recognition settles over her. She's seen me before, and I have a feeling I've seen her too in a different context. "We're just visiting for the day from the city." I'm seriously hoping she doesn't snap a photo of me here and post it online. If Jessalynn caught wind of where I am and who I'm with, they'd be furious.

"Wait a minute," the woman says, vowels stretched out like pulled taffy. "Drew and Nolan, right? It's me. Stephanie Hopkins. We went to school together. Pride Alliance and senior prom."

"Stephanie," Drew greets her congenially. "I thought that was you."

Memories sweep in. Drew and I didn't go to prom together, but we basically did. Our dates—Stephanie for Drew and Gemma for me—were girlfriends who weren't comfortable coming out to their parents prior to prom. They'd go away to Rutgers University the following fall and make it public, but at the time they needed dates who wouldn't be offended when they ditched them for their own slow dances and make-out sessions. Drew and I volunteered, which is how we ended up wandering away from the noisy dance floor and ultimately kissing.

"What brings you city people back to the burbs?" Stephanie asks, coming alive a little, then directing her next question at me. "Aren't you, like, famous now?"

"In some circles," I say. Because it's not like I'm starring in movies. Yet.

She snorts at that. "What are you doing here?"

"Visiting," I'm quick to reply.

"No, I mean *here*." Her hand spirals toward the fossils and the encased gemstones, the plaques and the posters. There's a suspicious tone to her voice as her eyes dart between us. "Are you two finally together?"

"Finally?" I ask, a healthy dose of curiosity and confusion sprinkled in my tone. I didn't even have feelings for Drew back then.

"Yeah," Stephanie says with an expanding smile. "The Pride Alliance had a little will-they, won't-they pool going for you two back in the day. Come to think of it, I should be kind of mad at you two. I bet good money you'd be boyfriends by senior prom. Gemma and I thought we were playing matchmaker."

If Drew was blushing before, he's on fire now, stammering slightly.

"How much did you lose?" I ask, simultaneously thinking back on all those conversations Drew and I had when we first came out about how two queer guys could be friends without romantic or sexual feelings developing. What was everyone seeing?

I knew in my heart that fate had brought Drew into my life, but up until two years ago in my real timeline—nine in this one—I never entertained anything other than friendship for us. Strange to think others had clocked something I hadn't a single sense of.

"Eh, probably only like ten bucks, but it was high school. We were all making minimum wage, dropping a hundred bucks on prom bids, and saving for college. That ten bucks was two trips to Starbucks," she says.

I laugh good-naturedly to brush off some of the awkwardness. "Sorry to spoil your slightly offensive romantic agenda both then and now. We're only here to see about some crystals."

Stephanie lets loose a dramatic sigh. "We've got plenty. Come on in." She gestures for us to follow her back around front where she pulls down the sign we saw earlier.

"Guess 'soon' was pretty accurate after all," I joke to no response.

Drew must be lost somewhere inside his head because all he says is, "Ha, yeah," before charging straight for the displays, which makes me wonder what version of that night Drew is replaying for himself. When he confessed his love for me at the hotel on the night of CeeCee's wedding, he said he'd been in love with me *for a long time*. Did he mean since prom night?

I would ask, but we're the only two in here, and I don't need Stephanie overhearing that vulnerable conversation. Besides, if we're trying to keep things as uncomplicated as possible, I can't be questioning Drew over practice kisses. It wouldn't be right.

I turn my attention back to the crystal hunt.

Dilapidated ceiling fans sputter overhead. Posters of scenic vistas and birthstone charts line the walls. Long-armed lamps shine down on hundreds of different, shiny stones available for purchase on tables draped in black fabric.

When we committed to this plan, I hadn't considered the number of variables at play. The right kind of crystal might not be enough. What if the shape is wrong? What if they need to be from a certain area of the world? I have no idea where Doop sourced those crystals from nor what they did to them afterward in that ridiculous lab.

Unwilling to stress out over the unknowable, I start browsing.

The metaphysical store displayed their stones like they were otherworldly adornment meant to be worshipped and worn with reverence and care. Here, the stones are no more than natural wonders. Completely of this earth, and not connected to any kind of higher power.

It just goes to show that the product doesn't matter. The story you spin around it is what you're selling. Doop knew that.

Stephanie throws her flannel over a creaky chair by the register and meets Drew and me by the largest bunch. "Anything in particular you're looking for?"

In my dream a few nights ago, I was overwhelmed with a kaleidoscope of orange imagery. It prompted the faintest memory of the crystal collection. "Do you have any orange stones?" It's not the best or most reliable lead, but it's not nothing.

"Tons," Stephanie says, pointing around.

Drew and I begin sorting, picking some up, passing others by. No one group stands out more than the other, so in the end, to pay Stephanie back for those lost Starbucks lattes, I buy one of each to cover our bases and sign an autograph for her before I go.

Chapter Twenty-Five

The hodgepodge of crystals jangles around on my lap as we sit in the back of another rideshare, another driver blasting pop hits—songs by artists I've never heard of with production that sounds wrong to my untrained ears.

Luckily, lyrical trends haven't changed all that much.

The female singer belts about dancing while we can and living for the moment, and considering it more closely, those themes have never been more relevant. I'm hit with flashes of prom. Our history is so robust you could fill an entire book with it.

Isn't it weird to be back here like this? I want to ask Drew, who's watching the neighborhood flit by out the window, drumming the rhythm of the song with his fingertips on the door's armrest, lips half-heartedly forming the lyrics. I don't ask because, while he may be experiencing my turmoil by proximity, he has no idea how supernatural it is to be twenty-three in the body of a thirty-year-old and going to your childhood home.

The driver pulls up in front of the mailbox. It's a gray house with a short driveway and overgrown shrubbery. It's not like Dad to let those laurels get so tall, nearly blocking the view from the living room window.

After CeeCee's college graduation, I avoided this house like I avoided the kid in my third-grade class who brought lice back from summer camp. The one feature I wasn't insecure about as a child was my hair, so I did *not* want a buzz cut. I don't have the face shape for it.

Now, I stand in the driveway behind a compact green car that doesn't look familiar to me. Mom must've traded in the family-friendly SUV at some point, too bulky for just her and Dad.

While home has made me queasy over the last few years in my timeline, it's never made me downright nervous. Which is why I'm all out of sorts as I notice the solar panels, the keypad beside the door, and other techie advancements that seem more a product of time than an addition or expense Mom and Dad were happy about.

"You coming in with me or will you go see your mom?" I ask Drew who's been very quiet since Stephanie mistook us for a couple.

Drew shakes his head. "My mom moved out of town a few years ago. She got a condo closer to the beach. But if it's okay, I think I'd like to go for a walk."

"Of course that's okay," I reply. These trips have been somewhat intense. Hunting for rocks that may or may not work. Teetering between rebuilding a friendship and knowing whatever happens in this timeline may be nothing more than a false future.

"Call me when you're done," Drew says, taking off in the direction of the neighborhood's entrance. I watch him disappear over the crest of a hill, and he takes a little chunk of my heart with him as he goes.

When I ring the bell, a robotic arm slithers out of the keypad. It's the Ring home security camera mixed with Doc Ock from the Spider-Man series. In a way, I feel a bit like Venom in this timeline, wearing a suit that's somehow turned me evil.

The lens on the camera scans my body, and the screen pings with my identity.

A ding sounds, and my profile pixelates out to make way for an image of Mom. "Resident has been alerted of visitor." But nobody comes to the door. My nerves escalate.

After minutes pass, I walk around the gate in the side fence. When I'm not even halfway through undoing the latch, a beeping sound blares.

Good thing these contraptions didn't exist when I was a teen, or I'd never have been able to sneak out or sneak friends in without my parents knowing.

I hear Mom's voice. "Nolan, is that really you?"

Worry torpedoes through me. I feel entirely discombobulated as I set the latch back and turn to find her skeptically smiling beneath a jaunty sun hat. Soiled gardening gloves are tucked underneath her armpit.

"It's me, Mom." The words are barely above a whisper as I take her in.

Seven years from your twenties to your thirties seems to fill you out and set your features. Seven years from your late fifties to your midsixties seems to be a balancing act of preservation. I can tell Mom's hair has been dyed recently to keep the gray away, and the tan she used to have year-round looks more uneven, hinting that she's either been in a tanning bed recently or lathered on a tinted cream this morning.

She's still Mom. Same bright smile and Martha Stewart fashion sense, but she also looks a bit like an actress hired to play Mom in a biopic of my life, purposefully made up to be aged down so she can still believably pass as the mother of a twenty-three-year-old.

Clearly astounded, Mom runs in for a hug, and I'm confused since this isn't what I expected. "Oh, Nolan, it's so good to see you. You have no idea how many times that blasted security camera CeeCee and James had installed tells me someone is you when really some media outlet has sent a look-alike journalist out here to get a ridiculous inside scoop on you."

Pleasantly surprised by this warm welcome, I mime pulling out a tiny notebook and pencil. "Say here, Mrs. Baker, tell us something scandalous about your son's riveting dating life." Mom's forehead creases in response. "Sorry, it was a joke."

She shivers at that. Those old stand-up sets didn't just throw Drew under the bus. They ran over my entire family without hitting the brakes. It's like one of those ethical trolley-problem situations where instead of choosing one track over the other, I somehow hit one and then swerved and killed the rest while I was still in command.

Mom has every right to be wary of my presence here, yet she invites me inside, without hesitation, for lunch, and I decide not to tamper with that by bringing up the past. Even if I want to tell her everything, ask how often we've spoken, or if I've visited at all, I stay mum as she lays out a spread of deli meat, cheese, and two different types of bread—"White or rye?"

I choose rye.

There's a new light that hangs down over the sink, a large air fryer, and a fridge that looks like the basic model of the one I have in my swanky apartment. In the living room, there's a new smarter-than-smart TV, mounted to the wall over where the brown TV stand used to be. The couch, where we sat to watch movies and award shows and Super Bowls, has been reupholstered but not replaced.

"What brings you home?" she asks, setting the plate of sandwiches down at the two ends of our rectangular table. The place where CeeCee and I would fling peas at each other or do homework or make ice cream sundaes when we made good grades on our report cards. I hate that I need a reason to be brought home.

"Overdue for a visit," I say before taking a bite, letting the melty mayo swiped onto the toasted bread sluice down my fingers.

Mom hands me a second napkin with a tentative smile. "Four years is a long time to be away from home."

I nearly choke on my sandwich at the shock. I figured it had been a while, but that's extreme, even for me. Regaining my bearings, I croak, "It's really been that long?"

Her nod is calculated, making clear that she doesn't want to throw a rain cloud over our afternoon. "By my count, yes, with all your touring and various shows, but what does that matter? You're here now and you look well."

What a strange compliment when it feels like I exist in a constant state of stupefaction. "You too, Mom."

"It's the new color," she says, toying with ends of her still-short hair. There's a reddish hue to the natural brown. "I needed a change." It sounds so much like the Doop slogan, which reminds me of the last time I saw Mom—outside on the garden terrace at CeeCee's wedding. At least that's one fight that's not still simmering seven years later.

"It's really nice. I bet CeeCee loves it," I say, knowing the compliment will do her good and wanting to slip CeeCee into the conversation since she hasn't written me back.

"CeeCee hasn't seen it yet. I got it done last week, and we haven't had a chance to video chat," she says while she scrounges around in the pantry for a bag of chips that aren't just crumbs. She returns with veggie straws.

"CeeCee hasn't visited recently?"

"CeeCee and James are so busy since they moved out to Colorado." I still can't help but wonder what my urbanite sister is doing in Colorado of all places. "Then, when Imogen was born, it didn't make sense for her to be flying a newborn across the country every few months, so we stopped doing our special brunches."

Imogen. I have a niece. A whole tiny human blood-related to me was born during the time that I skated over.

"Do you have a recent picture of Imogen?" I ask, stealing a veggie straw and attempting to hide the fact that this will be the first time I've ever seen her.

When Mom hands me her phone, which is so high-definition it nearly hurts my eyes, there's a photo of a girl with stringy brown hair in a pink dress with watermelon juice dripping off her lips, turning the leftover rind into a second smile. She looks so much like CeeCee that I'm almost convinced this is a photo of CeeCee that I've never seen before. One that got replaced in a picture frame when I came along and my baby photos got half the real estate CeeCee once monopolized.

It would be gauche for me to say that CeeCee begrudged me for being the younger sibling. But I did often get the impression that I was a rat in the kitchen of her life. And not a helpful rat like the one in *Ratatouille*. Instead, a rat where Mom and Dad—head chef and sous-chef, respectively—had to set traps for me so I didn't cause too much havoc while she—junior chef in training—stewed beside the overflowing pot of our family.

"She's adorable," I say, swiping to the next photo. It's Imogen in a blow-up pool playing with a mermaid doll beside James, who's wearing a captain's hat and blowing bubbles out of a pipe as his daughter giggles. A backyard. A picket fence in the distance. Domestic bliss. Is that what CeeCee wanted?

It dawns on me that we never talked about it back in my timeline. She got a job. She got a man. She got serious. I got shitty tips and shittier hours but better gigs. The line of communication became a string with two cans attached to the ends, and the center of the thread just tore and tore and tore until…

"She'll be four soon, can you believe that?" Mom asks as I hand the phone back, unable to look anymore. I'm uncomfortable peeking through this window into CeeCee's life when, judging by the social media blockings, she's shut the blinds to keep me out. "Her party is going to be fabulous. Just like your special!"

I'm smiling to cover up a grimace, knowing I didn't get an invitation to Imogen's birthday party. CeeCee has cut me off, which is what prompts me to say: "There are no jokes about you in the special. Any of you." It's important I make that clear to her.

Part of me wondered why I'd pivoted from the confessional family material while learning the jokes for this taping. Mom's admission of my absence makes everything clearer. There aren't jokes about them because the jokes are about my life, and my life no longer includes them in any meaningful way. I must've made a choice: fame over family.

"Nolan, I learned that jokes are not truths a long time ago," she says, devoid of resentment. She sounds at peace, which makes me happy but also jealous. I haven't known peace since I woke up in this timeline. "Look, I know CeeCee took the whole thing harshly, but your dad and I... Well, it's your life too. Do we wish you didn't share every one of our mistakes with the world? Sure. Did it take a few years of counseling to make peace with it? Also, sure." Hearing Mom and Dad sought out counseling is both surprising and reassuring. They came from a generation that didn't take mental health into consideration. "But..."

I rip apart the last of my sandwich, stomach blocked. "But what?"

She stares deep into my eyes. I know she's drawing back the curtains of my persona and seeing me still as the boy she raised. "My only want as a mother was to see my children succeed to the point that they surpass us. To shine and be stable, and you've done that. I don't spend my nights worrying about if you're making rent anymore. I don't feel the urge to send you care packages every month just in case you've run out of ramen or mouse traps." For a moment, I wonder if she sees the twenty-three-year-old stuck inside here. The lights of her eyes sparkle knowingly, and I'm about to question it and confide in her when she continues. "You've carved out your inde-pendence. I may not approve of the crasser content, but I support you and I love you always."

Those words find a home inside my sternum, undo some of the barbed wire that's been fenced around my heart since the jump. Learning of my exploits has been shocking and confusing. How can everything I ever wanted come with such a price? But knowing that Mom and Dad still support and love me after taking our family's past and turning it into punch lines means I haven't lit a match and burned down every bridge.

It took two sandwiches and one conversation to help me realize that seven years of good luck mixed with bad decisions doesn't have to define the seven ahead of me, or the seven I hopefully get to redo. I decide what happens next.

Which means I'm going to make positive change in this timeline before I go. I don't know what I'll leave behind once the crystal hunt is complete. Will a different version of me pick up where I left off? Will this reality cease to exist entirely once I'm back? No matter the case, I'm here right now, so I should treat this timeline like practice for the healthier choices I'll make once I return.

"Will you come?" I ask Mom, unprompted. The first positive change I can think of, even if I plan on returning before then. "To the special taping. It would mean a lot to me if you and Dad came. You might have to plug your ears for some of it, but I can warn you. Send you a copy of the set in advance. Anything."

"That sounds nice. I can certainly try to make it," Mom says, not committing fully. I know New York City makes her anxious. Traveling in general, actually.

"What about Dad? Is he here, by the way?" I figured Mom would've gotten him from the shed out back by now; that's where he went to work on his model trains on weekends when he wasn't at the hardware store. The shed was a whimsical place where I would sit some Sunday mornings and stay as still as possible while Dad labored. I wasn't often allowed to touch or participate, but I could wait until the product was finished. Hearing that first whistle as the model revved up always gave me goose bumps.

Sometimes, I'd have dreams where I shrank down to action-figure size and rode around on those trains that Dad built.

Though I guess at this point, he could've given up on those. Depression can make even your passions seem like burdens.

"No, he's not here," Mom says, clearing the plates and crossing the kitchen. "But I'll make sure he knows you stopped by."

"Do you think he'll be back soon?" I ask, checking the time on my phone. There's still a bit of a buffer before I need to be back for rehearsal, which is the last place I want to be anyway.

"You know him. He's out. Could be an all-day ordeal. Don't wait around."

"Okay," I say. "Would you mind maybe giving me CeeCee's new number? I'd like to call her and invite her to the special too." It's a lie, but a small one in the scheme of things.

Mom seems hesitant, but hopeful. "Sure, hon." I save a new contact for CeeCee in my phone as Mom reads off the digits to me.

While I wish I could stay longer, offer my help out in the garden, ask Mom to go on a walk, watch a movie, do any number of things we did before the move and the jump, it seems I might be on the verge of overstaying my welcome. Mom's mood has shifted.

Before I make a graceful exit, I ask if I can go to my old room. I proffer a lie, a half-assed statement about needing some old mementos and photos for the opening credits of my special.

She doesn't follow me down the hall, and when I nudge open the door, I'm bowled over by nostalgia. Everything is exactly as I remember it, from the secondhand paperbacks gifted by Drew on the bookshelf to the *Curb Your Enthusiasm* poster on the corkboard beside the desk. Participation trophies for all the talent shows I performed in line a shelf affixed to the wall, coated in layers upon layers of dust. Even the bed—the space-patterned duvet and star sheets—hasn't been updated.

Which makes me think other areas haven't been shuffled or rearranged since I moved out either. The bottom drawer of my desk had a keylock on it. Some leftover piece from my grandfather's childhood. When my dad moved it into my room, he gifted me the key with a knowing nod. "For whatever. Keep this in a safe place."

I stashed notebooks in there with crude jokes, pictures of shirtless, sweaty celebrities I used up all the ink cartridges for on the family printer, and maybe most importantly…

"Aha!" I cry as I pluck a baggie of weed out from underneath a photo of Zac Efron in swim trunks. Stashing rolling papers, some old photos, and a pen in my bag of crystals, I shut the door behind me.

"Get everything you need?" Mom asks when I'm back at the front door.

"Yeah," I tell her, heart feeling full from our conversation. "In more ways than one."

Chapter Twenty-Six

Drew doesn't answer his phone when I leave, which is fine, because I think I know where to find him.

When I come around the corner, marching toward my old elementary school, there's Drew, legs dangling off the top of the look-out tower on the playground, cloud-watching.

Drew didn't fit up there even when we were teenagers, sneaking out, full of angst about everything. Now, he's Alice after she eats the mushroom, bursting out of the White Rabbit's house, limbs and head poking through the slats.

So as not to alarm him, I clear my throat. "If you were running away from me, you picked a bad hiding spot."

Drew's eyes flick from me to his phone, where a missed call notification blinks. "Shit, sorry. I must've dozed off." I join him right as he points above us. "Doesn't that cloud look like a dove?"

"Sort of," I reply, closing one eye and outlining its wings with my pointer finger. "Might look more like a dove once we smoke this." I pull the weed out from my bag.

Drew's hooded eyes flicker with mischief, like he's tapping into his early twenties self. Then, he reconsiders when he sees how crumbly and dry the weed is. "How old is that stuff?"

"I barely even know how old *I am*. You think I know that?" I ask. "What's the harm? If anything, we just won't get very high."

"Probably for the best." Drew sits up on his elbows, yawning.

"Yeah, old men need the weak stuff," I joke as I begin rolling the paper up into a little tube. I've never been great at this.

"For the sake of both your cover and my ego, let's refrain from that kind of talk." Drew's laugh makes some of the cannabis spill as he taps it out of the baggie below the filter, taking over from me.

Long fingers pinch with precision to make sure it's enclosed before he licks the end paper, which is so erotic I have to look away. Heat blossoms up from my pelvis and into my sternum. Never have I wanted to be an inanimate object so badly before.

"Do you have a lighter in that treasure trove?" he asks, kneeing the paper bag.

My face falls. "Shit."

"A joint without a light," Drew recites like it's poetry. "There's a metaphor in there somewhere." Rolling my eyes, I hop down the ladder, kicking through the mulch. "What are you doing?"

"It may be 2030, but kids can't have changed *that* much," I say, getting on my hands and knees so I can inspect the low-hanging tire swing beneath. "I'm sure this is still the number one smoking spot in town." Reaching into the inner ring, I find exactly what I'm looking for. "Told ya." I shove a Post-it-note-pink BIC lighter in his face.

"Watch, it doesn't work," he says, joint waggling between his teeth, drawing my attention to his enticing lips even more. Rocketing memories of our kiss at CeeCee's wedding and our practice kiss at prom to the forefront of my brain. To discard those, I prove him wrong by lighting him up. His first drag causes bliss to whisper over his features, smoke to puff out into the air. "Maybe your luck is changing after all. How did it go with your mom?"

"Good. Really good, actually." Aside from when Drew agreed to help me, my time with Mom was the only moment in this unprece-dented experience that has felt sincere. "I got CeeCee's new number, so I can try to call her, but also I found out she has a *kid* in Colorado."

Drew nods, handing me the joint. "Yeah, I would've said some-thing, but I didn't think it was my place. The reason I had her per-sonal email address is because she and I talked a lot when things first blew up with you after the wedding. Your parents had to be impartial. CeeCee needed someone to vent to. So did I."

The hurt of the lost years was not my doing, but the wedding fiasco was completely my mistake. To witness how much hurt spi-raled out of that one heat-of-the-moment choice is harrowing. "I'm glad you had each other."

"She moved pretty shortly after Doop imploded. I think she needed to start over," he says, staring off at another cotton-candy cloud lingering over the roof of the redbrick school building. "We lost touch when Imogen was born. She was becoming a mom and I was becoming a business owner, so life got in the way and your comedy stopped being about us. It was a natural end." The way Drew tells it—the throaty rasp of his voice—clues me in to the fact that he may not have many friends. He was never a social butterfly before. What if my public blasting of his love for me caused him to crawl into his shell even more, like a turtle in protection mode?

The beard. The glasses. The store with its murdery vibes and crime scene display windows. I wonder if it's all his way of redefining himself. Like Mom's new hair. Like CeeCee's new address. Little things to distance themselves from the people I wrote jokes about. The people I hurt.

"I wish I could take it back," I whisper, a thousand more words backlogged in my windpipe.

"I know." Drew kicks at the crystals. "Maybe you can." There's a nervousness that underscores his statement; for the first time, I wonder if he's also having reservations about the efficacy of our plan, but I can't find the words to ask.

As I'm staring at the bag beside his clean, off-white sneakers with red racing stripes across them, his hand finds mine on the board between us. Not a full hold. Not a clasp. Not even a cover. Just a single finger brushing back and forth, causing goose bumps to chase each other up my arm and across my clavicle.

"This isn't how it was supposed to go," I say. "Strange that I got the funhouse-mirror version of everything I ever wanted." I stop myself to consider this, the weed doing its work to unwind me. "Well, I guess not *everything*."

Drew exhales; swirls of smoke carry the familiar skunky smell in my direction. They make my head whirl and make this reality seem even more carnivalesque. "What more could you want?" Drew says, suppressing a cough. "You got the fame, the money, the comedy special, the dog."

"CeeCee and a niece in my life, for starters," I admit. Largely, I took CeeCee's antagonism as judgment, but maybe it was never more than misplaced care. A need for a sense of control over everyone and everything—playing at being the quintessential older sibling from a '90s movie. Completely unhealthy, but not intentionally harmful.

The niece part...well, it's not like I ever vision-boarded being an uncle—a *guncle*. But I knew from a young age I never wanted kids of my own. A corgi was enough of a responsibility in the grand life plan. Now, in this timeline, I'm completely missing out on an entire branch of my family tree.

"And for enders?" Drew asks.

After a hit and a silent dare to be brave, I say, "*You*." So I don't have to see his reaction, I rummage around in the bag until I find one of the photos I took from my bedroom. It was folded in half, almost ruined, but it's one of Drew and me at prom, outside the venue in the Stone Museum gardens in sharp suits, hair tamed, bow ties in different bright colors.

I hand him the crumpled, glossy piece of paper. He clutches it between shaking fingers. "We look so young here."

"I'm *still* young, thank you kindly," I joke to diffuse some of the agonizing tension filling the springtime air alongside clouds of pollen.

He forces out a laugh, and then his mouth snaps back into a straight line. Too serious. "Nolan." I prepare for the absolute worst. "You have no idea how long I've waited to hear you say that you want me."

An exhale saws out of my lungs. The words make me even braver. "I do." Hearing it back, I realize how I'm betraying myself. I swore I could rekindle a friendship but not a flame with Drew. Not in this temporary timeline. Yet words pour out of me before I can sop up the spill. "I want to choose you. I've wanted to choose you for the longest time, but I promised myself I'd get my shit together before I could be worthy of you. Before I could take the risk of ruining our friendship."

"Nolan, on what planet would I have ever let romantic feelings ruin our friendship?"

"I don't know, but I was scared about it," I admit, shrugging off some of the insecurity like soaked layers after coming in from a torrential storm. "I was scared about everything." My whole career was rejection after rejection. I couldn't bear the possibility of that in my personal life from the person who meant the most to me.

Drew grabs my hand suddenly, interlaces his fingers with mine, breaching his own rules about our closeness. "This is going to sound like a line, I'm sure, but there really haven't been many since us. Since *you*. I don't... I don't experience attraction like most people. When we lived together and went out, I didn't approach guys or ask them to go on dates because I couldn't be attracted to them on the spot like that. And the guys I did make exceptions for, the ones willing to take it slow, I never wanted book-level romance with them. I kept it going sometimes because I thought that's what a single gay man in New York City was supposed to do. But it was always different with you."

Always different with you. My heart balloons beyond my rib cage. "Wow," I say, stunned.

"I didn't completely know until prom," he clarifies. "I had been talking to Chris Oleander, an artist and the son of one of my mom's friends, for most of the spring term."

"I could never forget that," I butt in, circling back to all the thoughts I had at the Stone Museum today. "You made me proof-read every text you sent him for three months straight. Even the spicy ones!"

He lets out an embarrassed laugh. "I was nervous I would say the wrong thing, even if I was basically paraphrasing lines from Tessa Dare books. Anyway, I was scared about meeting him for the first time that summer before college at the beach because I knew he'd want to kiss me and…and then, you offered to kiss me at prom, so I wasn't putting so much pressure on it."

It's clear his memory of that night is as vivid as mine. "You had once told me practice kissing was one of your favorite tropes," I say. That night, I thought I was doing Drew a favor. Now, I wonder if I was wrong. Maybe that kiss was as much for me as it was for him.

"Not so much anymore," he says honestly.

"What takes the top spot now?"

He hits the joint before saying dreamily, "Friends-to-lovers."

My breath catches in my throat. Is it the weed or is it elation causing me to feel floaty? I laugh, because of course we're bringing this back to romance novel tropes, and, wow, it just occurred to me how much I missed the mushy-gushy nerd he was before he hardened into crime-fiction daddy. This Drew, sitting beside me, is *my* Drew.

"I like that one too," I say softly.

Drew's calming blue eyes meet mine. "You never had to be anything more than what you were to be worthy of me, and I hate that you thought you did."

The magic spell reminiscing cast over me breaks immediately. "Drew, are you kidding?" I ask, stubbing out the joint and standing. The hand-holding abruptly feels far too intimate for the feelings I've been harboring. "I couldn't keep a pair of socks together, let alone a relationship."

Drew doesn't immediately come to comfort me. I appreciate that. He hangs behind, holding space, breathing in loudly. When I'm ready, I turn back, and he says something that makes my heart levitate. "So you couldn't keep a non-holey pair of socks together, so what? I couldn't be bothered to put on pants and go out past 10:00 p.m., but you forced me to. You live without a shell. I live inside mine. That's why we worked as friends."

"But," I protest, scared of upending the sweetness, "I ruined it before opposites attract could *become* friends-to-lovers." *Or a happily ever after*, but I don't say that part out loud.

Dazed, he steps toward me, narrowly missing the rock collection, and clamps his hands onto the yellow metal bars on either side of me. His body is a barrier to the world. Backed into the corner of this kiddy playset, I'm not twenty-three-years old trapped inside a thirty-year-old's body and he's not thirty-year-old Drew either. We're something outside of that. Suspended in a glittering void for only us.

Timeless.

"What I'm hearing is you *did* read all those romance books I shoved at you over the years," he says, voice light, eyes heavy with desire.

"Some of them," I say, "yeah."

He quirks a brow. "Why'd you lie?"

"Because," I reply, sounding schoolboy snotty to cover up the fact that I read those books to feel close to him. To run my fingers across the sentences that he underlined and loved. "Reading's for nerds."

He throws his head back, laughing. "Is kissing also for nerds?" he asks, voice rumbly and intriguing. Maybe it's the weed. Maybe it's the enchantment of being back here after all these years and admitting these things we'd never thought we'd admit.

I promised myself that I wouldn't get involved beyond a friendship because it will make leaving this timeline that much more impossible. But with every second that passes, I lose more of my resolve to stop this. Perfect moments in life are so rare regardless of timeline. I can't let this kiss—our fourth—go unfulfilled.

"Kissing is *definitely* for nerds," I say, summoning my best screw-it attitude.

He steps closer. Age has emboldened him. "Good thing I'm a nerd then."

My breath hitches. "Good thing I am too."

And just like that, we're kissing beside a plastic slide atop a children's castle where we used to dream about being this age and count the stars. Right now, the only stars I'm counting are the ones bedazzled onto the insides of my eyelids as our lips clasp and part, press and tug. Teeth grind over sensitive skin. Tongues brush but don't linger. It's heady and heavenly, and before this goes too far, I pull back and whisper, "NERD. Not. Even. Remotely. Dorky."

Another laugh, louder this time, rolls out of him. "Interesting theory. I was thinking: Naughty. Erotic. Romance. Doms."

"Daaaaamn. Very smut-erotica. Okay, *Daddy*," I playfully name-call, gripping a handful of his T-shirt, stunned by how much I like this new confident side of him that can make sexy jokes and corner me on play sets.

He presses into my hand, but shakes his head sheepishly. "Oh God. Don't call me that." He covers his face with his palms. Not quite as embarrassed as he'd have been seven years ago.

"Why not?" I ask partly in a purr, knowing he's secretly enjoying this kind of attention. I peel his fingers away so I can see him fully. That face I'd never, ever want to forget. "You're seven years older than me, you know. You're kind of a DILF."

"I'm not a dad!"

"Okay, so a cougar."

"That's for women."

"A jaguar then?"

"That's a car!"

"Fine. A cradle robber."

"*That's*...concerning!"

And we laugh.

We laugh so long and so hard before he pulls me close, lays me down, and starts kissing me again.

Chapter Twenty-Seven

I'm in deep shit with Jessalynn.

And also Harry, our producer, the network, and the venue.

I missed rehearsal because Drew and I were too busy playing horny teenagers all over our hometown. Once I realized the time (maybe that weed was effectual after all), there was no way we were making it back to Brooklyn before it wrapped.

And yet…I couldn't care less.

That night, I try calling CeeCee because a deep part of me wants to hear her voice. I want to apologize and confess everything and talk with her for hours the way we did back when all we cared about were boys, TV shows, and if we could get a ride to the mall that weekend. However, all my calls go to voicemail, and I'm too unrehearsed to spew it all out in a single message without fumbling my words.

Resigned, I sit at my computer and write CeeCee yet another email. It has almost become meditative. A journal of sorts.

Drew kissed me for the fourth time.

And the fifth, sixth, seventh…

I know you're probably thinking that I've lost my mind. Maybe I have, but if this is what losing your mind is like, I don't know if I want to find it again!

I know you know about the first time Drew and I kissed, but did I ever tell you about the second? Probably not. We were mostly estranged at that point. You in Jersey City. Me in Queens. Two planets with the solar system of Manhattan between them.

It was New Year's Eve two years ago. We were at a party where we found ourselves as the unpaired queer folk who didn't want to be left out of the midnight make-out. As the countdown started, we locked eyes across the room and shrugged. I assumed it would be a light peck, a quick hug, but when the clock struck midnight, it was like our mouths were speaking a language brand-new to both of us. (TMI, I know...sorry!)

I wanted to say something, but Drew excused himself to refill his drink and then the holiday high wore off and things went back to normal and I convinced myself that was for the best. From afar, I couldn't fuck things up with him, but now...

Now I know I was wrong? At least partially? Maybe?

I don't know what any of this means! I fucking time traveled, and the crystals to get me back are the thing that brought us together! And I might lose everything I've just built with Drew when I go back in time to the wedding night I ruined.

I don't know what to do.

All of this is to say...I miss you. I know that's unfair, but I do. I would give anything to sit on the beanbag chair in your room and vent while you paint your toenails like we did at the beginning of high school. To look at the 1989-era Taylor Swift poster on your wall and know that no problem couldn't be fixed with ice cream and a "Shake It Off" dance party.

"Where were you?" Jessalynn asks as soon as they find me in the office of my apartment, ready to pounce. I send the email and turn toward them.

"Visiting my mom," I say, which at the very least is not a lie.

They narrow their eyes at me. "Is that code for something?"

"No," I say, shaking my head. "Why would it be?"

"Because you haven't *visited* anyone in the last few years. You once said, 'People outside of New York City don't exist.'"

While that doesn't sound like *me*, it certainly sounds like this costumed version of me. "I've changed my mind." It's dinnertime for Milkshake, so I head toward the kitchen—without getting lost. I pour some dog food into Milkshake's bowl, and he comes bounding into the room, tail wagging, tiny feet clacking on the wooden floor. "Speaking of change, I'm updating the set."

The conversations with Wanda and Mom and kissing Drew all made clear that this may not be my reality, but it's still real. Though I have faith that the crystals will work their magic again, I can't completely ignore the possibility that I could get stuck here. At least for a time. And I'm responsible for this timeline while I'm living in it.

"For the special?" they ask, sounding borderline infuriated. "Like hell you are."

Now that Milkshake is fed, I search around for some nourishment of my own. Jessalynn is breathing down my neck. "It's my words coming out of my mouth, and I should get the final say over them."

"No," they say, furiously stabbing something into their phone.

I grab a chia pudding from the fridge. "What are you going to do, ventriloquist-dummy me then? Pull a *Singin' in the Rain* and force me to mouth the words someone else is saying offstage? Some of those jokes are mean-bordering-on-cruel, and I won't say them."

They roll their eyes. "Oh, so one trip to visit Mommy and you're suddenly questioning your morals? Give me a break."

I hate how snide their tone is. Maybe I used the same one before arriving inside this body, but no more. I refuse to be ruled by pessimistic hate.

Things are finally looking up in this timeline. Drew is on the way to fully forgiving me, or at least he kisses and texts me like he is. Mom might be coming to my special taping. I still have made no headway with CeeCee, and I haven't seen Dad, but I want to leave this timeline better than how I found it.

Again, it's good practice for when I'm back.

"I'm making edits. End of discussion," I say, borrowing some of my onstage confidence. Wanda's encouragement gives me the bravery to stand my ground here.

Jessalynn sighs with the strength of a cyclone. "The network approved the jokes. The director approved the jokes. Our editor—responsible for knowing your jokes inside and out so they can be spliced—has committed the set to memory. Why must you do this to me?"

"To you?" I ask, dropping my spoon in my cup. "You know, when we worked at the Hardy-Har Hideaway and we made fake plans for the future, dreaming of all this"—I motion around me, at the excess and the luxury and the stupid automatic vacuum—"you always said we'd be partners. This feels a bit like you're bullying me into what you want, and that's not okay with me." Maybe time travel is exactly what I needed to finally grow a backbone, enough of one that Jessalynn backs down slightly.

"We were children then. You have a fan base. I have a business," they begin, less fight to it. "We have people to answer to. If it were up to me—"

"It's not," I say, cutting them off. "It's up to *me*."

They slip their phone into their bag with a huff. "Fine. Make your changes," they say, putting sunglasses on. "But they better be done before the next rehearsal or else."

Their warning follows them out, but I'm undeterred because a massive weight lifts off of me for finally getting rid of those jokes that aren't me. That won't be me ever again. I can promise myself that much.

Only now I have to do the hard work of editing them to reflect this positive confidence.

.₀ † ✦ † ˙°

After several SOS texts to Drew, he tells me to come by the store so I can workshop my edits while he mans the register and, from what I've overheard so far, argue with a fickle man about folding chairs.

"No, I promise you, sir, I did not fill out the form incorrectly," Drew says sharply yet politely into his phone. "I'm a triple-checker. I would not have put five when I need fifty. I own five chairs, so it would be quite silly of me to hire your company to provide something I already have." Tucked into one of the jade-colored wingback chairs across the way with my notebook open in my lap, I'm in perfect eavesdropping distance. Even though I should be scrubbing through these setups.

"No, that doesn't mean I only need forty-five. I would like fifty matching folding chairs delivered by Thursday afternoon at the absolute latest," Drew says, a heart-shaped stress ball deformed inside his fist despite his voice being morning-dew calm. "Yes, noon would be excellent. Thank you. All right. Have a good day."

When Drew sets the phone down, he slips off his glasses and massages his temples. I set down the pen I've been gnawing on and go to him. "May I approach the bench?" I ask, gesturing to the hefty antique checkout counter where bookmarks, stickers, and postcards are displayed for purchase.

"Proceed."

I extend a hand toward him, and he takes it without hesitation. "Everything okay?"

He nods. "I'm really banking on this author event being a success. The grand unveiling of the author's identity. It's going to get a lot of media coverage and could bring an influx of shoppers to the store. Everything needs to be perfect."

That need for perfection leads him to drop my hand and scurry over to a disorganized stack. Instantly, he's rearranging the titles, making sure they're displayed properly even if no one has been in here since I arrived.

"Sounds like you're doing everything right," I say.

"Except getting people to attend," he says, forlornly looking around. It's true his store isn't a super-popular business, but he's got his book club, his regulars, and some curious tourists. Enough cash flow to keep the lights on. "I have to pull in numbers."

I whip out my phone and click open the first social media app I see. "How does two point six million sound as a number?"

He laughs. "I don't think the fire marshal would be happy about that."

"I mean, what if I posted about the event?" I hand him my phone. "I've got the platform. I might as well use it."

Drew bobs his head, shoulders joining in. "I don't know. Not sure the audiences really overlap." I know it shouldn't sting, but it does a little. "Not in a negative way. I'm just saying that it's not like it's an event for you, or an event you'll be at."

"It is most definitely an event I'll be at," I tell him. "Where else would I be? I'm obviously coming to support you." It stings more that he'd assume I'd skip out on an important event of his. My skipping-out days are behind me. Chaos ensues when I do. I have categorically learned my lesson.

"Even still," he begins, swapping out one of the books in the new window display promoting the event, "it's not for or about you. Your fans would only come if it was."

An idea pops into my head when I realize he's not going to be able to focus on the crystal hunt with this humungous responsibility hanging over his head. "What if it was about me? Indirectly, anyway."

"Clue me in."

My heart pirouettes when his old words hit my ears. It's phrases like this that let me know the twenty-three-year-old Drew is still jammed underneath the button-downs and facial hair.

"I could moderate the talk," I offer. "Think about it. I'm already reading the book. It's excellent. Freakishly reminding me too much of CeeCee's old workplace, but still good." A panopticon reception desk. A secret hallway. A *guru*.

On the way back to New York, while playing footsie, we both dove into the book club pick. Drew was about four chapters ahead of me, given my ADHD makes focusing—especially in a highly stim-ulatory environment like a train—difficult, so his slight gasps and chuckles made me pause and whisper, "Spoiler alert."

"Reading," Drew said with an air of knowingness, "is entirely subjective. My gasp may be your groan." And, I had to cross my legs at that because suddenly my mind was overrun with all the acts we could do to each other that would elicit a different type of groan.

To ward off the reminder of those stirring feelings, I resume my argument. "I could come up with plenty of questions to ask, or you could draft some and I could memorize them. You know that's my number one skill." I hold up my notebook chock-full of material as concrete proof.

"You're not a bookseller, though."

"So what? That doesn't mean I'm incapable," I counter. "I know how to engage a crowd. I can throw in a few jokes. It'll be a riot."

He's a veritable bobblehead of indecision. "I don't want to draw any attention away from the author."

"Oh, and your bright hair and dashingly handsome face aren't going to draw *any* attention?" I ask, putting on the charm but meaning every word of it. His blush is my absolute favorite sight. His cheeks are shiny red apples I want to take bites out of. In a sexy way. "Come on, let me do this small favor for you. You've helped me so much already with the crystal hunt."

"Where are we at with that, by the way?"

"You're changing the subject," I protest, not wanting to battle with myself over what going back means and what I'll be leaving behind—or is it ahead?—when I do. "But we're five-sevenths of the way there. I'm pretty sure I slotted in the fifth crystal from Stephanie's stash."

Stephanie offered me a helpful cheat sheet to be able to identify them, which led me to several minutes of internet-searching stone names before remembering Drew left behind the mystical blue light glasses made by Doop.

Colors blurred by on the screen until I was looking at a listing for citrine: a light-orange stone with golden flecks and tumbled rounded edges. It was a bit before I found a match, but when I held the sixth stone from the bag up to the image, I knew I had it.

"Citrine is a sunny stone known for optimism and opening your mind," I tell Drew, but refrain from adding that I've opened my mind to the possibility of being stuck in this timeline. While not ideal, it's becoming less appalling as the days go by.

"Two more away from you going back," he says in a near singsong. Not a happy one though. More like a dirge. And it takes everything in me not to climb over the counter, throw my arms around him and reassure him that everything will work out somehow. Though even I'm not entirely convinced.

Suddenly, those stones from the collection—my potential tickets back to my usual timeline—are rough reminders in my stomach. We have little idea how this time-vacation has rippled the universe. Is this a Scrooge situation where everything I'm experiencing is a hyperreal premonition? Or is this a true *Back to the Future* situation where my actions could have real effects on the life I drop back into?

There's only one way to know: try.

And if we're successful, that means goodbye all over again, with no guarantee of an impending hello on the other side.

"Considering I have no recollection of what those final crystals were and we aren't 100 percent certain the ones we have are correct, I think it's safe to say I'll be here for at least a bit longer." It's not nearly as comforting as I want it to be, but it's all I can offer. That, and using my presence as bait for attendance at his author event. "Which means I'm fully free to interview this mysterious author about his twisted book. If you'll let me." Drew holds my eyes for a moment. Thoughts skitter across his expression as it shifts from delight to surprise to stoicism like slides on a projector. "What are you thinking about?" I ask.

"Just that I forgot how much I missed knowing you."

Those words uncork me, and before I can even question it, I'm jumping over the counter and kissing Drew with everything I have. Even though this body is on loan, it lights up with intense pleasure when it presses into Drew's. At our contact points, he gradually relaxes, leans into the kiss, and presses a huge hand firmly to my sacrum, heaving me tighter to him so our hips are flush.

"And, somehow, I missed this, too," he says wistfully, visibly contemplating something.

I'm caught off guard. "But we never—"

"In my dreams, we did."

Instantly, I'm on fire for him. My hands are in his hair, messing with the styled perfection until it's sticking up, the heat of the moment leaving it slightly damp with sweat. It's like we're dancing, and even though I initiated it, it's Drew who takes the lead, waltzing us over to the door, where he breaks the kiss to flip the OPEN sign to CLOSED and to turn the lock.

My head is woozy, knowing where this is going.

"Come." It's a quiet command that I'm more than happy to follow.

He leads me by the hand up the sweeping staircase and into the loft, where there are more books, more displays, and, more importantly, a theme-appropriate red-velvet fainting couch that would be right at home in a creaky Victorian mansion.

With a gentle push, he lays me down on it and begins kissing my neck, his beard tickling the sensitive skin beneath my chin.

His body presses down on me, the world's sexiest weighted blanket, and his bulge grazes my inner thigh. The plush couch beneath me bounces when he comes up to meet my mouth again, tenderly taking my lower lip between his teeth.

There's no necessity here as we hold each other in the middle of a bookstore, surrounded by shelves, wrapped up in the scents of mahogany and the Earl Grey tea Drew's been drinking all afternoon—the canister left open near the electric kettle.

In the privacy of the loft, I finger the hem of his shirt before he gets the hint, hiking it up over his head to reveal smooth, milky skin, a small tuft of red chest hair, and two perfectly pink nipples. I pitch forward and take one in my mouth, which makes Drew groan so deeply that I back off, worried.

"No, do it again," he growls. "I like that." And it occurs to me again that Drew isn't the guy I left back in 2023. He's sitting on seven years of experience. Eighty-four months of kisses and touches and orgasms from himself or from partners or multiple partners in beds and in cars and God knows where else.

There is so much of Drew's life in this timeline that is still a mystery to me, and right now I get clues on how to unlock him. Exhibit A: When I run my tongue over the shell of his ear, he curses. Exhibit B: When I palm the front of his jeans, he grinds and writhes with pleasure. Exhibit C: When I undress, his eyes never leave mine, even as the underwear comes off. Because it's abundantly clear that it's not the body I'm in that matters.

It's me.

He wants *me*.

And he takes me. In his hand. In his mouth. On the fainting couch. On the floor. Against the bookshelf, where a sliding ladder becomes a rickety gripping post, jostling the titles.

Paperbacks topple over, and my body shudders when I grip the nearest table, finally releasing in his beard and on his chest with a sigh that echoes through the shop with melodic clarity. And Drew smiles so wickedly, so charmingly, that my pumping and shuddering doesn't stop until he's finishing too, carefully dribbling into his hand as his chest heaves and I kiss him while laughing into his mouth.

Laughing because this is how the night of CeeCee's wedding should've ended. He and I spent and breathless, sprawled together in a perfect embrace because we'd finally given ourselves over to the love we'd each been privately clutching.

Laughing because, as I look around us, we somehow turned his murdery bookstore into a place for love stories—*our* love story—in the end anyway.

Chapter Twenty-Eight

Bound by Mayhem Books is no longer the sex den it was a few days ago.

Eager readers and fans line up down the street and around the block. Jessalynn, who unenthusiastically let this happen, is beside me. High heels clack menacingly on the pavement, and a bodyguard stomps right behind us.

"The fans can get wild," Jessalynn said. "It's for your safety and my peace of mind. Gotta protect the assets."

I made no snide remark about how they referred to me—inadvertently or not—as a product and not a person. Zipping my lips at that was hard, but I didn't want to risk them changing their mind about this event. If I can help Drew and his store, I have to so I can make up for being an ass over the course of seven years.

It helps, too, that the media is reinterested in Drew's involvement in my life since that photographed sniff outside Lucille's business. I take this as a small chance to overwrite some of the long-standing hurt that hovered over him during my ascent to fame. I hope this will show the world what Drew made for himself in the face of it all.

Inside, rows of the requested matching folding chairs are set up around the tables, stopping at the start of the stacks. A small make-shift stage sits in front of the right-side window display. There's a wired microphone on a stand, its cord snaking into a nearby amplifier, which is currently cranking out music.

The air is sweet with the smell of homemade cookies. I spy Jolene from book club arranging her baked goods—which also happens to be the name of my fanbase, Nolan's Baked Goods (BGs for short)—to perfection. Upon closer inspection, they're sprinkled and iced to match the colors of the book cover. Now that I think about it, they closely resemble the colors of the old Doop logo, too: peacock-blue and gold.

"Nolan, nice to see you," Jolene says, offering me a cookie on a plate with a napkin, which I accept.

Jessalynn, on the other hand, purses their lips, shakes their head, and looks around for something stiff to drink. Too bad for them, this is a sober event.

"Wow, Drew did an amazing job. This place looks incredible," I say after taking a bite of the cookie, which is the right ratio of chewy-to-crumbly.

"You didn't hear it from me, but he upped the budget when he onboarded you as the interviewer," Jolene says, glancing over her shoulders. I don't spot a red beard anywhere in the bunch. "That's why he went a little overboard with everything, but it looks like it was worth it from this turnout."

When I glance out the window, I notice fans holding poster boards up to the window reading "NOLAN BAKER, HAVE MY BABIES" and "ROAST ME, NOLAN BAKER." Both make me laugh, so I wave at them and they scream back.

Despite the excited throng here for me, I'm here for Drew, even if I haven't seen him for most of the week. Sure, a text or two here and a stolen lunch there, but Drew was consumed with getting this event squared away, and I'm in the throes of major tech for the special, which—worrisomely—tapes four days from today. Even if our hearts want to be together, our situations have partitioned us.

Instead of loving on Drew and finding those last couple crystals to test, I spend my days in camera-blocking rehearsals as people in headsets run around checking lighting fixtures and setting up microphones through various areas of the audience, each meant to pick up laugh tracks.

The budget and production value is unmatched. I vacillate between being awed at what I've garnered and disgusted by how it came to pass. My anxiety swings like a pendulum from (a) getting out of here before the special tapes so I don't have to go through with something so false and permanent to (b) losing Drew, once again, before we even have a chance to properly begin.

Could losing seven years but gaining confidence and love be a worthwhile trade?

"Drew seems really taken by you," Jolene adds with a coy smirk.

Even though that gap in my memory persists—all that time I flew over thanks to the crystals—hindsight remains strong. I was so afraid of crushing Drew the lovebug that I became a self-fulfilling prophesy. I courted him as my date to CeeCee's wedding, and then I didn't watch where I was stepping. *Splat.*

Now, what if staying is my best option?

If Drew was able to be honest with me at the playground and have sex with me in this very shop, then he must be asking himself the same question. Right?

Jolene checks her silver watch. "Oh! Drew roped the entire book club into assisting, so I think it's time we take our posts and start letting people in. You can find Drew in the back office. Looking forward to it. Break a leg."

Jessalynn hooks me by the arm before I can break toward the back room. "You told me this was strictly professional."

"I lied," I say, with one question still overtaking my mind.

"You can't lie to me," they tut. "You pay me to manage you."

"I could stop paying you. Would you prefer that?" I ask, warning laced into my voice.

They narrow their eyes. "I have a contract."

"And I'm certain I have very powerful lawyers who can loophole my way out of it," I say, unwilling to take their bullying any further. I'm certain their new personality was a by-product of mine, but I'm committing to being better. I'm in love. Again. Against all odds. In a timeline I traveled to via freaking crystals. "Nothing matters. Time is meaningless. If you're afraid me finding someone I care about and turning toward kinder comedy is going to tank the career you had a hand in building, maybe neither of us deserved this to begin with."

"You realize that someone is the person you used to publicly bash during your sets," Jessalynn says through gritted teeth. "I don't know what magic you pulled out of your ass to get that kind of forgiveness, but I can see it for what it is."

"Which is?"

"Someone using you for your platform." They point to the fans.

I shake my head. "Using the fans was *my* idea."

"Who even are you right now?" they ask, features contorted into an unnatural scowl.

"I could ask you the same question," I say, voice low so none of the incoming patrons hear me. "You used to be my friend, and I refuse to let you become the villain of my story. So get on board or politely bow out."

They clam up, speechless.

Satisfied, I continue on, bumping right into Drew's broad chest as I open the back door. Sturdy and tall as a skyscraper. Instead of backing away, I simply sling my arms around his torso, pressing my cheek into the blue cotton of his button-down. I inhale his clean scent and exhale a hello.

"Hello to you too," he says, settling into the embrace. "Didn't realize how nervous I was until you started hugging me."

"I can tell." His heart *puh-plunks* against my ear before I straighten up to kiss his bearded cheek. "Is the author here yet? I want to go in and introduce myself, run some questions by him."

"It's actually time to get started. I'd like to introduce you, get the hoopla out of the way, and then bring out the author. The grand reveal. Is that okay?"

"Of course." I kiss him on the lips and then tilt back to watch his face turn crimson. "I'm here for you. Whatever you want works great for me."

As expected, my introduction applause goes on for a while. A sense of pride comes over me, knowing that this applause is for the right reasons. I'm using my celebrity for good instead of rude comedy.

I could stay here, do more of this, and use my money from the special to invest in Drew's business. I could find purpose and fulfillment with that life, couldn't I?

I shelve that idea for later.

The audience has leaked into standing-room-only. People are up in the loft. Others are snaked through the stacks, phones raised, eyes alert. We're definitely breaking some safety codes, but it's all worth it to support Drew, given how everyone in attendance is holding a copy of the book and slipping bills into the donation box.

When the crowd dies down, Drew goes on: "Here at Bound by Mayhem Bookshop we are so pleased to introduce to you for the very first time the author of the bestselling thriller *Fare-Thee-Wellness*. Here he is, R. U. Low."

Except the person who steps out from the back to hoots and hollers isn't R. U. Low.

Well, he is.

But he's also someone else: Ryan from the receptionist desk at Doop.

My jaw drops.

Chapter Twenty-Nine

"They worked," Ryan says, awestruck, as soon as we're in the back office again, away from the crowd.

My head spun through the entire interview as I tried to remain calm, ask questions, be personable. The difficulty was alarming and went both ways. Ryan seemed as rattled as I was. The clues were all laid out in his book—the New York City setting with West Coast vibes, the description of the office, and the fictional products that sounded familiar. I'd just chosen to take all the details as coincidence. I should've known that nothing when it comes to Doop is a coincidence.

Drew's face twists with confusion. "What is he talking about?"

"As soon as we made eye contact, I knew," Ryan says, inching his face closer to mine so he can stare deeper into my eyes. In search of something I can't figure out. Uncomfortable, I step back but slam into a hard, metallic shelf.

Suddenly, Drew's hand is on Ryan's chest, pushing him back. "Whoa. Hey. What's going on here?" I don't have a moment to relish Drew stepping into the protector role because I'm too freaked out by this.

"When I started to write my book, I wondered. I'd see ads for your shows on my phone and consider if the crystals had something to do with it."

Drew puts his body between Ryan and me, looking only at me. "He knows about those?"

"He gave them to me," I clarify.

Ryan's eyes have a mad-scientist quality to them that chills me to my bones, reminding me of the first impression I got from him when I arrived at the Doop offices before one of CeeCee's fittings. He knew something then, and maybe he knows more now. "I can't believe you jumped seven years. It has been seven years, hasn't it?"

I nod. "Yes, I woke up here about six weeks ago." Keeping track of time has been difficult considering a calendar is nothing more than a worthless, universal organizational tool, but my rehearsal schedule and the crystal hunt has kept me abreast with some structure.

"Whoa," Ryan utters. His epiphany seems far less pressing than my personal crisis. "Seven stones, seven years. Suddenly my satire isn't all that funny."

"You're seriously thinking about your book right now?" I ask. "I'm twenty-three trapped in this thirty-year-old body because of you!"

Ryan holds up his hands in surrender. "Hang on, all I did was fill the goody bags and hand them out. I didn't make the products, nor did I force you to use them. All I did was a little snooping while I stuffed and tagged, so I knew you got the crystals."

"So how did you know about the time travel, then?" Drew asks, arms folded across his chest in a stance that says *I demand answers*.

Ryan shifts uncomfortably. "There were rumors going around the office. Doop had a secret, special lab locked behind retina scan. We were told not to go there and not to ask questions," he says. "But everybody had their own theory. Everything from embezzling to cultish offerings to witchcraft."

"See!" I say to Drew, pointing right at Ryan. "The Go to Sleep, Bitch candle!"

"Those candles came out of the lab," Ryan confirms. "What did they do?"

"They made me pass the fuck out and start a fire. That's what they did!" I shout, spiraling over this situation and the fact that my suspicion about that secret back hallway had been right. Did CeeCee know that and was covering, or did she seriously think snooping wasn't worth her time and energy?

"Look, I don't know any more than what I've told you. I kikied with the cult camp. That's how I got the idea for the novel, fictionalized the details, and skewed them just enough to get away with it."

I deflate. "Basically you're saying you can't help me get back."

He gives me a half-shrug. "Have you tried the crystals again?"

"They disappeared," I tell him, at a loss. Every time I say it, I feel salvation slipping away. "I've been trying to remember which ones were included so we could start a new collection. Try them out." Drew is pacing behind his desk, biting his thumbnail, probably lost in thought. In contrast, I'm unable to move for fear our only informant might bolt.

"That's not a bad idea," Ryan says earnestly.

"The problem is that the internet has been no help, my memory is unreliable, and Doop has completely disappeared." I sigh. "We think we're on track, but there's no way to know for sure without that damn scroll."

There's a knock at the door. Jolene pokes her head inside. "Sorry to interrupt, Mr. Low, Nolan, but they're ready for your signings."

I almost forgot that there's a room full of people out there waiting for us to be on. Smiles. Signatures. How am I supposed to care about all that shit when I feel hopelessly stuck without any more answers?

"They'll be out in a moment," Drew says, crossing to the door and shutting it behind Jolene. He presses his back to the wood and looks at us both, understanding passing wordlessly between us.

Before we compose ourselves enough to get back to it, Ryan adds, "Doop shut down because they were bleeding money and didn't want an investigation." His voice dips almost as if he misses it. "I kept a journal during my time there, a personal one, completely unrelated. I did occasionally jot down information, a lot of which I used to write the book." He offers us an apologetic half smile. "If I remember correctly, I think there was some stuff about crystals in there around the time of your sister's wedding. It wasn't relevant at the time, but I might be able to dig it up if that would be helpful."

"Yeah, it would," I say, burrowing my claws into any shred of promise. "Thanks."

Chapter Thirty

A day later, an email arrives during rehearsal.

I excuse myself, stepping out of the pool of pink light the designer is trying to adjust. My stand-in—a man who could be my twin—switches with me, offering a warm smile. For a second, I consider the possibility that he's another me, and instead of time-jumping, he got flung through a portal and stumbled into my universe, which isn't even *my* universe.

After my conversation with Ryan, the possibilities seem endless.

In the wings, I click into the email. There's no signature, and the address is a series of jumbled, random numbers and letters, but the attachments tell me everything I need to know.

Scanned in are pages from Ryan's journal with information about the crystals and CeeCee's wedding.

Pulling up the most recent photo of my own crystal collection, I cross-reference Ryan's notes with my stash. His handwriting is crooked and sloppy, but I decode the gist, and when I get to the part about the goody bags, I'm reassured that the ones we collected are right and there are only two left to find: malachite and pyrite.

The images that populate from my search for malachite show stones with mesmerizing emerald and black swirls. They are meant to be used for transformation—fitting in more ways than one—but also for letting go of negative habits and unhealthy patterns. How, then, have I found myself in the life of a playboy?

The other stone, pyrite, is considered "fool's gold." Its shiny exterior makes me laugh. This sucker is the one. I can feel it. The stone that twisted my intentions into the *Black Mirror* version of my life. Though, in fairness, my intentions may not have been all that pure to begin with.

What's my next move? With only two-and-a-half days left before the special taping, I want to meet my deadline, even if there's an anxious heartbeat thrumming underneath every step I make, I can't live with the uncertainty of what these crystals could do.

I race to the bathroom to put on a performance that rivals anything I've ever done onstage. After locking the door, I fake-retch and groan, loud enough so the PA stationed outside the door sends for help.

Right on time, Jessalynn is banging their fist and calling through the door, "You all right in there?"

"Not really," I yell back, clutching my stomach even though nobody can see me. "I think I ate something bad."

"Ate something bad," they shout back over the whirring of the fan I flicked on, "or drank too many something goods?"

"Jesus, Jessalynn, it's not even noon." The playboy conundrum comes barreling back at me. How did crystals meant for healing make me into a giant bruise on the back of society? Would I be able to undo that completely if I got stuck here?

"Time has never been a deterrent for you before. Though now I guess that you're cleaning up your image, you're making healthier choices too." A real groan escapes them. "Shall I call the medic?"

"No, just give me a minute." I use that minute to dampen my forehead, ratchet up my breathing, and exacerbate my sickness. Not like my inner turmoil isn't enough to give me a clammy sheen and perpetual cramps.

When I open the door, Jessalynn visibly cringes. "Jeez, I've seen you look better after a three-night bender." Which inspires them to send me home for an early lunch and nap on the stringent condition that my assistant keep an eye on me. I need to be back—bright-eyed and bushy-tailed—for the second half of rehearsal later. A full-fledged dress rehearsal that has me nervous beyond anything.

By the time I'm back at the apartment, decked out in lounge-wear, I've already hatched an escape plan. I send my assistant out for a brand of stomach medication that doesn't exist. A goose chase that will last just long enough to get me out of the apartment, down-town, and back in time to have made a miraculous recovery. Very *The Lizzie McGuire Movie* without the fake European pop-star part.

Lucille is surprised to see me again so soon when I arrive at her place, out of breath. She says her regular clients usually need more time between readings to really sit with what she's told them. In her lap, an orange cat purrs before hopping down, circling my legs, and leaning its head into my shin. Its fur reminds me of Drew's hair, and its affection sends a thrill through me.

Completing this hunt is for us. For a redo.

"She likes you," Lucille says of the cat, impressed. "She hates grown men usually. It's why I keep her in the bedroom when clients come through. It's why you didn't meet her when you were here last. Her name is Tigress, and she's clawed more than her fair share of middle-aged men in the time I've had her."

"Maybe it's because I'm not a middle-aged man," I say without thinking. Lucille's office, for lack of a better word, has an ethereal hominess. It's what makes people comfortable enough to ask her vulnerable questions during their readings and imagine futures that can be foretold through palm ridges. It's what keeps them coming back…and what prompts me to explain my situation this time.

I don't skimp on the details because I know she'll believe me. I'm paying her to believe me, essentially, and withholding information has been constricting my muscles, driving me wild.

Lucille appears completely unfazed by my admission. Or perhaps she's deemed me unhinged, in which case she's trying not to make any sudden movements for fear I might pounce on her. Tigress is no match for this CrossFit bod I've been lugging around on loan.

"Say something?" I ask meekly, dropping my shoulders. I'm treating her like a therapist with an on-call telephone line to the cosmos.

She rests her chin on her fist and appraises me. "Nothing I can say will change your truth. If you want me to say I believe you, I think you know I do." She points to her rock collection, her crystal ball, her burning incense, and her tarot deck. The tools of her trade that supply her with a spiritual—if not concrete—tether to a universe of knowledge beyond the norm. "Crystals have healing powers, vibrations. I've never time traveled myself, but I've also never parachuted out of a plane or hiked through Greece or swam with sharks. Does that mean those life-changing experiences aren't possible?"

"I think you're overlooking the part where I said I went to bed seven years ago and woke up here." My voice is a wavering scrape, worn out from rehearsals.

"And I think you're conflating what's perceived to be possible and what truly is," she says. "Not everyone believes in ghosts, but there are plenty who've had interactions with the supernatural. How do we explain that? Who's to say airplanes aren't simulators that cover up the fact that teleportation is real and if the commoners knew, they'd use it for unsightly gain?"

"If ghosts are real, I bet the Wright brothers are in this room and flipping you off right about now."

A witchy cackle echoes through the room. "Let them. The spiritual realm doesn't scare me, just as time travel shouldn't scare you."

"That's out of the question. I've been scared out of my wits ever since I woke up here. Scared of how I got here, how my life turned out like this, how I could've possibly hurt all these people I loved so dearly." I sigh heavily. "If crystals are meant to be about freeing the self and making positive change, how come I turned out to be such a frivolous ass?"

Tigress leaps up onto my lap, snuggles against my chest, and stabilizes my heart rate while Lucille prepares some tea for the two of us. "Crystals are not powerful on their own. On a shelf or in a store, they are ornamental only. It's not until someone charges them and sets their intentions that they're able to become more than a beautiful, natural element."

"Does that mean because my intentions were selfish, the crystals could only match that energy?" The thought had occurred to me before, but I didn't put much merit to it. That night I said I wanted to prove people wrong, I was awash in negativity, convincing myself that I'd made the right choice regardless of cost, and maybe that distorted everything.

Her nod isn't definitive either. "There are no exact rules or science. If there were, their magic and abilities would've been adopted by all, don't you think?" While she has a point, I still wish there were a manual that I'd been handed when I woke up. At least I would've known I wasn't alone in this peculiar experience. "Why are you stalling? What is it you really came here for?" she asks, and I'm slightly unnerved at her ability to break apart my intentions like a KitKat bar.

I show her the crystals on my phone. "These are the last two I need, but again—"

"You're scared because you're in love," she says, finally sounding definitive. It leads me to wonder if she's a mind reader among all her other otherworldly talents. "Don't make that face. You don't need a crystal ball to know the man you were in here with the last time loves you beyond measure."

With that, I tell her the truth about my real timeline. About leaving the wedding and losing Drew. Just saying it how it happened, not how I painted it in my head, frees me of some of my guilty conscience. "What if I double back, make better choices, and we still don't end up together? At least now I know I have him."

Lucille wraps her shawl around her torso, eyes scanning the ceiling as if there really are ghosts up there whispering down celestial messages to her. Oh wait, that's a medium, not a psychic. "What's meant to be will always come to pass. Time does not dictate destiny."

"It doesn't?" I built my whole life plan around time, around meeting goals by certain ages so I could prove to those who doubted me that the pursuit of my dreams was not wasted. Had that all been for nothing?

Without a word, she walks out of the room with Tigress close behind.

As I sit there alone, swirls of steam rising off the mug of tea she placed before me, I consider, as she said, all the wonders in my original timeline that I've never encountered. Hot-air balloons. Hallucinogenics. Free soloing.

Any number of those things could've unlocked a part of me, led me to new discoveries, knocked me off the course my life was taking. Maybe there was always magic around me. It just took a lavish wedding, a wellness company, and some crystals to set me up to believe.

When Lucille returns, she sets small malachite and pyrite stones in my hand. I go to pay her, but she stops me. "When you get back to your true life, you come and see me. I may not remember, but somehow I'll know, and that will be payment enough."

Lucille seems entirely unsurprised when I hug her. She even hugs me back. Tigress, cuddler that she is, meows as she joins in as well. I scratch her between the ears before I go, bounding down the sidewalk with faith rolling around at the bottom of my bag.

Chapter Thirty-One

"I have to try, right?" I ask Drew.

If I let this unknown linger, I'll be a wreck, even if the worries I voiced to Lucille remain true. I might lose Drew. Mom might not forgive me the way she has. I might never get a comedy special as extravagant as this one. But...

Time does not dictate destiny.

I remind myself of that as Drew and I inspect the crystals laid out in a decorative, ceramic bowl on the windowsill. Lucille instructed me to let them soak in moonlight, to write out my intentions, and then when I can't keep my eyes open or my mind awake any longer, sleep.

I had my final dress rehearsal with the lights and the sound cues and the cameras flying and rolling in from all directions. Even though the jokes were nicer, the experience still made my skin crawl.

It's well past midnight. Nighttime has crept in through the windows, and uncertainty has overtaken my brain. Drew, shiny, light-led Drew, is the only bright spot in the hazy gray middle-space I'm inhabiting.

"I think you'll regret it if you don't," he says, a note of sadness resonating beneath his words.

My chest seizes with worry. As if he can sense my heart switching into overdrive, he places a hand to my sternum and holds it there. The shuddering settles, but not enough to help me relax.

Part of me wants to ask him if he's sure, if he realizes that me going back might mean a permanent ending for us. But those words keep retreating into the recesses of my mind because we did all of this *to* get me back.

"You're right," I say. "Except I'm never going to be able to sleep with the not-knowingness towering over me like the grim reaper from those tarot cards. At least last time I expected nothing, and I was exhausted from...well, from *everything.*" The memory of why all this happened eclipses the moment.

"Nolan, I know you're nervous, but I'll be right beside you all night. We can marathon old seasons of *Drag Race* or take Milkshake for a walk or go down to the gym and run on the treadmill," he starts listing.

"Okay, I know it's been seven years, but I still only run when my life depends on it," I say, nudging into his side as we sit on the California king bed.

He glances down at my torso-hugging tank top, blushing all the while. "Clearly that's not the case anymore."

"Excuse me, Drew Techler, did you just check me out while I'm in the middle of a full-on emotional crisis?" I ask, moving up onto my knees so our heights are more matched.

"I..." He loses the thread of his sentence as I challenge him with my eyes. "I'm not going to lie to you, so yes. I did. For a second. I'm sorry." The apology is so genuine and cute that I tackle him and begin to tickle his sides. "Wha—Ha, ha... Hey! What are you doing that for?"

His laugh lightens the mood and intoxicates me, so much so that I continue because he's not telling me to stop. His ear-to-ear smile says he's enjoying it, and I'm desperate for a distraction.

Milkshake hops off his doggy bed in the corner, clearly confused and amused by the two adults acting like teenagers at a sleepover, and begins barking happily, his tail wagging a mile a minute.

Right when I let up, captivated by the sliver of pale, freckled skin that reveals itself as his shirt wriggles higher, Drew retaliates. His fingers become weapons of mass laughter, striking all my hotspots.

"You want a tickle fight, Baker?" he asks over my own loud laughter, voice dropping low and causing a stir in my gut. "I'll give you a tickle fight."

My body spasms with delight. "That'll certainly tire me out." I can barely get the words out between euphoric gasps for breath.

A shadow falls over Drew's face and a closed-lip smile spreads seductively. "You know what else will tire you out?" he asks, tickling me one last time.

Before I can make an educated guess, his shirt is off and his lips are on mine and our bodies, already warm from the wrestling, glide over each other's. My breath, once panicked, is now heavy for entirely different reasons, and it wafts up the side of his neck before I lightly bite him there. He yips a little before nipping me right back.

As he helps me out of my shirt, he remarks, "This is not the body of someone who does not run." His large hands swipe over the ridges and valleys that are still completely alien to me.

I stop what I'm doing, suddenly self-conscious. "Are you saying I need abs to be sexy?" I know it's a ridiculous question, but it's a valid one. "If I go back, these go away," I say.

"Oh my God. No." Drew helps me off him, sits cross-legged across from me, and grabs the closest hand, kissing the center of my palm repeatedly. "You would be sexy in any size in any place in any timeline because you're Nolan goddamn Baker."

I nod, unconvinced.

He uses his hand to tilt my chin toward his, so I can't avoid his eyes, which are burning with a passion so bright it's nearly blinding. "I said you are the sexiest man I have ever met or ever will meet. Twenty-three or thirty or three-hundred-and-seven. Do you understand?"

My heart speeds up. "I understand," I say, feeling myself and him and this.

"Good." He's tickling me again, stealing laughs and asking for kisses until I'm kissing down his torso of my own accord, taking him into my mouth.

He groans as he touches his own pale-pink nipples, and I don't stop as I watch him give himself over to me. An act that can't be easy, given all he's told me about his relationship to attraction. I feel special that of all the people in the world, Drew is attracted to me because of our bond, a bond that has transcended the rules of linear time and miraculously grown stronger in the process.

And soon, he's so uninhibited that he's hiking his legs up by the knees and asking me to tongue him lower, to open him up and fuck him.

The Drew I left back in 2023 was not a prude by any stretch of the imagination. He read erotica, for God's sake, but he didn't often talk much about his own sex life. Maybe there wasn't much to talk of. Not that it concerned me. Now, I'm starring in it alongside him and noticing how beautiful he looks with sweat dripping down his brow, red hair sticking to his forehead. Gorgeously letting go.

"I'm ready," he says when I slide my fingers out from the warmth between his legs. "I want it."

And I let him have it. However he wants. Wherever he wants. Because we only have tonight for certain, and I'm intent on making it count.

Until the countdown starts, the pressure from beneath builds, and Drew's mouth switches from an "o" to an "O," unable to say anything else besides, "Fuck, fuck, fuck."

Fuck, fuck, fuck indeed as he releases and then so I do.

He was right. That did tire me out.

I lie there, panting, reaching to check the time on my phone.

Late. Nearly 3:00 a.m.. How long were we at it? Does it matter?

No. Not when Drew is sitting up beside me, naked, catching his breath and running a towel down his beet-red torso.

"I'm too tired to get up," I say, legs weak and head woozy.

"So don't," he says, planting a kiss on the crown of my sweaty head. "Just stay there."

He comes back with a damp, cool washcloth, which he uses to clean me off. He pats me dry, pulls the sheets up, and grabs the bowl from the windowsill, where the moon still spotlights the crystals. "Lift your head," he instructs, placing the crystals one by one beneath my pillow.

"Are you leaving?" I ask, afraid again. Afraid of losing him. Afraid of going back. Afraid of the unknown. I've always, always, always been governed by fears. I wish I weren't, but they clutch tight to me the same way I clutch tight to his forearm right now.

"No," he says, brushing a hand across my cheek, tracking down to the point of my chin. "I couldn't do that. I'm going to go make some coffee so I can stay up until you're asleep. I want to be awake in case anything happens. Is that okay?"

My heavy head nods, and my eyes flutter shut as he pads out of the room.

Once he's gone, I speak my intentions into the universe, but I don't fall asleep right away. My head is too busy screening a one-night-only presentation of our time together here as thirty-year-olds. Shots of Milkshake and Drew and the Brooklyn Academy of Music, which maybe I'll never get to perform at. Maybe I'll make it there regardless.

There's no going back after this. Whatever waits for me when morning comes is the reality I'll have to accept. My mind is still at war over where I truly want to be. I never imagined I'd win something so beautiful in this timeline that I'd be scared to lose it, but I have.

Time doesn't dictate destiny.

Lucille's mantra becomes a lullaby with a melody so soothing I almost pass out from mental exhaustion, until the mattress ripples again. I open my eyes, just for a second, to see Drew fluffing the pillow and setting his freshly brewed coffee on the bedside table, which smells dark, rich, and heavenly.

He cracks open a book, and at first I think it's a thriller. Perhaps his next book club pick. But then I notice the pastel colors and the cartoon characters and the large type, and I realize it's a romance.

Drew's reading romance again.

The fear of what's to come fizzles out, and I whisper, "Good night, Drew. I love you."

He puts his finger to the sentence he's reading to hold his place, looks down at me, and says, "I love you too, Nolan. Good night and goodbye."

The last thing I see before I fall asleep is the smile that powers my days, keeps me up at night, and never ceases to buoy me.

PART FIVE

MALACHITE

Unlocking your inner strength

Chapter Thirty-Two

When I wake up with the first licks of morning light, groggy and sore, the first thing I check for is the nose splint.

The second thing I check for is Drew, curled up on the other side of the bed.

Neither of them is there.

Chapter Thirty-Three

I find Drew standing in his sleep clothes in the living room, looking out upon the ashen sky as raindrops pelt the windows. A relentless sound score of *rap-rap-ra-rap*.

Milkshake is spread out on the floor beside him, back legs winged out as he rests his head on his favorite toy—a yellow stuffed bird.

The crystals that were still under my pillow are cradled in my shaking hands. "They didn't work," I croak, voice raspy from sleep.

Drew doesn't turn to me as he says, "I waited all night for a sign—a spooky light from beneath your pillow or for you to levitate out of your body and zip away, but nothing. Nothing more than you, lying there, looking peaceful as you slept." I wish he would turn around and look at me, move to me, wrap me in his arms, kiss my hair, and tell me it's all right. Instead, I spot a glass of brown liquid trembling in his hand in the reflection of the window, the rest of him immobile.

"A little early for that, no?" I ask, knowing that in this timeline, alcohol for breakfast was probably the least of my sins. However, it's still shocking to see that Drew is a tipsy mess when he finally shows me his face. Bloodshot eyes. Hair pointing out every which way. He looks as unraveled as I feel.

"I've been brainstorming," he says. Whiskey. I see the half-drunk bottle on the counter. The drink that inspired the crystal quest—the fix we now know failed. "I didn't sleep at all. I tried to read but I couldn't focus. Every hour I spent mulling over what could've gone wrong. Was it the intentions you set or the specific crystal shapes we gathered?" That's when I see the pile of crumpled papers littered all over the coffee table, a ripped-clean legal pad with a pen from Drew's shop on top of it.

He holds out the only unwrinkled piece of paper with half a ring stain in the top right corner. Sitting on the floor, I pull up the front hem of my shirt, creating a tiny pocket to drop all the crystals in. Their weight, one by one, in my lap is a tiny, crushing avalanche of failure. Milkshake nuzzles against my bare legs as I try to read, but I can't make out this chicken scratch. "What is all this?"

"I have a plan. I made a list," he says, pacing now. "I think we should start with the orange crystals that we got from Stephanie. We have a few different shapes and shades of those. We can rotate them in and out in various combinations."

"Tonight? After the special taping?" I ask, squinting at the paper, noticing how his writing got larger and sloppier the farther down he got.

"No. Now," he says. It's clear he's not thinking straight. What happened to his two-drink rule?

"Drew, it's dawn. I can't go back to sleep," I say, finding a place among the mess to set down the crystals and then standing.

"I thought that too," he says. He rushes to the bathroom and returns with an orange bottle I haven't investigated before. "You have sleeping pills, so it's not a problem."

"Jessalynn will be here soon, I'm sure. There's press and photo shoots and last-minute tech to run," I say, voice pitching higher the more frantic I become. It's a lot, but I know it's *a lot* I can handle with Drew by my side. Only he's spiraling before my eyes, scaring me. Usually I'm the messy one. I don't know how to navigate this new dynamic.

"Who cares? This is more important," he says. "I promised I'd get you back before the special taped. I'm not going to give up now. Here, I laid out the crystals we've got and labeled them." The other orange crystals are set in a row, Post-it notes stuck to each. The more I take in, the more I see that Drew has turned my apartment into one of his bookstore displays—the scattered work of a veteran detective out to crack the grisly case.

I can't help thinking: What if there's no case to crack?

"Drew," I say after a shaky breath, ready to tell him where my mind has been at. "What if…what if I just stayed?"

Drew comes to an abrupt halt. When he looks at me, he's instantaneously sober. Frighteningly so. "We can't leave you like this."

I think about reconciling with Wanda and Mom. I think about growing closer, both physically and emotionally, with Drew. I think about the Harvey Theater and the hordes of adoring fans who purchased tickets to see me tonight, who will be surprised by the friendlier comedy I've written thanks to my time here.

I always wanted it all, but didn't know how to get it. Maybe Doop gave it to me in the form of this time-jump. I just had to work hard at untangling the old me before I could have it all as the new me.

The me I am right now.

"What if that's what I want?" My voice is tissue paper thin. It seems simpler, easier. God, I could use simple and easy for a change.

Drew's eyes widen. "To live trapped in a body that's not yours in a life you didn't earn?" The question whips at me, even if it's mostly truth.

"But aren't I working toward earning it?" I ask, desperation and fear circling like they're about to start a duel in my stomach. "I've been reaching out to CeeCee. I helped Wanda at the club. I've been chipping away at Jessalynn's exterior, trying to pull out the Jessie I used to know. I even edited my stand-up material to reflect the honest me that you helped find in this timeline. Doesn't that mean anything?" The air between us grows hotter and harder to breathe.

Drew's eyes fall down as he slumps against the counter. "I can't be a part of a half-life, Nolan. I worked too hard to build this one without you."

I place my palms on my chest, stopping my heart from falling out onto the floor. "If this is it—if I'm stuck here—are you saying that there's no place for me in your life?"

"I let myself have this because I thought it was temporary," he says, hanging his head. "I realize that was a terrible mistake. I thought if I could get you back to your original timeline, we could start over with a clean slate. That was wishful thinking. I knew it was a possibility, but I never considered what would happen if it didn't work."

"I did," I'm quick to say, stepping closer to him even as he shrinks. "Drew, I love you."

"That's the trouble," Drew says, visibly grasping at straws, blue eyes growing darker and harsher. "I don't believe in love like that anymore. I told you as much in my shop, and I meant it." He drains the rest of his whiskey in an efficient gulp.

The romantic, rose-colored pipe dream shatters when Drew glances at my outstretched, upturned hand and actively chooses not to take it.

My heartbeat roars inside my ears, which have grown hot to the touch. "Then what happens now?"

He pauses for what feels like an eternity as my eyes well up. "I have to go. I don't want to be the subject of think pieces where writers deconstruct how you hurt me and then I took you back anyway. I don't want to be the playboy comedian's latest conquest. You wanted the fame. I only ever wanted you."

Even though his excuses sound flimsy, loss pounds its fists at the walls of my rib cage. "You can have me."

"Not this way, I can't. I won't." A fire takes up residence in his eyes, two eyebrows sloping downward right above. While collecting his coat and his shoes, he adopts the detached tone he used on that first day in his shop. "I told you I would help you, and I did. We tried, we failed, and I'm sorry. I—I can't do it anymore. Goodbye, Nolan."

The door shuts between us. Again.

I don't call for him or run after him. He was pacing like a caged animal. Trying to keep him here, locked in this ivory tower he so openly detests, would've done no good for either of us.

Without him, I'm left with the mess of his mind. Papers. Crystals. Even the romance novel he didn't read is on the floor. Milkshake must've gotten to it.

I want to sob, but I don't get the chance, because I hear the doors to my private elevator sliding open. Jessalynn's loud voice bounces off every wall. "Today's the big day, superstar! Let's get a move on."

Chapter Thirty-Four

I'm perched in a swivel chair in my dressing room at the Brooklyn Academy of Music while a makeup artist named Hanson attends to me with careful precision. A playlist—curated by my assistant—loops across the room, giving the space a party vibe that couldn't be more unwanted.

There's a large fridge fully stocked with alcohol whirring across the way. A massive, faux-fur Lovesac takes up the other half of the room. Its cloud-like comfort brings me no joy. Every available surface is overrun with flower arrangements and cards wishing me luck, but it truly feels like my luck, if I ever had any, has entirely run out.

"Look up," says Hanson, effortlessly applying my eyeliner.

A blond girl with rosy cheeks gives me a hand massage to de-stress, but I'm a pack of quaking nerves and live-wire emotions that no amount of pressure could resolve in the wake of Drew's and my fight.

Across the room, a wardrobe assistant makes last-minute adjustments to my peacock-blue suit, reminiscent of the one I wore to CeeCee's wedding but with black accents and more luxurious fabric.

It makes me think about the twenty-three-year-old I was before, and how he'd be pinching himself over this venue, the star treatment, and the distant thrum of the anticipatory crowd. But right now, even with the edits I made to the jokes, this means nothing. I feel hollowed out.

"This is why I told you not to get involved with him," Jessalynn scolds again with so much I-told-you-so energy I could scream. "Anti-love on stage, anti-love off. It's easier that way, darling. He hurt you once before. It was obvious he would do it again."

I don't have the energy to tell them how wrong they are. Drew never hurt me. Sure, the sight of him leaving the hotel room crushed every bone in my body, but I deserved that. I made a choice. I paid the consequences.

Here, now, those consequences have expanded, unfolded into a life so unrecognizable that I could almost imagine I was an actor in a movie. I wish I were because then I'd have more objective perspective. I could see a way out that the protagonist couldn't.

But I can't. I'm stuck. I'm alone. That's that.

"You're right," I say, because maybe it was obvious. Just not in the way Jessalynn thinks.

Drew said it from the beginning. Our time together wasn't about rekindling a flame. It was about returning me to the proper timeline. We had a mission. Feelings and kisses and sex clouded that mission, but it still had an end goal.

Admittedly, I thought the bond we'd fused this time around would be strong enough to withstand one setback, but it wasn't a minor one.

Maybe at twenty-three, you're willing to change your entire life for love, but at thirty, you have different priorities.

I wouldn't know. I'm not fully grown up yet. Everyone realized that but me.

"I'm glad you're finally seeing it my way," Jessalynn says, slightly smug.

More than before, I wish I had Jessie the friend back. So I could vent. So I could cry on their shoulder. So I could bomb tonight and it wouldn't crush us both, financially and professionally.

But I'm to blame. You are who you surround yourself with. Jessalynn is a by-product of a different me's bad decisions.

It's unfair that I'm carting around the weight of that different me's life.

"How's it look?" Hanson asks, turning me in to the mirror where the bright bulbs blind me.

"Good. Fine. Thanks," I say, because no matter how many layers of foundation he put on me, the face underneath, filled out and maintained with plastic surgery, is a Halloween mask. Bare or beat, it makes no difference. It's not mine, and I wish I could rip it off.

"Let's get you dressed," says the wardrobe assistant, helping me into a pair of perfectly tailored pants. Someone else slips on each of my shoes, tying them with surgeon-level attentiveness.

And as I put one arm at a time into the jacket that fits so well and makes my shoulders look broad, I know my transformation is complete.

This is my life now.

It makes me sick.

"I've got to jet, but you're going to be great, darling," Jessalynn says. "I just know it. I'll see you out there." The door glides closed behind them.

Jerome, my nighttime assistant, has been watching the clock, ensuring my hospitality rider is taken care of every few seconds, almost as if he's afraid if he stops working, I'll fire him.

"Can I have the room?" I ask Jerome. "To myself? I, uh, want to warm up in private."

Jerome nervously checks the schedule and then snaps his fingers. Everyone, even those who don't work for me directly, scurries out of the room without a trace. "I can give you twenty, but that's it. Is that all right, Mr. Baker?"

"Yeah, great. Thanks," I say. "Oh, and you can tell the box office to release Mr. Techler's ticket. He won't be coming." The hurt pierces all over again, spiking the image of him walking out of my apartment and out of my life for the second time.

"You've got it," Jerome says, making a note.

"And can you ask if my parents picked up their tickets yet? I haven't heard from them." I check my phone again, but still no word.

"Absolutely."

When I'm alone, I expect to break down, but find my tear ducts jammed up. I shouldn't ruin my show face anyway. Instead, I grab my laptop from a nearby bag, open my email browser, and begin typing.

CeeCee,

It's all gone to shit.

Drew's and my plan didn't work.

When I saw my name on the dressing room door, I started crying. My manager thought they were happy tears. They were wrong.

I'm lost. Drew's gone. I'm expected to perform for eight hundred people who paid almost two hundred dollars a ticket to see me be funny.

I don't feel funny.

Truthfully, I feel like I may never laugh again.

And I know it's wrong to say this, but I wish I could hug you. I wish I could tell you I'm sorry to your face so you know I mean it. I wish we could be siblings again. For real this time. Because I love you. I know I didn't show it.

But I do and I always will.

In this timeline. In the last. In the next.

There's a knock at the door.

"Come in."

Jerome pokes his head in. "The box office says none of the held tickets for Baker were picked up tonight."

"None?" I ask. That's not like Mom to leave someone hanging without a lengthy voicemail explaining why and apologizing profusely. "Not even one?"

"No, sorry, Mr. Baker," he says. "The stage manager should be by shortly to give you your ten-minute call. The theater is filling up quickly."

My chest tightens. "Okay. Thanks for checking."

There are a million buzzing thoughts clogging up my brain. I can't imagine what could be keeping her and Dad. I send my email to CeeCee and then, with shaking hands, I tap into Mom's contact.

It rings and rings and rings and then...

Chapter Thirty-Five

"Your father had a fall" was all Mom needed to say before I was escaping the theater, still in my show suit, hopping back into the limo and instructing the driver to take me to New Jersey, leaving behind the noisy theater and an even noisier life.

Now I sit in a scratchy, uncomfortable chair in the hospital waiting room, which is its own kind of noisy. Phone calls. Rolling wheels. Clipboards clanging into holders. Nurses chatting by their station.

I drown them all out and try praying to a god I don't believe in while wondering how, in the intervening years, no one has thought to redesign hospitals so they aren't the dingiest, most depressing places possible.

I would use my phone as a distraction for the sudden flooding of unwelcome thoughts, but I've shut it off. I know I've left behind a PR nightmare. Ticket refunds. Crew payments. An angry streamer. An angrier manager. This must be a breach of contract, and I've certainly blown the chance of a lifetime, but what does that matter when my family needs me? What does that matter when I'm finally showing up for the right reasons?

When Mom appears from around the corner, wringing her hands, wearing a lovely black dress that she saves for special occasions, I stand and rush to her. Holding her tight, I ask, "Are you okay? How's Dad?"

"He's stable." She motions for me to walk beside her as she charts a course toward the vending machines, fishing for cash in her purse.

"Allow me," I say, handing her some of my own, which might as well be Monopoly money.

Pulling a pair of readers from her bag, she cranes her neck closer to the smudgy glass, inspecting her choices. No one gets between Dana and her candy, so I let her make her decision before pressing her for answers. I've been in the dark over so much in the last seven weeks. What are a few more minutes in the scheme of things?

She tears into a bag of peanut butter M&M's with her teeth before handing me the Sour Patch Kids. My absolute favorite. It's warming that she remembered, even if they feel too relatable right now: sour, sweet, and too far gone.

"Dad's going to need surgery. He's fractured his hip."

"Jesus, how did this happen?" I ask when the puckering sourness of the candy passes.

She takes a sharp inhale. "One of the medications he's on has side effects, and he tried to get up too quickly without the home care aide…" Her hands fly up, as if she's at a loss. "I was already on the train. I had to get off at the next stop and take a taxi here. My car is still at the train station."

My mind gets stuck on three words: "Home care aide?"

Shaking out some more M&M's into her palm, she says, "CeeCee convinced me. The Alzheimer's dementia has only progressed."

This news causes me to rock back on my heels. It seizes my chest. "What?" I never thought his occasional memory loss would evolve like this.

He's Dad. Stoic. Stable. A builder. There's no way a disease like Alzheimer's could take someone so strong without warning. Though maybe the depression was a huge warning nobody was properly paying attention to. Ever since the jump, my hindsight has sharpened well past twenty-twenty.

"I'm not a professional," Mom says, "so I can only handle so much, can only make him so comfortable. Love does not reverse the clock."

Neither can crystals, apparently.

"It was a good fix for a while. I fought CeeCee's original plan to consider a memory care facility because I wanted to keep him home where he's comfortable, but this fall proves that's not an option anymore," she says. Sorrow causes her words to take on a breathless quality.

"Why didn't you tell me?" I ask, even though I can think of at least two reasons. One, ever since I was little, Mom was a grade-A worrier. Helicopter parent of the highest order. But she never, not once, let CeeCee and me worry about her or Dad. That often meant keeping us in the dark about what went on when grown-ups talked after bedtime. Two, even if I'm missing seven years of memory, it's clear I've been MIA when it comes to my family. I no longer hold a stake in their lives.

"You had a special to worry about. We were managing okay. He goes through bouts, and this is a bad one. There was a long wait list for any of the good memory care facilities and a deposit needed," she says. It's unspoken that the deposit is pricey. An expense that would impose a burden on them. "It was hard at first, finding the inner peace to let go a little, bringing him to adult day care so I could get a break. Then it was hiring the nurse. Now I have to accept that this is moving into late-stage." I realize the therapy she mentioned when I visited wasn't just for overcoming the way I chipped myself off the family block for good. It was for making peace with Dad's illness. CeeCee's distance. Learning how to be independent again.

That beautiful garden I saw her tending to was perhaps a project, a place to put the energy she used to give to parenting and being a loving, supportive spouse. That's not to say that Dad's gone; he's obviously not. He's down the hall being looked over by a team of top professionals. But she can't be everything for everybody anymore.

Is that my problem? Trying to be someone for everyone except *the one* for the people that matter?

"This is life now. The house has been so quiet and still when he's not in it. Even on his bad days, your father always makes me laugh. I think that's why I was so overcome when I saw you the other day."

It clicks. "And when I asked where Dad was…"

Guilt creeps across her expression. "He'd been having good days. I didn't want to worry you, and I didn't want to spoil the surprise of you showing up." The M&M's bag crinkles in her fist. "I wanted to pretend for a little while. I hope you can understand that."

Instantly, I do. I've been pretending this whole time. I know how easy it can be to slip into a role you didn't expect to be playing.

I hug her again while nodding, letting her know without words that whatever happened in the past, I'm here for her now. Nothing is going to tear me away. "Can I go in and see him?"

"He's resting, but I'm sure he'd like that," she says, walking me over to the room.

Just as we arrive, a doctor comes out. He talks us through a lot of incomprehensible jargon, runs down some vitals, and mentions they've scheduled Dad's surgery for the morning—details about rods and screws and incisions that make me light-headed just thinking about them.

He tells us he has high hopes for recovery and then rushes off to his next patient.

"Why don't you go get some rest?" I suggest when Mom tries to follow me in. "Grab your car from the train, and go home to get in bed. Sleep will help."

She shakes her head. "I can't leave him here overnight like this."

Inside, I pause, taking in the sight of Dad in a hospital bed, hooked up to machines, mouth slightly open, tubes escaping his nostrils. He's nearly unrecognizable. Time and disease have reshaped him. This can't be the same man who taught me the difference between model railroad scales and helped me with my math homework. Who quietly believed in my comedy dreams as hard as I did.

"I'll stay with him. You heard the doctor. You've done everything you can," I assure her. "I'll stay."

Mom's eyes take on a grateful glow. "Are you certain?"

"Yes," I say, both because I know she needs the break and because I'd like to be alone with Dad for a while. After tonight, I know if I go back to the apartment, people will be waiting for me. If I turn my phone back on, Jessalynn will be in my inbox or at the hospital in an instant. At least now, away from my reputation, surrounded by IV bags and paper gowns, I can make believe I'm the Nolan I am inside.

Mom gives me a kiss on the cheek. "Thank you, sweet boy." Then she goes.

I set down the Sour Patch Kids and pull up a chair beside his bed. "Hey, Dad." I keep my voice low, as not to wake him up. "It's been a while. Gosh, I don't even know where to start." The air is stale with antiseptic mixed with fragrant get-well-soon flowers. When I look at the card stuck on a plastic stem, it reads: *See you soon, Dad. Love you.—CeeCee, James, and Imogen*

So they're coming. Last night, I thought I wouldn't have to face CeeCee until I was back in my true timeline, but now I'm stuck, and I'm going to have to talk with her here. She won't even return my emails or pick up my calls.

There's a stirring from the bed, and I remember that my long-standing feud with CeeCee is the least of my worries. I have to be here for my parents right now. No running away. No dodging the situation.

Dad's eyes flutter open, heavy with sedation. A wrinkle forms between his brows.

I'm arrested by his hazel eyes that match mine. It's like looking in a mirror, one that Doop might've made, that shows my future. A more distant one than the one I'm inhabiting now. "Hey, uh, hi. It's Nolan."

Recognition doesn't come. Neither do words. I should've been prepared for that. *Late-stage.* I may not have known with any certainty what Mom meant, but it's well-defined now.

I skootch my chair closer to the bed, place my hand near his, and, using the voice he used when he'd read me bedtime stories in childhood, I say, "You're never going to believe what's happened to me."

Chapter Thirty-Six

I'm stirred awake by the door banging open.

I sit up straight in the rigid chair and try to gain my bearings. Where am I again? Oh, right. The hospital. Dad's across the way, and as I rub the sleep from my eyes, there's the blurry outline of a nurse on the far side of the bed.

No, not a nurse.

Dark-brown hair. Medium height. Deep-set glower pointed right at me.

CeeCee.

My heart pounds as I take her in. She looks just as I expected except more world-weary.

Gone are the Doop-approved outfits. She's a mini-Mom, dressed in beige pants and a flowy top. She even carries a Coach tote bag in a fake leopard print—the kind of purse that oozes New Jersey even though she's just flown in from Colorado.

I can't believe she made it here so fast. They must've taken a nonstop red-eye, which would explain her droopy eyes and the slump of her shoulders.

"Morning," I say, just as she says, "What are you doing here?"

Before I can answer the first question, she asks a second: "Where's Mom?"

I know I shouldn't be surprised by the third degree, but it burns all the same. The way she's regarding me it's obvious that what she said out on the garden terrace at her wedding was true. She's kept that grudge going for far longer than I would've hoped.

"I told her to go home and get some sleep so she could be rested for today," I inform CeeCee. "I knew she wasn't going to want to leave his side after the surgery, so I offered to stay the night."

"So much good that did. You were asleep," she huffs, jerking her oversized bag higher up her shoulder.

"He was asleep too," I point out, but not in a nasty way.

Her hands shoot up like an electric shock has just gone through her. "Sorry, we took a really late flight, Imogen was sleep deprived, and it was a nightmare, and now I'm here and *you're* here, so this is all feeling a bit like *The Twilight Zone.*"

"In more ways than one," I say, reminded again of my unfortunate situation. Not only am I stuck here, but I'm overwhelmed by this new development.

She squints at me. "What?"

"Have you…have you been getting my emails?" I know it's a long shot, but there is a fraction of hope left inside me. The hope that whispers, *Dad will be okay,* and *CeeCee will have answers.*

Exasperation bursts from her immediately. "Our dad is about to go under for hip surgery and you're asking me about emails? No, Nolan, I filtered out your many addresses years ago. Have you even spoken to a doctor this morning?"

I'm disappointed and uncomfortable. She hasn't read my emails, which means she knows nothing about my situation. The whispering hope inside me promptly shuts up. I check my watch, attempting not to anger her any further. "There was a nurse in here about an hour ago. She said they'd start prepping him around nine."

"Okay, well, it's eight thirty now. Where are they?" She's moving back toward the door with clear intent. "I'm going to go talk to somebody about this."

"Eight thirty is not nine," I say, standing, pulling my loosened tie from around my neck and stuffing it into my pocket. A physical reminder of where I should've been last night. If I were the true thirty-year-old me, I might be waking up hungover beside Harry right about now. I cringe at the thought.

CeeCee turns up her nose at me. "You've been on a hiatus from this family for God knows how long, so please don't come in here and start talking to me like you know anything, okay?"

I reconsider my words. They were flippant. "You're right. I'm sorry," I say to her back as she's barreling toward the door.

She stops in her tracks, absorbs what I've said, nods to herself, and then exits.

Mom arrives about an hour later, holding hands with a little girl I only recognize from the photos she showed me.

Imogen is the spitting image of CeeCee, who hasn't come back yet, and it's even more apparent up close. Her thick hair curls subtly at the end and is parted to the left. She has round cheeks and a big smile. She also shares CeeCee's affinity for muted colors with bold patterns, judging by her salmon T-shirt paired with polka-dot leggings.

As soon as Imogen spots Dad in the bed, she freezes, half-moon eyes going full. "Why ith Gram-puh like that?" She points ineloquently across the way, except before she gets a suitable response, she snaps her head in my direction, noticing me for the first time. My breath catches. Suddenly, she's real to me, and I'm real to her, and it's too mind-boggling to make sense of.

Imogen skitters behind Mom's leg, using Mom's dangling purse as a shield. "And, and, and who ith that?" She's got a slight lisp like CeeCee used to before she went to speech therapy in the second grade.

"That's your Uncle Nolan," Mom says with a smile.

Uncle. The word chills me. Not because I never thought I'd be one, but because in this timeline, I've been one for almost four whole years and this is the first time I'm even sharing the same space with my niece.

Surely a tour of mine stopped in Colorado, or at least passed through. Couldn't I have visited? Perhaps a meeting or two would've quelled some of the fear Imogen is experiencing right now at the stranger sitting next to her *Gram-puh.*

But maybe CeeCee told me to stay away. Maybe I self-isolated from them for reasons beyond me. I'm not sure which is worse, honestly.

"I have an uncle?" she asks, so much inquisitiveness packed into such a tiny body. She looks up at Mom with a sense of wonder I haven't experienced in ages. It's the first time it clicks that Mom is *Gram-muh* now too.

Mom nods. "Indeed you do, and here he is. Say hi. Can you say hi?"

Imogen offers the smallest, floppiest wave imaginable, so I offer the same kind back, which makes her giggle. We find ourselves in a waving war until there's a groan from the bed. Dad adjusts but doesn't open his eyes, and for some reason, I can sense all three of us holding our breath, watching, waiting.

Then, CeeCee enters in a tizzy. "They're coming in now to start the prep…"

Dad's gone still again, pulled back into slumber.

"I have an uncle!" Imogen shouts excitedly as James enters the room. He's gotten a bit stouter, eyes a little more sunken, and hair-line a little farther north of his forehead. He looks like most of my friends' dads from grammar school. Still handsome in a little-league-baseball-coach kind of way.

"That's great, sweetie," James says, as if I'm the class pet she brought home to take care of for the weekend. He throws me a long-time, no-see head nod.

CeeCee, unsurprisingly, seems displeased by her daughter's revelation.

She's clearly unhappy about our meeting. I wish I could talk to CeeCee about this, but it's a terrible time, and despite my emails, I still don't know exactly what to say to her face-to-face. We're practically strangers who share parents.

"They're about ready to move him. We should wish him luck now," she says.

Dad's eyes open, but we can all tell he's still out of it. One by one, we wish him luck, kiss his hand. He doesn't react, really. At least not perceptibly. But I can see something in his eyes as they land on me, and I say, "See you on the other side, Dad."

He'll be just fine. I don't know how I'm sure of it, but I am.

Being famous has its perks.

I get us a private family waiting room with all the amenities, including a small office off to the side with a desk. As soon as we learn that Dad's surgery is underway, I step inside and turn my phone on—nervous beyond measure.

A billion notifications pile up on the screen, and a billion more conflicting feelings pile up in my gut.

Nolan Baker Skips Special Taping Then Drops Off the Grid: Is This the End of His Comedy Reign?

I might've been around for its inception, but I never ruled, so the baiting, sensational headline barely gets a rise out of me.

Ignoring the texts and emails about that, though checking hopefully for word from Drew (none), I glide my thumb over to the contacts and call Antoni.

"Cancel everything else I have scheduled for the week," I say. "Something's come up."

"Jessalynn isn't going to like that," he says apprehensively.

"It's a family emergency," I clarify. The line goes quiet. "Did you hear me?"

"Yes, it's just… You don't see your family. Did you get kidnapped and you're being held hostage? Do I need to call the FBI?"

"No, don't be ridiculous. I'm serious. Tell them, please?"

"But the special…"

Losing the opportunity of a lifetime doesn't wallop me in any way. I have too much else to worry about. "Tell them."

"They're really angry…"

"Tell. Them."

"Sure thing. Send my best," he says before hanging up.

And three, two, one…

Bringgg. Jessalynn's contact comes roaring up on my phone screen.

"Okay, I came around on the book event. I even agreed to the set changes, but I draw the line at screwing up the biggest opportunity you've ever been given," they spit out in rapid-fire fashion.

"I don't care about the special," I say with resolve. The true twenty-three-year-old inside me would yell blasphemy if he heard me saying those words, but in this moment, it's true. I should've never let anything come between me and my family.

"Mm-hmm. Mm-hmm. The special we worked for years to get under the exact right conditions that would please Your Highness?" they ask with a dollop of sarcasm on top. "Please, tell me again how you don't care about the special."

"Right now," I say evenly, "I don't care about the special. My family needs me."

"Do you know how much shit we're in? Do you know how furious the theater is? Do you know how much *money* we lost?"

"Take it up with my *business manager* or whatever," I tell them.

"We are so done. Do you hear me? Done! Finished!"

I hang up.

I'm overrun with missing Jessie, the twenty-four-year-old who made a mean cosmo, flirted with everyone, and supported me even in my lowest moments. I don't think the Jessie I knew would approve of how we ended up either, and it pains me that I'll never know for sure.

When I turn back, I find a mini eavesdropper and a grown-up eavesdropper in the doorway. I hadn't heard it open over Jessalynn's shouting. They wear matching confused expressions and near matching shirts. This is what happens when the American Girl Doll generation is allowed to have children.

CeeCee clears her throat, pretending not to have overheard, but it's abundantly obvious she has. "I came to tell you that we're going to get lunch down in the cafeteria." There's no invitation in that statement, so I take it that I'm not included.

I nod. "Okay, I'll stay behind in case there are any updates. I'm not hungry anyway." It's a lie. The only thing I've had all day is a pudding cup I snatched from a leftover tray outside a room, which felt felonious, but the pudding hit the spot, so I didn't care.

Imogen asks, "Who were you talking to?"

"My boss," I say. "Well, not exactly my boss. I'm kind of *their* boss. It's complicated."

She nods thoughtfully, the way children do. "You thounded bothy, tho it maketh more thense if you're the both." CeeCee snorts at this.

"Fair point," I concede.

She seems undisturbed by the stench of sickness and the sounds of far-off beeping machines. If I was a three-year-old in a hospital, I'd have probably begged to go home by now. "What job do you have?" she asks, lacing her fingers through her mom's nearby hand.

"I'm a comedian."

"Whath that?"

"I tell jokes."

"Oh," she says, thinking for a second. "I gueth I'm a comedian too." CeeCee snorts again, slightly kinder this time, and I swear a hint of a smile inches onto her face.

"Oh yeah?" I ask. "What kind of jokes do you tell?"

"Knock, knock joketh mothly." She says this very earnestly. I wonder if that's how I looked in my late teens and early twenties when I talked about comedy: all stern and focused and demanding other people see me as such.

"Can you tell me one?" I ask Imogen.

She looks up at CeeCee for approval, which she gives, along with the first genuine smile I've seen from her all day. I wonder if CeeCee notices that I'm trying extra hard to make a good impression with Imogen, to show her that no matter what went down between us in the last seven years, I'm not the asshole she remembers. Maybe she gathered a morsel of that from the phone conversation she over-heard. I would ask, but it's still a terrible, uncertain time to dredge that up.

"Knock, knock," Imogen says, rapping her tiny knuckle on my leg.

"Who's there?"

"Shore."

"Shore who?"

"Shore hope you like knock, knock joketh!" she cries, letting on that maybe she doesn't entirely get it, but she heard it somewhere and now it's embellished on her brain.

"That's a pretty good one," I say with an unaffected laugh because, heck, the kid's got good delivery.

"Mom," Imogen says, tugging on CeeCee's hand, "I'm going to be a comedian when I grow up like Uncle Nolan."

"Let's not get ahead of ourselves," CeeCee says before they turn to go, leaving me behind.

Chapter Thirty-Seven

Through all of this, I get good at a skill I never thought I'd have: waiting.

So good, in fact, that if I wasn't a formerly beloved, currently disgraced stand-up in this timeline, I'd entertain a career change into one of those professional line-sitters you pay to get you *Saturday Night Live* tickets or Broadway tickets or whatever other kind of tickets are hard to come by but rich people want anyway for the *experience.*

The opportunities to practice are plentiful.

Waiting for Mom, CeeCee, James, and Imogen to come back from the cafeteria. Waiting for the surgeon to tell us all went well and Dad will be moved from the PACU back to his standard room in a few hours. Waiting for Dad to be discharged in a few days (fingers crossed).

And, finally, waiting for Drew to send a message of any kind, but that's a private sort of waiting meant only for me.

Tonight, I sit in my dad's old shed surrounded by disused model trains in front of a ring light with my phone on it. My finger hovers over the "live" button on this hot, new social media app I've never used. I'm about to broadcast an apology to two point six million people for vanishing without a trace, and the pressure is on.

I'm ignoring the advice of my PR team and everyone else trying to tell me to lie low until the frenzy blows over and we can reschedule. The last thing I want to do is reschedule.

In the front-facing camera, I look ghostly—sheet-white and sleep deprived—but I'm ready to make a statement, so I begin.

"Hey, Baked Goods," I say into the camera once the red light blinks on and the followers start pouring in. The comment feed is split—half hearts and kind messages of support and half mean names and thumbs-down emojis. "I know many of you are disappointed over the cancellation of my Netflix stand-up special. Anyone who purchased tickets to the in-person taping is eligible to receive a full refund from their point of purchase. I wish I could say hang on to them for when we can announce a new date but…"

I start getting choked up over how real this is. How there are hundreds of thousands of people on the other end of this live stream who adore the mean-spirited celebrity I became. Hopefully one day I can have this kind of platform again for the right reasons and use it for good.

"I'm struggling," I admit to the faceless audience that is listening to my words from all over the world. "Without going into too much detail, I'm facing a really hard struggle alongside a family member who needs me now more than ever."

A couple of awful comments roll in:

Don't tell me your helicopter mom is helicoptering on your ass again!

I bet it's your naggy sister! Tell her to piss off and do the show anyway!

I block those posters, but I'm not fast enough to click away the others.

Is that ginger dude making you quit or something?!

This relationship between me and my fans may be parasocial, but I'm starting to see that it's parasitic as well. Maybe they wouldn't have approved of my friendlier material after all. I would've gone out onstage, bombed in front of the Netflix camera crew, and ended up disgraced anyway.

Regardless, I refuse to feed these negativity leeches any longer.

"Look, if you have nothing kind or productive to say in the comments, please refrain from posting," I say as levelheadedly as I can. "I spent many years spewing lies about the people I loved because I had convinced myself that they had rejected me. I somehow thought if I could reject them more loudly and more publicly, then I would win. But that's…not how life works. There's no winning. There's no losing. There's just trying your best to play the game."

More comments:

Are you trying to tell us you're going to host a game show? Such a fucking sellout.

Stop toying with us! Tell us jokes!

I take a deep breath, honing in on my last shreds of patience. "Right now, life doesn't feel very funny, and if I can't find the humor, then I can't make you laugh. And if I can't make you laugh, then I can't be a comedian. So, I'm sorry, but this is it for now. Wishing you all love and joy."

I sign off, blink back abrupt tears, and let out a sigh of relief.

At least that's dealt with. Partially.

Once I've composed myself, I go and chill out on my parents' back patio, listening to the wind rustling through the trees of my childhood, to the ripple of water in the open pool, and the grill cover as it flaps against metal. I rock back in my chair, sinking my weight into the cushion I brought out with me, and look up at the night sky.

"What's up there?" I ask myself. Stars and planets and the sun and the moon, sure, but are there portals and other universes too? After all this time, a concrete answer would still put to bed some of my unease.

But any concrete answers are hard to find when you're sharing your childhood home with your sister who hates you, her husband who barely knows you, and your niece who can't yet comprehend the complicated dynamics of adulthood.

Neither can I, honestly. I'm twenty-three. Maybe that's why Imogen is the only one I've had more than a ten-minute conversation with since we all started cohabitating.

It only made sense. The house is close to the hospital, free, and can fit all of us. I suggested I get a hotel nearby, but Mom wouldn't hear of it. "Family needs to stick together right now," she'd said, and we all adhered and adapted.

That's how CeeCee and James end up sleeping in Mom and Dad's room (Mom having requested a roll-away cot at the hospital to stay by Dad's side), Imogen in CeeCee's old room, and me sleeping in the double bed that was a perfect, makeshift trampoline for jumping contests between CeeCee and me in elementary school. The double bed that cradled me during my first struggles with insomnia in high school. Drew and I shared that bed during sleepovers, careful to leave a pillow barrier between us lest our wandering limbs touch in the night, which is so silly to think about now that our limbs have been entangled on more than one occasion.

That mattress might as well be memory foam because it's chock-full of memories that encroach on me in the dark.

That's why I'm out here, avoiding that room like the plague, hoping an email comes through from the care center or a text or call comes through from Mom or Drew. Anything to distract my mind from my current state, the seven-year gap in my memory that might last forever now, and the permanent memory loss Dad is suffering through. The disease that means he may never know me fully again.

I may never know me fully again.

The sliding glass door whooshes open behind me, sending a chill of air-conditioning out into the slightly muggy spring air.

CeeCee joins me. She's wearing sleep shorts and her hair is up in a messy bun. A mug with our old high school mascot—the badger—on it is in her left hand.

"A little hot tonight for tea," I say.

"I put ice cubes in it," she says. I raise an eyebrow at her in the hazy glow of the only light that's affixed beside the door. "What? We didn't have any iced tea, and it would be wine, but." She sips, almost as if she's said something she shouldn't have.

Which leads me to the only logical conclusion: "You're pregnant again." I don't know where the assumption comes from. Maybe a nugget of our sibling telepathy is still intact. "Wait, does Mom know?"

"Yeah, great idea for me to spring that on her in the same call where she tells me Dad's fallen and probably needs surgery. She'd be in the hospital right now too if I did that. I was planning to tell her the night of your special taping, to counteract whatever... You know what? Never mind. That's not why I came out here."

I wonder about that. How she planned to tell Mom and Dad on the night of my taping, but I can tell she has something more important on her mind. This is the first time we've been alone together since she arrived, and I don't want to risk her running away by asking the wrong question.

"Why'd you come out here then?" I ask instead, nervous about her answer.

She takes a long sip. "Because I saw your live stream. Then I found your emails, and I read them."

"From your tone, I take it you don't believe me." Just like Drew, she has every reason to assume I'm pulling a fast one on her for a laugh. I wish that wasn't my reputation, but it is. I know now I can't just edit that. Every person is a calculated amalgamation of their past, present, and future. You can't lop one off because you don't like it.

Her head falls to the left, hair swishing slightly in her face. "Not true. I don't have a choice but to believe you."

"Because you're my sister," I fill in for her, half-joking, half-surprised.

"No, dumbass," she retorts with an offhanded laugh that's not as mean as I assumed it'd be. "Because I had an inkling everything was fishy when Doop immediately agreed to use my wedding as a marketing campaign."

"How did that even come about?" I ask, realizing that instead of having a conversation with her at the time, I simply wrote it off as another blessing for the always-perfect firstborn. Mom and Dad didn't have to foot the bill. It piggybacked off a promotion. The golden girl became even shinier with a gold band on her finger.

CeeCee sets her cup down on the table between us, hugs one knee to her chest, and sighs. "I was drowning when I got that marketing position. The rapid expansion of the company mixed with the heavy pressure to perform started to mess with me." It's eerie how much this sounds like what I was going through with my comedy dreams. "James surprised me with a weekend getaway to upstate New York where he proposed at this beautiful winery. I was so swept up in excitement that I forgot I had a major presentation to give on Monday. It wasn't until I was in the meeting room, sweating my makeup off, that I remembered. As soon as my boss, Kerry, asked me to start, I looked down at my engagement ring and offered them the first idea that came to mind."

"Shit," I mutter.

"They loved the angle of selling the fairy tale. That if you used Doop products and subscribed to the Doop lifestyle, you too could find love and have a lavish wedding," she says. "James was…less than thrilled."

"I didn't know any of that." My heart lurches as it dawns on me that perhaps I didn't *want* to know any of that.

"Maybe because you never asked." Her eyebrows raise accusatorily. "We made it work, but the closer we got to the day, the more secretive the Doop team became. Everything was being run by me at first, and then suddenly, the flower arrangements had changed, then the signature drink and the bridesmaid dresses, and I realized I'd effectively given over my wedding in exchange for a raise that was making me pull my hair out. Thank God for extensions," she says. I thought her wedding hairstyle was a choice, but maybe it was thrust upon her by the Doop team.

"Why didn't you stop it or say no?" I ask. High school CeeCee was outspoken, dance team cocaptain, and a real go-getter. She wasn't the kind of person who would let a business walk all over her. What changed for her in college that led her to be amenable in the face of dissatisfaction?

"Because my job was hanging in the balance and, uh, you've met our parents," she says with a shake of her head that says *duh*.

"Yeah," I snort out. "The parents who harp on me and treat you like you're the winner of the womb. The perfect first try while I came out the half-baked second act." My cheeks burn with that admission.

CeeCee's stunned eyes peek over the top of her mug, which has paused halfway to her lips. "Is that seriously what you think?"

"It's been obvious for forever, yeah." I wish I didn't sound so bratty about it, but I've been holding on to the feeling since high school. It's like the memory of my teenage self supersedes the twenty-three-year-old inside, contorting the voice of the thirty-year-old me, until I'm trembling and confused.

She slowly shakes her head at me. "You think Mom and Dad's helicopter parenting was exclusive to you? That's cute. I was the trailblazer kid, the trial-and-error baby."

"That seems like an exaggeration."

"Oh, yeah?" She folds her arm across her chest. "Then why is it when I went through the guest room and shimmied down the storm pipe into the back garden to sneak out to see my high school boyfriend, I got grounded on the third try and banned from going to Jessica Miller's sweet sixteen, but when you did the same thing two years later to meet Drew, Mom and Dad fully knew and said nothing?"

"Oh, come on…" I say, losing a bit of my fight.

"Or how about when I told Mom and Dad I wanted to go to college to study dance, and I was met with an immediate no?" she says. Of course I remember her being the cocaptain of the dance team in high school, but I always thought it was a hobby she only picked up because her friends were doing it.

"I didn't realize." I worry my bottom lip, combing back through my memories, guilty that I may have perceived everything all wrong.

"Probably because by the time you came out and befriended Drew, you relegated me to the sidelines of your life," she says, almost as if she's rehearsed that exact line. It's not lost on me that CeeCee is speaking of the Nolan I was, not the Nolan I became. Those actions she's referring to are *my* actions from *my* timeline. Maybe this version of me isn't as far off from who I was as I originally thought. "And I don't blame you for that. I went away to school. I met new people. But I was your first best friend, Nolan, and Mom and Dad's first kid. It hurt knowing that you were pouring all your friendship into Drew and Mom and Dad were pouring all their parental concern into you."

All this time I thought Mom, Dad, and CeeCee were a three-ring circus of stability and I was the sad boy left outside without a ticket, but it turns out CeeCee also felt that way. Perhaps because I carried myself like the ringleader, convinced myself I was a showman, she was able to believe it.

"I guess I always thought you were the perfect child in their eyes. That everything I did was always being put up against your accomplishments," I say. I was too loud and too focused on myself to see it differently.

"Mom depended on me," CeeCee confesses, sighing heavily. "First by confiding in me about Dad's depression, and then by asking for help getting *him* the help he needed."

"What do you mean by that?"

"When I graduated, I took on this silent burden. Mom and Dad poured a lot of money into my tuition, which I appreciated, but that money, well, they needed it too. Mom's health insurance was kind of shitty, so I pushed myself to get the highest-paying full-time job I could in the shortest amount of time possible so I could help her," she says.

"So you didn't seek out Doop?" I ask, shocked and not trying to cover it up.

She snorts. "No. Not even close."

"I just assumed since you seemed so... *in it*." She spread the good word of Doop like her life depended on it.

"That was part of the job. Selling the brand, living the lifestyle," she says. "Having everybody fooled was how I knew I was good at it. How I knew I'd be able to rise through the ranks—while there were still ranks to rise through, anyway."

In hindsight, it seems so obvious. CeeCee never had an affinity for meditation or twelve-step skin-care routines. What I perceived as willful change was necessity.

She continues. "Mom was adamant we didn't tell you. 'He can't handle this stuff. Not like you,' she'd say. For a while, it felt like I was an only child, having to keep that from you, even when we'd both moved out. It weighed on me, and I took it out on you without ever explaining."

"I never really gave you the chance to, did I?" My breathing becomes labored.

CeeCee shakes her head, crossing to the railing and looking out on the yard. When she turns back, she's got one palm pressed to her belly and the shimmer of tears rimming her eyes. "I don't want them to end up like us. Imogen and the little one in here."

"Me neither," I say, because even though I don't know exactly what got us here, I was there for the decision that catalyzed it all. And if I'm stuck here like I think I am, this is the only relationship with CeeCee I'll ever know. There's no undoing what's been done.

"Imogen asked constantly about when she'd have a sibling, and every time she did, with those big, wise-beyond-her-years eyes, I thought of you and how you'd hurt me, and how I never wanted her to experience something like that," she says, trailing off for a moment. "Though, I guess, it wasn't *you*, was it? If what you said in the emails is true?"

"No, it wasn't me." I'm adamant about that, even if remorse bites at me.

"It started with a scar cream," she says, abruptly changing subjects. Maybe because the tears subsided. Maybe because she realized what she wants to say can only be said to the thirty-year-old me. At times, I wish I was him. For real. Things would be so much easier. I'd have my memories. I'd have (hopefully) matured. I could take ownership over my actions and properly make amends. All things I'll have to let go of or make exceptions for.

"What did the scar cream do?" I ask.

"Removed scars overnight like some sort of cosmetic miracle elixir," she says, obviously still baffled by it. "When one of my bridesmaids messaged me about it, I said, 'That's the Doop guarantee,' and then left the rest of her messages on read. I didn't know any more than she did."

"Jesus."

"When James and I got back from our honeymoon, I started asking questions at work, and the higher up the ladder I went, the cagier and more cryptic the responses became. When no executive would talk to me, I tried to get access to the Doop lab at the end of the secret hallway with no success. I even attempted to make friends with development associates I knew worked in the lab, but they were under strict orders not to speak about their projects. Company policy or some shit. I watched as everything I was told to want, everything I helped build, crumbled because there was so much going on behind a curtain. Some serious Wizard of Oz–level nonsense."

"What exactly happened?" I ask, riveted.

She runs her tongue along her top front teeth, stuck in some bout of intense thought before she speaks. "The more messages I started getting about the wedding favors, the more I knew it wasn't a fluke. The scar cream had gotten rid of the scar. The Go to Sleep, Bitch candle had put people to sleep. The blue light glasses Drew got really did minimize your blue light exposure by reading your mind. And for some reason, none of it scared me."

"Why not? I'd have been freaked out," I say, heart rate jumping up. "I *am still* freaked out."

"Because I heard they were working on memory-enhancement chews," she says. "They were trying out new cognitive-support dietary supplements, and if I was to believe my wedding guests who had these out-of-body experiences, then these should've been magic too. I stole some…for Dad."

I nod with somber understanding. "Did you get caught?" I ask, leaning in.

"No, or at least I don't think so. If anyone knew, they didn't care because I'd signed an NDA," she says. "They knew I wouldn't snitch. There would be legal consequences if I did."

"Did they work? The chews, I mean?"

"Yeah," she says with faltering certainty. "Maybe? It's possible I was just seeing what I wanted to see, wanting to believe Doop could make Dad better, help him retain his memories. Anything to block out the noise of your jokes and fame and whatever else."

My body tenses knowing that I brought so much extra stress to CeeCee's life by using her as fodder for jokes. I know that once she went off to college, I largely stopped considering her. She became a person outside of me. An adult who had her act together and was constantly making me look bad—or so I thought. If this jump has shown me anything, it's that I didn't need anyone's help looking bad, even back then. I was doing a fine job of that on my own.

"I'm sorry," I choke out.

"It wasn't you, Nolan."

"But leaving your wedding? That *was* me. That's what got us here, what got me into this mess," I say, exasperated. Angry that I could unravel not just my own life, but the lives of those around me with one rash decision.

"Like I learned from those damn memory chews, I don't think you can outrun fate," she says sagely. "Time has a way of serving you everything you deserve—the good and the bad—no matter what you do to change it or stop it."

"Are you saying I should just accept that I'm here now?" I ask, the whiplash of it all causing my neck to crick.

She shrugs. "I'm saying you've already lost seven years. Don't waste another second."

· ✦ ✦ ·

The next day, I call Antoni and have him bring Milkshake to New Jersey.

Imogen's happy screech can be heard around the world when I introduce the two.

"I have an uncle, and now I have a dog!" she shouts. It warms my heart.

Her excitement renews each time Milkshake's tiny paws clack across the hardwood floor toward her. Even in the face of Dad's illness, we all find joy in puppy-Imogen playtime. Squeaky toys thrown and retrieved. Laughs shared by all.

Imogen, curious and precocious, starts keeping a journal of Milkshake's "business" schedule, and I don't mean his boardroom meetings over the necessary frequency of treats. She insists on three walks a day, even in the rain, and while she's not at the level that she can write words just yet, Imogen draws Milkshake's "business" with crayons and construction paper. It would be concerning if it weren't so darn cute.

CeeCee says as much on one of our morning walks—Imogen keeping pace with Milkshake up ahead, studying his waddle and mimicking it to the best of her ability.

"Do you think Imogen likes Milkshake more than she likes me?" I jokingly ask.

"Until you grow a tail and a snout, I think that's a pretty safe bet," CeeCee says before taking a sip of coffee. I was pleasantly surprised when CeeCee took me up on the offer to join us on our first walk of the day, reigniting my hope that maybe we can find a path back to friendship through all of this.

"I hear they have cosmetic surgeries for stuff like that now," I say while chuckling.

"Now that I'd like to see," she says, inadvertently reminding me of the first day I set foot in Drew's shop when he basically called me a dog, angrily pointing at the sign on the door.

I tell CeeCee about that, and to my delight, she listens. She listens so intently that I share all the bits about Drew that I left out of my emails. When I'm done, she offers me gentle, sage advice like she used to.

"You should reach out to him," she says.

"I don't think that's a good idea," I say, half-upset over Drew and half-thrilled that CeeCee and I are spontaneously having a heart-to-heart after all these years of tension and separation.

"Nolan, he loves you," she says with conviction, nails tapping against the side of her thermos.

"I'm not so sure," I say, calling to mind the anger and upset caked across Drew's face when he left that mammoth Upper West Side apartment the morning of Dad's fall. Those weren't the words or expressions of someone in love.

"I am," she says knowingly. "I'm sure for you."

Her words make my brain short-circuit. I want to ask what she means by that, but we're quickly interrupted.

"Uncle Nolan! Uncle Nolan!" Imogen shouts. "Number two time! Number two time!"

"I got it, sweetie," CeeCee says, pulling a small, pink baggie out of her daughter's pocket. For the remainder of the walk, CeeCee listens as Imogen details what kind of dreams she thinks Milkshake has at night, little legs moving in a speedy run to nowhere. I hang back, soaking this in.

By the time we return to the house, I'm left wondering why I ever begrudged CeeCee for acting like a second mom when she was clearly just a naturally nurturing person to begin with. Maybe I was looking for an excuse to justify my unwarranted feelings.

Once Milkshake is settled, I call Jessalynn, and after some futile protesting on their part, I fire them.

"This isn't working for me anymore. I'm sorry," I say, even if I'm really not. "One day, I hope we can move past this and be friends again, but for now, our business relationship has run its course. Thank you for all your work, but I won't be needing your career guidance any longer."

I'd like to say we've left things on good terms, but I know that's not the truth. And I'm only interested in the truth now.

. $\cdot \, {}_{\circ} + \, \blacklozenge \, + \, {}^{\circ} \, \cdot$

Dad's recovery is slow and uncertain, but we've been told the surgery itself went well and they'll need to keep him a little while longer to monitor his progress.

Mom, CeeCee, and I take shifts at the hospital. James works remotely from Dad's old shed in the backyard, careful not to disturb what's left of Dad's model trains, mostly coated in dust or packed away by Mom. We get a table set up in the corner with a monitor, a keyboard, and everything else he needs for the time being.

"Thanks for your help," James says when we're finished.

"No problem," I say. I'm looking forward to getting to know him for real this go-around.

Imogen is missing most of preschool, but it's just shapes and numbers anyway, so we sit her in front of educational TV shows for a few hours and make sure her brain isn't becoming mush in the process.

At night, after family dinner, we play brainteaser games, and if Imogen can't focus, we read books about road trips and dragons and candy factories aloud to her until she falls asleep with Milkshake curled up on his doggy bed, which is never more than a foot away from her.

It becomes a routine, and I forget, at least for a while, that this isn't the life I'm supposed to be living right now. If I had to choose between going back to my career and staying here once Dad gets better, I think I'd choose the latter.

Even in the face of surgery and disease, this time together has been all the proof I needed to know that putting comedy—which I admit was more of an obsession than a pure dream—over my family was wrong.

The only one of us keeping track of the day of the week is Imogen, who, before bed one night, reminds us: "My birthday ith next week."

CeeCee looks stricken. "Oh gosh, you're right, sweetie." Time, yet again, has proven elusive.

"Will we be home in time for my party?" Imogen asks innocently, but her eyes betray her. I think she knows the answer, and I want to comfort her.

"Sweetie, I'm sorry." CeeCee shakes her head. "We'll have to stay here until Grandpa's better. I'll have to call everyone and let them know of the change."

"I can help," I say, stepping up. My days are free now, and I want to be of use.

"Thanks," CeeCee says. "Maybe we can reschedule?"

Imogen isn't enthused by this feeble offer. "It ith okay, Mommy. Can we do thomething here with Gram-puh?"

CeeCee checks the calendar on her phone. "If the doctors are right, he should be home by then. I think that's a great idea." She settles down on the bed beside Imogen, cradling her head close and stroking her hair. I know she wishes she were delivering better news to her daughter.

"Let's plan something together. Would that be cool?" I ask, taking the lead so as not to add any more to CeeCee's plate. "Anything you want."

Imogen's eyes light up at me. "Anything?"

"Absolutely anything," I say, delighting in playing the role of the fun uncle.

"Within reason!" CeeCee interrupts with a laugh before gracing me with a tentative smile and mouthing a genuine *thank you* over Imogen's head.

Chapter Thirty-Eight

Imogen insists her birthday party be comedy themed.

It doubles as a welcome-home party for Dad, so we go all out.

While Dad's far from fully recovered, looking weary as he's rolled into the house in a wheelchair, we're all set to help manage his pain and keep him comfortable until the memory care facility calls, which should be any day now.

Currently, he sits in a hospital bed we've rented and set up in the living room, just enough space for a tray and his bevy of orange medicine bottles. None of them are a cure, but all of them a blessing anyway.

The night nurse sits on the far side, red hair pulled up and away from her round face. That color makes me miss Drew more than I already do, makes me wish he were here to support me through this, which is selfish, I know.

For years, I mistook Drew's seeming stability as a leaning post. I see how unfair that is now. Too little, too late, perhaps. I hope he's okay, and I would reach out to know for sure, but I'm respecting his boundaries.

I wish he'd give me a second (third?) chance to prove that our love, much like my familial love, can flourish in this timeline if we work at it, but I realize that I've been flung into the future and the past is not mine to manipulate.

"Hello, everybody!"

Imogen is standing in the center of the living room, holding an old toy microphone from the plethora of toys I had still stashed in my room, and is wearing a rainbow wig from CeeCee's dress-up box, which we found in the basement. Me, Mom, and CeeCee are squished in on the old couch. James is in the recliner nearby, the one Dad used to occupy every night when the ten o'clock news came on.

Over the last few days, I helped Imogen come up with five minutes of her best knock-knock jokes collected from her friends, her dad, and the internet. While I'm not a proponent of plagiarizing material, I told her, a lot of comedians learn by watching other comics. Much like a painter might recreate a masterwork to examine brushstroke techniques, some stand-ups borrow material in a class setting to work out timing and joke construction. Imogen yawns when I tell her this, and I have to hand it to her, it's the best laugh I've had in a while.

To get the house ready, we find low stools and an adjustable microphone stand on Facebook Marketplace. I string up an old red tablecloth as a curtain between our living room and dining room and get Antoni and Jerome to source us some workable stage lights that give the place a club vibe.

After crafting construction paper tickets and programs done entirely in marker, it is time for the main event.

"Knock, knock," Imogen says into the mic, while wearing a frilly floral dress and a matching headband atop the rainbow wig. She insisted CeeCee help her look show-ready, which included a ridiculous amount of blush that makes her already rosy, freckled cheeks look like fresh-picked strawberries.

"Who's there?" we all call in response. We've got plates of store-bought birthday cake in our laps, cans of soda resting on coasters on the coffee table.

"Who."

"Who *who*?"

"When'd'ja get all thethe owlth?" she shouts, laughing already at her own joke. It's bliss distilled.

Five jokes later, Imogen gets bored and complains the wig is too hot and itchy. I instruct her to take a bow, and everyone except Dad climbs to their feet to give her a standing ovation. Even CeeCee, who seemed mildly annoyed her daughter would want to emulate me of all people, looks misty-eyed. Though I suppose when you're a parent watching the petite human you grew inside yourself do just about anything, you can become misty-eyed.

"What a great warm-up act," Mom says, eyes flicking toward me with anticipation.

"That was the only act in our program," I say, waving the purple paper James was dutifully told to fold and hand out by his daughter as he accepted tickets.

"Well, since your special didn't happen, I was thinking you could do it now. For us." The only person in the room who appears indisputably excited by this is the home care aide, and probably only because this will make a good story later.

"Oh, I don't think so. It's Imogen's day," I say with performance anxiety I don't usually have. Onstage with a mic stand in front of strangers, I can speak freely. Here, even if the jokes aren't at my family's expense, they are infinitely more vulnerable. The lack of a laugh will hit harder.

James says, "I wouldn't mind a good laugh right now."

CeeCee peers at him, first with shock and then with what looks like agreement. She turns to me and offers a full smile. "Get on up there, Nolan," she says encouragingly.

I shake my head. "I don't know." Like I said in my live stream, I don't feel funny right now. Taking the spotlight after Imogen feels like the opposite of what I should be doing.

But then a pair of tiny hands land on top of mine, which are folded in my lap. Two doe eyes stare up at me from beneath a flurry of unkempt bangs. "*Pleathe*, Uncle Nolan. It would be the betht birthday prethent ever."

How can I say no to that face?

I take the microphone, which isn't plugged into anything, don the rainbow wig for confidence, and take a deep breath. There's a charge of anticipation through the room like a heartbeat at rest. Like not just my family is there ready to listen, but so are the walls and the floors and the photos, the furniture and the plumbing.

And as I begin to tell the jokes, it feels…good. I skip the saucier material for everyone's sake, but give them the highlights of the special. Delivering this kinder material to my family means more than doing it wearing a fake smile in front of expensive cameras for millions of people.

Millions of people don't matter. The five people in this room do.

It dawns on me that I spent such a significant portion of my late teens and early twenties trying to outrun this place. I'd convinced myself that stages and clubs and sticky floors and stale beer would provide a better foundation than this town and these people ever could. But I never stopped to consider that without them, this life that I'm stuck in right now would've never been possible.

And at the very least, for that revelation I'm grateful.

. ⁺ ✦ ⁺ ˚

A surprise guest knocks on the door right as we're cleaning up the party.

"Nolan! It's for you," Mom says, which catches me off guard.

When I enter the foyer, still wearing the rainbow wig from earlier and holding a filled-to-the-brim trash bag, I find Drew standing in the doorway, holding a gift bag with balloons all over it, tissue paper spewing out the top, and a second smaller brown paper bag.

My entire body lights up at the sight of him. What Doop product did I use this time to magically materialize him out of the blue? I can't figure out if I'm awed or worried. The erratic pounding of my heart tells me it's a lethal combination of the two.

I'm so stunned that I can't get any words out.

"Hi," Drew says, winded. "Sorry I'm late. By the time I got CeeCee's message, I had to close the store and then the train was delayed. I'm a mess." I notice the stains under his armpits, sweat darkening the lush purple fabric. Even disheveled, he's heart-hammeringly handsome. "I hope I haven't missed it."

CeeCee's message? I turn and catch a glimpse of brown hair and long legs dipping into the kitchen. CeeCee was up to this. I should've known.

I'm sure of it for you, CeeCee had said on our walk. Between visiting Dad, getting him home, squaring things away with the memory care facility, and Imogen's party, I haven't had alone time with CeeCee to ask about it, but maybe now I have my answer. I think back on those emails Drew sent CeeCee during our crystal hunt. I may never know what they said verbatim, but I can almost read the words written across Drew's flushed, half-smiling expression that dazzles in the glow of the dim porch light.

"The birthday girl is in bed, but don't worry, she'll accept belated gifts." I take the bag from him and gesture for him to come in, but quietly.

Dad has finally dozed off into dream world where he can be at peace at least for a few hours before his next round of meds. So as not to disrupt him, I tell Drew to follow me up to my room, which is something I wouldn't have batted an eyelash at before but now— with two quasi-breakups under our belt—feels loaded.

With each creak of the stairs, my heart rate elevates. That fight we had felt so permanent, but he's here, and I still have no idea why, and all I want to do is hug him for eternity and never let him go.

"It's like a museum in here," Drew says, and I realize he's referring to how nothing's changed since our sleepover days.

"An exhibit of who I was," I say somberly, remembering how he told me my present incarnation was completely incompatible with his. Does he still believe that, or is he going to take it back? CeeCee wouldn't have invited him here to break my heart all over again, right? My defenses fly up anyway.

"So…" I say, unable to bear the extended silence.

"I like your hair," he says with the tiniest laugh.

"Oh," I chirp, finally yanking the wig off. "Thanks."

"Can I sit?" Drew asks, nodding toward the desk chair.

"Sure. Go for it," I say, crossing the room and sitting on the bed as far away from him as possible, erroneously thinking that any upsetting words can't hurt me from such a distance.

He sets his bag down on my desk and meets my eyes for the first time since arriving. For the first time in weeks, actually. "I owe you an apology."

"Okay…"

"I'm sorry I left."

"I didn't exactly give you a good reason to stay." In the nights since, I've replayed that morning before falling asleep, and every time I rewatch it, I notice how selfish I sounded.

His head bobbles, maybe in agreement but maybe not. "I owe you an explanation as well."

"I'm listening," I say, uncertain what he could be referring to but open to hearing him out.

"Did I ever tell you about my dad?"

"No," I realize, which is weird considering how long we've

known each other. I'm also unsure what this has to do with that morning and him leaving.

"I'm sure you know that my mom and dad weren't really *together*-together when my mom got pregnant with me, but she gave him the opportunity to be in my life." He pivots his torso in toward me, shoulders back, chest open. I can sense he rehearsed this. "My dad was in a band that was taking off, so he chose the road over me, and at a young age I swore to myself I'd never fall for someone who'd make me feel that way again: choose their career over a relationship. Choose to leave."

"Drew, I didn't realize." There is a wavering quality to his voice that cuts through me. I see how my actions in both timelines triggered that old wound, those latent feelings. Even if I accidentally stepped on an emotional land mine, I should've checked for casualties. The night of CeeCee's wedding, as soon as our fight started, I knew my actions had shifted something in Drew. If I had been looking harder, maybe I would've noticed the same shift the morning after the crystals didn't work. The drinking. The legal pad. My selfishness blinding me to him.

I was the one who was stuck. *I* was the one who asked for help. *I* was the one suddenly changing my tune after turning his current life upside down. I never considered what the fallout meant for him. I resent myself for that.

"I didn't expect you to," he says. "And I know this is shitty timing, but I just wanted you to know because…I should've told you all this instead of leaving the hotel that night. And I should've explained the morning after the crystals didn't work instead of hiding behind the excuses my tipsy, sleep-addled brain spat out. I was panicking, so I blamed you. It took some time, but I realized I was trying so hard not to end up with someone like my dad that I turned into him instead. I'm the one who chose to leave. Twice."

"Hey," I say, taking his closest hand, overcome that he's finally trusted me enough to tell me his truth. "It's okay. I'm not upset with you. And listen, you may have left, but you also did what he couldn't: come back."

Drew's hopeful eyes lift to meet mine. It's like my words have unencumbered him. At least a bit. "You'd take me back?"

I laugh, happier than I have been in weeks. Dad's home. Drew's here. A tingling races up my spine. "You took me back after a version of me told jokes about you all over the country. I know what scared feels like. I'm not going to hold that against you. Drew, I love you too much to do that."

"I love you too." Just hearing those words sparks hope in me that there is a future for us after all. He stretches out his long arm, grabs the brown paper bag from earlier, and hands it to me. In response to my questioning eyes, he says, "Open it."

Inside, I find a picture frame with the photo of Drew and me from the senior prom inside. I hadn't realized he'd kept it. My eyes begin to water.

"After thinking long and hard about my dad, about how I didn't want my past to define me, I realized I would be a hypocrite if I judged you by a past you weren't even fully a part of," he says, which lifts my spirits but brings on more tears. "I saw the articles about you ditching the special taping for your family, and then I watched your live stream…"

I wipe my eyes. "I hope you didn't read some of those awful comments."

"I've got thick skin in this timeline," he says, and I believe him. "Trolls like that can't hurt me, okay?"

"Okay."

He stands from the chair, crosses to the bed, and sits beside me. Close enough to touch. Far enough for me to be able to breathe without breaking into a sob.

"It's that thick skin that reminded me that I wasn't always this way. I changed over time. I grew that thick skin. That doesn't mean I'm not still the shy boy my dad walked out on, the scared, closeted teen you met at fifteen, the out-and-proud high school senior in this photo." He taps the glass above his smiling face with his pointer finger. "The twenty-three-year-old so in love with you that it kept me up some nights. The twenty-six-year-old who became a business owner to live out his dream and prove he wasn't broken."

"Drew..." I whisper. He strokes the back of his hand across my cheek, swiping away a stray tear I didn't even realize had escaped.

"I'm also the thirty-year-old you see now who is irrevocably changed because I knew you again. Exactly as you are. Not trapped, like I thought, but brand-new in this body," he says, cracking a small smile that makes me feel proud. "Maybe that's what Lucille meant by that card reading. It wasn't a real death the grim reaper was signaling. It was your ego that died."

This revelation washes over me alongside relief. He's right. He's also wise. When did he get so damn wise? "I agree. But what does this all mean for us?" It's a vulnerable question that causes my hands to shake.

Drew notices and takes them in his, and even though his are shaking as well, it's better that we're frightened together than frightened alone. "It means that I want you in my life, Nolan. Whether that means trying again to get you back to our past or building our future from this point onward, I'm here for the long haul."

Overwhelmed with love, I squash the space between us, wrapping him in a hug and kissing the side of his head a million times. He smells like sweat and tea tree oil and *him*. I don't even try to hide the fact that I'm inhaling his scent this time. "I love you so much, Drew," I whisper into his ear.

He leans back so our eyes meet, and then he kisses me so deeply I could faint.

When I finally break our kiss and regain my senses, I take a deep breath and say, "Now I guess I just need to figure out if I can live without those seven years or not." The precarious situation sits between us.

"Well, we'll figure it out," Drew says, wrapping an arm around my shoulder and heaving me in to his side. My head slips into the crook of his neck where it belongs, and like always, just his nearness makes my heart rate slow and my thoughts stop racing.

That's until I replay what he just said, *We'll figure it out*.

"We," I whisper into his neck.

"Yeah," he whispers back. "*We*."

Finally, we're a *we*.

Chapter Thirty-Nine

"I helped you with Drew," CeeCee says as we walk through our neighborhood a few days after Imogen's birthday. Imogen and Milkshake are, as usual, trotting a few steps ahead, Imogen blissfully lost in her own little world. "Now I need your help with Mom."

"What with?" I ask, locking Milkshake's retractable leash before he gets too far.

"James and I talked, and we want to move back to New Jersey," she says.

"Oh my God," I yelp, excited by this news. "That's great."

CeeCee nods. "I think so too, but I know Mom is going to push. She's going to say our life is in Colorado. Imogen's school and friends are in Colorado but…" CeeCee tilts her chin toward her daughter. "Aside from when we were at the hospital, I haven't seen her happier. She needs her family. *I* need my family."

"Retweet," I say, shaking my head. I learned that lesson the hard, magical way.

"You know Twitter is barely a thing anymore, right?" CeeCee asks. "God, Drew and I are going to need to give you a crash course in 2030 etiquette. Properly catch you up to the times, you relic."

I laugh, and then return us to the real topic at hand as we cross the street, sun shining down on us. "Whatever you need from me.

I got you." With my career on hold and with Drew standing by me, I feel sort of invincible. I've come to terms with time travel. I could move mountains, probably. "I'm with you," I tell her, squeezing her shoulder.

And she squeezes right back.

. ⁺ ✦ ⁺ .

"I need a change," CeeCee says to Mom the day before they're scheduled to fly back to Colorado. "We're moving back to New Jersey."

It's the speech CeeCee practiced with me in my room the night before, because the truth is that CeeCee knows the loneliness will eat away at Mom. Mom's at her happiest when she has someone to helicopter, and lord knows CeeCee and James will need the help with a second kid on the way.

"I'm comfortable here," CeeCee tells Mom between bites of turkey and cheese on rye. "I want to be able to visit you and Dad whenever I want."

A few days ago, we got Dad settled into his new place at the memory care facility fifteen minutes away. The staff did their best to create a comfortable, safe space for Dad where assistance is never more than a button-push away. We brought his favorite reclining chair, his TV set, and one of his model trains. His memories may be waning, but setting up that train beside CeeCee with Dad's interspersed help is a memory I won't forget. At the first whistle of the train, Dad's face broke out into a wide smile, and I will carry that sight with me forever.

"You can't just pull Imogen from school, from her friends," Mom protests, which CeeCee and I knew she would. "I'll be fine."

"Fine is not good enough for you, Mom," I say. "We're gunning for great and will settle for good."

"I'd like to see Imogen graduate from the same high school I did," CeeCee continues, sounding excited about this new chapter of her life. "Bring both kids to the playland at the rock museum. It's settled."

Mom ultimately relents.

CeeCee, James, and Imogen fly out to Colorado first. Drew and I aren't long to follow.

Drew decided he could use some time off from the shop and knew CeeCee could use an extra pair of hands with the packing. I think, too, now that we're committing to this—each other—fully, he wants to use this time to reconnect with CeeCee as well. They were friends for years after the wedding thanks to my boneheaded public persona. I want that again for them.

Mom stays behind to be close to Dad in case he has trouble adjusting.

By the time Drew and I arrive, the house, a cute two-story, is already on the market. James has gotten approval to work fully remote, CeeCee has been transferred to the New Jersey branch of her company, and they've secured Imogen a spot in a highly coveted preschool. All that's left to do is box up their entire lives. A massive undertaking.

Our world becomes consumed with packing tape, takeout food, and bubble wrap. Not necessarily in that order. And not necessarily in that line of priority either.

Imogen sits for hours popping bubbles. One day, after a lunch of burgers and truffle fries, I ask her what she's doing, and without missing a beat, she says in a complete deadpan, "Helping." I reiterate the story to the entire family but nobody laughs. I can't quite get her delivery down. Damn, I've got a lot to learn from that child.

On the third night, pulled from sleep yet again by Imogen's loud white-noise machine blasting through the wall, I creep out of bed

and downstairs in the dark for a glass of water. Ever since Dad's surgery scare, I haven't gotten much rest.

Unlike the first two nights, I notice a light on in the basement.
The house is old, but doesn't give off distinctly haunted energy, so I
slip on my shoes, which I've left by the front door, and sneak down
to investigate.

The basement is half-finished. One of those projects that surely
got put on the back burner when Imogen arrived—a nursery being
more important than a hangout space. CeeCee stands in a pair of
pink sleep pants and a tank top, hair in a top bun, looking around at
a mess of boxes. It's nothing like the upstairs, where everything was
arranged with perfect precision before we began hauling it all onto
trucks and into pods.

"CeeCee?" I call. She spins around as if broken from a trance.
"Everything okay?" I ask.

"Yeah," she says with a severe lack of conviction. "Couldn't sleep,
so I figured I'd make myself useful." Her eyes dart around the gray
space as if she's overwhelmed. A chill cuts through the cold floor,
making me wonder how she's standing there in only thin slippers.

"Need some help?" I offer.

"Sure," she says, using her knee to nudge a box in my direction.
I pull a string on a second overhead bulb, and the pool of light illu-
minates even more mess. Christmas decorations. Deck chairs. An
old mailbox. I didn't realize we had so much more to do. "I want to
get out of here as soon as possible, so the quicker this all goes, the
quicker I can breathe again."

"Did you like living here?" I ask, mostly to fill the space.

"I tried to, but you can only like a place so much when you
move there out of necessity." Her bun slips a little further out of its
holder as she inspects some cushions that will probably end up in
the dumpster parked in their driveway.

"You didn't want to come out here?" I ask, surprised.

"We told people the move was for James's work, but really, we were running away out of embarrassment over Doop folding and…" Her fingers wiggle in my direction like she's casting a spell on me. Before the split in our relationship, I often thought of CeeCee as a twin. Someone whose mind I could read in any situation. I know she's referring to my jokes and similar consequences to the ones that plagued Drew.

The remorse doesn't weigh on me as much knowing that our relationship is on the mend. That some of that pain has been scrubbed away.

I take that in as I wander over to the finished section of the basement, where the concrete gives way to brown carpet. On the far wall, there's a closet, which I'm certain is chock-full of junk, yet the first thing I see when I open the accordion door is CeeCee's wedding dress in a transparent hanging bag. Perfectly preserved. Just the sight of it floods me with memories.

CeeCee comes up beside me. "I thought about selling it at one point. We needed the money, and it was just…there. But I couldn't. I don't know why. I couldn't part with anything from that day. I was scared someone from Doop would come after me if I did." She rolls her eyes at herself.

We dig through the remnants. A digital photo frame. A cake plate. The signage that still reads like an ad for oatmeal. Beneath all that and other miscellaneous keepsakes, I notice bag handles poking up from beneath a swath of fabric. What I pull out makes my heart stop.

"Are those…?" CeeCee asks.

"I think so," I mutter.

Leftover goody bags.

Awed, she says, "I had no idea those were down here, I swear."

With shaking hands, I part the tissue paper in each one, setting aside candles and creams and oils and supplements. It's in the bottom of the very last bag that I find a smaller velvet bag that feels smooth to the touch and looks strikingly familiar.

I undo the drawstring and into my hand plops a collection of crystals.

Different colors. Different shapes and textures than the ones Drew and I painstakingly collected. The same scroll as the original bag from Ryan, but with different words.

In this collection, you will find pink tourmaline, peridot, sodalite, serpentine, anhydrite, citrine, and fire opal. These specially shaped crystals were chosen in consort to help the user make peace with their past.

Instructions:
Hold the crystals close to your chest.
Set a strong intention. Speak it into the universe.
Visualize the ideal outcome.
Place crystals under your pillow for sleep.
Wake up rejuvenated and ready to begin again.

"This can't be a coincidence, right?" I ask. My thoughts are of two minds: I'm still on that really elaborate prank show I dreamed up when I awoke into this reality, or those folks at Doop played a long con on me. Reconciling with Drew, my family, and finally my sister led to my ultimate escape.

Well played, Doop. Well played.

CeeCee's eyes scan the instructions. "Those fuckers…" Her laugh is sardonic. "Maybe you were supposed to get both, and Ryan messed up with the goody bags." CeeCee's tone suggests that, even as she's saying it, she doesn't buy it. "Are you going to use them?"

"Not tonight," I say quickly, worry impinging on me. "I–I need some time with them. With this." I know she'll know what I mean. "This" includes Mom and Dad and Imogen and Drew and her. "All the relationships I restored in this timeline will be lost or changed if I turn the clock back. Embark on my own daylight savings." I roll my eyes at how cheesy that sounds.

"Yeah, of course," she says, taking me seriously. Finally.

"I don't know if I want to give this up," I say. "And if I do want that, I don't know if I'm ready to just yet."

"That makes sense," she says. "It's your life, Nolan."

We work in silence until we're both a barrel of yawns and worry, the crystals becoming heavier by the second in my pocket. We drag ourselves upstairs and back to our respective bedrooms, and before we part ways, CeeCee hooks her hand in mine. A level of tender we haven't shared since high school.

Even in the darkness, her voice barely above a whisper, I know she's crying. "I would give anything to not have lost seven years of this." She shakes our joined hands. "You know what's best, and I'll support you in whatever you choose, but I just had to say that."

Without another word, she pulls me into a hug that lets me know the sins of my past have been forgiven. Or, at least, forgiven enough that we can start over. In whichever timeline I decide on.

Chapter Forty

When I'm back in New York, I don't go out and party and drink and make a general ass of myself. I stay home to cook Drew and me a dinner we always loved: spaghetti bolognese. I was never much of a chef beyond instant ramen and instant oatmeal and anything else with *instant* in the title, but I collect the ingredients from a nearby organic market, I watch a YouTube video walking me through the steps, and when I'm finished, it feels like I've meditated. Zen sweeps through my veins as I set the table and pour the expensive wine, ignoring the mess I've made of this luxurious life.

Without Jessalynn on my team, everything pretty much goes to shit. Nobody knows what to do or what to say or what needs paying for or who needs to pay me. I appoint my assistants as the leaders of damage control, tell my business manager to "figure it out," and get a new phone with a new number with five contacts: Drew, Mom, CeeCee, James, and the memory care facility.

I sneak Milkshake a wayward noodle that landed on the counter. He happily slurps it up, tail thumping against a nearby cabinet. I'm going to miss him. Because even if there's another Milkshake, it won't be this exact Milkshake. If that even makes sense.

"What's all this for?" Drew asks when he walks through the door, rumpled from a day at the store. He'd texted earlier to let me know the store manager he promoted in his absence had done a decent job, but Drew is a perfectionist, so of course he had to work extra hours to get everything back to his liking.

As I stand here, sweating with nerves, I hope my gesture is to his liking as well. "I wanted to do a little something to celebrate us."

His smile sends a bolt of love straight down to the ends of my toes. We take our seats, lay down our napkins, and I can't help but notice how my utensils are shaking as I serve us both. Drew, clearly clocking this, remains mum. Really, I'm worried about what he'll say when I show him what I've been hiding for the past week.

By the time I set out dessert, I decide I can't take it anymore, and I place the bag between our plates of flourless dark-chocolate tart (not made by me, but hand-selected while starving and rolling a cart by the bakery section).

Drew's brows furrow. "Did you get me a gift?"

"Not exactly," I say, before urging him to open the bag and see for himself. I wouldn't be able to find the right words to explain the serendipity.

He's surprised by the number of items that roll out of the black bag, but when he realizes what they are, his surprise visibly doubles. "How did you get these? Did Ryan send them?"

"They were in CeeCee's basement, buried beneath all her wedding keepsakes," I say, watching as he realizes I've withheld this.

"Why?" is the first question that unfolds from his mouth.

"Because," I pause for what feels like an eternity. "Because I wanted us to make this decision together. The last time it didn't work, you…" I can't bring myself to say that he left. It was for a good reason, but he still did. And it hurt me. "There are too many unknowns," I say instead.

He nods. "Almost everything is unknown. I was worried that if you stayed twenty-three, aging independently of your body, there was no way I could be sure that you wouldn't make the same mistakes of those seven years, but the one thing I'm certain of is that you have grown. The way you dropped everything to be there for your family. Even the way you worked to help me with my event. I wanted an excuse to run, so I ran." His glassy eyes bore into mine. They only alleviate a fraction of my worry. "Even if the crystals don't work, I'm not going anywhere this time."

"Right. A guaranteed happy ending for us. If they do work, though," I say shakily, "this may not happen again. We may never find our way back to each other."

"That's true." His eyebrows furrow.

"On the other hand, if I don't at least try, then I'll definitely lose seven years with my dad." My heart aches at the thought. "I'm not delusional. I don't think I can go back and cure him or whatever, but I see now how precious the time I had with him was and how much of it I wasted."

Drew nods thoughtfully, taking his time to respond. "If I were in your shoes and it were my mom, I know which choice I would make."

Words don't come right away; tears threaten to fall.

"Nolan." He says my name like it's sacred. "If that's the decision you make, I have no doubt that your growth will help us find happiness again."

Overcome, I lean across the table and kiss him, because I don't know what else to do and I have nothing left to say. Never have I been surer that nothing matters more than my family and Drew.

No. Wrong. Drew *is* and always has been my family. My home. And our love bled romantic long before we tried to compress the wound and stop the spillage.

Now, we're overflowing with the stuff, even if it hurts.

For the rest of the evening, we drink whiskey, we take Milkshake for a walk, and we make plans like I'm a wealthy English teenager about to embark on a tour of the European continent to stoke adventure and learning.

If I end up staying, we'll sell my apartment, move into Drew's, and I'll help out at the bookstore. I'll disavow my celebrity, return to the Hardy-Har Hideaway, and start over from scratch. My name may still carry weight, but I'll create a new persona. No suits. No man-child. No meanness. Just me and a microphone. Like it was at Imogen's party. Back to basics.

If I go back, well, there's a lot of uncertainty there. All I do is make a promise that I'll right my mistakes as best I can. The shift in my priorities is sedimented in my soul. Even if I forget this experience, the lessons they taught me won't go anywhere.

I call Mom to check in on her. Imogen can be heard rehearsing knock-knock jokes in the background. The kid caught the bug, and I'm not apologizing for it. When Mom has exhausted her topics—the garden, the food at the memory care facility, the pickup lane at Imogen's new pre-K—she puts CeeCee on the phone.

"What are you typing?" she asks when she hears the clack of my keyboard.

"I'm sending you an email," I tell her.

"We're literally talking right now," she says with a snort. "Can't you just say what you need to say and save the dramatics?"

"Me? Save the dramatics? Never," I say and hit Send. "Check your computer."

In come the sounds of CeeCee walking around, stealing into the bedroom, and announcing that she'll be closing the door. A slight gasp rings through the phone when she sees what I've sent. "Holy shit, Nolan. What is this?"

"Half is to pay for Dad's care and half is a college fund for Imogen," I say.

"No, duh. I got that," she says. "But...but why?"

People seem insistent on asking me that today. "Because you deserve a little back after helping Mom and Dad all these years. Because I love you and I love Imogen and I want her to succeed. Even if I won't be there to see it." I hope this one small act will offer my family some security when I'm gone.

Will I be gone, or will I be replaced? Will this timeline go on without me? Gah, too many existential questions for my already fried and frazzled brain. I promised to leave this reality better than how I found it, and this is a part of that.

CeeCee brings me back with a gentle "Oh."

"Yeah," I say. I understand all too well the sadness embedded beneath that *oh*.

Our goodbyes morph into good lucks, and our good lucks morph into I-love-you's. Before she hangs up, she says, "I can't wait to see you on the other side."

Peace washes over me.

At midnight, Drew and I open a second bottle of whiskey, Drew produces a joint, and Milkshake joins us to curl up on the couch. The three of us catch up on a season of *RuPaul's Drag Race* that I missed during my seven-year gap, and Milkshake barks loudly at the TV when he sees his favorite queens.

We laugh and kiss and snuggle and kiss some more. It's the perfect cap to a whirlwind experience. And after brushing my teeth and putting on pajamas, we crawl into bed with the intensity of two scientists who are nearly out of funding and desperately hoping for the right results in one final trial.

The late hour mixed with our uneasiness gives the room a pulsating sense of possibility. I launch my body into Drew's and latch on. My arms wrap around his soft-in-all-the-right-ways torso, inhaling his lavender-tinged detergent scent. "I don't want to let you go."

"You won't have to," he says with certainty, running a large hand through my soft hair.

"You don't know that," I say, nuzzling into the fabric of his T-shirt. "Our love may feel like magic, but that doesn't mean it is."

Gently, he cups my head in his hands and leads it up to his. He plants a kiss on my lips that tastes like whiskey and promises and forever before guiding me back to my own pillow, letting my head loll as I look up at him. My gentle giant. My no-longer-gangly gentle giant.

"Magic or not," he says, sinking down into the sheets beside me so we're eye-to-dazzling-eye, "our love is *inevitable*."

That's all I need to hear before I kiss him, take his hand in mine, and close my eyes, hopefully for the last time in this timeline.

PART SIX

HEMATITE STONE

Beautiful, balanced alignment

Chapter Forty-One

When I wake up with the first licks of morning light, refreshed and excited, the first thing I check for is the nose splint.

The second thing I check for is Drew, curled up on the other side of the bed.

Only one of them is there, and it's not the handsome, bearded man with tiny imprints on the bridge of his nose where his glasses usually rest.

"Aha!" I shout, springing off my floor-level mattress and launching into a happy dance, which results in me stumbling over Mount Ve-*shoe*-vius, which has erupted, once again, out of the accordion doors, causing absolute chaos across my cheap, crumb-laden Target rug. Even the sting of landing hard on my ass doesn't outweigh the utter elation roaring through my chest.

Footfalls echo through the apartment, and my door flies open. Drew, thankfully, does not have the extinguisher this time.

A relieved exhale saws out of me.

He's here. Thank God, he's here. That must mean I haven't jumped to after the wedding. He hasn't left. I get a redo, and that means the grand plan I thought up last night before falling asleep can still work.

Drew stands there in pajama pants and a sleep shirt. I take in his eye crusties and that unbearded baby face. "What happened? What broke?" he asks, immediately coming to help me up.

"The space-time continuum, but who cares?" He looks at me funny, while I look at him with love overflowing. "What's today?" I ask to be certain like I'm Scrooge.

He looks at me even funnier. "It's Saturday. Today is CeeCee's wedding."

My heart jumps for joy, and so do I, taking Drew with me. "My sister's getting married today!" My voice is a giddy yelp that's probably penetrating the quiet morning of our next-door neighbors.

"Okay, who are you and what have you done with Nolan Baker, my cynical-yet-motivated best friend?" Drew asks.

"I left him in the future," I say.

This must stump Drew. Cute creases materialize between his eyebrows. "Shouldn't you say you left him in the past?"

"No, because this is the past."

He scratches his head, a funny show of befuddlement. "No this is *the present*. Are you sleepwalking or something?" He follows me into the kitchen, where I begin brewing coffee.

"Maybe," I say with a playful shrug. "But I'm living my dream." Back here. Back with Drew.

He pauses, hands splayed on the counter, eyes scrutinizing me as the aroma of breakfast blend fills the air. "Okay, now you're offi-cially scaring me. What inspired this sudden change of heart over your sister's nuptials?"

"First off," I say, grabbing the oat-milk creamer from the fridge. "Please refrain from ever using the word 'nuptials' again. Second, believe it or not… *Doop*." A laugh bursts out of me.

"That's it. I need to get to the bottom of what kind of body swap comedy you're starring in right now."

"Body swap?" I ask with a laugh, pondering which Doop product from the secret lab could do that. "Now there's an idea…"

"I'm serious. I'm going to get to the bottom…"

I thrust a hot mug toward him. "The only thing you need to get to the bottom of is this cup of coffee so you're properly caffeinated for the long day ahead of us." He blinks, maybe considers if I've done something weird to the coffee (I haven't), and then hesitantly accepts it. "I'm fine. Trust me." I plant a kiss on his cheek and go to get ready, delighted to be right where I belong and ready to tell him everything.

Soon. Later. Tonight.

"I have some business to take care of, but could you grab my suit before you leave and I'll meet you at the wedding venue?" I ask.

"Business to take care of?" he asks. "You're seriously weirding me out. We're not going to ride over to the hotel together?"

I sip my coffee before saying, "I have to do something. It's important. I don't know how long I'll be, but I don't want to be late, so I won't have the opportunity to stop back here before CeeCee's call time."

"Call time?" he asks with a chuckle. "It's not a show. You know that, right?"

"I know. I'm just saying I have an itinerary to stick to," I say, certain I'll make good on that this time around.

· ✦ ·

When I come up from the subway station in Midtown, I call Harry.

I don't need the directions open on my phone because I know this walk by heart. Feeling my lungs expand as I pick up my pace, I rejoice that I'm back in my twenty-three-year-old body. While it's not as groomed or as sculpted, it's mine, and I love it.

I make a silent vow to myself to treat this body with as much kindness as I treated my thirty-year-old-loaner body. Less instant ramen. More fresh vegetables. And it really wouldn't kill me to go on more walks.

My call to Harry goes straight to voicemail, which doesn't surprise me. I hurt him in both timelines, and though he only knows about one of those hurts, it still makes sense, he wouldn't care to hear from me.

After the beep, I say, "Hey, Harry. It's Nolan. Look, I'm calling because I wanted to apologize for the shitty way I left things between us." I pause at an intersection, taking in the city that I love, feeling renewed. "It was wrong of me to ditch out on dinner for a stand-up gig. I'm sorry for treating you like a second thought. I was desperate for a wedding date and in no place for a relationship, and I brought you into the crosshairs of my own awful actions, so seriously, I'm so sorry."

I'm approaching my destination, shoes stomping down the gum-covered sidewalk at a hurried pace so I can make it there and to the wedding on time. I wrap this up. "You may never listen to this, and that's cool, but if at some point you hear this and think, 'Hey, that Nolan guy isn't a scourge of the earth like I thought,' hit me up anytime. I'd love to get coffee, apologize face-to-face, and maybe, I don't know, try to be friends? Sorry if that sounds cringey. I'm sorry for everything again, and be well."

Shoving my phone back into my pocket, I push through the front entrance into a familiar club and make my way to the back office. I knock twice on the ajar door before entering.

"Nolan?" Wanda asks, looking up from her laptop screen. "Shouldn't you be getting ready for your sister's wedding right now?"

"Yes, but first, I came to rescind my two weeks' notice."

Wanda appears surprised. "What brought this on?"

I spare her the fantastical truth and say, "The Hardy-Har Hideaway has been a home-away-from-home to me for so long, and leaving it isn't the right option for me." This may not be my forever job, and working here may sting a bit as I cut back on my stage time, but I still care deeply about this business.

"Consider your notice rescinded then." I can tell she can't contain her smile.

"Great. In that case, I'd also like a promotion." I summon some of my self-assuredness, the kind I developed standing up to Jessalynn in the future timeline. It's certainly coming in handy.

"Feeling bold, are we?" Wanda asks.

"Yes. Over the years, I think I've proven myself. I want more responsibility. I can handle it," I tell her. "I'd like set hours, better pay, and if you can swing it, benefits."

"Benefits?"

"Never know when I'm going to get hit in the face with a swinging door again," I joke, pointing up at the splint I somehow couldn't be happier to be wearing.

She rolls her eyes at me good-naturedly. "I'll see what I can do, Nolan. Now, get out of here, and send my congratulations to your sister."

"Thanks, Wanda. Will do."

I leave, certain that I'm setting myself on the right path.

Chapter Forty-Two

After the ceremony, which is even more beautiful the second time somehow, I don't indulge in a cocktail out on the balcony. I don't banter with Drew about line dances and kiss him with my whole heart, body, and soul.

Instead, I make my way down that familiar corridor and into the tiny room where I saw Doop employees stuffing wedding favors the first time around. I'm prepared to rid this party of miracle creams, mind-reading glasses, and time-traveling crystals by any means necessary.

Except, when I barge in, no one is here. All the favors have already been packed up. Every bag is the same color—white—and when I peek inside the nearest one, all I find are concealers, hair-brushes, and decorative clocks.

The same in the next, and the next, and the next.

Nothing concretely magic remains.

Was it all in my head?

Clive's call comes in at almost the exact same minute as last time, even though I've already altered the outcome of tonight.

"You in or you out?" Clive asks as I stand in the housekeeping closet in the Flamhaff Hotel once again.

"I'm sorry, but I'm out," I say confidently, and then reconsider the first part. "On second thought, I'm not sorry. My sister's wedding is today, and I know you're going out on a limb for me, but I've got to put my family first. I hope you understand."

I can almost hear Clive nod. "I respect that, man. Send my blessings to the happy couple."

"Will do. Thanks."

I hang up relieved.

Back out in the event space, I take a cleansing breath and take it all in, the faces of those who love CeeCee and my family joined together to celebrate. Why I had to be such a curmudgeon about the whole thing the first time around is beyond me. This is my do-over, though I guess it's more of a redo. Because too much has changed already.

As dinner is served, I sneak over to where Mom and Dad are sitting with James's parents.

"How's it going over here?" I ask like some sort of hired party-starter. Mom and Dad look up from their salmon with smiles. Seeing Dad coherent and happy again is a lot for me, but I rein in the emotions. While I know there's no way to reverse the disease that's eventually going to take him from us, I can soak in as much now-time as possible. I won't let another second slip away from me, much less seven years.

"Good, just enjoying our meals," Mom says, dabbing her mouth with her napkin. "Everything okay, sweetheart?"

"Of course. Just wanted to say hello," I say. "And that I've been thinking, and I'd really like us to start up our family brunches again."

"Thought you said you were too busy," Dad grumbles.

I shake my head. "I'm going to talk to Wanda. I might be eligible for a promotion, so I'll see if I can have my work schedule sorted out around it." I don't tell them that the work excuses have mostly been lies. I'm trying for 100 percent truth in this timeline, but I think 98 percent is better in this instance. "I'd love to help out with the garden if you're still up for making one, Mom. And, Dad, CeeCee mentioned you just got a new model train. Maybe you could show me how to put it together like in the old days."

He leans back in his chair. "I distinctly remember a fourteen-year-old boy telling me trains were for dweebs and refusing to step foot in the model shed."

I shrug, embarrassed by my past self. "Yeah, well, maybe I'm a dweeb now."

At that, he laughs a raucous laugh that I store in my memory banks for safekeeping. I should start recording what he says on my phone so that when his memory goes and his motor functions cease, I'll always carry a piece of him with me. Memories can falter, but recordings can stay. I learned that the hard way when I had to sit down and watch all of those insulting stand-up routines I did aimed at Drew and my family.

I won't make those same mistakes again.

"All right then. But you're making the waffles," Dad says.

"I'd be glad to," I say with a tiny regal bow.

Mom seems charmed. "We'll start up again when CeeCee gets back from her honeymoon."

"No." I shake my head, impatient. "Let's start next Sunday. She can join us again when she's ready."

Mom raises a sly eyebrow. "Whatever you say, Nolan."

I pivot on my heel to head back to the bridal party dais, feeling light, knowing I've just secured myself, hopefully, at least seven more years of Sundays.

CeeCee turns to me when I've sat. "You've barely touched your food."

"Yeah, been busy socializing," I say. This time around at dinner, I don't take the passive-aggressive care of our distant relatives to heart. I accept their concern as love manifested in a way that may not be helpful to me, but feels right to them.

Just this small change in attitude has opened me up to the joys of the day. But I pull back from being an overbearing attention hog. This is CeeCee's show. I'm only a supporting act, and this time, I like it that way.

"You have been unusually chipper," she says. "You're not high, are you?"

"Nope," I assure her. "Just high on love." That statement sends my eyes darting over to Drew, who is midconversation with my great-aunt Laurel, a woman with a southern drawl and a penchant for Hallmark movies. She's blushing, which means only one thing. He's turned on the signature Drew Techler boyish charm.

"I didn't expect you to bring Drew," she says.

"Neither did I," I reply. "But life is like that. Surprising sometimes." I take a deep breath. "Dad seems good today."

"Yeah," CeeCee says, raking her fork through steaming farro.

"I don't want to work for Doop," I confess abruptly. CeeCee's eyes go wide, but I cut her off before she can speak. "*But* I am demanding better-paying, more consistent work at the club. I can still pursue comedy without making it my entire personality. Without ruthlessly chasing after it at the sacrifice of everything else in my life."

"That's...very mature of you," CeeCee says, taken aback.

"And I know things have been hard on you, helping Mom out with Dad's health."

She leans in, whispers, "How did you know about that?"

"I don't know," I say because truthfully, there's no other way to explain it. I learned it from the future? Even I'm not stupid enough to say that. "I just do, and I'm sorry you've been bearing that burden alone. I want to be there for you. I want to be stable enough to help."

"Wow, I was not expecting you to say that."

"I love you, CeeCee. I'm here for you. And I'm sorry if I made your life harder by not making that clear," I say.

There are fresh tears in her eyes, so she turns away and snatches a hanky from James. Blotting at her eyes, she says, "Waterproof, my ass." She laughs. "I love you too, Nolan."

"Oh, and if, when this is all over"—I paint the air with my palm—"you're still drowning at Doop over the promotion they gave you, maybe find a new job." I don't bring up how the business might not even exist in a few years. I don't know how my change in actions will butterfly-effect out. Either way, I don't want her to take it as a jab. I'm only looking out for her. Always and forever now.

"Wait, how did you know about *that*?" She clearly thinks I'm a mind reader. I can live with that assumption.

I suppress a chuckle. "Let's just say I had an inkling it would be coming sooner or later. And now that we've had this lovely bonding moment, it's perfect timing for me to make my post-dinner mister of honor speech, and…" I show her my cracked phone screen, which blinks the time. Damn, I really do need to get that fixed now that I'm resigned to being a new kind of adult. "Right on time." I know CeeCee loves nothing more than a perfectly aligned schedule, and I'm finally getting this timing thing down pat.

I stand and tap the butter knife to my champagne flute like I've seen supporting characters do in countless romantic comedies. A hush falls over the room as utensils are put down; hands and heads turn in my direction. The band leader runs me a microphone.

Clearing my throat, overcome with both emotion and gratitude, a thought pops into mind: this was the gig of a lifetime to begin with.

No stage in the world could compare to uplifting my dearest family and friends with amusing anecdotes and well-timed, *kind* jokes.

So I speak from the heart.

And I absolutely, positively *crush it*.

Chapter Forty-Three

When the confetti clears, CeeCee and James have left for their honeymoon, and "Doop There It Is" has finished rattling the floorboards, the jazz band takes the stage once more.

"This one goes out to Nolan Baker and a very special someone," says the lead singer, a Judy Garland look-alike, as she pulls the microphone from its stand.

A cover of "You Make Me Feel So Young" starts, and I zip through the crowd to where Drew is standing, holding CeeCee's bridal bouquet, which he caught on the fly. I may or may not have hip-checked him into it, knowing his height would reign supreme over the bridesmaids in attendance.

"Would you do the mister of honor the honor of this dance?" I ask, palm upturned toward him. Gentlemanly.

Without putting his flowers down, he joins me on the dance floor among the lingering couples who aren't done partying just yet.

It takes a second for us to decide who's leading, but once I fall into his rhythm and steady foot pattern, we're out-dancing everyone. Even Mom and Dad, who once took swing dance lessons together, can't match our marvelous moves.

"Thank you for being my date," I say during a break in the lyrics, swaying and utterly swept up. In the magic. In the moonlight. In Drew's dreamy eyes.

He smiles a toothy smile. "Happy to."

"I think," I begin, trying to remain coy when really, I'm vibrating with emotion, "I'd like you to be my date for all future weddings." I spin him out and then back in with pizzazz.

"Are you planning on attending many more weddings in the near future?"

"Sure. And birthday parties and holiday gatherings and galas and fundraisers and carnivals."

"Since when do you go to carnivals? I thought you said you don't trust rides that can be moved."

"I stand by that. Okay, not carnivals, but at least circuses and fairs and communions and concerts and the occasional funeral."

He stops dancing. Goes unmovable, even as I attempt to take the lead. "This took a dark turn."

"Life can take a dark turn." I think about Dad's Alzheimer's. About fleeting time and shifting priorities and bookstores and the dark side of fame. I step closer, feeling brave. "Let me make it a little brighter by saying this. I'd like you to be my date to all functions in perpetuity, because…I love you, Drew. I've loved you for a while now, in a romantic way, but I've been too chickenshit to tell you because I was afraid that I wouldn't be able to live up to the lofty heights of the heroes in your romance novels and that I'd somehow mess it all up because I wasn't worthy, wasn't this hotshot successful comedian, but I realized that the only way I could mess this up was by not being honest. So, here it is, honesty…"

Drew's stunned silence draws out through the end of the song and into the next. Another wedding classic I recognize but can't think up the name of.

Growing worried that this timeline has been skewed and Drew

doesn't return my feelings after all, I notice the flowers Drew's still clutching, so I pluck a pretty, dangling petal to busy my free hand. "He loves me," I say, wistful. And then pluck another. "He loves me not. He loves me. He loves me not…"

Right before I run out of petals, Drew stops my hand from dismembering the flower completely and instead does it himself. "He loves you," he says sweetly, kissing the last petal before letting it float to the floor alongside my worries. "*I* love you, Nolan."

Drew leans down and kisses me as we start to sway to the music again, finding our way back into each other's arms, falling into a natural rhythm. The rhythm of our life together. The beautiful music we can make by embracing our unique love story.

That's when I recall the song title, and I'm so goddamn tickled by it that I pull away right as the chorus comes in with just enough time to sing: "It had to be *Dreeeeew*." I'm flat, but I don't care, and an incredible smile spreads across Drew's face; red rushes across his cheeks. Utterly adorable enough that nothing else matters. "Wonderful *Dreeeeew*."

He laughs the only laugh I'll ever long to earn.

The laugh I want to grow old listening to.

"It had to be *Drewwwwwww*."

As the song comes to a close and the floor starts to clear, I kiss Drew's beautiful face once more. Everything seems settled.

Well, almost everything.

My mind whisks back to the empty closet, the missing crystals, and whether or not the future I lived inside was nothing more than a product of my imagination.

Then I remember two things from that dreamlike timeline: an omniscient voice and a promise.

They both echo loud and clear inside my head, and they spur me to act.

"Are you up for an adventure?" I ask Drew with an air of mischief, still holding tight to his hand.

"With you?" he asks, smiling. "Always."

We race out of the venue to grab a cab, and a short time later we find ourselves in a waiting room awash with dark reds and the smell of incense. "Hello?" I call into the room beyond a beaded curtain.

"Where are we?" Drew whisper-asks, sounding concerned but still excited.

"You'll see," I say, nudging him forward.

It's late, but I knew she'd still be open.

An orange cat appears from beyond the beads before a person does. The cat is smaller than the one I'd previously met, but just as striking with emerald eyes. It meows when it sees me, brushing up against my leg, which I hope means she remembers me.

"Do you have an appointment?" comes a familiar voice above the sound of footsteps.

"No, we're just dropping by for a tarot reading," I say, crouching down to pet the cat, who is shedding a lot but also living for the attention.

"I don't usually do walk-ins this late," the woman says as she enters. I don't look up right away, afraid of what I might find. I take in her black, heeled boots that stick out beneath a flowing crimson skirt, and urge the universe to please answer my final question. "Tigress never takes to men right away like that." The woman's voice comes out shocked. "You must be special."

"Yeah," I say. "I think I am."

When I look up, I half expect Lucille to hug me or burst into tears, but all she does is gesture for us to follow her back to her table. The room is slightly less cluttered than I remember it being in the future timeline, yet it still has that ethereal quality to it that helped me to trust her in the first place.

Drew volunteers me to go first since he's clearly still unsure what we're doing here, so I shuffle the deck of cards and pass it back to Lucille, who lines up three cards facedown, just like last time. Even though I know how this works now, and I'm not desperate for crystals, I'm still jittery.

"For the past," Lucille says, flipping the first card. It showcases a naked woman beside a small pool; the night sky shines above her. I notice it's upside down. "The Star reversed tells us that you were stuck in a period of hopelessness. You lacked faith and you lost yourself."

Unlike last time, Drew doesn't hesitate to comfort me physically when he registers her jarring words. He grabs my hand and grounds me, which I appreciate. "And the present?" I ask.

"The Ace of Cups, which symbolizes a release and an outpouring of love and connection. This is a good card. You're lucky. You've found emotional fulfillment." Lucille's eyes flit between me and Drew. I feel my cheeks grow hot. "Everything is as it should be."

"I couldn't agree more." I shift further into Drew, gripping his hand tighter.

I think about where I was, where I am, and how I got here. I let the past wash away and the present embrace me. I take a deep, gratifying breath.

Lucille pauses before revealing the final card. She gives me a long, hard look. A grin plays on the edges of her bright-red lips, and something akin to recognition sparks in her eyes. "Would you like to see the final card, Nolan Baker?"

At that moment, I realize that I never told her my name in this timeline…

We share a secretive, affirming smile as she overturns the last card in the reading and shows me my future.

PART SEVEN

CITRINE

Sunny days and good vibrations

Chapter Forty-Four

2030, AGAIN

I'm awoken, like I am most mornings, by a scratchy tongue on my cheek and the thumping of a tail against the old gray comforter. When I open my eyes, Milkshake's adorable face lights up, knowing I'll groan once, stretch twice, and then slip out of bed to feed him breakfast.

Except this morning, Drew's taken the day off from the store, so he's a lump of pointy joints and messy hair as he lets out a ginormous yawn that makes Milkshake yelp. "Good morning, sleepyhead," I coo, running the back of my hand over his full, red beard. "It's nice to have my two men home on a Saturday morning." Simultaneously, I kiss Drew and scratch Milkshake between the ears, showing my affection the best way I know how.

It's a big day, so I bypass the stretching and get to it. Food clangs into Milkshake's bowl from the automatic feeder, and he scarfs it down with impressive speed. I turn on the coffeepot before grabbing a yogurt from the fridge. Sunlight spills in through the kitchen window of our modest one-bedroom apartment right above the bookstore.

It's not the opulence I once wanted for myself by thirty, but sometimes what you want and what you need aren't the same.

In the shower, I do a speed-through of my thirty-minute comedy set, careful not to let any wayward shampoo get in my mouth while I do. I've been practicing for months, perfecting my material at the

Hardy-Har Hideaway, but today is the day I put it to tape. I couldn't be more happily anxious.

"Room for one more?" Drew asks, sliding the curtain back and standing there all freckly and naked and beautiful. Lucky. I feel lucky.

"Always."

He joins me in the steam and the spray, smiles at me, and I bask in one of the many simple pleasures of living with the one you love. Intimacy never more than a step into the shower away.

Dried, dressed in a taping-appropriate outfit, and with Milkshake in his carrier, we head downstairs through Eight, Three, One Books, the romance-only bookstore Drew and I opened together almost two years ago to the day. It has echoes of the lost Bound by Mayhem Bookshop from a different dimension: the same rental space, the same dark wood, the same blood-red fainting couch. Except, now, that blood-red accent color doesn't read like a grisly crime scene. It reads like hopeful hearts. Like love made manifest.

Like *us*.

Jolene, the store manager, waves from her perch behind the register, where she's reading a late-in-life romance about a ship captain and a fisherwoman. A bowl of rose quartz sits on the counter in front of her. The crystals may not be magic, but their vibrations are wholly welcome here.

"Good luck today, Nolan. You're going to do great!" Jolene says.

A regular customer, Bart, comes over to the register with his purchases, a tall stack of titles from our Staff Picks section. One of them is *I Wish You Wellness* by R. U. Low—a buzzy romance title about two men who fall in love thanks to time-traveling crystals. I have absolutely no idea where he could've come up with such a concept.

"What's the occasion?" Bart asks.

"I'm filming my stand-up special today," I tell him with a knowing smile before we bid everyone goodbye and duck into the SUV waiting for us at the curb.

Drew gets into the passenger seat since there won't be room for him in the back.

"Uncle Nolan!" Imogen shouts from her booster seat as soon as I open the door.

"Hey there, cupcake," I say, giving her a little tickle. It's not a private car with a hired driver, but the company is definitely better.

CeeCee, shining with a pregnant glow, smiles warmly from the other side of the car. "Buckle up. We're going to be late."

Doop shuttered a few years after the wedding. Turns out marketing a lavish, unattainable event to the masses does not churn out as many sales for body scrubs as one would hope, especially when that blushing bride puts in her letter of resignation a few months after the all-expenses-paid honeymoon.

CeeCee and James never moved to Colorado. Instead, they moved into a two-bedroom apartment in Jersey City to make space for Imogen, and now with kid number two on the way, they're eyeing a second move to the suburbs, not far from Mom and Dad. That works out fine for CeeCee because she flipped her degree and pivoted back toward her passion. She now works remotely as an outreach coordinator for a dance nonprofit.

I'm happy for her and even more happy to be a part of the life she built.

We speed out of the city and make it to New Jersey in a little under an hour and a half. By the time we step inside, Mom and Dad's living room has been rearranged to make way for professional lighting and a single camera. A man we hired holds a boom mic in one hand, his phone in the other. The couch has been pushed flush against the wall, and mismatched chairs are set out in curved rows.

Jessie, Wanda, and Harry all greet me with hugs and pats of encouragement.

"Okay, the crew is set. We'll need to do a lighting check, and then of course vet everyone's wardrobe choices," Jessie says, acting the part of the friend/manager I always wanted them to be. "Last thing we need is wavy stripes or distracting polka dots in the audience reaction shots."

"You'll never take away my polka dots!" Imogen harrumphs, appearing suddenly beneath us. Then, she runs off screaming, arms overhead. That girl is a natural clown, and I love it.

"We'll put a blanket over her or something," Jessie says with a laugh.

Harry steps forward. "We threw around the idea of doing a rehearsal, but we want genuine reactions for you to play off, and we only have the crew for the few hours we could fund for, so if you flub or go up on anything, take a beat and restart. We'll edit around it."

To my delighted surprise, Harry took me up on the offer of a face-to-face apology over coffee seven years ago, and we've been casual friends ever since. As he's built up his directing résumé, it only made sense I'd hire him for this job.

"And, Maggot…" Wanda says with audible pride.

"Yeah?"

"Time to fly." Her support and generous financial contribution mean the world to me. She may no longer be my boss, but I know she's my friend and mentor for life. She winks at me before moving out of the way for Mom, who pushes Dad in a wheelchair, a home aide not far behind.

Positing it as preventive, I slipped into conversation over one Sunday brunch that I'd read a recent study about Alzheimer's screenings and cognitive testing.

"Have either of you gotten one?" I asked, adding pepper to my scrambled eggs.

A few weeks later, we had Dad's diagnosis. An early catch won't cure him. I know that. But it got him into a clinical trial that seems to be prolonging his mental functions and slowing the overall progression.

All I can ask for is time. Sweet, untamable time.

"This is quite the production," Mom says, inspecting the circus that is her living room.

"We'll be sure to put everything back where it belongs," I say while hugging her.

She *pshes* me and then goes to find a seat by Imogen, James, and CeeCee.

Jessie takes me up to my childhood bedroom, which has been rebranded "Dressing Room" with a golden paper star on the door. It's not extravagant. There's no Lovesac or fridge of top-shelf alcohol, but it's perfect.

"We'll come get you when we're ready for your big entrance," Jessie says before shutting the door behind them.

As I sit at my childhood desk, reading through my notes and jokes while listening to the voices and footsteps of family and friends filing in downstairs, pleasant jitters overtake my body. I spent so many years hoping and praying that I was making all the right moves so someone would open the door of opportunity for me. Well, I crowdsourced, got together a group of my friends, and I'm kicking down that door on my own with a self-produced comedy special that I'll post online.

Maybe one person will find it. Maybe a million. Who cares? I'm just happy I get to do what I love.

Fifteen minutes later, as I stand at the top of the staircase, rocking on the balls of my feet with anticipation, I take a moment to appreciate how far I've come in seven short years. Adulthood will always be hard, but it isn't as harrowing with a support group of amazing people sitting, smiling, and waiting for you to tell them jokes. Letting you shine and spread laughter while making their lives a little easier by being present.

"Gentlefolk," Drew announces, "please welcome to his own living room, a class-act and a comedy cool kid all grown up, in his very first comedy special. Here he is…"

Imogen steals the mic. "Nolan Baker!"

And I absolutely, positively *crush it*.

Acknowledgments

Writing a book is an act of magic and manifestation that wouldn't be possible without a fierce group of believers.

Thank you to the team at Sourcebooks Casablanca, including but not limited to: Mary Altman, Letty Mundt, production editor India Hunter, copy editor Diane Dannenfeldt, proofreaders Patricia Fogarty and Melissa Thorpe, Alyssa Garcia, and our talented designers, especially Monique Aimee, who never fails to perfectly capture my characters in stunning cover art.

I'd like to extend my gratitude to Kevin O'Connor and the team at O'Connor Literary for jump-starting my career, and to Samantha Fabien and Root Literary for plotting the next chapter beside me.

I'm especially thankful for the writing community that has supported me through every setback, cheered me on through every triumph, and inspired me with their fearless, beautiful stories: Alison Cochrun, Gina Loveless, Anita Kelly, Lisa Roe, Courtney Kae, Helena Greer, Xio Axelrod, Annabeth Albert, Chloe Liese, and Chip Pons.

I'm indebted to the booksellers-turned-friends who have been instrumental in getting my books into the hands of passionate readers, including Kirsten Hess and Maddie Hess at Let's Play Books and Laynie Rose Rizer at East City Bookshop.

Thanks a million to the online book lovers whose friendship and cheerleading are indispensable and wholly appreciated—Kasee Bailey and Simone Richter.

Thank you to my parents and family, who have encouraged me and guided me tirelessly and lovingly, and to the best friends a guy could ask for—Melanie Magri, Tarah Hicks, Julie Matrale, and Kelsey Scanlon. I love you all!

Every romance I write is inspired by my partner, Robert Stinner. Thanks for the banter, laughs, love, and everything in between.

Thank you to my therapist, without whom writing would be an insurmountable feat.

To the readers—old and new—who take the time to engage with my words and receive my characters with open minds and hearts, you're the reason I get to do what I love.

Finally, to anyone like Nolan who's feverishly dreaming of a brighter tomorrow, don't forget to breathe in and be grateful for today.

About the Author

©Rebecca Phillips

Timothy Janovsky is a queer, multidisciplinary storyteller residing in Washington, DC. He holds a bachelor's degree from Muhlenberg College and a self-appointed certificate in rom-com studies (accreditation pending). When he's not daydreaming about young Hugh Grant, he's telling jokes, playing characters, and writing books.

TIMOTHYJANOVSKY.COM
Instagram: @TimothyJanovsky
TikTok: @TimothyJanovsky
Twitter: @TimothyJanovsky